FAKING LOVE
WITH THE
BILLIONAIRE BOSS

by

SERENITY WOODS

CONTENTS

Chapter One

Heidi

It's Tuesday the twenty-sixth of July, the first week of the English school summer holidays, and I'm in the kitchen making bread when my phone vibrates in the back pocket of my jeans, announcing the arrival of a message.

Assuming it's another unwanted text, my heart sinks as I take the phone out with floury fingers. I do a comical double-take when I see it's a Facebook message from Lawrence Oates.

I feel a wave of relief, then a flutter of pleasure deep inside. My heart racing, I go over to the sink and wash my hands, then pick up the phone and bring up the message. It's short but sweet.

Your Royal Highness! Don't suppose you'd be around for a Zoom call at 8 p.m.?

I laugh at his greeting. My full name is Heidi Rose Huxley, and the first time we met, he commented that my initials were HRH.

Still smiling, I sit on the kitchen chair, bring up his Facebook profile, and study his picture.

His real name is Lawrence, but everyone calls him Titus. He got the nickname from the Antarctic explorer of the same name who sacrificed himself for his teammates in 1912 by going out into a blizzard. That Lawrence Oates was nicknamed Titus after the English priest who invented a conspiracy to kill the English king, Charles II, in 1678.

How do I know all this? Because when I was sixteen, tipsy on one glass of sparkling wine at my brother Oliver's twenty-first birthday party, I asked his gorgeous mate for a kiss. Instead of getting exasperated with the irritating young teen who was trying to pretend she was sassy and sophisticated, he proceeded to kiss the living daylights out of me. Shy and innocent, I'd never even had a boy kiss me on the cheek before, so to be French kissed by a gorgeous older guy completely blew me away.

After the kiss, I found out everything I could about him, convinced I'd found my Prince Charming and that we were destined for a happily ever after.

We weren't, of course, and unsurprisingly after the party he didn't contact me and declare his undying love. We did see each other relatively frequently over the years, either at Oliver's business club or at my parents' house. Every time our gazes met with a mischievous smile as we both clearly recalled that kiss, although we never spoke of it openly.

We've been friends on Facebook for some time, although we've never communicated on there. Two years ago, I moved to England, and I haven't spoken to him since. He was the first guy to burst my girlish, romantic bubble, but he wasn't the last. Einstein said insanity is doing the same thing over and over and expecting different results. I think, from that definition, I'm pretty bonkers, as the English like to say.

His profile picture is an old one, taken when he was at university, of him with his arms around Oliver and their friend Mack. It's a bit blurry and doesn't do him justice. I remember him as tall, dark, and handsome, and being impressed because he'd been approached to play rugby for the Auckland Blues. The only other thing I remember about him is that his mother is Scandinavian, and he has Viking tattoos down each arm.

As I scroll down through his Facebook feed, I can see why I've never read any posts from him—he hardly ever goes on there. Oliver has mentioned him in passing when I've spoken to him on Zoom over the past two years, but I don't know anything about what he's been up to, apart from that he works with computers.

Why on earth does he want to talk to me?

Then it comes to me—it must be about Oliver's wedding. Oliver is marrying his girlfriend, Elizabeth, next month, and I'm flying to New Zealand for it. Maybe Titus is organizing something he wants me to be a part of. Yes, that would make sense. Much more sense than him deciding he wants to chat up the tipsy teenager he snogged eight years ago.

Blowing out a relieved breath, I reply to his message.

Hey Titus! Sure! 8 p.m. your time or my time?

He responds almost immediately: *UK time.* He includes an invitation to the Zoom call, then says: *Great, speak to you tonight.* Wow. Captain Concise.

Putting the phone aside, I return to making the easy-bake bread, adding a can of beer to the flour with the baking powder. I mix it all up and tip it into the loaf pan.

Then I scoop it back into the bowl, add the salt and sugar I'd forgotten, and put it back into the loaf pan again. I top it with grated cheese and salt and pepper, and slide it into the oven.

Then I remember I haven't added any olive oil, take it back out, drizzle the oil over the top, return it to the oven, and set the timer.

Even though it's clearly not a romantic call, he has me all flustered.

I huff an irritated sigh at myself and check the time on my phone. It's nearly ten a.m. now, and I'm due to have another Zoom call with my sisters. I go into the living room and collect my laptop, then take it out of my tiny cottage into my even tinier garden, and set it up on the plastic table under the umbrella.

I've learned that summer in England can be extremely variable, especially where I live, in the county of Devon in the southwest, where the hills of Dartmoor generate mild, wet weather. Last year, it rained the whole of July and a good part of August. This year, June proved to be one of the wettest on record, but the weather has miraculously cleared up for the start of the school holidays, and today the sky is the color of bluebells.

I click on our Zoom link and discover that two of my three sisters—Chrissie and Evie—are already there, waiting for me. There's a moment of delay, and then their pictures spring up on the screen.

"Hey!" They smile and wave as they see me, and I grin and wave back.

"Hey you lot!"

"Ooh, it looks like a lovely day there," Chrissie says.

"It's a beautiful summer morning," I reply.

Evie shakes her head. "It must be so weird to have summer in July!"

"You get used to the seasons being reversed," I tell them. "Christmas in winter wasn't as strange as I thought, because our cards Down Under tend to feature wintry scenes despite it being in summer. And it makes sense that Easter takes place in spring here, with all the lambs and chicks being born."

"I guess," Evie says. "But Halloween in autumn? That's just weird."

I smile. I can't imagine that either Evie or Chrissie would take to living in England. There's a tendency for Kiwis to think of the English like cousins because so many of us have relatives back in the UK, but the fact is that the two cultures are very different.

Chrissie is thirty-three and, like me, a schoolteacher, although she teaches science at a large secondary school, which is a world away from my position teaching five-year-olds at a tiny Devon primary school. Evie is twenty-seven and a police officer, bossy and no-nonsense. They're both quite frank and outspoken, and I think they'd struggle with the way most English people are reticent and reserved.

"Where's Abigail?" I ask, referring to our oldest sister.

"She's in the South Island with Sean at the moment," Evie says. "They decided to have a weekend away to celebrate their third wedding anniversary, so she won't make it tonight."

"Oh, that's a shame. Have they taken Robin with them?" Their little boy is eight months old.

"No, they've left him with Mum and Dad," Chrissie replies.

"I can't wait to see him," I say longingly. Robin is my first nephew, and I'm desperate for a cuddle.

"Not long now," Evie says cheerfully. "It'll be great to see you. We've missed you so much."

"Yeah, me too. It's going to be such fun. Hey, do you know if Titus is organizing something for Oliver?"

Chrissie shrugs. Evie says, "What do you mean?"

"I don't know. I've just got a message from him asking if I'm free for a Zoom call tonight. I assumed it was something to do with the wedding."

"Are they having a stag do?" Evie asks Chrissie.

"Not as such. Hux says he didn't want one," she says. Even though his first name is Oliver, everyone calls him Huxley or Hux, except me. It always feels odd to me, especially as my surname is Huxley too. "He says he's too respectable," she adds. Evie and I snort. Chrissie grins. "When we go to Lake Tekapo, the night before the wedding, the guys and the girls are having some kind of separate wine and whisky event. That's all he wanted, as far as I know. And Mack's organizing it, so it's nothing to do with Titus."

"Hmm." Now I'm puzzled. "What do you know about him?"

"He's got a big knob," Evie says.

My eyebrows shoot up as Chrissie bursts out laughing. "Jesus," I say. "Evie!"

"What?" she grins. "You asked."

"I meant, you know, his personality, what he does for a living."

"Oh… sorry."

"How do you know how big his knob is, anyway?" Chrissie asks. "I didn't think you were in the knob business."

"Claire referred to it once," Evie says, ignoring the jibe, used to her sister's teasing about her sexuality. "She's his ex," she explains to me. "They were together for a couple of years, but they broke up a while ago. I met her at Huxley's club one evening. She was absolutely out of her tree, and she told us she called his dick 'Sir Richard' because it was so big."

"Oh my God," I say, as Chrissie dissolves into giggles. "Now I'm not going to be able to think about anything else while I'm talking to him."

"I wonder what he wants," Evie says curiously.

"He works with computers, doesn't he?" I ask.

"He doesn't just work with computers," Chrissie says. "He's the CEO of NZAI. New Zealand Artificial Intelligence?"

"Oh. Wow."

"He started the company not long after leaving university. You know that Mack Hart created New Zealand's fastest supercomputer?"

"Yes, I knew that."

"Well, Titus works with him in developing Artificial Intelligence. At the moment they're also working with Elizabeth on an IVF project. Something to do with using AI to choose the best embryos or something. Elizabeth did explain it to me, but it went a bit over my head."

My brother's fiancée, Elizabeth Tremblay, is a chemist who runs her own pharmaceutical company. He told me about her IVF project the last time I talked to him, a few weeks ago. "Didn't they get an offer of some serious funding from an English company?"

"Yeah," Chrissie says, "and they wanted Elizabeth to move to the UK and head the project from there, but she decided not to go. That's why Titus is over there. He's meeting with the company to discuss it."

I blink. "Wait, what? He's here, in England?"

"Yeah," Chrissie says. "Sorry, I assumed you knew."

"No! I had no idea. Where is he?"

"Don't know. London, I'm guessing. When Elizabeth turned Acheron down—that's the name of the pharmaceutical company—they asked Titus if he'd spearhead the project instead. They want him to move there for two years, but obviously he has his own company to run, so I guess he's trying to talk them out of it while keeping the money."

"How much is the funding?" Evie asks.

"Oliver said it was five hundred million dollars," I reply.

"Wow. That's a lot to turn down. Mind you, I think he's a billionaire. He could just pay for it himself."

"It doesn't work like that," Chrissie says, amused. "He's like Dad and Hux—a lot of their money is tied up in stocks and shares. Besides which, I think Acheron is promising more funding if the research goes well."

"Hence Titus's trip, I guess," Evie says.

"I still don't understand why he wants to talk to me," I comment.

Evie shrugs. "You might be the only person he knows over there."

"I doubt it," Chrissie says. "He's got a lot of connections. All joking aside, he's big news in the AI industry. Have you heard of *Atamai Tuatahi*?" When we shake our heads, she continues, "It's the Aotearoa AI Summit. It features leading industry speakers, panel discussions, all that kind of thing. It's a huge event."

"He went to it?" I ask.

"He was the keynote speaker last year."

"Oh." Now I'm impressed.

"He also spoke at a conference on Robotics and AI in Melbourne, another one in Toronto, and the AI Summit in Seoul. He's big news in the industry."

"Didn't you snog him at Hux's twenty-first?" Evie wants to know.

I blush. "Might have. That was a long time ago, though, before he became so intimidating."

"He's not that scary," Evie says. "I chatted to him at Mack's wedding on the yacht. He got drunk, knocked over Mack's grandmother's wine glass, then fell asleep and snored for the rest of the night. They left him there when everyone went to bed, and he was still there in the morning, apparently, covered in dew."

I chuckle. "Sounds like he needed a rest."

"He works hard," Chrissie says. "Twelve to fourteen-hour days usually, like Mack."

"So what's he like?" I ask curiously. "I remember him being really tall and kinda gorgeous."

"He's still tall and gorgeous," Evie says with a smile. "He plays a lot of rugby."

"Didn't he trial for the Auckland Blues at university?"

"Yeah. They wanted to sign him, but he said no because he thought it'd take him away from his studies."

"I partnered him at a tennis tournament in January," Chrissie states. "I wasn't anywhere near his league. He could have won if he'd had a better partner, but he was very kind about it and said it was his fault because his serve was off."

"That was nice," I say.

"He's a lovely guy," Evie replies, "when you get him talking. It takes a bit of doing. He's quiet and sorta brooding. Elizabeth said he's like the Dark Knight without the cape."

That makes me laugh.

"I don't think he's moody," Chrissie says, "I think he's just preoccupied, you know? He's like Mack—all he thinks about is work."

"Like Mack used to be," Evie corrects. "Now he's met Sidnie, he has other things on the brain."

My lips curve up. "She's managed to drag him away from Marise?" I know that Mack was obsessed with his supercomputer.

"Amazing what the power of the pussy can do," Chrissie states. "From what I've heard, the two of them hardly get out of bed."

I grin. "So is Titus dating?"

"Don't think so," Evie says. "He went out with a girl called Maisey, but Hux said that Titus told him she talked all the time—even during sex. I mean… Jeez. Poor guy."

"I thought most men liked dirty talk," I say, amused.

"No, apparently she used to list what she needed at the supermarket."

Chrissie and I dissolve into giggles. "Not so bad if it's whipped cream," I comment. "Less interesting if it's bleach for the loo."

"Loo," Evie echoes with a chuckle. "You sound more British each time we speak to you."

"Still enjoying it there?" Chrissie asks. She says the same thing every time we have a conversation.

"Yes, but I'm looking forward to coming home for a bit."

I don't like being too effusive about the UK when I'm talking to them, as I know they miss me, but the truth is that I love my job in the tiny primary school, and I adore the picturesque village I live in. There are a lot more people in the UK—sixty-seven million compared to New Zealand's five million, and the countries are a similar size—but most of New Zealand's population is concentrated in the biggest cities, and so traffic and overcrowding is as much of a problem there as it is in the UK.

But the most important thing is that I love being surrounded by history. In New Zealand, the oldest building is Kemp House in the Bay of Islands, which was constructed in 1821. In the UK there are prehistoric, Roman, Saxon, Viking, and Medieval buildings. My degree is in history, and it's a dream come true to be able to wander around castles and churches in my spare time.

"Mum and Dad will be pleased to see you," Evie says.

"Yes, I'm looking forward to seeing them, too."

"Once more with feeling," Chrissie says wryly.

I scrub at a mark on the bottom of my keyboard and don't reply.

"Are you going to see Dad?" Evie asks.

I don't want to. But I do want to go to Oliver's wedding, and to see my mother and sisters and the friends I left behind, so I'm going to have to see him at some point.

I don't like talking to them about it, though, because I know they don't fully understand why I feel the way I do. It's not their fault. I haven't told them everything.

"Can we change the subject?" I ask.

They exchange a glance, but Evie says, "Okay, how are Gran and Grandpa?"

"They're great." Our mother comes from England, and much of her family still lives there. "Gran's taken up pottery making. I've got odd-shaped bowls all over the house. Grandpa caught a thirteen-pound bass last week. I'm guessing he sent you a photo."

"I think he sent one to everyone in New Zealand," Chrissie says.

I laugh. "He was very proud of it."

"When's your flight to New Zealand?" Evie asks.

"A week Wednesday. Third of August."

"Have you got anything planned until then?"

"Nope," I say cheerfully. "It's been a hectic term, and the trip's going to be busy, so I'm taking it easy. Reading, some sightseeing, and lots of cream teas!" And panicking about seeing Dad again, obviously.

Chrissie clears her throat. "And… what about you-know-who?"

"Yeah," Evie says, "has Voldemort gotten the message yet?" Her attempt to make light of my breakup with Jason doesn't hide her concern.

My smile fades, and I look away, across the lawn to where a thrush is trying to pull a resisting worm from the grass. There must be something about me that makes men think I'm weak and helpless and easily controlled. I'm not as small as Oliver's fiancée, who's tiny. I'm five-foot-five. But I am slender and have a girlish figure, and I can easily pass for seventeen or eighteen, even though I'm twenty-five now. I broke up with Jason over three months ago, but he's refusing to take no for an answer.

"I'm working on it," I tell them.

My sisters fall silent for a moment, though, and I know they don't believe me. I can feel their worry seeping through the screen.

"Have you been to the police?" Evie asks.

"Not yet. I will, if it gets worse."

"Did you contact that helpline I sent you?"

"Yes," I say, although I haven't.

Evie glares at me. "I wish you'd do as you're told."

I poke my tongue out at her. "Yes, Mum."

"You shouldn't make light of it," she tells me. "These things can turn serious very fast."

I don't reply, because I can't argue with her when she deals with problems like this on a daily basis in her job. I shouldn't have told her, because now they're both worried.

Jason has never been violent, he's just persistent in sending me texts and messages on social media. Nothing threatening, and no dick pics or anything. If I were to show anyone else the messages, they'd look innocuous—he chats about his day, talks about movies and music he thinks I'd like, sends me funny memes and jokes, and occasionally asks me out. Whatever Evie says, I can't help but think that the police would wonder why I hadn't dealt with it myself rather than run to them— surely they have more serious problems to deal with?

"Enough about me," I say cheerfully. "What are you two up to?"

Evie tells us about a training course she's being sent on, and Chrissie chats for a bit about the school inspection she's preparing for. We talk until my timer goes off to say the bread's ready, and then we say goodbye, excited to see each other soon.

I take my laptop inside, retrieve the bread from the oven, then glance at my phone as it buzzes again. This time it is a text from Jason, and I pull it up with a sigh.

Don't suppose you want to go to the cinema this evening? he asks.

I answer with: *No thank you.*

He comes back immediately: *Come on. I know you want to see that new sci-fi.*

I feel a surge of irritation. How do you convince someone it's over? I suppose I could block him, but it feels like a massive overreaction. I don't want things to turn nasty. I just want him to leave me alone.

I turn off my phone, leave it on the counter, and go out into the sunshine with a book. I'm not going to think about him again. I'm going to think about Titus and Sir Richard.

Smiling, I open my book and begin to read.

Chapter Two

Titus

My first week in England has proven to be super busy, filled with meetings, conferences, and industry talks, and Tuesday the twenty-sixth turns out to be more of the same.

In the morning, I attend a symposium on Interpretation and Knowledge Representation at University College London in Holborn. Then in the afternoon I give a lecture on Artificial Intelligence Reasoning and Decision Making for the college's Master's students. The lecture theater is packed out for the whole of the two-hour talk, and afterward I answer questions for a further hour, until eventually I have to beg for a break to have a cup of coffee.

It doesn't end there, though; half a dozen members of staff and a gaggle of students follow me to the coffee shop, and I end up talking with them for another couple of hours before I finally tear myself away and head back to the Rosewood Hotel. There I have dinner with the CEO and two other directors of an AI and Data Science Consultancy, and it's nearly eight p.m. before I finally excuse myself and make my way up to my suite.

I'm staying in the Garden House—a suite with a private garden terrace. I call room service and request a latte, and when the butler arrives with it, I ask him to take it out onto the terrace. I set up my laptop on the circular glass table, thanking him as he lights some of the lamps and the deck heater as, even though it's July, I've learned that the evenings tend to be cooler than they are in summer in Auckland.

He withdraws, and I sit in one of the chairs, stretch out my legs, enter the Zoom meeting room, and turn the video on. There's about an hour until sunset, and the darkening sky behind me is brushed with orange, but the lamps mean that I'm clearly visible.

I'm tired, which is unusual for me at eight p.m., but I still haven't gotten over my jetlag. I should have said I'd call Heidi in the morning, but hey ho. I doubt it'll take long.

In under a minute, she joins the meeting room. Her picture pops up, the same one she uses for her Facebook profile. It's a couple of years old, of her with her three sisters. After a few seconds, she appears in the flesh.

We first met at Huxley's twenty-first birthday party, held at his parents' house because they have a large pool. Ever the host, Huxley introduced his four sisters to all his friends, then promptly told us to keep our hands off them on pain of death. I had no trouble doing as I was told with sporty Abigail, outspoken Chrissie, and somewhat aggressive Evie, who I discovered preferred women anyway. But Heidi was a whole other matter.

Just sixteen, with straight blonde hair that was so long she could sit on it, Heidi's lips permanently curved upward. I also remember that the bikini she wore was a startling fluorescent orange. Funny what sticks in your mind.

I watched her for a couple of hours, getting in and out of the pool, hovering on the edge of the party, too old to play with the children, too young to join in with Huxley's friends, and thought how beautiful she was, like a spring goddess, a budding rose full of promise, a soft fruit close to being ripe.

When I went into the kitchen to get myself a beer and discovered her there helping her mother organize sausages and burgers for the upcoming barbecue, I hung around until her mother left the room, then went and leaned a hip against the countertop next to where she was preparing a salad for the table.

"Hey," I said. "I'm Titus."

She glanced up at me and blushed. "I know who you are."

Flattered, I said, "And you're Heidi Rose Huxley. HRH. Should I call you Your Royal Highness?"

She gave a little laugh and tucked a strand of her long hair behind her ear. Then she turned to rest her butt against the counter, leaning her hands on the edge. "I like your tattoos," she said, her gaze brushing down my arms like a feather, making me shiver.

I looked down. I was wearing a sleeveless tee, mainly to show the tattoos off. I'd gotten them just six months before—a stylized dragon on my left arm and a wolf on my right, both wrapped around Norse great axes. "My mum comes from Norway," I said.

"The Striking Viking," Heidi teased. "Isn't that what Elizabeth calls you?"

"Yeah." I grinned at her, then offered her my bottle of beer. "Want a sip?"

"I shouldn't. I've already had a glass of sparkling wine."

"Do you always do what you're told?"

Her eyes met mine, and she held my gaze as she reached out, took the bottle, and had a swig. When she'd done, grimacing slightly at the taste, she wiped her mouth, her gaze dropping to my lips.

"Would you like to kiss me?" she said, bold as anything.

I don't know whether she expected me to act the gentleman and say I couldn't possibly, and to walk out of the room. Or if she thought I'd look shocked, maybe tell her off for being so audacious.

Instead, with all the confidence and foolishness of youth, and inspired by at least two beers, I said, "Fuck, yeah," put the bottle on the countertop, and moved up close to her, taking her face in my hands. Her blue eyes widened. "You're sure?" I murmured, half-expecting her to shake her head. Instead, though, she just nodded, her eyes full of excitement, and so I lowered my lips to hers.

I remember hers being incredibly soft, and to this day I can recall the heat that surged through me when she gasped, her lips parting. I brushed my tongue into her mouth, and her soft moan sent fireworks off in my belly that made me give a low growl as I deepened the kiss and slid my hands into her hair. She rested her hands on my chest, and we exchanged a long, luscious smooch that must have lasted a good fifteen seconds before someone suddenly said, "Oh! Sorry!"

As shocked as if someone had thrown a bucket of cold water over me, I stepped back, lowering my hands. It was Elizabeth, who was staring at us with much amusement.

Alarm rang through me, and all I could think was that if Heidi's brother found out I'd just snogged his sister, he was going to murder me in front of both his parents, and if he didn't carry it through, I had no doubt that Peter Huxley would finish the job. Huxley had commented several times how protective his father was of his youngest sister.

"Don't tell Huxley," I said. Which, on the face of it, wasn't the most romantic thing to have come out with.

Elizabeth just grinned. I glanced at Heidi, whose face was scarlet, then turned and walked out, back to the party.

And that was that. I saw her several times socially over the next few years, but we didn't get the chance to talk alone—we exchanged amused glances when we said hi and that was about it. She moved to England two years ago, and I haven't had any contact with her since.

So it's been a while since I've seen her, and I have to admit she's fixed in my mind as Huxley's kid sister. I'm therefore shocked when her image forms on my laptop screen. She's wearing a cherry-red T-shirt, and her blonde hair is now cut in a chin-length bob, parted on the left, with the shorter side tucked behind her ear, and the longer side hanging down like a shining curtain. She has large hoops in her ears. Her lips still curve up naturally, and she still looks younger than her years, but she's matured into a summer goddess, gray eyeshadow giving her sexy smoky eyes, and a touch of gloss making her lips look soft and kissable.

"Hey," I say softly. "Long time no see."

She stares at me for a moment, and I wonder whether I've changed as much as she has. Then she smiles, which lights up her whole face, and says, "Titus! Oh my God, it's good to see you! I didn't realize you were in the UK. Chrissie told me this morning."

"Yeah, I'm over here on business." Behind her is a series of bookshelves. She looks as if she's in a study, or maybe a living room. "Are you at home?" I ask.

"Yes. I've got the tiniest cottage in a little Devon village called Briarton. It's wonderful—it has oak beams from the Armada, and a coffin hatch in the ceiling." She tilts the laptop up to show me the square shape above her head. "It's so if you die in your sleep, they don't have to get your stiff corpse down the spiral stairs."

"That's amazing."

"It's actually a converted Saxon longhouse. It's made from cob—straw mixed with cow dung. You can't smell it though." She grins, then says, "Where are you? In London?"

"Yeah, I'm staying at the Rosewood Hotel in Covent Garden."

"Ooh, snazzy. Where are you right now?"

"Just outside. It has a garden terrace." I turn the laptop to show her.

"Jesus," she says, "that must have cost you a fortune." Then she grimaces. "Sorry. Oliver's always telling me not to mention money."

I grin. "I think you're the only person apart from your parents that calls him Oliver."

"Well, technically you can call me Huxley too."

"Ah no," I reply mischievously, "I'll always think of you as Your Royal Highness."

That makes her laugh, and her eyes dance. "Eight years," she says, "and I still blush when I think of that afternoon. I can't believe you kissed me."

"You asked me to," I point out.

"I did. You could have said no."

"I absolutely should have."

"Do you regret it?"

"Nope." I smile, and she giggles.

"This is a bolt out of the blue," she says. "What made you contact me today?"

I scratch my cheek. "Actually, I've got a favor to ask you."

"Oh?"

"You're not leaving for the wedding for another week, right?"

"Yeah. I fly out on August the third."

"Well, the reason I'm here is to meet with a company called Acheron Pharmaceuticals."

"They're the ones offering funding for your IVF project, right? Chrissie told me this morning."

"Yeah. The CEO, Alan Woodridge, lives just east of Exeter, and he's invited me to stay for the weekend. He's holding a cocktail party on Friday night, a murder-mystery evening on Saturday night, and then on Sunday morning he's organized a hot-air balloon ride across Devon."

"Wow, sounds great."

"Yeah. Monday I'll get a tour of the company, and we're meeting with the board in the afternoon for a more formal discussion. But anyway, so I've got to go to these events, and... well... I'm on my own, and I don't know anyone else here. And so I was wondering whether you'd like to come with me."

She stares at me. Her lips part, but no words come out.

Concerned that she thinks I'm hitting on her, I add, "Not as a date, just as a friend. Absolutely no obligation at all. I'm sure you're busy, and it's the last thing you'd want to do."

"It's not that," she says. "Did Huxley ask you to check on me?" She doesn't look annoyed, just suspicious. I decide honesty is the best policy.

"Yes, he did, and I promised I would. But it was a kind of kill-two-birds-with-one-stone thing. I don't want to spend the weekend at this house alone, and I thought it would be a chance to catch up and have a bit of fun."

Her lips curve up. "I see."

"I think if Huxley knew I'd ask you out, he might have had second thoughts about asking me to contact you."

"I thought it wasn't a date," she says.

"Ah… yeah, nah, obviously it's not, because we live on opposite sides of the world. It's purely platonic."

"How dull. In that case, the answer's no."

I laugh. "You haven't changed."

"I'm going to take that as a compliment."

"You should." I smile. "Will you come?"

"Well, how can I pass up the chance to go on a platonic date with the Striking Viking?" Her eyes twinkle.

I feel a surge of pleasure. "Excellent. Well, like I said, there's some kind of cocktail evening on Friday night, so I thought I could pick you up in the afternoon and…" I trail off as I hear a doorbell, and she looks past her laptop.

"Fuck," she says.

"Everything all right?"

She bites her bottom lip. "Someone's at the door. I'd better answer it."

"Okay."

"Give me five minutes and I'll call you back?"

"Sure."

"Thanks." She folds down the lid of her laptop—but she doesn't close it completely. I don't think she's realized she's still transmitting. I can't see anything, but I can still hear what's happening in the room.

I stare for a moment, my cursor poised to end the call. But then I hear her say, "What the hell are you doing here?" and I lower my hand, concerned.

If she'd been anyone else, I might have told myself it was none of my business, and waited for her to call back. But before I left, Huxley took me to one side and said, "Can you do me a huge favor?"

"Of course," I replied.

"Can you check on Heidi?" He gave me her phone number, email address, and physical address. "Just a phone call would be great, but I'm worried about her."

He'd already told me that she'd broken up with her boyfriend a few months before, but this was the first time he'd expressed concern. "Why?" I asked.

"She won't talk to me about it," he says, "but she's told my sisters that her ex is harassing her."

"Oh no. In what way?"

"I think it's mostly online. Evie said she's trying to get her to report it to the police, but she doesn't think Heidi's called them yet. I'm worried it's more serious than Heidi's letting on."

"Have you talked to her about it?"

"She changes the subject. I worry about her, that's all."

"I'll contact her," I told him. "Although I don't know that she'd be likely to tell me any more than she'd tell you or her sisters."

"I dunno," he said, "you two seemed to click last time you met." He gave me an amused look.

"That was eight years ago," I replied wryly, "and the only conversation we had was with our tongues." I blanched as his eyebrows rose. "I mean… ah…"

He rolled his eyes. "Anything you can do would be greatly appreciated." And that was the end of the conversation.

So being in the middle of talking to her when it sounds as if her ex might be at her door has put me in a difficult position. I wait and listen, prepared to close the laptop as soon as I know she's okay.

A male voice says: I need to talk to you.

Her: I'm busy.

Him: What do you mean? Have you got someone there?

There's a bang, and an exclamation.

Her: What the fuck? Jason! You can't just walk into my home.

I stiffen, alarmed. Shit. What should I do? Phone the police? I pick up my mobile, ready to call them.

Him: Where is he? Who is it?

Her: There's nobody here. I was on the phone.

Him: Who were you talking to?

Her: It's none of your business. I want you to leave.

Him: Don't do this. I just want to talk.

Her: Well I don't. There's nothing to talk about. We're done. You've got to stop this and accept it.

Him: I'm never going to accept it. I want you back.

Her: You can't browbeat me into going out with you again. You've got to stop calling and messaging me. What you're doing—it's harassment, Jason. It's stalking. Do you understand that?

Him: That's bullshit! I love you. And I'm trying to show you. It's not harassment!

Her: Are you drunk? Jesus. You're fucking drunk.

Him: Who were you talking to? Tell me.

Her: An old friend.

Him: From New Zealand?

Her: Yeah, but he's in London, and we're going to meet up.

Him: Do you have feelings for him?

Her: We're just friends. But if you were a fraction of the man that he is, we might still be together.

I'd have blushed if I wasn't so worried.

Him: Don't say that. I love you.

Her: Don't you fucking touch me.

She sounds furious, but I know that doesn't mean she's safe. What the hell is the emergency number out here? It's 1-1-1 in New Zealand. 0-0-0 in Australia. 9-1-1 in the States. I think it's 9-9-9 here?

Him: Please, I love you…

There's the sound of a scuffle, shuffling feet, a squeal from Heidi that makes me leap to my feet, and then a deep male groan.

Him: Ahhh Jesus… Oh God…

Her: Get the *fuck* out of my house.

Him: Heidi…

Her: GET OUT! Stop calling me. Stop texting me. And stop messaging me on social media. We're done, and if I see you here again, I'm going to ring the fucking police, do you hear me?

There's more scuffling, then the bang of a door closing.

I slowly sit again and stare at the screen. It sounds as if she threw him out. Good on her. Do I wait for her to open the laptop and see that I heard everything?

I hear footsteps, then the squeak of the sofa as she sits.

Then, to my horror, she bursts into tears.

Her sobs are deep and heartrending, and my insides twist as I listen to her, one hand over my mouth. At least she's safe, for now anyway. She wouldn't let him in if he knocked again, would she?

The sofa squeaks, and then the connection is cut—she's closed the laptop lid.

I sit back and look up at the darkening sky. Will she call me back when she feels better? I wait for fifteen minutes, but the screen remains blank.

I pick up my phone, dial her mobile number, and put it to my ear. After a few rings, it goes to voicemail. She's turned off her phone. I end the call without leaving a message.

Maybe she'll answer if I call in the morning. But she doesn't want to talk to me right now, and I need to honor that. I'll talk to her tomorrow, when she's hopefully feeling better.

I let my gaze drift over the rooftops, up to the night sky, fighting with my natural instinct to take action. I think of her deep sobs, and Huxley's concern for her. She has family here, and plenty of friends, I'm sure. She doesn't need me riding in on a charger to rescue her. It sounds as if she can handle herself just fine. She doesn't need me.

If you were a fraction of the man that he is, we might still be together.

Pursing my lips, I pull up Google calendar and see what I have planned for the next few days.

Chapter Three

Heidi

I awake with a start. It's dark, and I'm in the living room, on the sofa. I look at my watch; it's 1:03 a.m.

I groan. After Jason's surprise arrival and our subsequent argument, I cried for thirty minutes non-stop. After that, I was so exhausted from all the emotion that I must have crashed out.

My laptop sits on the coffee table, next to my phone. Ah, Jeez, Titus. I told him I'd call him back. I was so upset, and worried that Jason would try to call or message me, that I turned off my phone, too.

I pick it up, hesitate, then turn it on. My stomach flips with worry as I wait for any messages to download. Tomorrow I'm going to block Jason's number, and I'll also unfriend him on Facebook and block him on all my social media channels. I'm done trying to be nice.

He's sent me two texts, but I ignore them. Instead, I pull up the one that's waiting from Titus.

Hey, hope all is well. Let me know when you're up in the morning and maybe we can chat. T.

I rest my forehead on a hand, cursing myself. I should have cut Jason out of my life as soon as we broke up, and then I wouldn't be in this position. What must Titus be thinking? I know that Oliver must have told him what's been happening in my love life. I'm sure the last thing he wants is to spend time with someone recovering from a bad breakup. It wouldn't surprise me if he withdrew his offer to go with him for the weekend. Dammit.

I decide to send a reply to his text. I'm going to be totally honest. There's no point in trying to squirm my way out of it.

Hey, I know you're probably asleep now. Just wanted to say sorry for not getting back to you. Can we chat tomorrow? I'll understand if you've changed your mind, though. H x

I add the kiss and send it before I think better of it. Oh well. I tend to wear my heart on my sleeve, and I'd rather be myself.

I should go to bed, but I feel discombobulated and decide to make myself a cup of tea first. I go to get up, and then to my surprise my phone vibrates, announcing a text. It's from Titus.

Him: *Hey, glad you're okay. Would you mind if I called you now? No worries if you're off to bed though.*

Me: *Sure, I'm just having a cuppa.*

I flick on the kettle, trying to calm my breathing. No doubt he just wants to make sure I'm okay. Damn Huxley for telling him about Jason. Even from the other side of the world, my family still manages to make me feel like the baby sister.

My phone vibrates again, and I answer the call and put it to my ear. "Hello?"

"Hey," he says. "Hope you don't mind me calling."

"No, of course not. Look, I'm so sorry for not getting back to you."

"It's okay." There's a strange noise in the background. It sounds like cars. I know his room has a garden terrace, but the traffic sounds more like a motorway.

"Where are you?" I ask curiously. "In your hotel room?"

"Ah, no. Actually I'm on the outskirts of Exeter, in the service station."

My eyes widen. "What?"

"I was worried about you. I was going to come to your house and make sure you were okay. I settled up here and hired a car. But when I got to Exeter, I realized you'd probably be in bed, and the last thing you'd want after an argument with your ex is a stranger turning up at your door. I decided to get a motel room, but they're fully booked. So I thought I'd crash in the car and then call you in the morning."

My jaw drops as I think over what he's said. Then something strikes me. "Wait, how did you know I'd had an argument with my ex?"

He doesn't reply for a moment. Then he says, "I have an admission to make. You didn't completely close your laptop lid, and it didn't end the Zoom call."

I cover my mouth with a hand. "You heard the whole thing?"

"Uh, yeah. I know I shouldn't have listened. I was going to hang up, but then I heard him come into your house, and I was really worried about you. Shit. I'm so incredibly sorry. Now I sound like a fucking stalker. Look, just forget I even exist, okay?"

"Titus," I say softly, "it's okay. I'm touched that you were concerned. I know that Oliver must have told you all about my breakup."

"Only that your ex has been harassing you. And I'd never have forgiven myself if something had happened to you. I was close to calling the police when you threw him out."

"Look," I say, "do you know where I live?"

"Yeah, Huxley gave me your address."

"Why don't you come here? It's only about fifteen minutes from Exeter. I've got a spare room, and I make a mean cooked breakfast. You'd be better off staying here than sleeping in your car, anyway. Tomorrow we'll find you a hotel."

"Heidi, I couldn't do that after the night you've had."

"I'm fine. Honestly, it wasn't all about tonight. I hadn't really processed the breakup, and I've been in denial about his harassment. It just all came crashing down on me. I'm okay now. I mean I have panda eyes, but I'm all right. I won't go weepy on you."

"Ah, I wouldn't mind. But you don't want a stranger in your home."

"Christ, you're not a stranger. I've known you for eight years. You're one of Oliver's best mates. Evie and Chrissie had nothing but good things to say about you this morning." I smile. "I can't believe you left your posh hotel for me, that's so sweet. You should know that my house is incredibly small, not what you're used to at all."

"Well, size isn't everything."

"I don't know about that," I say mischievously. "I've heard the rumors about you."

As soon as the words are out of my mouth, I can't believe I've said them. God, what is it with this man? Why does my brain refuse to function when he's around?

But he just gives a deep, sexy chuckle. "Glad to hear my fame is spreading," he teases. "All right, I'll head off now. You reckon about fifteen minutes?"

I'm glad he can't see me blushing. "Yeah, about that. There isn't any parking right outside the house, but there is a small car park just down the road."

"Okay. I'll see you soon."

"See you." I hang up.

I sit there for a moment, totally bemused. He listened to my argument with Jason? Oh my God, what did I say? I try to remember, but it's all a blur. I recall Jason trying to slide his arm around my waist, and I yelled not to touch me. Titus said he was close to calling the police, so he must have heard that bit. I decide there's no point in worrying about it. Although he shouldn't have listened in, I'm kind of touched that he did. Now, though, I need to get ready for his arrival.

I dash around tidying up, then go up the stairs to the spare room. The furnishings come with the house, which I rent from my headmistress at the primary school. I've never used the spare single bed, and it's heaped with boxes containing books and other personal effects I've never bothered to unpack. As quickly as I can, I move them into my own bedroom, stacking them up in the corner. There's a spare duvet in the laundry cupboard, rolled up in a black bag, and I take that out and quickly stuff it in a fresh cover, and make up the bed. Finally I put on an oil burner with a few drops of lavender and bergamot to make the room smell nice.

I check my appearance in the bathroom mirror, wincing at the state of my mascara. I take out a wipe and clear up the worst of it, brush my hair, then go back down to the kitchen. I pop a couple of slices of the bread I made today in the toaster, just in case he's hungry.

The poor guy must be absolutely shattered. I can remember when I first came over from New Zealand—I woke up at four a.m. and had to go to bed at seven p.m. for what felt like weeks before I gradually adjusted to the twelve-hour difference. It makes his four-hour journey all the way from London even more impressive. How on earth did he manage to hire a car at this time of night?

Then I remember Chrissie's comments about him speaking at conferences in Australia, Canada, and South Korea, as well as being the keynote speaker in Auckland. I keep forgetting how important he is. He obviously wasn't staying in a hostel. No doubt the kind of top hotel he'd been in would be used to organizing requests like that.

I check my watch; it's been nearly twenty minutes. He should be here soon. I put some Miles Davis on in the background, then open the front door and go outside. The road is quiet; there's very little traffic at this time of night. It's a narrow street, as the houses on both sides have medieval origins. A Norman church sits on the hill up the road, overlooking the village. Down the road, the street splits around a central clocktower, the right-hand fork leading up toward the moors, the left-hand down to the river.

There's not a lot of light pollution here, and the sky is brilliant with stars. I turn to the northwest and find Ursa Major, the Great Bear—also known as the Big Dipper and the Plough—and follow two of the stars—Dubhe and Merak—to Polaris, or the Pole Star. These stars aren't visible Down Under, and I always get a thrill when I see them.

Then I drop my gaze back to the road, and I inhale at the sight of a lone man, walking toward me.

It's been a few years, but I recognize him immediately. He's tall—I think he's six three—and built like a rugby player, with powerful shoulders, muscular arms, and big thighs that stretch the material of his jeans. He was wearing a suit when I talked to him on Zoom, but he's obviously changed, and now he's wearing a gray T-shirt, which means his gorgeous tattoos are visible on his forearms.

His hair is short at the back, fashionably styled on top to make it look like he doesn't give a damn, or maybe he genuinely hasn't touched it since he got up this morning, it's hard to tell. He's clean shaven, although as he gets closer I can see the shadow of stubble, suggesting he didn't stop to shave before he left this evening.

Oh my God, I assumed I'd imagined how handsome he was, but my memory is better than I thought. He's absolutely gorgeous.

He smiles and lowers the bag he's carrying over his shoulder as he nears. Just in front of me, he drops the bag onto the pavement. Then he walks right up to me and takes my face in his hands.

For a moment, I think he's going to kiss me the way he did when I was sixteen, and I inhale like I did back then, my heart skipping a beat. But he just stares into my eyes as if he's shining a flashlight into the corners of a cave, looking for buried treasure.

"Are you okay?" he whispers. "Really?"

I nod, emotions welling inside me at his concern. "I'm all right."

"Thank God," he says, and then he pulls me into his arms and wraps them around me.

He's warm and solid, and as I press my cheek against his T-shirt, I can smell his really nice aftershave. It's lost its intensity after his long drive, but it's still rich, sensual, and spicy. Three words I'd definitely use to describe him.

Embarrassed that he might be aware I've just sniffed him, I go to draw back, but he doesn't release me, and so I slide my arms around his waist and let him hug me for a while.

I hadn't realized until I came to the UK how different the men are here to Kiwi guys. Don't get me wrong, I love Englishmen, and, on the whole, they tend to be self-effacing and polite, while plenty of them play sports, or have jobs outdoors. But Kiwi guys *are* different. They're matter of fact and practical, open-hearted rather than reserved, and speak their minds rather than holding back out of politeness. Also, because the weather tends to be nicer up in Auckland and the Northland, much of our childhood is spent outdoors, and even if they don't have Māori blood in them, the guys usually have light-brown skin. He looks young, fit, and healthy, and he's a connection with my homeland that I hadn't expected. Although I love it here, and I haven't thought too much about New Zealand, a sudden wave of homesickness makes tears spring into my eyes.

"I promised I wouldn't go weepy on you," I whisper, fighting not to let the tears roll down my cheeks again.

He rubs my back. "It's okay. I'm just glad you're all right."

I lean my forehead on his shoulder, and he rests his hand on the back of my head.

"You cut your hair," he murmurs, running a strand through his fingers.

I nod without looking up, waiting for him to echo my family and say something like *What a shame.*

"I love it," he says. "You look all grown up."

Aw, this guy is killing me. I put both hands on his chest, unable to miss the hard, defined muscles beneath my fingertips, and push back. "Come in," I say, smiling, and I back away into the house.

He follows, bringing his bag, and I close the door behind him.

"Wow," he says walking into the center of the living room, "you weren't kidding."

"About the size?" I grin. "No. She's super small. But she has a lot of character."

He puts his bag down and turns around, looking up at the coffin hatch, then at the big black beam over the fire. "That's from the Armada?"

"Yeah, a lot of the houses in the street have them."

He runs his fingers across the bumpy cob wall. He's so big—he seems to fill my tiny room. I can't believe he's here, larger than life. I love the way the sleeves of his tee stretch over his biceps, and his gorgeous tattoos. I'm having trouble tearing my eyes away from him.

"You'll have to watch your head on the way into the kitchen," I announce, because I can't think of anything else to say.

He glances up at the beam, then back at me and smiles. Then, as he turns away, he tips a picture on the wall with his elbow. As he hurriedly tries to stop it swinging, he bumps into a shelf and knocks two of the books onto the floor.

"Sorry," he says, bending to pick them up. "I'm a bit like Gandalf when he visits Bilbo in the hobbit hole."

"You must be tired," I say, chuckling. "Do you want to go straight to bed? Or would you like a coffee and a slice of toast?"

"Toast sounds fantastic. I'm ravenous, and it smells great."

"I made it this morning."

"The toast?"

I lead him out into the kitchen, making sure he ducks beneath the beam. "No, the bread."

"Really? With all the kneading and rising and stuff?"

"No, this is easy bake. No yeast—you use beer instead."

"Beer? In bread? Now you're talking."

I chuckle, take the slices out of the toaster, and retrieve some Lurpak from the fridge. "Spread that on," I tell him, "nice and thick, and I'll make the coffee."

We stand side by side, him buttering the toast while I make the espresso and steam the milk. I feel as if I have a celebrity in my home— a rock star, or a member of royalty. I've known him for so long, and he's my brother's mate, but I feel shy now he's here, and more than a little tongue-tied. I sneak a glance at him, and he meets my eyes, takes a step closer, and bumps my shoulder with his. I chuckle and pour the milk over the espresso, trying not to blush.

When we're done, we take the mugs and plates into the living room. He sits in the lone armchair, and I sit on the two-seater sofa, the only furniture that will fit in the tiny living room. The lit candles on the coffee table cast flickering shadows across his face, and the jazz music spirals to the beams as we crunch our toast and sip our coffee in companionable silence.

I have to say something. I wipe some crumbs from my bottom lip. "Titus…"

"Yeah?"

"Thank you. For being concerned, and driving all the way down here. There aren't many guys who would have done that."

"You're Huxley's kid sister," he says as an explanation. He takes a bite of his toast, his eyes gleaming. "And I was influenced by our romantic history."

That makes me laugh. "I still can't believe you did that. I'd never kissed anyone before."

It stops him in his tracks, and he stares at me. "What? Seriously?"

"Nope. I thought you were going to give me a peck on the cheek. I didn't expect a full-blown Frenchie."

"Shit. No wonder you looked so shocked."

"I was. You totally corrupted that innocent sixteen-year-old."

"Something to put on my CV," he says, and we both laugh.

"Huxley says you're doing well here," he comments. "You've settled in well at the school?"

"Mm. I love it there."

"Have you got citizenship here?"

"Yeah, because Mum is British."

"Ah of course. What age kids do you teach?"

"It's called Reception or Year Zero—after nursery, which is what they call kindy here, and before Year One. Kids start school here the year they turn five, so some of them are five in September, when the school year starts, and others have only just turned four in August."

"Still babies then really."

"Oh yeah."

"How many in a class?"

"I have twenty-one this year, and I have a teaching assistant to help. It's a tiny school, just over a hundred pupils. It's a state-funded faith school."

His eyebrows rise. "Christian?"

"Yes."

"I didn't realize that was still a thing."

"Oh, over a third of the twenty thousand funded state schools in England are faith schools."

"Wow, really?"

"Yes, I know it's strange for us because religion isn't part of New Zealand's school curriculum. Almost two-thirds of the faith schools are Church of England, and a third are Catholic, and a few follow other religions. Ours is a lot more relaxed than some because our headmistress is very open-minded. Children of any religion—or no religion—can attend, although priority is given to Christian families in the first instance."

"Do you teach Creationism?" he asks curiously.

"No, by law schools have to teach Evolution as part of the science curriculum. We also teach about other religions in the Religious Education lessons, although obviously we concentrate on Christianity. We have a close connection to the church up the road, to encourage children to feel part of the community, and we have a daily collective act of worship."

"I didn't think your family was religious," he says. "Huxley's not, anyway."

"No, Dad's not. Mum's English, as you know, and she was christened. She didn't go to church in New Zealand, but she used to tell me some of the Bible stories. I was hardly steeped in it, though, and I was surprised to get the job. I got on very well with the headmistress, though. This is her house."

"Oh, really?"

"Yeah, she rents it out to teachers, and it just happened to be available when I started. She liked what I said at my interview about my teaching ethos."

He tips his head to one side. "Which is?"

"The importance of friendship, justice, courage, perseverance, and forgiveness, and the value of human life." I flush. "It sounds a bit pretentious, but—"

"Not at all. Religion may depend on morality, but morality doesn't necessarily depend on religion, right? I would imagine it's as important to have teachers with a strong moral code in faith schools as it is to have those with a religious background."

"That's pretty much what Lucy—my headmistress—says." I warm all the way through at his understanding.

He leans his head on a hand. He looks super tired.

"Come on," I say, picking up his plate and mug and taking them out to the kitchen. "Bedtime. We can talk in the morning."

I turn the light on to illuminate the stairs before blowing out the candles. He picks up his bag and follows me up the curving staircase. "There's the bathroom," I say, pointing to the right. "This is your room. I'm sorry it's so small."

"I could sleep in a cardboard box," he says, going in and dropping his bag on the floor. "It looks great. And it smells nice."

I lean on the door jamb. He slides his hands into the pockets of his jeans, and we study each other with a smile.

"I'll see you tomorrow," I say.

He nods. "Glad you're okay," he murmurs.

I smile, go out, and close the door behind me.

Chapter Four

Titus

I don't even remember my head hitting the pillow. I sleep right through without stirring, and I only wake up when my phone goes off, telling me that someone is calling me on FaceTime. It's 07:27 a.m., and the screen tells me it's my father.

Pushing myself up in bed, I answer it, still half asleep. "Hello?"

"Lawrence? Did I wake you?"

My history teacher at high school, who had a fascination with the Antarctic and knew everything about the Terra Nova expedition to the South Pole, called me Titus, and it stuck. Only my father calls me Lawrence, insisting my nickname is childish and unprofessional.

I stifle a yawn and run my hand through my hair. "I was just rousing. Everything all right?"

"Fine. I thought I'd see how you're doing."

Of course, it's early evening there. "Are you still at the office?"

"Yes. I'll leave after our call. How's the trip going?"

"Very well, thanks."

"George Barnard contacted me. He said you canceled your talk today."

Dammit, I'd forgotten he knew Dad. "I did," I say. I refuse to apologize to him, even though I know he's expecting me to because he set up the visit.

"What happened?" he demands.

"I decided to take some time off to visit a friend in Devon."

He frowns. "You blew off the principal of King's College for a social visit?"

"It was a one-hour talk to a small group of students, and my friend needed some help." I don't bother adding that I haven't taken a single hour off to sightsee while I've been here, because I know how he'd respond to that.

Dad surveys me coolly. "This friend, is it a girl?"

"A woman, yes, not that it's relevant."

"Jesus, Lawrence. Can't you keep your dick in your pants for five minutes? Do you know how that's made me look?"

Fury blasts through me, due in no small measure to the fact that even though he's married to my mother, I'm pretty certain he's banging his secretary, and has been for several years. Six months ago, I finally plucked up the courage and confronted him about it. He denied it heatedly, tore me a new one, and called me a 'disrespectful, ungrateful little shit.' I'm convinced he's lying, but there's not much I can do about it without any proof.

He's brought me up to be polite and respectful, and never to give in to my emotion, but it takes every ounce of willpower I possess not to tell him to fuck off and hang up. "I spoke to him personally and explained the situation," I say icily, "and he was fine about it."

"I don't care. You've embarrassed me. I expected better of you."

This conversation sums up our relationship together. It doesn't matter that I've spent the past week working flat out, that I've received compliments left, right, and center, that I've had staff and students hanging on my every word, and that my work in AI is receiving attention internationally. Dad will always find fault, somehow.

I'm twenty-nine, a grown man, so why does he make me feel like I'm sixteen whenever we talk? Even though I owe him a lot, mainly because he funded my studies and invested in my business at the start, the fact that my bank balance includes nine zeroes has little to do with him. He knows nothing about the computer industry, and even less about AI and my work within the field. All he cares about is his image and how he can use me to further his position in the political arena.

"I hope you're not throwing away your career for a woman," he says. "I thought I'd brought you up better than that."

"I have to go," I say flatly.

"Lawrence—"

I end the call.

It takes me a few minutes to calm down. I regret hanging up, because I know he'll lob it back at me like a hand grenade next time we talk and criticize me for losing control and being rude.

I've done my best to stand up for myself over the years, but despite everything, he's my dad, and I do appreciate his support, his money, and his contacts. Still, how long do you have to put up with abuse because you feel you owe someone? If he'd given me one compliment, or said he was proud of me, just once, I might be prepared to keep overlooking his cruelty, but I'm close to telling my mother about his affair and cutting him out of my life, because I don't think I can bear much more of this.

It makes me think about Heidi. Huxley has told me that their father had a tighter hand on the reins with her than he did with his other children. For the first time, I wonder whether that had anything to do with why she moved to the UK.

I cock my head, listening, wondering if she's up. I think I can hear her moving around in the kitchen. Also… I inhale, just managing to catch the aroma of frying bacon. She's cooking breakfast.

Nothing will get me out of bed as quick as the promise of a fry-up, and I leap out, go into the bathroom and take a fast shower, get dressed in a new tee and a pair of comfy track pants, and head down the funny, winding staircase.

"Morning," I say, ducking under the oak beam into the kitchen.

"Hey! Sorry, did I wake you?"

"No, not at all. I slept really well." I lean a hip against the counter. She glances at me and smiles, then returns her gaze to the frying pan. Some more of her delicious, toasted beer bread lies buttered on two plates that are already topped with scrambled egg. As I watch, she lifts the pan and adds a couple slices of bacon, two sausages, a spoon of baked beans, and a heap of fried mushrooms to the plates, then picks them up and places them on the small kitchen table and gestures for me to take a seat while she goes over to fetch two mugs of tea standing on the counter.

I sit, thinking how bizarre the situation is. I drove down last night in a kind of dream, and when I arrived at her village, I felt as if I'd somehow gone through a wormhole into the past somewhere along the A38. The roads are narrow, and the houses are squeezed together, many of them portraying features that announce their origins lie in medieval times or even earlier. The pub by the river even has a thatched roof, and I'm sure I saw a standing stone in its garden, although whether it's actually prehistoric is another matter.

Heidi's cottage is miniscule—you could fit the whole house in my living room. But it's beautiful, with its oak beams, real log fire, coffin hatch, and spiral staircase. The windows in my bedroom were double-glazed, but the walls were bumpy cob, and the ceiling was slanted. I know I'm going to brain myself at least once on the low beams, but it's a small price to pay to stay somewhere so historic.

Heidi looks fresh as a daisy, and has obviously been up for a while. She's wearing a bright yellow sleeveless top and denim shorts, and her blonde bob shines golden in the sun slanting through the high kitchen window. She's slender, with a girlish figure that's nevertheless still sexy. She's absolutely stunning.

She's also Huxley's kid sister. I can see myself repeating that like a mantra all the time I'm with her.

"This looks amazing," I say, trying to distract myself.

"Do you cook much?" she asks, sitting opposite me, and sipping her tea.

"Nope. I love eating food. I don't know the first thing about preparing it."

"So you live on takeaways?"

"No, I have a housekeeper who makes and freezes meals."

"Wow," she says, "you're a spoiled brat." I chuckle, and she grins. "HP Sauce?" she asks, showing me the brown bottle. "It's great with bacon."

"Mm, sure." We can get it in New Zealand, but I haven't had it in years.

"Did you know it stands for Houses of Parliament?" She shows me the drawing on the front, and I realize it's of Big Ben and the Palace of Westminster.

"I didn't." I reach for the bottle and knock it over. "Dammit."

"You really are clumsy, aren't you?" With amusement, she stands it back up.

I lift it and add a dollop on the side of my plate. "Did you know that you have a touch of an English accent now?"

"I do not!"

I grin. "It's faint, but it's there. It's nice. Kinda sexy." I wink at her.

She lowers her gaze to her plate. "Lawrence Oates," she scolds, "how come you can still make me blush?"

"Skill."

She laughs and starts cutting up her bacon. "So…" She stops cutting and moves the scrambled egg around her plate. "I've got something I need to say."

"Oh dear."

"No, it's nothing bad. I just want to say that after what you witnessed last night, I'll understand completely if you'd prefer to withdraw your offer to go with you for the weekend. It's no fun being with someone who's been through a breakup, and I'm sure you don't want a miserable girl tagging along with you."

I sit back. "First of all, you're not a girl anymore. That much is obvious."

She looks down at her bust, then back up at me and raises an eyebrow.

"I was actually talking about your ability to stand up for yourself," I point out. "Jesus. I hope I'm more subtle than that."

She giggles. "Sorry."

I give her a wry look. "And secondly, maybe it's what you need to cheer yourself up. It sounds like it's going to be fun."

She wrinkles her nose. "As long as you're sure."

"I'm sure."

"Okay. I'll come then."

"Cool." Pleased, I tuck into my breakfast, which is excellent, the bacon crispy, the scrambled eggs just liquid enough, and the toast done to perfection.

"So what do you have planned for the next couple of days?" she asks.

"I should really go back to London. I'm supposed to be attending a conference this afternoon, and I have two meetings tomorrow."

"How long have you been in the UK?"

"Just over a week."

"Is it your first time in England?"

"No, I've been to London a couple of times, although I haven't been anywhere else."

"So you haven't been to Devon before?"

"No."

"Have you seen much of London?"

"Hardly anything," I admit. "I've spent most of the time either in meetings or giving talks."

"That's a shame."

"I know. I'm a bit one-dimensional."

"But you love your work?"

"I do."

"And you're very good at it, from what I hear."

"I do okay." I smile.

"Taking time for yourself doesn't come easy to you, does it?"

"No," I say truthfully.

"When's the last time you took a vacation?"

"Ah… what year is it?"

"Oh! That's shocking. All work and no play…"

"Yeah."

"Evie told me that at Mack's wedding you fell asleep on the deck and were still there in the morning."

I laugh and cut into the toast, scooping up a forkful of scrambled egg and bacon with it. "That's true."

"You didn't pull, then?" she teases.

"I didn't even try. I was knackered. It had been a busy month."

"The IVF project?"

"Yeah."

"I suppose it's made things harder for you, with Elizabeth getting pregnant."

"Yeah. I wouldn't say it to her, of course. Acheron will take me, but they really wanted her to come and head the research."

"So are you thinking of moving here?"

I meet her big blue eyes for a moment. I can't be sure, but I think there's a touch of hope in them. I clear my throat and look back at my plate. "No, I'm hoping to persuade them to invest, but that they'll let us run the project from New Zealand."

"Ah."

"I'm sure it would be a great experience, but my company is based there, and all my friends and most of my family are there."

"Of course."

"Well, you know what an upheaval it is, moving countries."

"Sure," she says, "and I didn't run a company. I was a free spirit. Still am." She laughs.

"That must be nice."

"Aw," she says, "don't tell me you regret all your hard work. I can see how much you love what you do."

"No, I don't regret it. But I know I'm a workaholic. I find it impossible to switch off, I don't know why. There's always something work-related I could or should be doing."

"Which makes it even more important that you take a few days off." She leans back and has a sip of her tea. "I have an idea. Cancel your meetings and stay here with me for a few days. I'll take you on a sightseeing tour around Devon."

My eyebrows rise. "I couldn't do that."

"Why?"

"You must be busy…"

"Not at all," she says. "I was going to have a few days off myself. Not all those who wander are lost, you know?"

"You're a Tolkien fan?"

"Big time."

"Do you have an English degree?"

"No, History, but I'm interested in a lot of things."

"Like?"

"I read all the time, fiction and nonfiction. I paint a bit. I play the guitar, and listen to a lot of music. I love astronomy."

That makes me sit up. "Seriously?"

"Yeah. You too?"

I nod. "I've been working with the Royal Astronomical Society, using artificial intelligence to search for exoplanets by studying the variation of a star's brightness over time."

"Jesus. I look at the moon through a very cheap telescope. It's not quite the same thing."

I chuckle. "Even so, it's cool to know you're interested in it."

"I'll show you my observatory in a minute." Her eyes twinkle. "So, can you take a few days off?"

I study her, slightly taken aback. There's no reason I can't cancel the meetings—I've already attended the most important ones, and the conference was something I signed up for to fill in time. But is that what I want? To stay here, in Heidi's tiny cottage, and spend a few days doing nothing but pottering around Devon, looking at the sites?

I discover that actually, yes, it sounds like something I very much want to do. But there is a problem.

Asking her to go with me for the weekend was one thing—I'd have asked the same of Huxley's other sisters if they were the only person I knew in another country. But staying in her house… spending time alone…

The thing is, I like her. A lot. She's young and sexy, and I have a sneaky feeling she likes me too. I think we could have had a lot of fun together. If she wasn't related to my best mate.

"I don't know," I say softly. "You're Huxley's kid sister, and you're recovering from a bad breakup. The last thing you need is… complications."

She meets my eyes, and we study each other for a moment.

"Just to make things clear," she says, "sex isn't on the table."

My eyebrows rise. "Right."

"Or on the bed or the floor or anywhere else in this extremely small cottage."

That makes me laugh. "Okay."

"We aren't going to do anything that involves removal of clothing."

"Got it."

"We're friends, aren't we?" she adds.

"Of course."

"And I'd like it to stay that way."

"Definitely."

"I didn't want you worrying," she says. "It's always best to be direct."

"Absolutely."

"We're grownups, right? We can spend time together without getting involved. Even though we're attracted to one another."

"You're attracted to me?"

"Um… no…?"

We both laugh. "You're right," I tell her, trying not to think about her admission. "Best to be open."

I think I can see a glimmer of hope in her eyes, and it occurs to me then that she might be glad of my presence here because it'll be some protection for her if her ex comes knocking again. Not that she can't stand up for herself, because she obviously can, but it might give her some peace of mind. And I think Huxley would like that.

"All right," I say, "I'll stay, and you can show me around."

"Great!" She beams. "So anywhere you fancy going?"

"Dartmoor, I guess. I don't know what else is here."

"What are you interested in seeing? Nature? Cities? History?"

"History, definitely, as we don't have much in New Zealand." I check my watch. "I should do a bit of work before we go out, if that's okay. I need to cancel those meetings, and catch up on emails."

"Of course. What about if, when you're done, we take a walk through the village, and maybe have lunch at The Monolith? It's a pub."

"The one with a standing stone? I thought maybe it was fake."

"No, it's real, and it dates to about 2,500 BC. Legend has it that if you touch it, you either die, go mad, or fall in love."

"Not sure which I'd prefer."

She grins. "The pub does great food, including cream teas, which you absolutely have to have in Devon. Then we could take a drive across the moors. And I'll find something interesting to do this evening."

"Okay, sounds great. First though, I'll help you wash up, and then you can show me your observatory."

She laughs, goes over to the sink, and starts running the hot water. "I was joking. It's not a real observatory."

"I gathered."

"It's pretty cool, though. Do you have a telescope?"

"I do." As I pick up the tea towel and start drying the clean crockery she puts on the draining board, I think about my Celestron Equatorial Schmidt-Cassegrain, which I love almost beyond all things. "I've been into astronomy since I was a boy. My mum's dad works at the Institute of Theoretical Astrophysics in Norway, and whenever he's visited, we go stargazing."

She slots a plate into the stand. "He must be really proud of you."

"Yeah, I think so." I watch bubbles rising from the sink, rainbow-colored in the sunlight. One lands on her arm and pops. She has elegant hands, with long, tapering fingers and neat nails painted a sparkly pink. I can't help but think of those fingers on my thigh, sliding up over my skin to take me in hand…

She lifts her gaze to mine, and I realize she's waiting for me to say something.

"Ah, sorry?" I say. "I zoned out for a moment."

Her lips twitch as if she can guess what I was thinking, but she just says, "I asked if you can speak Norwegian."

"Yeah, not quite fluent, but enough to make myself understood there."

"You've been there?"

"Yes, a few times. It's where I got the tattoos." I hold out my arms. She drops her gaze to them. "That makes sense. They're magnificent."

"Thank you."

"I love the wolf." She reaches out a wet finger and brushes it against the wolf's head. A frisson runs all the way up my arm and then back down my spine. As if she felt it, too, she glances at me, then lowers her gaze and slides her hand back into the water to finish off the last mug.

I take it from her and dry it, hoping I'm not doing the wrong thing by saying I'll stay with her. She was right—we are grownups, and we should be able to control ourselves. It's not easy though, when all I can think about is kissing her.

The dishes done, she hangs up the tea towel and says, "Come this way," and leads me through the kitchen and out the back door into the garden.

It's tiny, with a paved patio bearing a round plastic table and two chairs, and a rectangle of grass that's the size of the rug in my living room. At the bottom, though, is a greenhouse, and she crosses the lawn in her bare feet, opens the door, and lets me precede her inside.

It's a makeshift observatory, with a small, beginner's refractor telescope standing on a plastic table in the center. "Not quite in your league, I'm sure," she says, a little embarrassed.

It's not a patch on my Celestron, but what impresses me are the star charts she has spread out on the benches all around the greenhouse. They're very detailed, mapping the constellations visible in the northern hemisphere, and she's annotated them with the positions of the planets throughout the year, as well as marking things like the phases of the moon.

"I watched the Perseid meteor shower the night before last," she says. "So many shooting stars, it was spectacular."

"You've been looking at Messier 13, too." I tap the chart showing the Hercules globular cluster she's marked with a Post-it Note.

"Yeah, it's an excellent target for observation at this time of the year because of its high altitude at night. Although you know that, obviously."

"It's a great setup," I say. "I'm impressed."

She nudges me. "You don't have to give me false flattery."

"I don't do that."

She laughs. "No, I forgot you were a Kiwi guy. Oh, mind out!" She just catches the telescope as I knock into it.

I wince. "Sorry."

"I need to bolt everything down when you're around. It's like having a young colt in the house."

"Are you comparing me to a stallion?"

"Jesus, are we back to Sir Richard again?"

We both laugh, and I follow her back out and across the lawn to the house.

"Okay," she says, "you crack on with your work and then we'll go out a bit later."

"Do you mind if I set up in the living room?"

"Of course not. I'm going to do some baking. Do you like muffins?"

"I like food, Heidi, I don't care what sort it is. I'll eat anything."

"Right, then I'll make some muffins." She starts opening cupboard doors and taking out ingredients.

I retrieve my laptop from my flight bag, bring it downstairs, and plug it in by the sofa. Then I open it up and start checking my emails.

Heidi comes in and says, "Do you prefer to work in silence, or shall I put some music on?"

"I don't mind noise. Music would be good."

She goes over to what I realize is a record player, selects an album from the cupboard beneath it, and puts it on before returning to the kitchen. Stevie Wonder's voice starts singing *You Are the Sunshine of My Life*, and Heidi joins in, her voice like the sunlight filling the house, bright and uplifting.

I stretch out my legs and prop my feet on the coffee table, surprised that I feel a mixture of happiness and contentment. Usually by now I'm knee-deep in meetings or immersed in computer code, and it feels like a vacation just to do something different.

I spend a couple of hours working, canceling the meetings I had planned for the next few days, answering emails, and reading a couple of reports my team have emailed to me from New Zealand. Halfway through, Heidi brings in a cup of coffee and a warm banana-and-chocolate muffin dripping with butter, which I eat with pleasure while I finish the reports.

"Want any washing done?" she asks. "It's a nice day to hang it out on the line."

"Are you sure?"

"Yeah. It's not often I get the chance to fondle a gorgeous guy's boxers."

I laugh and get up. "You're a naughty girl."

She grins at me, and I roll my eyes and go upstairs to fetch the clothes I've worn over the past week. I bring them down and give them to her, and she takes them out to the laundry.

Sometime later, when I finish the last report, I close the laptop and lean it against the chair, get up and stretch, then go into the kitchen. I can see Heidi through the window in the garden, so I cross to the doorway and lean against the post, my hands in my pockets.

She's hanging up the washing on the rotary line. As I watch, she picks up a pair of my boxers, shakes them to get rid of the creases, and pegs them up. When she's done, she puts her hands on her hips and studies them, then gives a soft laugh before she turns to collect another item from the basket. Only then does she see me and straighten.

I raise my eyebrows, and to my delight she turns completely scarlet.

"No need to ask what's going through your mind," I say, amused.

"Can you blame me?" She's obviously determined to pretend she isn't blushing. "I've heard about Sir Richard." She lifts her eyebrows. "Is it true?"

"Not at all. Two, three inches max." She giggles, and I give a wry smile. "Who told you that?" I'm pretty sure she's not in touch with my ex.

"Evie bumped into Claire. Apparently she'd had a few and was happy to share some details about your family jewels." She laughs and turns to hang a shirt on the line.

I don't say anything. When she's done, she picks up the empty laundry basket and comes to stand in front of me.

"Don't look at me like that," she says. "I wouldn't be human if I wasn't intrigued."

"Please don't talk about my family jewels. It gives me goosebumps."

She chuckles. "I only said we wouldn't have sex," she points out. "I didn't say we couldn't talk about it." She winks at me and squeezes by to go into the laundry room.

I sigh and follow her in. I'm beginning to realize I'm subjecting myself to a form of torture by staying here. It's easy to tell her we're not going to get involved. It's a lot harder to carry it through when she's teasing me, and looking up at me with those gorgeous blue eyes.

SERENITY WOODS

She's Huxley's kid sister. She's Huxley's kid sister.
Say it like a mantra, dude, and maybe it'll eventually sink in.

Chapter Five

Heidi

Shortly after, we head out of the cottage. "Let's go up to the church," I suggest. "It's such a beautiful little building, and it goes right back to the Normans."

"I know it sounds weird," he says, "but I'm finding it hard to get my head around all the history. The Normans—that makes it nearly a thousand years old. That's incredible!"

"Some of the prehistoric stuff is going to blow your mind, then. Did you come down here along the A303 or via the M4/M5?"

"The M4/M5."

"Aw, so you missed Stonehenge. You'll have to take that road when you go back to London."

It's a beautiful morning, a true English summer's day, warm and bright. We're both in shorts, and he's wearing an All Blacks rugby shirt. I'd forgotten how tight the new ones are. Man, he has an impressive physique. I'm tempted to take him swimming just so I can see him with his clothes off.

I'm already regretting my insistence that we're not going to have sex. But I know the fact that I'm his best mate's little sis is on his mind, and I don't think he would have stayed if I hadn't said that. Besides which, it makes sense for us not to get involved. After all the hassle I've had with Jason, the last thing I need is to fall for the Striking Viking when he lives on the other side of the world. Some people can have sex without being emotionally attached, but I'm not one of them.

We arrive at the fence of iron railings that surrounds the church, and I open the gate and go in. "There's been a church here since Saxon times, and they think it burned down in a Viking raid."

"Wow."

"The west end has a Norman entrance—you can see that because it's round rather than arched. The rest of it is fourteenth century, with some later additions."

"Can we go in?"

"Of course. Come on."

I take him inside, and spend some time showing him the features: the fifteenth-century octagonal font, the painted and gilded pulpit, and the tombs of local landowners with their carved stone effigies.

"This knight has one leg crossed over the other," I say. "That means he fought in the Holy Land."

"Oh, really?"

"Mm. And look at these carved bosses. There's a pope, a bishop, a nobleman, and a king, but can you see the one at the end? It's a Green Man. Look at the oak leaves around his face."

"Isn't that a pagan symbol?"

"Oh, definitely. That's what I love about England. It's like a businesswoman dressed in a perfectly respectable suit who's wearing naughty underwear underneath."

He chuckles. "Trust you to have an analogy like that."

"Oh, there's plenty more where that came from." I grin and lead him back along the nave. "What do you think?"

"It's wonderful."

I smile, glad he likes it, open the church door, and go back into the sunshine. "Come on. I'm getting hungry. Let's have some lunch at the pub."

We walk slowly through the village, with me pointing out the sights as we go. There's an old market cross that's been restored as a war memorial, the Town Hall, the Mission House, and the Devon House of Mercy for reclaimed fallen women.

"They're saving me a spot," I tell him, and he chuckles.

About halfway down, I lead him along a side road and stop outside the primary school.

"This is where you work?" he asks.

I nod. "There's my classroom." I point to the one on the right, nearest the office block. In the window is the long picture I did with the class at the end of last term of African animals—elephants, lions, giraffes, and zebras.

"It's nice to be able to picture the place," he says.

"Miss Huxley!"

We turn at the sound of a young girl's voice and see Tara, one of my pupils, running up with her mum a few steps behind.

"What are you doing here?" the girl asks, astonished.

"Miss Huxley doesn't disappear when the holidays start," her mum says, amused, and we both laugh.

"I live in Briarton," I tell Tara. When she looks up at Titus, I add, "This is my friend. He's come all the way from New Zealand. Do you remember where that is?"

She nods and says to him, "Miss Huxley showed us where she was from on a globe. It's underneath."

He grins. "That's right."

"Is everyone upside down there?" she asks.

"Yep," he says, "we all walk on our hands."

I chuckle. "He's teasing," I tell Tara. "It's exactly the same as here."

"Except the moon's upside down," he says.

"Best not to complicate matters." I smile at the girl and her mum. "I hope you have a lovely summer holiday."

"Thank you," the mum says, and Tara waves as the two of them cross the road.

We continue walking down to the river. "I don't think you're brooding," I tell him.

"Er, thanks?"

"It's how Elizabeth describes you. Apparently she said you're like the Dark Knight without the cape."

"Seriously? I don't know how I feel about that."

"I'm sure there are worse ways to be described. But I'm just saying, I don't see you like that. You're not brooding at all. I find you very warm and funny."

"You bring out the best in me," he says, and smiles, and I smile back. He probably doesn't mean it, even though he promised he doesn't give false flattery, but it's a nice thing to say.

Eventually we reach the river, and cross over the bridge to The Monolith. He crosses the lawn to the standing stone.

"Over four thousand years old," he says in awe. "Unbelievable." He reaches out a hand to touch it.

"Careful," I warn, "or you might go die or go mad. Mind you, not sure how we'd tell."

"Haha. With my luck I'd fall in love. The ultimate disaster!"

I smile, because I'm meant to, and we head into the pub. The outside is whitewashed cob; inside, it's all oak beams and low ceilings, with a huge fireplace. In the winter the logs would be crackling merrily but today because it's warm, the double doors are open to the beer garden, so we decide to sit outside.

Under my direction, we order two cream teas, and we let the warm summer breeze blow across us as we watch two house sparrows hopping around beneath the tables looking for crumbs, while a wood pigeon coos softly from its perch in the lower branches of a nearby horse chestnut tree.

Titus closes his eyes, tips his head back, and breathes deeply. I imagine he's inhaling the scents from the nearby herb garden—mint, rosemary, and thyme. I study his light-brown skin, clean-shaven jaw, and Adam's apple. When he passed women in the street, their gazes were drawn by his height, his powerful shoulders, and the fact that he walks with confidence, not stooping like some tall men do. And he's so handsome. He looks like a movie star on vacation.

At that moment he opens his eyes and looks straight at me, catching me looking at him. Caught out, I just smile, and he smiles back.

"So tell me why you think falling in love is a disaster," I say.

He chuckles. "I was being facetious."

"You say that, but I sense some truth beneath it. Some girl has scarred you. Was it Claire?"

He looks at the beer mat on the table, picks it up, and turns it in his fingers. "Did you ever meet her?"

"Yeah, once or twice. I thought she was very nice. Pretty and smart."

He gives me a wry look. "You can be honest with me, Heidi. We're not together anymore. You won't hurt my feelings."

"She seemed like a bit of a bitch," I admit. "It surprised me that you'd end up with someone like that."

"We sort of fell into a relationship," he says. "We met through friends and went out a few times. She started staying over. And then one day she just didn't go home. I don't remember talking about it, but her clothes appeared in the wardrobe and her things were in the bathroom and that was it—we were living together. I didn't argue at the time because it was nice to have the... ah... company..."

"To have sex on tap, you mean."

His lips twist. "Maybe. But it turned out in the end that's all it was about. For me, anyway. Elizabeth told me she'd overheard Claire joking with a friend about hooking a rich guy at last. I confronted her about it, and she just shrugged and said I was naïve if I thought women wouldn't be interested in my money. I ended it that day."

I can't tell whether he truly liked her, or if he's more annoyed about her being attracted to his fortune.

"I'm sorry," I say. "I know both Mack and Oliver have had similar problems."

He shrugs. "It wasn't the only issue we had. She never really got me. She thought I was being contrary when I didn't just say yes to her all the time. She called me moody, which used to annoy me."

"I don't think you're moody. I'm sure you just get preoccupied with work."

"Yeah, that's pretty much it."

A young guy comes out with a large tray and sets it on the table between us.

"Thank you," I say, and he smiles and withdraws. "Shall I be mum?" I ask, picking up the teapot.

"Sure. Wow, this looks amazing."

Four large warmed scones rest on a plate next to two dishes containing strawberry jam and thick clotted cream.

"Dig in," I say, pouring the tea into two cups.

He takes a scone and pulls it apart. "Jam or cream first?"

"Ah, that's the question." I tip a little milk into each cup. "In Cornwall they prefer the jam first, and in Devon they put the cream. But apparently Queen Elizabeth used to spread the jam then the cream, so that's what I've always done."

"Fair enough." He spoons the jewel-like jam onto each half of the scone, heaps the clotted cream on top, and takes a bite.

"What do you think?" I say, amused at his white mustache.

"Mmph."

I slide a cup and saucer over to him. "I'm guessing that means you like it?"

He wipes his top lip. "It's wonderful."

"Oh, I'm glad." I help myself to a scone and begin the process of adding the jam and cream. "I ate so many of these when I first came here that I put on five kilos." I bite into the scone, filling my mouth with fruity, creamy sweetness, then run my tongue across my top lip to remove the cream. His eyes follow it, then meet mine for a moment before he drops his gaze back to his tea.

My pulse picks up a little. I know he's attracted to me. What a shame he's not going to stay in England. We could have had a lot of fun.

I have a sip of tea. "So you're single now?"

"Yeah. Work is intense, and I don't want the complication of a relationship."

"Fair enough." I study him over the rim of my cup. "So Maisey's not in the picture anymore?"

He lifts his eyebrows.

"I heard she liked to talk at inopportune moments," I add mischievously.

"Huxley and his big mouth. I told him that in confidence."

"Oliver can't keep a secret to save his life, you should know that by now. So she liked to give you her shopping list while you were having sex?"

He gives a short laugh. "It was rather... distracting. A man needs to be able to concentrate on the job at hand."

I grin, but I'm unable to stop a shiver running down my back at the thought of Titus and sex in the same sentence.

He has another bite of his scone and gives me an amused glance with his light-green eyes. "Stop thinking about sex," he scolds.

"You started it."

"You give me goosebumps when you look at me like that."

"Like what?"

"You know what I mean. The come-hither look."

"Jeez, where are you from, 1895?"

His lips curve up, his gaze still on mine. "You know we can't," he says softly.

"Yeah, I know I said that. I'm having trouble remembering why."

"Because you're Huxley's little sister."

"We could just not tell him."

He laughs and finishes off his scone. "So, about Jason."

I sigh and put my teacup down with a clatter. "Way to bring the mood down."

"Sorry, but I'm curious. Where did you meet him?"

"At a teaching convention. He teaches Physical Education at a secondary school in Plymouth."

"Those who can't do, teach. And those who can't teach, teach gym?"

I chuckle. "Who said that?"

"Woody Allen. Seems appropriate."

"Yeah. He's a wanker. Jason, I mean, not Woody Allen."

He laughs. "How long did you go out with him?"

"About a year. The first six months were okay. I mean, he was a bit possessive when we started dating, like, he'd put his arm around me if any other guy came up to talk to me. But I didn't mind that, I thought it was cute. But it turned unpleasant fast."

He frowns. "He was jealous?"

"Yeah. I mean, possessiveness can sometimes be attractive or flattering, because it shows a partner wants you. But he was just nasty with it. He hated me going anywhere without him. If I went out with friends, or stayed late at work, I'd get a hundred questions when I got in about who I'd been with. And then he'd…" I trail off.

He studies me, his smile fading. "Did he… hurt you?"

He means did Jason force himself on me. I shake my head, although there were definitely times near the end when there wasn't much pleasure in it for me, and it's the main reason I broke up with him.

He must guess I'm lying though, because his eyes flare with anger. "Huxley wanted to form a posse, come over here, and deal with it. I wish I'd let him."

Until now, I've struggled to match this gentle, funny, warm guy with the knowledge that he's a well-known, incredibly intelligent businessman who owns and runs his own company, but all of a sudden I can imagine him speaking to a roomful of employees, lecturing at a conference, or giving a member of his staff a dressing down.

"Would you ever think about coming back to New Zealand?" he asks, tearing apart his second scone.

Is he suggesting that if I did, he might ask me out? Or is it a genuine question about where I see my future lying?

I look back at my cup and sip my tea. It doesn't matter what lies behind his question. "Not at the moment," I reply. "I love my job here, and I'm happy."

"You don't miss New Zealand?"

"Not really, because England is so beautiful. Sometimes I miss the weather. We have fewer sunshine hours here in the southwest. It's often gray and cloudy, but I don't mind it too much."

"What about friends and family?"

"I miss Oliver and my sisters. And my mum."

He takes a bite out of his second scone. "But not your father?"

I pick up some crumbs with a finger. "Has Oliver told you anything about my relationship with Dad?"

"He's mentioned that he was controlling."

I blow out a long breath. "Yeah. Very. I came here to get away from him." The words burst out of me, still with a touch of venom I can't eradicate. "I think maybe it was because I was his youngest daughter. I know he meant well. He wanted to protect me. But I found it stifling. When I was at university, he'd come down to visit, and he'd talk to all my friends, and quiz them about how I was doing, who I was seeing... It was awful. He'd give me lectures about boys, and say things he'd never say to my sisters. Even when I left university, he tried to talk me into getting a job in Auckland so he could 'keep an eye on me.'" I put air quotes around the words. "I had to get away."

"Is that why you cut your hair?" he asks.

I tuck a strand behind my ear. "Yes. He loved it. It was a symbol, I guess, of my childhood. The day I landed here, I took a pair of scissors to it and lopped it all off."

His eyebrows rise. "Seriously?"

"Yeah. It looked awful, and I went to the hairdressers the next day. But that night, I lay in my hotel room feeling like a new person. It was the best thing I ever did."

"Maybe if you'd cut it in New Zealand, it would have been a signal to him," he says.

I hesitate. "I just couldn't. His displeasure would have been overwhelming. I'm not that strong. I'm not rebellious, and I don't like confrontation."

"It sounded as if you did just fine with Jason the other night."

"Maybe, but that came at the end of three months of harassment and frustration. Straw that broke the camel's... you know. And I'd just spoken to you. It gave me courage."

He smiles at that.

I break open my second scone and put half of it on his plate. "Finish that off for me."

"You're sure?"

"Yeah, I'm quite full, and I can see you have a healthy appetite." I wink at him before piling on the jam.

He chuckles and reaches for the spoon, knocks it off the dish, and spills jam onto the tablecloth. "Shit," he says. "Sorry."

I chuckle and scoop it up. "Don't worry, I'm getting used to it."

He sighs. "I'm sorry you've had a difficult time with men."

"I'm sorry you've had a difficult time with women. I think we're both a little ashamed of our sexes."

"Yeah. I don't understand men who want to control women. They should be protected, not dominated."

Protected is an odd word to use. "You think of us as the fairer sex?"

He thinks about that, licking his fingers free of jam. "Most of the women I know are strong and formidable. I don't know anyone who'd dare to call Elizabeth weak and feeble."

"Ha, no!" I give him a curious look. "What's your mum like? I've never met her."

"Fearless," he says. "She's always called herself a shield maiden, like Lagertha."

"Side question, but was Lagertha a real character, or is she just from the Vikings show?"

"A twelfth-century chronicler called Saxo wrote about her, but experts think she probably wasn't real, and that her tale was inspired by the Norse deity Thorgard."

"Mm. Interesting. Anyway, so you don't see women as weak and feeble?"

"Not at all."

"But you were ready to fly over here with Huxley to protect me?" I tease.

He finishes off his scone, wipes his mouth with a serviette, and picks up his teacup as he leans back. "Honest opinion?"

"Always."

"Today we're told that women can do anything. Mentally, I believe that to be true. Physically? I've yet to meet a woman who can beat me in an arm-wrestling match."

"Do you arm wrestle many women?"

He grins. "You want to try me?"

I try not to look at his bulging biceps. "No... but I get your point."

"It seems a shame to pretend we're exactly the same. You know what sexual dimorphism is?"

"The male is larger than the female?"

"Kind of. It's the difference in appearance between males and females of the same species. Size is one such difference. In spiders, the female is larger than the male. In humans, it's the other way around. It's a biological fact. Guys are—on the whole—bigger and stronger than girls. Today's society insists we're all the same, but I think that as long as men don't use it as a way to subvert women, our differences should be celebrated. It's a fine line, though, and I think men cross it without realizing how it's making women feel. Like your dad. Maybe I'm wrong, but I doubt he understood how he made you feel when he tried to control you. I'm sure he just wanted to look after you and protect you, but he didn't get how you might have felt dominated."

"Interesting choice of word. Are you into S&M?"

He blinks. "Jesus. How did you get that from what I said?"

"I extrapolated. Are you?"

"No, not at all. I mean, a silk scarf or two can be fun, but…" He trails off and shifts in his chair. "We really have to stop talking about sex."

"Sorry."

"You have a one-track mind."

"I can't help it. Your biceps make me all dizzy."

He laughs at that, and I grin, glad he's not offended. He's right, though. I shouldn't keep talking about sex. It's not fair on either of us, when we live on opposite sides of the world and neither of us wants to move.

It's fun though, and I can see from the gleam in his eyes that he's secretly enjoying it. I haven't enjoyed myself like this for a long time. So providing we both know the rules—no removal of clothing—surely it doesn't matter if we indulge in a bit of teasing?

Chapter Six

Titus

After our cream tea, we head out of The Monolith and start walking back through the village. We've only gone a hundred yards when Heidi stops and says, "Oh! I completely forgot about that!"

She's stopped to look at a poster in a shop window. I go back and look at it with her. It's advertising Shakespeare in the Park. A theater group from Exeter is performing *A Midsummer Night's Dream* in a variety of outdoor locations around Devon. And tonight, the performance just happens to be in Briarton.

"Oh," Heidi says, turning to me, "I'd so love to see that. Will you come with me?"

"Of course," I say good-naturedly, even though I've never been much of a theatergoer, and I've never studied Shakespeare.

"That's fantastic. We'll bring some cushions, and I'll make us a picnic. It'll be amazing."

I smile as we continue up the road, pleased to see the sparkle return to her eyes. I was actually quite shocked about what she told me of her relationship with her father. The fact that she cut her hair the day she landed here tells me how deeply her resentment runs. It also emphasizes how awful what's happened with Jason has been for her. All her life she's had to put up with men trying to control her. I resolve to make sure that in the short time we're together, I never put any demands on her in that way.

The play begins at six-thirty, and it's only two p.m., so Heidi suggests we take a drive across the moors.

"You want to take my car?" I ask.

"If you don't mind driving."

"Not at all—at least it's the same side of the road as in New Zealand."

"True, I was very relieved about that when I came over."

We walk up to the car park, and I press the button on my keys to open the car.

Heidi's eyes almost fall out of her head. "Your hire car is a Range Rover?"

"A Sport Dynamic SE. What's wrong with that?"

"Nothing at all. I keep forgetting you're a gazillionaire."

I laugh as we get in and close the doors, and I start the engine. "You're hardly poor, surely. Your father's one of the richest guys in Auckland, I would have thought." Peter Huxley is an investment banker, and he's made a fortune over the years.

"I don't want any of his money," she says, buckling herself in. "He insists on paying an allowance into an account for me, but I don't touch it." She looks out of the window. "I know it's not the same as not having money, because there's always the reassurance that it's there if I need it. But I've survived on my wages so far."

I reach out and take her hand in mine and squeeze it. She looks up at me with her big blue eyes, surprised.

"I'm sorry," I say. Then I release her hand, buckle myself in, and reverse out of the parking space.

She clears her throat and directs me to turn right out of the car park, and I head along the main road toward the western end of the town, and turn onto a B-road. "Tomorrow I'll take you to some of the other villages on the moors," she says, "but today we'll just have a look at the landscape."

I follow her directions along narrow lanes with high hedgerows, having to reverse twice when I meet a car coming the other way. After about ten minutes, we pass over a cattle grid, and she says, "We're on the moors now."

It's not long before the hedgerows clear, and either side of us the ground opens out to the upland area of Dartmoor National Park.

"This is all granite under peat," she says, "and sometimes it peeks out from the grassland and forms what we call tors. We'll go up to Haytor now—it's the best known one."

"Does it rain a lot here?"

"God, yes. There are a lot of bogs with cotton-grass and sedges— all that purple and pink, and the sprinkles of white. Fox Tor Mires was the inspiration for Conan Doyle's Great Grimpen Mire, you know, in *The Hound of the Baskervilles?*"

"Oh, really? I love Sherlock Holmes."

"Me, too! I've watched all the Jeremy Brett series as well as the modern ones."

"Yeah, same, and a lot of the movies, too."

We continue talking about our favorite portrayals of the fictional detective as I drive along the winding road through the vast, open moorland. At one point, I slow down as we pass a group of small, wild, Dartmoor ponies.

Following Heidi's instructions, I turn off and slot the car into a space in the Haytor car park, and we get out. I'm sure that usually it's a wet, rather miserable walk, but today it's *hot as*, the sun beating down on us, forcing us to don our sunglasses, and to apply the sun lotion that Heidi has brought in her purse onto our arms and faces.

"Don't forget your neck and ears," she says. "Bend down."

I dip my head, and she tips a little of the lotion onto her fingers and smears it across the back of my neck. I lift my gaze to hers as she rubs it in. "You're taking a surprisingly long time to do that."

"Gotta be thorough," she replies, giving me an impish smile.

When she's done, we continue walking up the path to the rocks. It only takes us five minutes, and then we're at the top of the hill, looking out across the amazing patchwork of colors forming the moors. Turning south, I can even see the sea. It's a fantastic view.

"Beautiful, isn't it?" she says.

I look at her profile, the breeze making her blonde hair dance around her face. Her cheeks are pink from the sun. She's still wearing her sleeveless yellow top and shorts and no jacket, and she shivers a little as the wind whips across the rocks.

"Stunning," I say, only half referring to the tor.

She doesn't notice. "There are several prehistoric settlements up here," she says.

"Really? I would've thought it would be far too cold."

"It was warmer back then, and the moorland was covered with trees. Neolithic farmers cleared some of the forests and established the first fields. And of course there are lots of individual standing stones, stone circles, and stone rows."

I look at the ancient landscape, awed to think a man could have stood here, on this spot, five or six thousand years ago. The New Zealand landscape can be breathtaking, but we don't have anything like this.

"I can see you're a teacher," I say as we begin to walk back down the path. "You make it sound so interesting. It makes me want to study archaeology."

"You should! There are loads of deserted medieval villages here, too. You should see some of the aerial photographs, they're fascinating."

I love her enthusiasm and her obviously vast knowledge. She looks so young, but her expertise reminds me that she's twenty-five.

Despite the sun, she shivers again, and I say, "Are you cold?"

"A bit. It's so breezy. I should have brought a jacket."

"Come here." I put an arm around her and rub her arm. I know I shouldn't, but I want to touch her. I can't help it. She fascinates me.

If she'd stiffened or pulled away, I'd have apologized and dropped my arm, but she doesn't; she nestles against me and slides an arm around my waist, and so we walk back to the car like that, borrowing from each other's body warmth. It's with some reluctance that I move away from her in the car park, and I'm sure I see the same unwillingness in her to separate.

We get in the car, and I head back toward Briarton. "We can have a couple of hours' rest before we go out this evening," she says.

"Yeah. I might have a snooze," I tell her. "I've never slept in the afternoon before, but I'm feeling tired."

"It's your age," she says.

I chuckle. "Thank you. I'm only twenty-nine."

"When's your birthday?"

"October the twenty-fifth."

"Oh, a Scorpio!"

"You're into astrology?"

She grins. "Only for fun."

"So what are Scorpios like?"

"Bold, creative, determined, and loyal. Mysterious and mystical. Passionate and sexy."

"You're making it up."

"No I'm not! You read any online description. They're the sexiest sign."

"Well that's nice to know."

"They're also supposed to be quite jealous, but you don't seem like the jealous type."

"I think you should trust your partner, and I don't believe in demanding to know where they are every hour of the day or who they're with. That's not to say I wouldn't get irritated if some guy tried to chat up my girlfriend. I'm only human. That's why I can see the advantages of being married."

"You don't see it as a ball and chain?"

"Not at all. It's a warning to other men. Keep away, she's my girl." I glance across at her. She meets my eyes for a moment, then looks away, out of the window.

"What about you, when's your birthday?" I ask, changing the subject.

"July the twentieth."

"Oh, I just missed it. So what star sign does that make you?"

"Cancer. We're sensitive and compassionate, and very domestic— we like cooking and baking, and art projects around the home. We have deep feelings, and we wear our hearts on our sleeves."

"I've never believed in astrology, but that does seem to describe you."

"You do seem like a Scorpio, too. You're very mysterious."

I laugh. "No I'm not. I'm an open book."

"You are. Some men are all sport and sex, but I think you have layers."

"I really don't."

"You only think about sport and sex?"

"Sport, food, technology, and sex. That's about it."

She giggles, and I grin.

It's not long before we arrive back at the village, and I park the car.

"Let's call in at the supermarket," she says, "and choose some things for the picnic later."

"Okay."

It turns out to be less a supermarket and more a local store, selling a limited selection of groceries. We opt for soft rolls, baked ham, a triangle of brie, strawberries, red seedless grapes, and, under Heidi's insistence, a large bar of Dairy Milk chocolate. Finally, we choose a bottle of wine—a decent champagne, under my insistence this time.

"I'll get this," I tell her, handing over my credit card at the till.

"Titus!"

"You've just told me you exist on your teacher's wages, and you're putting me up for free. It's the least I can do."

She grudgingly accepts that, and I take the bags from her and carry them up the hill to her house.

"I'm enjoying having you staying with me," she says as she puts her key in the lock.

"Like having a slave?"

She goes inside, casting a playful glance over her shoulder. "Does that include chaining you to my bed when you're not washing the dishes?"

"Your wish is my command, ma'am."

She laughs and comes up to take the bags from me. I hang onto them, though, and she gives me a wry look before I finally release them.

"Go and have a snooze," she says. "So you're all fresh for tonight."

"You want me to get fresh with you?"

"Now who's got a one-track mind?"

I chuckle and head upstairs. I keep telling myself I mustn't flirt with her, but it's impossible not to.

I go into my room, take off my Converses, and flop back onto the bed. My skin feels sun-kissed and wind-burned, and I'm pleasantly tired. I close my eyes, and in my mind I can see the beauty of the moors, all that vast landscape, and the thousands of years of human occupation spread out before me.

Then Heidi appears in my memory, her hair lifting in the breeze, her blue eyes looking up into mine. Her face lingers there, as sleep slowly descends upon me.

*

We head down to the park around six, and I'm surprised to find it packed with people, drawn out by the beautiful summer weather. It's roughly square-shaped, with a children's playground in the middle, and a river that runs down the right-hand side. Numerous trees—English oaks, beeches, chestnuts, and birches provide plenty of respite from the hot sun.

Near to the stage that's been set up, we find a spot partly in the shade of a large English oak, spread out our blanket, and toss the cushions we brought onto it. I put the chilly bin—or cool box, as Heidi now calls it—between us, and we start unpacking the picnic. We've just begun eating the ham rolls when a man steps out onto the stage to welcome us to the park. He introduces us to the theater company, and then the play begins.

I stretch out on my side, head propped on a hand, next to Heidi, who's sitting crossed-legged, and let myself be carried away by the atmosphere and the wonderful playwright's words. It feels slightly surreal to be lying there in the evening sun on the other side of the world, eating strawberries and drinking champagne, under this old oak tree that has no doubt seen many such couples lying beneath its lobed leaves.

I've never felt this conscious of history before. There's probably not an inch of land in England that hasn't been walked on. I've not thought about it much, but I feel incredibly conscious of the people who've lived here—in the Neolithic, Bronze Age, Iron Age, Roman, Saxon, and Medieval periods. So many men and women, who've lived, loved, died, and been buried in this ancient land. I can almost hear them: talking, laughing, arguing, kissing, making love, having children, growing old, and dying, ghostlike around us.

"You okay?" Heidi whispers, and I look up to see her watching me, her blue eyes concerned. "You look sad."

"Not sad. Thoughtful. Just thinking about history," I murmur. "It feels very... I don't know... pagan here, under the oak tree."

"I know what you mean. I'll take you to a village tomorrow that has a really odd blend of past and present." She smiles.

I smile back, and I have to fight against an instinct to lift a hand, slide it to the back of her neck, and bring her down to kiss her. The sun is setting behind her, and she's lit by a halo of golden light. Her face is in shadow, but I can still see the curve of her Cupid's bow, and the rose-petal color of her lips.

She leans forward then, and my heart thuds as I wait for her to kiss me, aching for it to complete this mystical, magical evening. She pauses, her face about six inches from mine, looking into my eyes, and my pulse races. At the last minute, though, she reaches down to pick up a strawberry from the bowl, and returns to her sitting position, biting into the fruit as she returns her gaze to the actors on the stage.

I stifle a sigh. She is, of course, right not to go through with the kiss. We promised each other we wouldn't get involved. So why do I feel so disappointed?

We finish the picnic and the bottle of champagne by the time the play finishes, and after we've clapped all the actors, we throw away our rubbish then begin to make our way back up through the village with the empty bowls packed into the cool box, which I sling over my shoulder.

It's growing dark now, and the streetlamps have all come on, casting yellow pools of light on the pavement. Moths flutter around them, and the several pubs we pass spill more buttery light, while music spirals up into the night sky.

"I really enjoyed that," I say to break the silence as we near the house, as she's been quiet since we left the park. "Thank you for suggesting it."

"You're welcome. It was a lovely evening."

"Are you feeling okay?"

"Yeah. A bit… wistful, I suppose. It's been such fun, and I wish…" Her voice trails off, and she stops walking.

I look at her, see her staring ahead, eyes wide, and follow her gaze. A man is sitting on her doorstep, his back against her front door. He looks in our direction, spots us, and gets to his feet. I can immediately tell from the way he struggles to keep his balance that he's drunk.

"Jason?" I ask her, and she nods.

"What do you want to do?"

Twin spots of red have appeared on her cheeks. "That fucking arsehole. He won't leave me alone." She marches forward.

I jog to catch up with her, and we both walk up to the guy leaning against the wall.

He's shorter than me, maybe around five ten, five eleven, with short brown hair, fairly good looking, although his eyes are slightly too close together.

"Heidi," he says.

"What the fuck are you doing here?" she demands.

He ignores her question and looks at me. "Who's this?"

"None of your fucking business," she says. "I told you, if you didn't keep away from me, I'd call the police." She pulls out her phone and turns it on.

Jason lunges for it, and it's the perfect opportunity I need to put an arm against his throat and thrust him back against the wall. He tries to push me away, but I'm big enough to keep him there, and after a moment he stops struggling and glares at me.

"I wonder what your school will think of a young woman reporting you to the police for harassment," I say.

Fear lights his eyes at that. He looks at her and says, "Don't do it."

She turns the phone to show him that she's dialed 9-9. "One more digit," she states. I don't know if he can see it, but she's shaking. "I'll do it, Jason, if you don't leave me alone."

He looks back at me. "Are you two dating?"

"Yeah," I snap, furious that he's upset her. I bang him against the wall, and he knocks his head and groans. "She's mine now. So stay the fuck away from her, or you'll have me to answer to."

He holds up his hands. I step back, wanting with every cell in my body to hit him in the face. He gives her one last look. Then he turns and heads back down the road to the village.

Heidi fumbles at her door with her keys, but her hands are shaking too much, so in the end I take them from her, insert the key, and open the door. We go inside, and I close the door behind us and slide the deadbolt across.

She goes out into the kitchen and places the cool box on the table, then goes over to the window and stares out at the garden. I walk slowly up behind her and pause a few inches away.

"Are you okay?" I ask softly.

She shakes her head.

"Heidi…"

She turns, and I see briefly that her cheeks are wet before she buries her face in my T-shirt.

"Aw… come here…" I put my arms around her. Hers are folded defensively against her chest, and she feels like a baby bird, fragile and tiny.

"Why won't he leave me alone?" she whispers between sobs.

"Because he loved you and then he lost you. He's a fool." I kiss the top of her head.

"I'm sorry."

"Oh God, don't apologize. You've been through a lot."

She heaves a shivery sigh. "All breakups are hard, but that was so awful. I should have cut all contact with him from the beginning, but I missed him."

It occurs to me then that maybe she isn't as over him as I thought. Perhaps once she's taught him a lesson, she might want to get back with him.

"I'm sorry I said we were dating," I tell her. "I thought it might stop him bothering you, but I should have asked you if you minded first."

"No, it's good," she says fiercely. "I hate him. I'm glad you were here. I hope he never comes back."

I'm not surprised by her vitriol, but it does make me suspect she wasn't honest with me before. I move back a little and lift her chin so she's looking up at me. The moonlight that comes through the window lies across her face in a sheet of silver.

"He was my first," she says.

My eyebrows rise. "Seriously?" Jesus. She was a virgin until she was twenty-three?

She nods. "While I was growing up, Dad was really strict with us about seeing boys. My sisters didn't care, and just did what they wanted." She scowls. "I hate how I sound so weak. But I was too terrified of him to rebel. At uni, everyone else was sleeping around, but I was too shy, so I just threw myself into my studies. It was only when I came here and met Jason..." She swallows. "I was relieved to get it over with. But I really picked the wrong guy for that." Her eyes shine.

"Tell me the truth," I say firmly. "Did he ever rape you?"

"No. But he used to like holding me down, and he was... rough sometimes." Tears spill out of her eyes.

Cold slices through me, as if the moonlight is a silver blade. "Did you ever say no?"

She shakes her head and looks down. Fucking hell, she's ashamed because she didn't ask him not to be brutal with her. Oh my God, the things men do to women.

"I'll be all right," she says. "I just need a few minutes." She moves away from me, goes through the back door out into the garden, and closes it behind her.

I wonder whether to follow her. My instinct is to comfort her, but equally I don't want to intrude if she wants some time alone.

I want to kill Jason. To be the girl's first and treat her like that. No—to be with any woman at any point in her sexual journey and treat her like that. Fucking bastard.

Gritting my teeth, I decide to give her five minutes, and I go upstairs and visit the bathroom. As I come out, my phone vibrates in my pocket, and when I pull it out I see it's a FaceTime call from Huxley.

I go into my room, close the door, turn the light on, and answer it.

"Morning," I say, sitting on the bed as his face pops up on the screen.

"Evening," he replies, and grins. "How are you doing?"

"Yeah, okay. Just got back from watching Shakespeare in the Park with Heidi."

His eyebrows lift. "Oh, you've been to see her?"

"I'm still here, I'm staying with her. She's had a bit of trouble with her ex, so I thought I'd hang around and make sure she's okay."

His smile fades, and his brow darkens. "He's still harassing her?"

"I think she might have seen the last of him now. She threatened to call the police, and I roughed him up a bit."

He nods. "Good. Thanks."

I blow out a breath. "Hux, she wouldn't say, but I think he might have assaulted her."

"Jesus Christ."

"She's only just intimated. I wish I'd known. I'd have broken both his legs."

"God, I wish she'd come home. I hate that she's all the way over there."

I sigh. "She seems happy, apart from this. She's doing well at the school, and her students love her. She adores her cottage, although it is the size of a postage stamp. I know your grandparents aren't far away, and she talks about meeting up with friends. I think if she can put this ghost to rest, she's going to be okay."

"Well," he says, "she'll be home soon. We'll have to do our best to convince her to stay."

Half of me agrees with him. The thought of having Heidi living in Auckland fills me with delight, and I know already that I'd ask her out like a shot.

But equally, I understand why she loves it here. "I don't know," I say. "She's flourishing now she's her own woman."

"You mean now she's away from Dad?"

"I didn't want to say that."

"It's all right. I know what he was like with her."

"She said it's why she cut her hair—the day she arrived, apparently."

He sighs. "Yeah, I thought that might be the case. Ah, maybe it is better she's there. I know it sounds old fashioned, but I hope she meets a nice guy who can look after her, you know? Something more trustworthy than her fucking ex."

I nod.

"So you're staying with her?" Huxley asks. "In her cottage?"

"Er, yeah." He looks surprised, so I add, "I'm in the spare room."

He gives me an amused look. "Relax, Titus. You're one of the good guys. I know I can trust you." He picks up a takeaway coffee cup and has a drink, still watching me. I can't tell if he's teasing me or if he's serious.

I clear my throat. "How's life in New Zealand?"

"Yeah, good. Busy."

"The wedding all arranged?"

"Mostly, yeah." Huxley and Elizabeth wanted to get married before the baby comes, so they're having a quiet wedding in the South Island. Originally they thought of Queenstown, but in the end they decided to fly their friends and family down to Lake Tekapo, not far from Aoraki Mount Cook, for a couple of nights in an exclusive retreat high up in the mountains, in the world's largest Gold Dark Sky Reserve. The stargazing there is going to be amazing.

"Looking forward to be Mr. Tremblay?" I tease.

He chuckles. "Yeah."

"How's Elizabeth feeling?"

"Yeah, good."

"How many weeks is she now?"

"Seventeen. Joanna's got this chart, and every time I see her she tells me how big the baby is. Apparently it's now the size of a pomegranate."

Joanna is his nine-year-old daughter by Brandy, a girl he had a one-night stand with at university. She seems thrilled that he's marrying Elizabeth and having a baby, which is great.

We talk for another few minutes about business, and then, conscious that Heidi is still outside on her own, I say I have to go.

"Look after her," Huxley says.

"Will do." I nod, end the call, slide my phone into my back pocket, and head downstairs.

I go out into the garden, half expecting to see her in the greenhouse, but she's sitting in one of the plastic chairs, looking up at the sky.

"Hey," I say. "I was just talking to Huxley."

She looks up at me. "You told him what happened?"

"I did mention it, I hope that was okay. He's worried about you."

"He wants me to go back to New Zealand."

"Yeah. I said you were doing fine, though, and he admitted it's probably better that you're here."

Her eyebrows rise. "Really?"

"He's aware how you feel about your father. I think he knows how difficult you've had it."

She swallows hard and looks away.

I'm so tempted to take her into my arms again. To hold her tightly, and to kiss her tears away. I want to do it more than anything.

But I hesitate, Huxley's words ringing in my ears, *You're one of the good guys. I know I can trust you.*

Fuck it. I can't make a move on her. Huxley and I are good friends, and I don't want to jeopardize that by seducing his sister, especially when she's been through so much.

Chapter Seven

Heidi

I feel Titus's presence beside me with every cell in my body. It takes all my willpower not to turn, slide my arms around his waist, and bury my face in his neck.

I don't want a white knight to swoop in and save me every time I'm even remotely in danger. I like to think I can cope alone—hell, I moved across the world, got myself a job and a house, all on my own. I don't need a man. But fuck, I love that he stood up to Jason for me. That he got physical, and thrust him up against the wall. I couldn't have done that, and Jason really, really needed someone to do it.

It's the first time I've thought that the nickname Titus suits him. I looked up the meaning years ago. It means 'of the giants.' Honorable, strong, a defender.

I want to feel his lips on mine. To have his big, strong hands on my body. Oh my God, I want to have him inside me. I dreamed about it last night in bed. I've thought about little else all day, and now I've watched him stand up for me, I'm not going to be able to stop thinking about it.

But I can't sleep with him. I know if I suggest it, I'll just embarrass myself. He only thinks of me as Oliver's little sister, and even if he did desire me, he's such a nice guy that he'd never make a move on me.

Plus, I know there's a possibility I'm only crushing on him because I've broken up with Jason and I feel vulnerable and lonely. It's just a rebound thing, maybe for him as well, as I know he didn't break up with his ex that long ago. He's only been here for one day, so what I'm feeling—this connection, this longing—can't be real.

He sighs, and he looks a little wistful. Is he feeling what I'm feeling? Or is he exhausted by this drama that has nothing to do with him? I thought he liked me, but maybe I misread the signs.

"How about we watch a movie or something?" he suggests.

He's trying to move past it. And that's fair enough.

I force my lips into a smile. "I'd like that."

"Come on then. Let's have a cup of coffee and you can choose what we watch."

So we make ourselves a latte, then take it into the living room. I sit on the two-seater sofa, expecting him to take the chair. To my surprise, though, he sits beside me. Okay, the sofa faces the TV whereas the chair is at an angle, but even so…

"What kind of movie do you fancy?" I ask, trying not to sound breathless. "Something sci-fi, as we've been discussing astronomy?"

"Sounds great."

We decide on *Gravity* with Sandra Bullock, and I put it on, then curl up beside him, knees pointing away so I'm not tempted to lean against him.

We don't touch for a while, sipping our coffee. Then, after about twenty minutes, he slides down a little, props his feet on the coffee table, and stretches his arm out on the back of the sofa, not quite around me, but almost. Feeling like I'm sixteen, I sit there for a minute, not daring to move, and then I look across at him. He meets my gaze, and something in his eyes makes my heart miss a beat.

He doesn't feel as if he can make a move on me, either because of Oliver, because he's only here temporarily and neither of us need that complication, or, more probably, for both those reasons. But I wasn't wrong. He likes me, and he wants to comfort me.

I curl up the other way, turning my knees toward him, and rest my head on his shoulder. He doesn't lower his arm around me, but he moves it an inch, so he's just touching my back, and he kisses the top of my head.

And that's it, we stay like that for the rest of the movie. The scent of his aftershave rises from his warm body, and I watch his chest rise and fall with each breath he takes. On the rare occasions that he says anything, I feel his deep voice reverberate through him, and I have to fight not to shiver.

I'm disappointed when the movie comes to an end, but feel a little thrill when he doesn't stir, but instead picks up the remote. He brings up the YouTube app, searches for 'ambience night sky', and chooses something called 'Stonehenge Starscapes', which show Astro-lapse scenes of the celestial sphere moving over the prehistoric monument, overlaid with gentle piano music.

Then he lets his head tip back onto the sofa, inhales deeply, and lets out a long sigh.

I rest my cheek on his shoulder again and, unable to stop myself, place a hand on his chest. I can feel his pecs beneath the soft T-shirt fabric, the defined muscles firm under my fingers.

"Are you feeling homesick?" I ask.

"No."

"Do you miss working?"

He waits a little longer before replying. "I wouldn't say miss. I feel a bit… I don't know, guilty, I guess. Vacations have always seemed self-indulgent to me, so I don't tend to take much time off. But I enjoyed today. Getting out, exploring the country. Being with you. I'm just sorry it had to end badly."

"It hasn't. Not at all."

He smiles.

I draw a heart on his chest. "Oliver said that Elizabeth feels guilty about not moving over here, as if she's letting women down, because she has this huge opportunity to help people needing IVF. Is that how you feel?"

"Yes, pretty much. Do you know Ben Prince?"

"Hmm, is he related to Hal King? Lives in Wellington?"

"Yeah, that's the one. Their family owns a toy company. Well, he married a woman called Heloise. She'd been married before, and she and her husband had been conducting research into a cure for melanoma. They'd gotten really close, but her husband had Motor Neuron Disease, and he died very young. Heloise had been nursing him, and she had a complete breakdown. She walked away from her research and ended up as nanny to Ben's daughter. She was vilified in the press, and most of her friends and family refused to talk to her."

"Oh, that's awful."

"Yeah, it is. I can associate with how she must have felt. I mean, don't get me wrong, I'm not saying I'm on the same level as her by any means. But our research at NZAI is important in lots of ways, not just in IVF. We're making revolutionary advancements in astronomy, and also in understanding climate change. We're helping to make a difference, and it's hard to walk away from that, even for a few days."

"It's funny to think you run a whole company." I like touching him, so I draw another heart on his chest. He looks down, watching my finger move. "How many employees do you have?"

"Twenty-two at the moment. We're relatively small, because most of our work is carried out in affiliation with other companies like Mack's and Elizabeth's."

He's in charge of twenty-two people. It impresses and depresses me a little at the same time. A guy like this is never going to be interested in me. He might have taken one day out of his busy schedule to be with me, but soon he's going to be back in Auckland, or flying around the world, speaking at conferences and inventing all these marvelous things to change the people's lives. There's definitely a physical attraction, but that's all.

I push myself upright and get to my feet. "Well, I suppose we should get to bed. Tomorrow we'll go to a few more places during the day." I pick the cups up, then hesitate. "Um… in the evening I'd arranged to go out to dinner with a few friends in Plymouth."

"That's okay. I can do a bit of work while you're out."

"Well, I, um…" I tuck my hair behind my ear. "I was wondering whether you'd like to come with me. No pressure at all, I completely understand if you'd rather not."

He meets my eyes, and his lips curve up. "Sure, why not?"

My heart leaps. I smile back, then say hurriedly, "Are you sure? I mean, I'll tell them we're just friends, but there might be a bit of teasing." I wrinkle my nose.

He chuckles. "I've had to deal with Huxley and the others for the last ten years. I'm sure I'll manage."

"Okay. Well, I'll see you in the morning."

He gets to his feet. "Night."

"Night."

He disappears up the stairs.

I take the cups out to the kitchen and put them in the dishwasher. Then I look out of the window, up at the stars. I can see Mars to the west, glimmering red, and just above it the half-moon in Leo.

Smiling, I lock the door, then turn and go up to bed.

*

The next morning, when I come down, Titus is already up, sitting in the armchair, feet propped on the coffee table, his laptop on his knees.

"Morning," I say, surprised. "Couldn't sleep?"

"I don't usually have more than five or six hours. I thought I'd get the emails out of the way so we can go out early."

"Oh," I say, pleased, "okay. Maybe you'd like to have breakfast out?"

"Yeah, sure. Where are you thinking about going today?"

"Exeter first. I thought we'd go to the cathedral, and the Roman ruins. Then take a drive up to the moors again."

"Sounds great." His gaze lingers on me for a second longer than necessary before he looks back at his screen. I'm wearing shorts again, my favorite ones that I have to admit are quite short and tight, with a bright pink V-neck tee that has little daisies around the neckline.

He's also wearing shorts—khaki cargo ones—and the gray T-shirt I washed for him yesterday. Wow, he has great legs, with sturdy thighs and impressive calves, all covered with a sprinkling of masculine hair.

"You're giving me goosebumps again," he points out without looking up, and I chuckle and walk out to the kitchen. "That's what you get when you expose your legs like that," I call back, and I hear him laugh.

I smile as I get ready to go out, happy at the thought of having the whole day with him. It's not long before he announces he's finished answering his emails, and he closes his laptop, retrieves his keys, and then we head out of the house.

"Are you sure you don't mind driving?" I ask. "I'm happy to, although my car is a lot less impressive than yours."

"We might as well enjoy the comfort," he says, unlocking the Range Rover, and I have to agree. The leather seats and pleasurable ride make it much more attractive than my old, rattly second-hand car.

He heads out of town and picks up the A38, and then it's a twenty-minute drive into Exeter. We drive through St. Thomas and over the River Exe, and I direct him to a central car park. We get out and walk slowly down the high street past all the usual stores, then turn off down a side road, and end up at St. Catherine's Chapel.

"Oh!" he says, staring at the red-stone building that sits just off the main pedestrian walkway. "Wow."

"This chapel and the almshouses were built in 1457 to house thirteen poor men," I tell him as we step down into the small building. "But there are much older remains here. Those two posts mark where a Roman timber watchtower stood. The Roman fort was built here to house the Second Legion Augusta in AD50."

"Holy shit, seriously?"

"Yeah." I smile at his obvious wonder at these relatively common English buildings. "And there are the remains of a fourth-century townhouse, too. It was bombed in 1942, unfortunately. They decided to leave it here as a memorial to those who lost their lives in the bombing."

"I can't believe you can just walk around it and touch it." He grazes his fingers against the ancient wall."

"Come on," I say. "If you like this, the Cathedral's going to blow your mind."

We continue walking along the pedestrianized area, and less than a minute later, we come out onto the Cathedral Green. We stop for a moment, and I let him take in the full beauty of the building.

"It's a cathedral because it's the seat of a bishop," I explain. "Its official foundation is listed as 1133, and the two towers are both Norman, but the rest of it was rebuilt in the thirteenth century in the Decorated Gothic style. Let's go around to the west end, to the main entrance, and you'll be able to see what I mean."

We walk slowly along the path, circling the stone building. Titus hasn't said anything yet. I think he's genuinely taken aback at the beauty of it. Even though he's been to London several times, I have the feeling he hasn't spent a lot of time sightseeing. And although St Paul's and Westminster Abbey are amazing, I love Exeter Cathedral, which sits surrounded by rolling lawns.

"How come it wasn't destroyed during the Second World War?" he asks.

"It was hit during the Baedeker Blitz in 1942. A bomb destroyed the chapel of St James, and there was a lot of other damage, but as you can see, most of it was untouched." I take him to one side of the path approaching the cathedral, and he looks at me, puzzled. "We're standing on top of a Roman military bathhouse," I tell him, and his jaw drops. "It was in the middle of the legionary fortress. They found the remains when they started constructing an underground car park in the nineteen seventies."

"Jesus."

"Yeah. They backfilled it with sand at the time so it would be protected for future archaeologists, but nobody's got around to excavating it yet." I smile. "Come on. Let's look inside."

I'd expected it to take us about ten or fifteen minutes to walk around the building, but Titus is so fascinated that it takes us nearly an hour. He's awed by the nave, especially when I tell him it's the longest uninterrupted medieval vaulted ceiling in the world. He loves the thirteenth-century misericords or wooden seats, the fourteenth-century minstrels' gallery, and he spends ages looking at the famous Astronomical Clock that's supposedly the source of the nursery rhyme Hickory Dickory Dock, which has a small door below the face for the resident cathedral cat to hunt mice.

By the time we come back out, we're both hungry, so we cross the Green to a café that has seats outside overlooking the view. We go inside and order a cooked breakfast and coffee, then come back out and sit at a table with an umbrella.

"What do you think?" I ask.

"I think it's amazing." He studies the cathedral, then drags his gaze away and looks at me. "You're amazing," he says.

I laugh. "Well, thank you."

"I mean it. You're the perfect guide. You have fantastic knowledge of the area. I don't mean this to sound patronizing, but I'm really impressed."

I blush, because I can't help it, glowing all the way through at his compliment. He notices, and I wonder whether he's going to apologize for embarrassing me, but he just smiles. Encouraged, I lift my gaze to his and meet his eyes, and he doesn't look away. There's heat within them, and immediately I know he's thinking about what I look like naked.

We're attracted to one another. It's not just because either of us is on the rebound. The connection began all those years ago, when I was sixteen, and it's still there now, an invisible thread that's drawn us together through the years, and that's continuing to wind around us, slowly pulling tighter with each minute we spend together.

Chapter Eight

Titus

We eat breakfast while we watch visitors coming from and going to the cathedral, while the sun beams down out of a brilliant blue sky.

Heidi tells me more about the history of Exeter while we eat, and I'm content to sit and listen to her, occasionally asking questions. She uses her hands a lot as she talks, her pink nails flashing in the bright sunshine.

Last night, I was a fraction of an inch from kissing her while we sat on the sofa. I hadn't planned to get close to her, but in the end it seemed harmless to cuddle up, as we're good friends, and she'd had a tough encounter with her ex.

But I knew I was kidding myself. Be honest, Titus. I want to get up close and personal with her because I fancy the pants off her. I like her sunshine-colored hair, her slender figure, her girlish breasts, and her long, light-brown thighs in her criminally short shorts that show off her butt. I like her girlish giggle and the way she seems young on one hand, and yet she's so knowledgeable and intelligent about her passions.

I know she likes me. She still looks at me the way she did all those years ago, when she asked me to kiss her, her big blue eyes filled with admiration and longing. I know she's not after my money, or to make connections, or because she wants to be seen with me amongst her friends and business acquaintances. And when I'm quiet or lost in thought, she doesn't get exasperated, or roll her eyes, she just smiles and waits for me to focus again before she continues.

Okay, I've only been here a couple of days. But right now, I feel nothing but attraction between us, and it's like this perfect summer day—hot, sweet, and full of happiness and hope.

Listen to me. I'm turning into an old romantic. Everyone knows it's easy to have a holiday fling. You leave all your cares and responsibilities behind, and nothing matters except pleasing the person in front of you. But they never last, especially when you live on the opposite side of the world.

I should pull back a bit, stop the flirting, and keep her at arm's length, but it's hard when she's such fun to be with. And she's intelligent, and she knows as well as I do that we can't get involved. She's just enjoying being with a friend from home, and I resolve to keep that in mind and not worry too much about it.

When we finish our breakfast, we walk through the city to the car, and then we head back past Briarton, taking the road to the moors. This time, we do a leisurely loop, driving up to Moretonhampstead, then take the road down to Two Bridges, where we get out and do a Pooh Bear and Piglet, and throw twigs in the river, then move to the opposite side of the bridge to see whose wins the race. After that, I drive to Dartmeet, which Heidi tells me is the center of a prehistoric landscape.

"There's a Coffin Stone up Dartmeet Hill," Heidi says. "Bearers placed their coffins on it while they took a rest on the way to burying them at Widecombe-in-the-Moor. The rock's split, and local legend says it happened when they laid the body of a wicked man there. God struck the stone with a thunderbolt, and He destroyed the coffin and cracked the stone in two."

"What a great story."

"I think so. Come on, Widecombe is next, and that's a lovely village."

It turns out to be a tourist destination, a little twee maybe, as if someone has designed their perfect view of an English country village, complete with pubs, village green, and its church, which is known as the Cathedral on the Moors because of its tall tower.

I'm surprised that Heidi seems so fond of it, but as we walk around and she tells me about its history, I begin to see why she loves this county so much. Maybe it's because she's a historian, but it's like she's an archaeologist of time, and is able to sift through the years and see all the different layers of occupation, all the people who have passed through this place. She talks about the prehistoric settlements, the field patterns and the stone circles, the Romans, the Saxons, and the deserted medieval villages. And she tells me about the spread of

Christianity, which gives the country a sound faith that nevertheless has beneath it a deep-rooted pagan undertone.

"Look at that roof boss," she says in the church, pointing up at a motif of what looks like three hares. "It's called the Tinners Rabbits. They each share an ear so only three ears are shown. It's a symbol of the Trinity, as well as fertility and the lunar cycle."

She also shows me four more examples of the Green Man—male figures with hair and beard made from oak leaves, which she says is a symbol of rebirth. "This land is ancient," she whispers, so as not to disturb the other visitors in the church. "I can feel all the people who've lived here, can't you?"

Her mouth is near my ear, and her warm breath brushes across my neck, making me shiver. I look down at her, and inhale at the sight of her covered in jewel-like colors, formed from the sun shining through the stained-glass windows. She's like England personified—a good person on the surface, kind, generous, and honest—but with an underlying sensuality that speaks of sun-kissed grain in the fields, ripening fruit, and sunlight on the rivers that tumble over the rocks.

I don't know what's wrong with me—maybe I'm still jet lagged—but I feel caught up in the magic of this place, as if I'm standing with one foot in the past.

"I wish you could have seen the May Day celebrations," she says as we make our way outside, "what they used to call Beltane. Children danced around the maypole, braiding the ribbons, and they chose a May King and Queen. In medieval times, young people would sneak off at sunrise to make love in the fields."

She meets my eyes. Her face is just inches from mine. Her lips are a rose-pink, and they look *soft as*. Jesus, I want to kiss her so badly.

"Titus," she scolds. "Don't look at me like that."

"Like what?"

Her gaze falls to my mouth. "Like you're picturing what I look like naked." She lifts her gaze to mine again. She looks amused and turned on at the same time.

Without meaning to, I lower my head, and now our mouths are only an inch apart. I stop, alarm bells ringing in my head. I can't kiss her. But I want to. Fuck. She doesn't move, and just moistens her lips with the tip of her tongue, so I know she's hoping I will.

We stand there like that for about twenty seconds while I fight with myself. I can smell her perfume. Her lips look so soft. Ahhh… it's so unfair…

Eventually, my brain beats my heart—or, more correctly, the organ located further down my body—and I lift my head.

"Dammit," she says. "You and your fucking principles."

I laugh. "Come on, I spotted an ice cream shop, in lieu of a cold shower."

She giggles, and we walk across the lawn to treat ourselves to a 99— whipped ice cream in a cone with a chocolate Flake.

"I wonder why it's called a 99," I say as we wander out.

"Apparently it was named for the Boys of 99," she says. "They were honored Italian heroes of the First World War, who'd been born in 1899. The shape of the Flake reminded Italian ice cream sellers in Britain of the feather the Boys of 99 wore in their caps."

"Really?"

"Yeah. I'm full of useless information like that."

I watch her lick her ice cream and have to look away. This girl… It must be the warm weather that's doing it. I haven't wanted a woman like this in years. Maybe ever.

God, this is so incredibly hard. How on earth am I going to make it through the weekend without touching her?

*

Heidi

When we finish our ice creams, we head back home so we can have a few hours' rest before we go out for the evening.

Titus declares he's going to do a bit of work and sets up his laptop, so I leave him to it, go outside, and spend a while gardening. I water the begonias in the hanging baskets, clip the hedge at the bottom, and weed the borders between the hydrangeas, roses, dahlias, and peonies.

When I'm done, I check my watch and discover it's nearly five p.m. I wash my hands, then go into the living room to find his laptop tucked next to the chair and the room empty. He must be in the bedroom. I run up the stairs, intending to go into the bathroom to freshen up, then stop short. The door's open, and he's in there, stripped to the waist, standing in front of the mirror, shaving.

"Shit," I say as he turns around, "sorry."

I was wearing a bikini top underneath my T-shirt today. I took the tee off while I was gardening, and I haven't put it back on, and he does a double take before lifting his gaze to mine.

"I'm only shaving," he says, amused, as I continue to stare at him. He looks back at his reflection, carefully drawing the razor up his throat. "What time do you want to leave?"

"I… um…" It's no good. My ability to form words has vanished. Wow, this guy has an amazing body. He's all tanned and muscular, and oh my God, I thought he only had tattoos on his arms, but he also has an amazing one across his back of a raven with its wings spread. I've never had a thing about guys with tattoos before, but there's something incredibly sexy about a guy who normally wears a suit having tattoos underneath. He looks like a Viking warrior, and he steals my breath away.

He looks back at me as he rinses his razor in the water, and stops as he sees the look on my face. "What?"

I just shake my head, unable to speak.

He meets my eyes for a long moment, then looks back at his reflection. He gives a couple of final strokes of the razor before bending to rinse the last of the foam from his face. I watch his muscles move across his shoulders and ribs, before finally he picks up the towel and mops up the drips.

I still can't speak. He rinses the sink, hangs the towel over the rack, and then unscrews the top of a bottle of aftershave. He tips a little onto his hands, rubs them together, and touches them to his face, wincing as it obviously stings. I feel entranced, as if he's put me under a spell, and I can't look away.

He picks up his tee, walks toward me, and turns to the side to squeeze past me in the doorway. Oh Jesus, he smells amazing. When our bodies are flush, he stops, the bare skin of his chest just brushing my nipples in the bikini top. The heat from his skin sizzles on my belly. He looks down at me the same way he did in the church, his green eyes hot, the pupils dilated. Oh… I want him to kiss me so badly. My pulse is racing so fast I'm sure he can hear it.

He takes a deep breath, then exhales in a huff. "You're like the fucking Temptation of St Anthony," he says, somewhat sulkily. He continues to move past me, goes into his room, and shuts the door with a little more force than is necessary.

My breath leaves me in a rush. Holy shit. I'm tingling all over. I've never ached for a guy like this. Never been so desperate for him to kiss me that I'm tempted to leap up into his arms, wrap my legs around his waist, and crush my lips to his.

I wonder what he'd do if I did that?

Going into the bathroom, I close the door and walk over to look in the mirror. I'm blushing, and oh no, my neck and chest have flushed, too, the way they do when I'm aroused. No wonder he looked at me with such exasperation.

I feel a touch of shame. It's not fair to be a prick tease. My brother's friendship means a lot to him, and as much as I want him, it means a lot to me that he's trying to resist his obvious attraction to me. I don't want to sleep with him and then have him hate himself afterward.

After freshening up, I quietly go out and into my bedroom and close the door. I spend half an hour getting ready, then take a deep breath and go downstairs.

He's sitting on the sofa, reading a book, although he looks up as I enter. He's wearing jeans and a long-sleeved dress shirt over the top that's a dark navy with a white paisley pattern, with the sleeves rolled up a couple of times.

"Hey," he says.

"Hey." I'm also wearing jeans with a white sparkly vest and a three-quarter sleeve black jacket. "You look nice," I add. "Very swish."

"Swish?"

"Sophisticated. Fashionable. Smooth."

"Thank you, so do you." He puts down the book—it's one of mine, I realize, from the bookshelf, a history of Anglo-Saxon England—and gets to his feet. "I want to apologize for what I said upstairs," he says.

I blink. "What do you mean?"

"About you tempting me. I hope you didn't think I was saying you were doing it on purpose."

"Oh. No." I tuck my hair behind my ear.

He moves a bit closer to me, and his eyes are gentle. "You know why we can't get involved, don't you?"

I nod. "I know Oliver means a lot to you."

"I promised him I'd look after you. He said he knows he can trust me, and I don't want to betray that trust."

I feel a flare of irritation toward my brother. "You know he probably said that to wind you up." He blinks, and I realize that hadn't occurred to him. "It's none of his business who I choose to date," I point out. Then I relent, "but it doesn't change the fact that I live in England, and you live in New Zealand. It makes sense not to start something we can't continue."

"Mm." His gaze drops to my mouth. He's thinking about kissing me again.

A car horn sounds outside, and I jump. "That's the Uber."

He sighs and grabs his wallet. "Come on, then."

Half relieved and half annoyed at the interruption, I retrieve my bag, and we go out and get in the Uber. It heads toward the A38, then southwest toward Plymouth.

"So who are we meeting tonight?" Titus asks.

"My friends Ally and Donna—they're both primary school teachers that I met in my first year at a training center. Ally's the same age as me, she's an artist, quite flamboyant, and she's dating Jack, who's a nurse. Donna is two years older, and her degree is in biology. She's married to Ian. He's a lawyer, but don't let that put you off—he's really nice." She smiles.

"I presume they know Jason?"

"Yeah, we went out a few times all together, but to be honest, Jason never really fitted in. He thought Ally was ditzy and Donna was bossy, and after we broke up, both Jack and Ian admitted they thought he was arrogant."

"Do they know I'm coming?"

"Yeah, I've told them about you."

"So where are we going?"

"It's a restaurant up on the Hoe."

"That's where Francis Drake played bowls, isn't it?"

"Yes, that's right. He circumnavigated the world, and he was second-in-command when the Spanish Armada was defeated."

"Should be fun," he says.

"I hope so. Thank you for coming with me. And I apologize in advance if they tease you at all."

"Don't worry about it. I'm a big boy."

"So I've heard."

He gives a short laugh. "Don't start."

"Sorry."

He smiles. "So, tell me about Plymouth. It was bombed during the Second World War, wasn't it?"

We chat about the city for a while as the Uber winds through the traffic, and it's close to six thirty by the time we get to the Hoe. I point out the red-and-white-striped Smeaton's Tower as we pass it, and then the Uber pulls up outside Seagulls Restaurant, and we get out.

It has a great view across Plymouth Sound, which is slowly turning orange as the sun sinks toward the horizon.

"They're already here," I say, seeing the cars out the front, and I wave as I spot them through the window. "Come on."

I surprise myself by feeling nervous as we go in, and I realize it's because I want them to like Titus. "Hello!" I call out as we approach the table.

"Heidi!" They all smile and stand to greet us. They kiss me on the cheek, but I can see that all they're interested in is the guy I'm with. "This is Titus Oates," I tell them.

"Like the Antarctic explorer?" Jack asks as we take our seats.

"Actually," I say, "that Titus was named after the priest who created the Catholic conspiracy to kill King Charles the Second in 1649."

"Does she drive you mad when she does that?" Ally wants to know as we pick up our menus. "She's always coming out with historical facts or quoting dates."

"Not at all," he says. "I'm learning a lot. By the way, Heidi, I've got a historical joke for you. How was the Roman Empire cut in half?"

"Dunno," I say.

"With a pair of Caesars." He grins.

I snort, and the others start laughing. "Don't encourage him," I tell them.

"He's going to fit in well," Ian replies, still chortling, and I meet Titus's eyes and smile.

It turns out to be an understatement. Titus is relatively quiet and thoughtful, and so I keep forgetting that he runs a company and is used to talking to groups of people. He doesn't dominate the conversation, and he's happy to sit and listen as we chat, but he isn't shy to join in, and his wry sense of humor keeps us laughing throughout the evening as we choose our meals, then sit and chat over a few glasses of wine.

"Another historical joke for you," he says while we wait for our desserts to arrive. "What's the most popular kids' movie about Ancient Greece?"

"Dunno," we all say.

"Troy Story."

I giggle, which makes Ally and Donna laugh.

He grins and says, "Excuse me, just going to visit the bathroom," and he gets up and leaves the table.

I watch him walk away, unable to tear my gaze away from his butt in the tight jeans, then drag my gaze back to the table to see the four of them watching me, smiling.

"What?" I say, embarrassed.

"He's lovely," Ally states.

I smile. "I'm glad you like him."

"He's really going back next week?" Donna asks.

I sigh. "Yeah, unfortunately."

"And you're just good friends?" Jack wants to know.

"Just good friends."

"Bullshit," Ally says. "He hasn't been able to tear his eyes away from you all evening."

I blush. "I'm not saying we wouldn't if we could… but I can't. Not after Jason."

Their smiles slowly fade. "Aw," Ian says. "You shouldn't let that fucker stop you having fun."

"No, I agree," I reply, "but Titus has to leave soon, and I don't want to get hurt."

"Fair enough," Ally says softly. "It's a shame though. He seems really into you."

Her comment warms me. I can see him coming back through the restaurant, and I have to stifle a sigh at the sight of him, striding confidently through the tables, the women in the room unable to stop casting him glances as he walks by. I like him so much. It's a shame our timing is so appalling.

"Can't you just have a holiday fling?" Donna whispers just before he arrives.

"Shh!" I smile brightly at him as he sits again, glancing around. A holiday fling… That would be dumb, wouldn't it? I'm pretty sure the Striking Viking would be a very easy man to fall in love with, and that's never going to end well.

Chapter Nine

Heidi

When we've finished our meals, Ally says to Titus, "So, are we going to be able to persuade you to join us?"

I give him an apologetic look and reveal, "They want to go to a karaoke bar."

He shrugs. "I don't mind."

I stare at him in delight. "Are you sure?"

"Yeah, of course."

So we pay and head out of the restaurant, then walk the short distance to the bar.

The sun has now set, and the waxing moon is casting a silvery path on the sea. We've finished off several bottles of wine between the six of us, and I feel mellow and happy as we enter the bar. Ally has booked one of the karaoke rooms, and we order drinks and take them inside. It's small with comfortable padded benches around three sides, tables in the middle, and a small stage at one end for whoever's performing. Flashing pink and purple lights turn the room into a disco.

We slide onto the benches, and then it's time to start with the songs.

The others go first, although we all sing along so the performer doesn't feel too self-conscious. Ally belts out Whitney Houston's *I Wanna Dance with Somebody*. Jack chooses Ed Sheeran's *Perfect*. Donna sings Amy Winehouse's *Rehab*, and Ian chooses Rick Astley's *Never Gonna Give You Up*.

Then it's my turn. I opt for The Pretenders' *Brass in Pockets*, a nod to *Lost in Translation*, which is one of my favorite movies. A tingle runs through me as Titus leans back and watches me, his eyes gleaming in the flashing disco lights.

I don't know if it's the few glasses of wine I've had, the strange, magical day, seeing Titus without his shirt earlier, or the flashing lights, but I feel hot and buzzy, and my heart's racing. I tell him I'm going to make him notice me, and that I'm special, while I move my hips to the music, and I'm rewarded by his steady stare, as if he can't tear his eyes from me.

When I'm done, he applauds with the others, and then Ally says, "Titus? Going to have a go?"

"You don't have to," I say breathlessly, sitting next to him.

"I'm absolutely going to," he says, getting to his feet.

Thrilled, I watch him choose a song. I have no idea whether he can sing or not, but I'm pleased he's having a go, and so are the others.

He chooses Marvin Gaye's *Sexual Healing*, which makes my heart skip a beat. As the music starts, he says, "Ah, now I'm regretting it…" He takes a deep breath to hit the powerful high note at the beginning, *Baby…* makes it, gives a relieved laugh, and then he's off and running.

I join in with the others and clap along, entranced by his sexy voice and his performance. Getting in his stride, he adds a few dance steps and a twirl, then manages to entangle himself in the microphone lead, but he just laughs and carries on.

We give him a huge cheer when he's done, and he comes and sits next to me, tapping his glass against mine when I hold it up.

"Well done," I say.

He grins. "Glad you enjoyed the performance."

After a few more songs, we head into the main bar and sit and chat for another hour over a last drink, and then finally call an Uber around ten thirty. We say goodbye to the others, who all say they hope they get to see Titus again someday, and then we get in the car and head back to Briarton.

"Thank you so much for coming," I murmur as the lights of the city flash by.

"Thanks for asking me. I really enjoyed it."

"My friends all liked you," I tell him.

He smiles. "I'm glad."

I open my mouth to say that I like him, too, then close it again. I've had a couple of glasses of wine, and I mustn't let it persuade me that coming on to him would be a good idea. Earlier I resolved to keep my distance, and I have to stick to it.

He meets my eyes, though, and there's more than a little heat in his. This is so hard. Maybe the hardest thing I've ever had to do. And I still have a whole weekend with him. How am I going to get through it without melting into a giant puddle?

We don't say much more as the Uber travels along the darkened Expressway, through the Devon countryside, then eventually turns off toward Briarton. My heart picks up speed as he nears my cottage, though. Will he go straight to bed? Or will he want to sit and talk, or watch a movie?

When we arrive, we get out and thank the driver, and I open the front door. Titus gestures for me to precede him. I say, "After you."

"No, after you."

We both hesitate, then move forward together, and give an awkward laugh as we bump shoulders. "After you," he says again, moving back, and I walk in hastily.

"Would you like a coffee?" I ask, heart racing as I toe off my Converses.

He clears his throat. "Yeah, that would be nice."

I light a candle on the table, then go into the kitchen, not bothering to turn on the light. He comes out with me, reaches up to retrieve a glass from the cupboard, and I turn and walk straight into his arm.

"Sorry," I say, and duck under it to fill the kettle.

He mutters something, but I don't ask what. There are butterflies in my stomach, although I'm not sure why. I take the full kettle back to its base and turn it on, then turn to get some milk out of the fridge, at the same time as he pulls out some water.

"For fuck's sake," he says.

My face flushes. "Sorry. I'm so clumsy."

"Not you, Heidi. I'm frustrated with myself." He puts the water on the counter, then rests his hands on his hips.

I let the fridge shut and turn so I'm resting back on the counter, puzzled at his words. To my surprise, he moves closer to me, until he's just a few inches away.

His eyes are blazing with something, I'm not sure what. I can smell his aftershave, warmed by his skin. The muscles at the corner of his jaw are moving, as if he's gritting his teeth.

"Everything all right?" I ask cautiously.

He inhales, then huffs a sigh. "I'm very disciplined," he states.

I'm not sure where this is heading. "Okay…"

"I rarely overindulge with drink or food. I don't smoke. I don't take drugs. I go to the gym several times a week, and I run on my treadmill most mornings."

"I see," I say, although I don't. I moisten my lips with the tip of my tongue, and as his gaze drops to them, he makes a frustrated noise low in his throat.

"So why am I finding it so hard to keep my hands off you?" he says. "Why are you so damn irresistible?"

"Skill?" I suggest, heart racing.

His lips curve up, and his gaze drops to my mouth. He gives a small shake of his head. "I can't stop thinking about kissing you," he whispers. "I've thought about little else all day."

Thrilled, I tip my head to the side. "I told you that we aren't going to do anything that involves removal of clothing."

"Yeah…"

I shrug. "I guess that means we can kiss fully clothed."

He's still looking at my mouth. "But nothing more."

"Of course not."

His gaze returns to mine, a tad helpless. "I don't want to take advantage of you."

"Titus, I promise, you won't do anything to me that I don't want done."

"Huxley trusts me," he says, so softly I think he's talking to himself.

"Forget Oliver. I'm not sixteen anymore."

"That is very obvious."

"It isn't any of his business. I kiss whom I please. The question is, would you like to kiss me?"

He leans a hand either side of me on the counter.

"More than life itself," he replies, and he lowers his lips to mine.

I hold my breath as our mouths connect. For a moment, he just holds his lips there, as if he's testing his resolve, waiting to see if he's flooded with regret, or whether I pull back, saying I can't go through with it.

I don't. I lower my lashes and, although my heart bangs on my ribs, threatening to burst through and bounce away, I stay still.

He moves back half an inch. I look up at him, dazzled, aching for more.

"Ah, Heidi," he says, and he cups my face in his hands. "You're so fucking beautiful."

"Kiss me again," I whisper. "Please."

"Oh I will. Last time I rushed it, though. This time, we're going to take it slow."

Ooh, what does that mean? Excited that he's not done, I rest my hands on his chest, my heart racing.

"Close your eyes," he murmurs. Obediently, I lower my lids, and the next thing I feel is his lips pressing on them, lightly, as if the butterflies from my tummy have fluttered up and are brushing across my face.

Slowly, methodically, he kisses my brows, my nose, along my cheekbones to my hairline, then follows the line of my jaw back to my mouth. I'm smiling by now, and I feel his lips curve up to match mine before he takes another step forward so our bodies are flush, and he lowers his lips.

Mmm… I drift away to a heavenly place where nothing exists except this quiet room, the flickering candlelight, and the man in front of me, filling every single one of my senses. I can taste the mint we had in the car, and the sexy scent of his aftershave sends my pulse racing. His hands on my face are warm, and now he's closed the distance between us, I can feel his hard, strong body pressed up against me.

Ohhh… he's so incredibly gentle. I know he's holding back on purpose, probably because of what I said about Jason. He just makes me melt. He presses his lips to mine, kissing from one corner to the other, then back to the center, and only then does he touch his tongue to my bottom lip. I'm more than happy to part them for him, and he slides his tongue into my mouth, where it entwines with mine.

Last time he kissed me, when I was sixteen, he went from zero to a hundred in seconds. This time, the heat builds between us slowly, my body stirring and responding to his subtle persuasion. I'm not a girl now, I'm a woman, and I'm not innocent; I know how to arouse a man, and how to be active rather than passive in a kiss. As he lowers his arms around me, the fingers of one hand splaying at the base of my spine to pull me away from the counter and close to him, so I raise my arms around his neck, lifting up onto my tiptoes so I can stretch out along him. He rests his other hand in the middle of my back, and now I'm touching him from my breasts all the way down to my thighs.

The hair on the back of his head is short and prickles my fingers as I slide my hand to the nape of his neck, and his answering shiver sends a flicker of pleasure through me. I'm affecting him as much as he's affecting me. The thought fills me with delight, and I'm unable to stop a purr of pleasure escaping.

Ohh… he liked that. He's trying to be gentle and go slow, but I feel a thrill as his passion flares. He answers with a growl, deep in his throat, and fire ignites between us. He lifts a hand to tangle in my hair as he tilts his head to change the angle of the kiss. His tongue delves into my mouth, and I respond with a thrust of my own, lowering my hands to clutch at his shirt, my body burning.

He slides his other hand beneath the edge of my top, his fingers brushing my skin. As they move up my ribs, my nipples tighten in anticipation, and he pushes me back—but we're further away from the counter than we realize. I stumble and meet the counter with a bump, and the shock breaks us apart as we both exclaim.

Titus takes my face in his hands again. "Sorry."

"It's okay."

He studies me, brushing my cheeks with his thumbs. "I don't know how you do it, but you make me lose myself."

I slide my arms around his waist and bury my face in his shirt. He sighs and wraps his arms around me, and we stand there like that for a long time.

"We should go to bed," he murmurs. "Our own beds, I mean."

"Yeah. I know."

"It's not that I don't want to…"

I move back, reach up, and kiss his cheek. "It's okay, Titus. I know. Thank you for the kiss." But I'm unable to suppress the bittersweet feeling that settles over me. My brain is calm and collected, telling me it makes no sense to get involved, because Reasons, Heidi—distance and Jason and Oliver, and it's only been two days, and I'm getting carried away, and I should know better. But my heart doesn't want to listen, and neither does my clitoris, goddammit.

The thought makes me give a short laugh, and he lifts my chin so he can look at me. "What?"

I shake my head. "Nothing. What time do we need to leave tomorrow?"

He sighs, lowering his hands. "I said we'd be there around four, and it's about ten minutes east of Exeter, I think. So, about three thirty?"

"Sure. Um, in the morning I'd like to call in and see my grandparents. I don't suppose you want to come?"

"Sure. Your mum's folks, right? I met them once when they came out to New Zealand."

"Okay. I'll say we'll be there around eleven?"

"Sounds great."

We study each other for a moment. The flickering candlelight highlights his face, so handsome it makes my heart ache. I wish I could take his hand and lead him up the stairs to my bed, but I don't want to ask because I can't face rejection. I don't want him to have to turn me down.

"I'll see you tomorrow," I say softly.

He nods. Ooh, the look in his eyes makes me melt. Poor Titus.

"Is Sir Richard giving you as much trouble as Countess Clitoris is giving me?" I ask.

That makes him laugh. "I'm sorry," he murmurs.

"It was worth it." I smile. "Goodnight."

It's not easy to walk away. But I don't have a choice. So I do my best to ignore his sigh, and head up the stairs to bed.

*

Titus

Ten thirty the next morning finds us on the road to Heidi's grandparents.

It's another beautiful morning. We've been so lucky with the weather, and it looks as if it's going to be nice for the next few days, too. All the news programs can talk about is the amazing heatwave, even though this is just an average summer day where I come from.

I worked for a couple of hours this morning, while Heidi did some baking. I'm holding the results of her endeavors on my lap in a tin—a fantastic-smelling lemon curd and blueberry loaf cake.

Heidi's driving us this morning in her rattly car, heading southwest to the tiny town of Ugborough, which I insist on pronouncing Uger-boruger.

She's wearing her short shorts and a crisp white T-shirt. Her blonde hair is like a slice of sunshine. She's gorgeous.

As the Devon countryside flashes by, I think about kissing her last night, how her lips felt beneath mine. How they parted for me, and the way the soft moan escaped her as she slid her hand into my hair.

"How's the Countess today?" I ask mischievously.

She laughs. "She's okay. I gave her a bit of attention last night, so she's not as sulky now."

Okay, so that backfired. I lean an elbow on the sill and massage my brow, and she giggles. "Oh come on," she scolds. "You can't say something like that and not expect me to have a comeback. Besides, don't tell me that Sir Richard didn't get to go jousting."

"Jesus."

"Do you deny it?"

"No. I'm expressing shock at your terrible euphemisms."

She gives me a longing look. It's obvious that the thought of me indulging in some DIY is as much of a turn on for her as the other way around.

I raise my eyebrows. Her lips twitch, and she returns her gaze to the road. "Maybe we should stop talking about... you know..."

"You think? You're extremely bad for my blood pressure."

"Ah, get some beta blockers like the rest of us, then you can daydream all you like."

I laugh and change the subject, and she chats away happily until she pulls into the village.

I send myself a warning though as I get out of the car and follow her up the path to the pretty little cottage. I really shouldn't flirt with her. I'm only making things more difficult for myself. I should shut down the conversation and move on, and she'd soon pick up on it.

But it's so hard when she turns on that impish smile, and when her eyes dance as she teases me. With some surprise, I realize it makes me happy. She makes me happy.

Well, isn't that something?

She doesn't go to the front door, but instead walks around the side of the cottage, past some roses bushes that scatter pink petals like confetti on the lawn as she brushes past them, and through a wooden gate to the back of the house.

"Hey," she says, and I hear an answering, "Heidi, my love," as I close the gate behind us and follow her around.

Heidi is hugging her grandmother, a slender, attractive woman in her early sixties, with silver hair that tumbles to her shoulders in waves. She has her arms around her granddaughter, but she's looking at me as I approach.

"Titus," she says, releasing Heidi and coming over to me. "How lovely to see you again."

"Hi, Mrs. Craven."

"Laura, please." She kisses me on the cheek, then moves back to look at me, holding me by the upper arms. "Goodness, look at you. You were such a skinny thing the last time I saw you. You've filled out nicely."

"Grandma," Heidi scolds.

"What? It's a compliment. And those tattoos. Wow. They're gorgeous."

"You should see the one on his back," Heidi says. "It's pretty amazing."

She turns away to greet her grandfather as he comes out, missing the way Laura's eyebrows shoot up into her hairline.

"I was shaving," I say wryly.

"Hmm." She gives me a mischievous look—oh ho, so that's where Heidi gets it from.

"Titus," Graham Craven says, coming over to shake my hand. "Good to see you, lad."

"Likewise."

Laura looks at the tin in my hands and says, "Ooh, is that for us?"

"Lemon curd and blueberry loaf," I tell them. "And that makes it sound as if I had something to do with its creation, and I didn't, obviously."

"Lovely. We've got some butter or whipped cream to go with it. Coffee or tea, Titus?"

"Coffee would be lovely."

"Heidi?"

"Tea, please." She grins as her grandparents go inside to make the drinks. "I'm turning English."

"So I see."

"Bloody hell, let's pop the kettle on and have a cuppa," she says in her best English accent, and I laugh.

"Your grandmother thinks we're sharing a bed because of your comment about my tattoo," I tell her.

"Oh shit, really? Sorry, I'd better put her straight."

"I tried. I don't think she believed me."

"Of course she didn't. I have a gorgeous, smart young guy staying in my home. There must be something wrong with me if I haven't jumped his bones." She crosses her eyes.

I chuckle, because I'm supposed to. But my gaze lingers on her as she tips up her face to the sunshine. She thinks I'm gorgeous. That warms me to the core.

After her comment this morning, it's impossible not to think about her lying in bed, closing her eyes, sliding her hand down her naked body, and pleasuring herself until her orgasm sweeps over her. I want to do that for her. I want to kiss her, and have her moan my name against my lips as I make her come, with my fingers, my tongue, and while I'm thrusting inside her.

God, why do I insist on torturing myself like this?

Chapter Ten

Heidi

"So," Grandpa says once we're all sitting with our drinks and a slice of the loaf, "you two are off to a castle for the weekend?"

"More like a large country house," Titus replies. He takes a bite of his cake, murmurs his approval, and removes some crumbs from his lip. "It's called Hawkerland Manor. The owner is a Kiwi, but his wife is English and from old money, I think."

"What are you wearing, Heidi?" Grandma asks.

"I meant to ask you what the dress code was," I say to Titus. "How smart do we need to be?"

"Alan mentioned a cocktail party this evening. Then tomorrow it's an Agatha Christie-style murder-mystery evening. Sunday he mentioned taking us to a local pub. Plus some casual events in between—the hot-air balloon ride, and he promised me some fishing in the river. And they have an indoor pool, so bring your swimming costume."

"I've got a little black dress for tonight," I tell him. "Not sure about the murder mystery."

"Apparently we'll get character descriptions, and he said something about having costumes to help us out."

"Sounds fun," I say.

"You should wear that silver dress you wore to Lisa's wedding," Grandma says with a twinkle in her eye. "Without the jacket."

I shoot her a warning glance, but she just grins.

"What's this?" Titus asks. "I think I need to hear more about the silver dress."

"It's sort of 1930s but with shoestring straps and it's a bit... ah... revealing."

"You should definitely bring that," he says. Grandpa laughs and Grandma giggles.

"If I do, I'll definitely be wearing the jacket over the top," I tell them.

"Spoilsport," Titus says, and smiles.

"So you're doing business with Acheron Pharmaceuticals?" Grandpa wants to know.

Titus nods. "I've been working with a colleague using Artificial Intelligence in IVF. Alan Woodridge from Acheron has offered to invest a significant amount of money in the research. His daughter apparently had infertility issues and had three unsuccessful rounds of treatment, and he's keen to help others in the same situation."

"How can AI help?"

"In the grading and selection of gametes, or reproductive cells— eggs in women, and sperm in men—and of embryos for transfer. Success is often based on an individual's ability to select the right embryos, but AI takes the subjectivity out of the process. It can also help in the formatting of a treatment plan."

As he speaks I can imagine him standing in front of an audience at a conference, delivering his talk. He switches into work mode, and he sounds authoritative and knowledgeable. And sexy, although that might be just me.

"Interesting," Grandpa says. "What's your opinion on using AI in art and literature?"

"Grandpa's writing a book," I explain.

Titus nods and stretches out his long legs, turning his coffee cup in his fingers. "Obviously it's a hot topic at the moment, and a sensitive subject. People don't like to think about computers being involved in the creative process. These fears have been around since the Industrial Revolution. But we're a long way from the scenarios you see in science fiction, where computers take over the world. And even though AI is being used in some basic art, it's done by programming in real artwork, so in that sense it's not the same as creating from scratch. The human's ability to put dreams on paper won't be superseded for many years, in my opinion."

"That's a lovely way to put it," Grandma says, and he smiles.

"What's your book about?" he asks Grandpa.

"It's a local history," he replies. "I'll show you some of my research if you'd like to see it."

"Oh Gray, don't bore the lad," Grandma scolds.

But Titus replies, "I'd love to, I've been getting more into history since Heidi's been showing me around," and so the two of them get up and go into the house.

Grandma smiles at me. "Gramps loves him," she says. "He doesn't show his work to just anyone."

"Titus is a nice lad," I reply. "One of the good guys."

Grandma meets my eyes, and her lips curve up.

"He also lives in New Zealand," I remind her wryly.

"But he's here to discuss the possibility of staying here for two years, isn't he?"

"He's here to try to convince Alan Woodridge from Acheron that he can run the project from New Zealand."

"Sounds like this Alan really wants him to stay though. Cocktail parties and murder mystery evenings and balloon rides? They're pulling out all the stops."

"Titus is pretty single-minded. I can't imagine him being talked into anything he didn't want to do."

"What about you, then? You've had a great adventure here. Might it be time for you to move back home?"

I hesitate. "I feel like I'm just settling in. I mean yeah, I miss home sometimes, but I love England."

"What happened with Jason hasn't put you off being here?"

"Of course not. There are obnoxious men in New Zealand too. Besides, Titus sorted him out. I don't think I'll be seeing him again."

"Ooh, did he get physical with him?"

My pulse picks up at the memory of Titus pushing Jason up against the wall. "Oh yes. He was quite… um…"

"Yummy?" She offers.

I giggle. "As good a word as any."

"He's lovely, Heidi," she says, "and he looks at you as if you're something precious. I like that."

"He does not," I scoff.

She smiles. "He's obviously very fond of you."

"He thinks of me as Oliver's kid sister, that's all."

"That might be what he tells you, but I think he wants to do much more than pull your pigtails." She waggles her eyebrows.

I glance at the window, where I can see him leafing through a book as Grandpa talks to him. "Well, actually, we did kiss last night…"

Her jaw drops. "Really? Oh my God, Heidi! A peck or a smooch?" Her excitement makes me laugh. She's always been like this—like my fifteen-year-old best friend, excited to hear about my love life. She made such an effort with Jason, but he just seemed to think she was weird, which made me very sad.

"Oh," I say with feeling, "it definitely fell into the smooch category."

"And yet you slept in separate rooms?"

I sigh. "I know he'd like more, and so would I, but we're both hesitant because we know it would have to come to an end, and neither of us wants that complication."

"It doesn't have to end. If it's meant to be, love always finds a way." She gives me a meaningful look, sipping her coffee as the two men come back out again.

I finish off my tea. It's a romantic thought, but not a practical one, and I'm not willing to enter a tunnel when I can't see the exit.

Still, it's nice to watch Titus talking to Grandma, laughing at her jokes, and responding with some of his own. He seems so at ease in whatever company he's in, able to converse with young and old, men and women. He's quite clever, I notice, at turning the conversation away from himself; he'll talk about his work, but he tends to divert personal questions away by asking the other person about themselves. With some surprise, I realize actually it might be because he's shy at heart, and uncomfortable talking about himself.

He's a puzzle, with many layers. A girl could take years peeling them away to discover what lies beneath.

We chat for another half an hour, and then it's time to say goodbye. I hug Grandma, and she turns to him and says, "We'll see you again at the wedding!" They're flying over closer to the big day.

"Of course," he replies. "I look forward to it."

She hugs him. "Take care of her."

"I will," he promises, meeting my gaze over her shoulder and smiling.

"Will you be staying with Titus in Auckland?" Grandpa asks as he hugs me.

I move back, and I know I've blushed scarlet by the heat in my face and Titus's amused glance. "No, I'll be staying with Chrissie."

"Oh, I thought you were…" Grandpa trails off as he looks at Grandma, and she glares at him. "Ah," he says, "trust me to put my foot in it."

Titus laughs. "We're just friends," he says.

"Goodbye," Grandma replies, "I hope the weekend goes well. And that he persuades you to stay!" she adds mischievously.

He gives her a wry look, and then we wave goodbye and head back to the car.

"Jeez," I say as we get in and close the door. "Sorry about that."

"He's getting a bollocking now," he says, amused. "Poor Graham." He looks across at me as I start the engine and back out of the drive. "He's worried about you."

"Because of Jason?" He nods. "Yeah," I say, putting the car into gear and heading toward the main road, "Gramps didn't like him much. Neither did Grandma, come to that, although they were both too polite to say so. I'm not quite sure what they didn't like, but you can tell, can't you?"

He nods, and something about his silence prompts me to look at him. "Gramps told you, didn't he?"

He glances at me. "Maybe."

"Go on, spit it out."

"He didn't like the way Jason treated you."

That surprises me. "Oh. I assumed you were going to say he was too arrogant or something."

"He didn't like that either."

I give a short laugh. "What did he mean, the way Jason treated me?"

"He said Jason put you down sometimes. And that you were his princess and deserve to be treated like one."

"Jesus. Grandparents."

"I think he was warning me," Titus says.

"Oh, I'm so sorry," I say, embarrassed. "I did tell them we were just friends."

"Heidi, I don't mind. I happen to think he's right. A man should always treat his girl like a princess."

He's looking out of the window as he says it, distracted by the view, so I don't think he's being sarcastic. My gaze lingers on him for a moment before returning to the road, a frisson running down my back. He says such nice things.

"How come you're not married with six kids?" I ask.

That brings his gaze back to me. "Haven't met the right girl."

"Maisey wasn't The One?"

He snorts, and I chuckle.

"Do you want kids?" I ask.

"I don't *not* want them. They're not on my radar at the moment. They seem like hard work."

"Yeah. You got that right. So you're not envious of Oliver, impregnating his girl?"

I meant to make him laugh, but instead he shrugs. "I admit to a twinge of jealousy."

"Really?"

"Yeah. He's getting ready to take his vows and promise to love her forever. They're going to be joined together forever metaphorically, spiritually, whatever you want to call it, by their baby. He's deliriously happy. So yeah, I envy him, a bit. I'd like to have that comfortable relationship. That contentment. I just don't want all the hassle that comes before it."

"I know what you mean," I say with feeling. "It's so bloody complicated. I hate dating with a passion. I think that's why I stayed with Jason for so long. I was relieved that I'd found someone, and I didn't have to worry about first dates anymore."

He doesn't reply, and so I leave it there. I signal to come off the Devon Expressway, and head toward Briarton.

"Nearly one o'clock," I say. "We'll have a couple of hours in, shall we? Do you need to sort out what you're wearing for the weekend?"

"Most of my clothes are already in my main case in the car, but I can do some work for a while."

"I'll make us some lunch."

"Sounds great."

Once we're home, I retrieve some wraps from the fridge, spread them with cranberry sauce, and add slices of camembert that I warm up in the microwave, along with a handful of green salad. Titus sits outside with his laptop, under the shade of the umbrella, and I take our plates out with two glasses of lemonade over ice, and sit and read my book while he works. After that, I close my eyes, resting my head on my hand, and doze for half an hour.

At one point, I hear a rustle as he gets up, and he quietly makes his way past me. He stops, and a shadow falls over me before I feel his lips on my hair. Then he goes inside.

*

At about 3:30 p.m., we're on the road, heading east to Alan Woodridge's country house, deep in the Devon countryside.

We're in Titus's Range Rover, and dressed smart-casual, Titus in beige chinos and a dark-blue short-sleeved shirt, me in white capri pants and a hot-pink top.

"Okay?" I ask when I see him glance across at me for the second time.

"Yep," he says.

"Something wrong with my trousers?"

"Nope."

"Out with it, Lawrence."

"They're very tight," he says.

I look down at them. "Are you saying I look like a slut?"

He gives me a startled glance. "How did you get that from what I said?"

"I extrapolated."

"You extrapolate a lot. It wasn't a complaint or a criticism. It was a statement. I shouldn't have looked, but they're tight, and you're gorgeous, and I'm only human." He sounds exasperated.

"Sorry," I say. "I should have worn a kaftan."

He scowls at me. "Don't think I don't realize you're doing it on purpose."

"I'm not!" Okay, I am, a little bit, but I'm not going to admit that to him. "I can't help it if you've got sex on the brain."

"I wouldn't have if you weren't sitting next to me wearing clothes so tight that they leave nothing to the imagination." That makes me giggle, and his lips curve up. "Minx," he says.

"Seriously," I reply, "I didn't realize they were that tight. Do you think I ought to change? I want to make a good impression."

"Not at all. You look amazing. You're right, it's my brain." He sighs.

"How long has it been since you had sex?" I ask.

"Nineteen weeks, four days, six hours, and about seventeen minutes."

Now I'm giggling nonstop, and that makes him laugh. "Don't mock me," he says. "I thought I'd be distracting myself by concentrating on business all weekend, and instead I chose to invite the most beautiful girl in the country to go with me. I must be mad."

I smile at him. "You say the nicest things."

He huffs a sigh, although he smiles back. "Distract me," he says. "For God's sake."

"All right. Tell me about Alan Woodridge and his family."

"Okay. He's in his late fifties, and he was born in New Zealand, but he met his wife, Vicky, when he came to the UK on his big OE, and he decided to stay here. They've got three girls, all married, and who've all had fertility issues, so it's a cause that's very close to his heart. The eldest, Carrie, has been trying to get pregnant for about eight years, and she's had three rounds of IVF, but it's not worked. She's taken it hard, apparently—he actually got a bit emotional when he was telling me about her. Unfortunately his middle daughter, Rowena, has just had her first round of IUI and it's failed. His youngest, Sarah, has gotten pregnant twice and had two miscarriages. He's determined to do anything he can to help them, which is why he wants to invest in our research project."

"Oliver said it was five hundred million dollars."

"Yes, and he told me there's more money there if the project goes well."

"But he wants the project to be run from the UK?"

"Yes. It's a fair enough request, and quite common to ask for a representative of the research company to be present. Obviously, Elizabeth would have been a better choice because she's the chemist behind the development of the fertility drug, but Acheron has an AI department, and their engineers are keen to learn more about the selection of gametes and embryos."

"Gametes being… eggs and sperm, right?"

"Yes."

"So how does AI help selection?"

"We use static images and time-lapse videos to identify early markers of quality. With eggs, that includes things like follicle size; with sperm, we look at morphology, concentration, and motility."

"What does that mean?"

"The ability to move efficiently."

"So… basically whether a guy's got good swimmers?"

He grins. "Yeah. We're hoping that AI will eventually compute the optimal sperm–egg combination in order to achieve the highest success rate."

"It's fascinating stuff."

"I think so."

"Alan is obviously serious about the research if he wants to invest that kind of money into it."

"Yes. He also said he's determined to convince me to stay, so I'm expecting him to be relentless. Businessmen like that usually are. Although to be fair, I've spoken to him on Zoom, and he's been nothing but pleasant."

We chat a bit more about his research as he takes the slip road off the motorway, and heads east into the countryside. The hedges rise around us, the roads narrow, and when we crest a hill, the view opens up, the fields forming a patchwork quilt of greens, browns, and yellows.

"Wow," Titus says, slowing as he approaches a large pair of iron gates. "I wasn't quite sure what to expect, but this certainly wasn't it."

"It looks like something out of Downton Abbey." I watch Titus lower his window and press the buzzer on the box to the side of the gate.

"Hello?" he says. "Yes, it's Lawrence Oates. Thank you."

The gates begin to open, and he raises his window, then eases the Range Rover into the grounds of the house.

"Do you think that's it?" Titus asks as a stone-built cottage appears on our left.

"I doubt it," I reply. "That's a gatekeeper's lodge. Like a Kiwi sleepout. Beautiful isn't it? Keep going."

He continues up the gravel drive, which is lined on either side by tall, straight, Lombardy Poplar trees. Then, all of a sudden, the trees end, the drive opens up, and...

"Holy fuck," Titus says, at the same time that I say, "Shiiiiit."

In front of us is an enormous Edwardian country house, built from pink granite with a clay tiled roof. It has two floors, a round turret on the left-hand corner, several tall chimneys, and a large wooden front door.

A river glimmers through the trees to the left of the house. Behind the building, wildflower meadows give way to the purple and green of the moors like a bruise beneath the light-blue sky.

Titus pulls up out the front and turns off the engine. Then he looks at me, and we both start laughing.

"Come on," he says. "Let's see if anyone's in."

As we get out of the car, the front door opens, and out comes a guy in his late-fifties, slender, about six foot tall, with short gray hair. He's wearing a light-blue polo shirt and navy trousers.

"Titus," he says, beaming as he holds out his hand.

"Alan." Titus goes forward, and the two of them shake hands, with Alan putting his other hand on top of Titus's.

"So glad you could make it," Alan says.

"It's good to be here." Titus turns and beckons me forward. "This is my friend, Heidi. Her initials are HRH, so feel free to call her Your Royal Highness."

"Titus," I scold, "honestly."

Alan laughs and shakes my hand. "It's great to meet you, Heidi. I'm Alan, and my wife's name is Vicky." He turns and calls over his shoulder. "Vic? They're here."

A woman comes to the door, medium height, as slender as her husband, with hair that's part blonde and part gray caught up in a clip that lets wavy strands frame her face. She's wearing navy-blue capri trousers like mine, maybe not quite so tight, and a white sleeveless top.

"Hello." Also beaming, she comes out and shakes Titus's and then my hand. "So lovely to meet you both."

"Come in," Alan says. "The sun's over the yardarm—must be time for a drink."

Chapter Eleven

Titus

I've been in some fancy places in my time—lots of top hotels and exclusive resorts—but hand on my heart, I've never been anywhere like this.

"It's so light," Heidi says as we walk into the reception hall, "like a cathedral."

"It's the high ceilings," Vicky says, "and it's south-facing, too."

"It sounds so strange," I reply, "because in New Zealand, all the best properties are north facing."

"Oh, of course," she says, "how weird that sounds!"

Beautiful oak paneling and polished granite tiles give way to a set of steps leading up to the next floor. Alan leads us all the way through to the rear of the house. I catch a glimpse of the kitchen—more English oak in the cupboards and tables, a huge AGA, a central island with a granite pillar as the centerpiece, and a breakfast area surrounded by exposed stonework with a glass roof above. Several people wearing white aprons are working at the counters, preparing platters for this evening.

"Come through to the sitting room," Vicky says, taking us into an elegant room with a wood burner set into an arched bay, more oak paneling, and oil paintings of old-fashioned hunting scenes.

"Champagne?" Alan asks, extracting a bottle from the bucket by the table.

"Ooh, yes please," Heidi says.

I nod, too, and he proceeds to open it and pour it into four narrow glasses.

Heidi accepts one of the glasses. "Your house is absolutely gorgeous."

Vicky looks pleased at her compliment. "Thank you, I love it so much. We'll show you around in a while, but feel free to come and go as you please this weekend. There's a pool and a gym that you must come up and use whenever you want."

Come up and use? The phrasing strikes me as odd. Where are we staying, then?

"We can't wait to introduce you to the rest of the family," she continues. "They all want to meet the couple from New Zealand. We didn't want to overwhelm you on your first night here with an intimate dinner party with everyone, though. We thought a cocktail party would be more informal, you know, drinks and nibbles so you can mingle."

Heidi glances at me. Assuming she's alarmed by the thought of a cocktail party, I wink at her.

"So how long have you two known each other?" Vicky asks.

"About eight years," I reply as Alan passes me a glass. "Heidi was sixteen. I kissed her at a party, and she turned the color of a tomato."

Heidi's eyes widen comically as the two of them chuckle. I grin and sip the champagne.

"But you didn't get together then?" Vicky asks.

"No," I say. "Her brother was one of my best mates and he'd warned us not to go near his sisters."

"It's understandable, I suppose," Vicky says. "Sixteen is quite young. I guess he doesn't mind so much now, though?"

"Yes," I reply. "I mean no." I'm not quite sure what she's asking.

"We've put you in the gatekeeper's cottage," Alan says, passing me a glass. "It's smallish, just the one bedroom, but nice and private. There are great views over the river."

Heidi catches my eye, and her eyebrows rise. Something's bothering her...

And then Alan's words sink in. Wait, what? I open my mouth to speak, but my brain has gone blank.

"Please excuse us for a moment," Vicky says. "Alan, can you double check with Sam that he's stocked the fridge in the cottage, please? I want to check with the chef that everything's okay for later. We'll be back in a couple of minutes."

"No worries," I manage to mumble, and the two of them leave the room.

Heidi immediately comes over to me. "They think we're a couple," she whispers urgently.

I blink. "I told him on the phone that I was bringing a friend."

"I guess he extrapolated," she says. Her voice holds a touch of sarcasm, but she seems more amused than annoyed.

"Why did he do that?"

"Maybe because you told them you kissed me?"

"Oh. Yeah. I thought it was funny. Shit."

"Why didn't you say something when he said about us staying in the cottage? That was the perfect opportunity to set them straight."

"I panicked," I reply. "I'm so sorry. I'll explain." I run a hand through my hair. I can't believe I've screwed up already. I really wanted to make a good impression, and this isn't a good start.

She inhales, then lets the breath out slowly. "Look, you don't have to say anything."

"What's the alternative?"

"One of us sleeps on the sofa?"

"It's not just about the cottage. They think we're a couple. We'd have to pretend to be an item all weekend." I can't say the idea doesn't appeal to me, but I'm here to get funding, not to get laid.

Heidi's trying not to laugh. "Honestly, you're such an idiot."

"I'm so sorry."

She rolls her eyes. "It won't be that bad. We can fake it, surely?"

My gaze slides over to her. "I hope you'll never have to do that with me."

"Jesus, really? You're cracking sex jokes when you've just bolloxed everything up?"

"It's a defensive mechanism. I'm dying a little inside."

She chuckles and, to my surprise, slides an arm around my waist. "It's not the end of the world. We're good friends, aren't we? We can fake love for the weekend."

I look down into her sparkling blue eyes, and my stomach flips. Oh shit. I've screwed up big time.

"We need to get our story straight," she says. "I'm assuming they think I still live in New Zealand, and we came over together?"

I'm distracted by the feel of her tucked under my arm. I put an arm around her shoulder, fighting the urge to kiss her. "I guess."

"All right. We started dating over a year ago, not this Christmas just gone, the one before. We live together in your apartment in Auckland. I teach in a primary school there, the one I did my training at."

"Okay. We're not engaged, though?"

"You haven't asked me to marry you yet," she says playfully.

"That's because I'm a fucking idiot," I murmur, looking at her mouth and watching her lips curve up.

"We'll have to make up the rest as we go along," she whispers. "And Titus, don't worry about it. If we screw up, we'll just tell the truth and say we were embarrassed. It'll be fine."

I'm not so sure, but I can hear Vicky coming back, and there's no time to argue.

"Relax," Heidi whispers, and to my shock she lifts up onto her tiptoes and presses her lips to mine.

"Aw," Vicky says as she comes in and catches the kiss. "Young love."

"Sorry," Heidi replies, pulling back. "It's hard to keep my hands off him."

"That's understandable." She smiles. "Come on, I'll show you around the house."

*

Heidi

Alan joins us as we leave the room carrying our glasses, and we slowly wander through the house, looking at the large living room with its beautiful bay window, a dining room that contains an oak table which seats ten and looks as if it has a central section that can be extended to make it bigger, a smaller, cozier living room through an archway that has a huge TV and looks as if they spend a lot of time there, and a conservatory overlooking a terrace and the gorgeous landscaped garden with its manicured lawn. Then we go upstairs, and they show us around the six bedrooms, including the one in the tower.

"We thought about putting you in there," Vicky confesses as the two men walk ahead, talking about fishing, "but I thought you'd prefer the privacy of the cottage. You can go skinny dipping in the river and nobody can see you." She chuckles.

I blush at the thought of seeing Titus naked and wet. "Mm."

"I'm glad you're here at last," she admits. "Alan has been looking forward to meeting you both. He's so excited about this project. I hope the weekend doesn't seem too daunting for you, but he insisted on pulling out all the stops. Between you and me, I know it's a lot to ask you to move over here for two whole years, especially when New Zealand is such a beautiful country, but he's really hoping Titus will oversee the project firsthand. It's because of our daughters, you see. I presume Titus has told you about them?"

"Yes, I'm so sorry to hear they've had issues conceiving. It must be very upsetting for the whole family."

"It's been exceptionally tough on Carrie, and she and Alan are close, so he's taken it hard. It's crazy when you have all this money and yet there's nothing you can do, you know? So when Alan heard about the Kiwi project, he was determined to help where he could. The new fertility drug is going to be essential, but it's the AI component that Alan's really interested in."

"Oh, I thought he wanted Elizabeth to run the project."

"No, he wanted Titus all along. Obviously, Acheron is a pharmaceutical firm, but Alan has always believed the major breakthroughs would come with AI, and Titus's project is going to be revolutionary. I don't know if you're aware, but Alan first saw him speak at the International Joint Conference on Artificial Intelligence in Vienna, Austria, last year. Titus was one of the keynote speakers, and he spoke about AI's role in IVF and fertility research. Alan was so impressed with him that he met up with him after his speech and told him right there and then that he wanted to invest."

"Wow. No, I didn't know that."

"It wasn't just that he was knowledgeable and erudite. It was that he didn't just give facts and figures and talk about the marvels of AI. He spoke about the emotional strain that continued IVF cycles put on couples, and how he hopes computers will ease that pressure. That was very important to Alan."

I knew Titus was smart, of course, and my sisters had told me that he'd spoken at conferences all over the world. But the way that Vicky talks about him, with respect and even reverence, brings goosebumps out all over my skin.

"And he's gorgeous," Vicky adds in a teasing voice. "You've really hit the jackpot!"

"I have," I reply. "He's a man in a million."

"And a boss in a billion, too," she says. "Alan's spoken to some of his employees, and they all sing his praises. He sounds pretty perfect. Does he have any faults?" She's teasing, but she looks at me for a genuine answer.

The guys are waiting by the top of the stairs, and they overhear her question as we approach.

Well, I think sarcastically, he's a bit dense when it comes to explaining his love life.

Titus's lips twist, suggesting he's reading my mind.

"He's exceptionally clumsy," I say. "I hope you don't have any priceless vases in the cottage, because they're likely to end up on the floor in a million pieces."

Vicky laughs. "No, nothing like that. I guess it's a small price to pay for him to be ninety-nine percent perfect."

"Don't tell him that," I scold, "he won't be able to get his head out of the door," and she and Alan chuckle.

We walk down the staircase, emerging into the reception area, and leave our glasses on a table. "Let's take you down to the cottage," Alan says, "and then you can have a rest before the cocktail party."

"What time does it start?" Titus asks.

"We've planned for six until nine, although it wouldn't surprise me if it goes on for longer."

"Sounds great," Titus says, and we follow him outside.

A beautiful, gleaming silver Merc is waiting outside. Alan opens the door and says, "Follow me down to the cottage."

"Okay."

"I'll see you later," Vicky calls from the doorway, and we wave goodbye.

We get into the Range Rover, and Titus starts it and eases it along the drive, following Alan down to the gatekeeper's cottage.

"Did you get the third degree?" he asks.

"Not really," I reply. "She mostly talked about you."

"Oh?"

"She told me how Alan saw you speak in Vienna."

"Oh yeah. That's where we first met."

"She was very complimentary."

"That's nice."

I look across at him. He glances at me, catches my eye, and his lips curve up. "What?" he asks.

"Nothing. It was weird, that's all. I'd gotten used to you being the clumsy guy who French-kissed me when I was sixteen. It's odd to hear someone talking about you like a mogul."

He laughs. "I like that word."

"She made you sound like Bill Gates, Elon Musk, and Stephen Hawking all bundled up into one."

"Wow. I'm impressive."

"Titus, I'm serious. I feel like I'm in the presence of a rock star. Can I have your autograph?"

"It won't go for much on eBay. Nobody outside the computer industry has a clue who I am."

"I don't know much about theoretical physics, but I know who Stephen Hawking is."

"Yeah, I guess."

I rest a hand on his where it sits on the gearstick. "It was nice to hear her talk about you like that. I appreciate that you've taken a few days out of your busy schedule to spend some time with me."

"It's been my pleasure, believe me. I haven't felt so relaxed in years." He pulls onto the small drive next to where Alan's parked his car, and we get out.

"This way," Alan says, and he leads us along the path, past well-tended flower borders, and up to the cottage's front door. He unlocks it, then gives Titus the keys. "Come in."

We follow him into the cottage, which is all one level. Ooh, it's beautiful. It has an open-plan kitchen and dining room, a white Neptune kitchen, one bedroom with an Oh-My-God enormous bed decorated in spring colors—peach, light green, and yellow—and a bathroom with a huge sunken bath. Oh my.

"The cupboards and fridge are fully stocked," he says, "but if you want anything at all at any time, please call the house—just dial zero on the phone. We have a permanent staff and a chef staying for the weekend, and someone will be happy to help."

"Thank you." Titus goes to the back door and looks out at the view. "It's beautiful."

Alan joins him. "It's quite pleasant to sit out on the deck looking out over the river. Tomorrow we'll go fly fishing. Heidi, you're very welcome to join us."

"No, thank you," I say, sure that he wants some time alone with Titus. "I don't know the first thing about fishing."

"Well I know that Vicky goes to a yoga class on Saturday mornings, if you'd like to join her, or you can swim in the pool, or go shopping, or just have some time to yourself."

"A yoga class would be lovely," I say enthusiastically, "if she doesn't mind me tagging along."

"Not at all, she'll love it. None of our girls are into it, and she's always saying she'd love to go with someone." He claps his hands together. "Okay, well that's sorted. I'll leave you to get settled in. Please, just call the house when you're ready to come up this evening and I'll send a car, then you won't have to worry about driving back tonight."

"Thanks," Titus says, and they shake hands. Alan waves goodbye, goes out, and closes the door behind him.

We stare at each other, then both blow out a relieved breath. "Phase one complete," he says. "Thank God."

"So far, so good. Shall we get our cases out?"

"Yeah, okay."

We head back out to the car, retrieve our bags, and bring them into the bedroom.

For a moment, we stand there looking at the giant bed. I glance at Titus and follow his gaze to the wardrobes. The fronts of the doors are mirrors, which give a perfect side-on view of the bed.

His gaze slides to mine.

"Don't say a word," I tell him, trying not to laugh.

"I wouldn't dream of it." Hurriedly, he slides open the doors, revealing the hanging space, and we spend five minutes hanging our clothes in the wardrobes before returning to the living room.

"Looks comfy enough," I tease, gesturing at the leather sofa. "Shall we rock, paper, scissors for it?"

"I'll be fine," he says. "My punishment for being an idiot."

I laugh, go through to the sparkling kitchen, and open some of the cupboards. "Oh my God, Titus, look at this." I show him the selection of groceries, which range from pantry items like pasta and rice all the way to boxes of chocolates, including several boxes of After Eight Mints—my favorites.

Titus opens the fridge and gapes at the array of fresh fruit and vegetables inside, along with several bottles of champagne and white wine. There's also a rack to one side with a dozen assorted bottles.

"Hold on," he says, and he strides into the living room. I follow him and watch him glance around, then walk over to a cabinet against the wall. He opens it and makes an odd kind of strangled sigh, the type

I might make if I saw him exiting the river *sans* clothes. I look at the contents. It contains a dozen bottles of amber-colored whisky.

"Fuck me," he says, taking one out. "It's a twenty-two-year-old rare-cask Ardbeg. That's, like, four thousand dollars. A twenty-one-year-old Lagavulin, six grand a bottle. And a limited edition twenty-year-old Mr. Porter Glenfiddich! Fifteen grand a bottle!" He stares at me. "They're all Islay malts—my favorites. How did he know?"

"I don't know," I say. "He also got my favorite chocolates—I love After Eight Mints."

He lifts the Glenfiddich out, holds it as if it's a priceless artifact, and strokes the label.

"Do you touch your women like that?" I ask.

He gives me an amused look, then returns his gaze to the bottle. "Is it too early to try it?"

"Touching a woman?"

"I meant having a whisky, but if you're game…"

I chuckle. "Alan said the sun's over the yard arm. Come on."

We go back into the kitchen, retrieve some ice from the freezer, and pour a generous measure of the Glenfiddich over it. I make him roll his eyes by adding a splash of cold water to mine from the fridge, and then we both take a sip.

"Ooh," he says, "caramel and creamy lemonade, and a touch of vanilla."

I wince. "If you say so. It's fucking strong."

"Philistine. We'll have to have a tasting session. I'll teach you how to appreciate a good malt."

"Only if I can teach you about gin."

He pulls a face but says, "All right." Then he grins. "Want to take a walk along the river?"

"Yeah, sure."

He has a mouthful of the whisky, and then says, "I'll finish that when I get back."

Leaving my glass beside his, I undo the sliding back door and head out into the balmy late afternoon.

"Phew," I say as we start walking slowly along the path beside the river. "It's so warm."

"Very Kiwi," he says. "Do you miss the weather?"

"It does rain a lot here. But I don't mind."

"Have you seen much of the rest of the country?"

I tell him a little about my trip to Kent and Sussex in the southeast, mainly to visit the remains of the Roman Saxon Shore forts, the site of the Battle of Hastings, and the medieval castles like Leeds and Bodiam.

"I'd like to go to Wales," I say, "and see Harlech Castle, and Caernarfon, and up to Hadrian's Wall, and Stonehenge, and all the sites I didn't see in London. There's so much history here."

"Should keep you busy for a while," he says.

I smile, but he looks away, across the river. We walk quietly for a while. Butterflies flutter around in my stomach. For the first time, I wonder whether he was secretly hoping that when we go back to New Zealand, I'd stay there? It's a big presumption. I know he likes me, but he's only been in Devon for three days. It's hardly the love of a lifetime. I wish I had the courage to ask him to kiss me, or to just kiss him, but I don't.

He's a mogul, for God's sake; a billionaire businessman who does keynote speeches at top conferences. I know he has an IQ of 159 because Oliver teases him that he's thick because it's less than Einstein's. He might want to get in my knickers, but he's not going to be interested in having a relationship with a primary school teacher, I'm sure.

Besides which, he's a guy, and guys tend to be able to sleep with girls without forming emotional attachments. The only person likely to get hurt if we were to have a fling would be me.

I sigh. Part of me wishes I'd said no to coming here with him, especially now we're supposed to act like a couple for a few days. It's just a bit of fun. But I have to make sure my heart stays locked away, because I'm pretty sure that if I let Lawrence Oates get anywhere near it, he could easily shatter it into a thousand irreparable pieces.

Chapter Twelve

Titus

Heidi sighs, and my stomach gives a strange flip. I can't deny that, deep down, I was hoping she'd had enough of England, and that when we go back to New Zealand, she realizes how much she misses it, and decides to stay.

But she speaks about the history here so passionately, and she loves her job, and I know she's not ready to go. I can't expect her to leave for a guy she barely knows, just because he thinks he sees the seed of something worth nurturing. It's hardly strong enough to build a future on.

I glance across at her. She's studying one of the moorhens that's gliding on the river, and she looks sad. Is it because she's also thinking that she doesn't want to leave here? Does she feel the same way I do— that there's a spark of something between us? Or is she thinking about Jason, maybe wondering whether she should try again with him?

Anger flares inside me. She wouldn't go back with that idiot, would she? No, of course she wouldn't. She's sad because she likes me, and she has feelings for me, and she can't bear the thought that our time together is limited. That's what I'm going to assume, anyway.

"Talk to me about your school," I say, because I want to return the smile to her face. "What does your typical day look like?"

Sure enough, she brightens as she starts telling me about her pupils, and how her day progresses. When she's laughing and joking around, it's easy to think of her as a young woman without a care in the world, but when she talks about her work she speaks knowledgeably and passionately, telling me about teaching standards, statutory assessment requirements, and differentiation—how she adapts her teaching to respond to the strengths and needs of pupils.

"They're very lucky to have you," I say, holding up a branch of a tree that's leaning across the path.

"Thank you." She ducks under it, then holds it up for me so I can pass beneath.

We continue on along the magical pathway that makes me feel as if we're miles from civilization, surrounded by bird calls and the occasional splash of a fish jumping out of the water. At one point, she stops with a gasp to point at a kingfisher sitting on the bridge crossing the water, its turquoise feathers glinting in the sunshine. As we go over it and start to head back, we spot a small mammal darting through the shallows that she tells me is a water vole. Ducks swim past, looking at us with interest, and elegant dragonflies with their diaphanous wings skim along the river's surface.

It's a beautiful vista, but it's still not as beautiful as the girl walking by my side. It's warm and humid out here, and her English-rose complexion glows. Her blonde hair gleams in the sunlight. It's the perfect length to draw attention to the soft, pale skin of her elegant neck. It makes me want to kiss it.

"Titus," she scolds.

"What?"

"Don't look at me like that."

"Like what?"

"You know like what. Like you want to kiss me."

She looks up then and meets my gaze. I stop walking, and she does too, turning to face me.

"I do," I say. "I can't help it."

Her lips curve up. "You're a naughty boy."

"Our clothes are still on."

She laughs. "That's true."

"The question is, would you like to kiss me?"

She sighs, repeating the answer I gave when she asked the same question. "More than life itself."

I move closer to her, and she slides her arms around my waist. "Well, if anyone's watching, we are officially a couple," I murmur, and lower my lips to hers.

Her mouth is soft, and her lips part for me, allowing me to slide my tongue against hers. I cup her face and deepen the kiss, and she gives one of her delightful half-sighs, half-moans, tilting her head, her tongue darting to stroke mine.

I lower my arms around her, and her arms rise around my neck as she presses against me. Ahhh… I stroke my hands down, following the line of her waist, the flare of her hips, fire licking up inside me, and I can't resist flicking up the hem of her top and resting my fingers on her bare skin. She gives a delicious shiver, and that's it, my erection springs to life.

We kiss for a while, in the afternoon sunlight, surrounded by the gentle quacking of the ducks, the honks of geese flying overhead, and the movement of water through the reeds at the edge of the river.

When I eventually lift my head, her cheeks are filled with a rosy flush, and her eyes look dreamy.

"Mmm." She presses her lips together. "You kiss like a god, Lawrence Oates."

"It's easy when I'm kissing you." I touch my lips to her cheek, then her lips once more, briefly. "Come on," I say softly. "Let's get back to the lodge."

We continue walking, but this time I put my arm around her, and she nestles against me with her arm around my waist.

"I was thinking while you were talking to Alan and Vicky that you seem quite shy sometimes," she says.

"Oh?"

"You don't talk about yourself much. I mean, you discuss your work, and you have funny anecdotes and stories, but I realize I don't actually know that much about you."

"What do you want to know?"

"I don't know. About your family? Have you got any siblings?"

"Nope. Only child."

"Do you have any other relatives in New Zealand?"

"Yes, my dad's a Kiwi."

"Oh of course, he's in politics, isn't he?"

"Yes, he's a lawyer, based at the Beehive. Most of my family is in Wellington. My dad's sister is a surgeon. Her husband is a computer engineer, and he's the reason I got into the field. He invented a computer graphics card when I was young that was the best-performing in the market at the time, which is where he made most of his money. When I was in my teens he started to get interested in AI. He's got three boys, and I spent a lot of time with them all, tinkering with computers and writing code, so it's not surprising we all ended up working in the field."

"They're all computer engineers as well?"

"Yeah. Saxon's actually on the verge of opening up a second branch of NZAI in Wellington with me."

Her eyebrows rise. "Oh, really?"

"Yeah. It's going to be health-focused, working with Wellington Hospital and looking at ways to use AI to help deliver better healthcare faster, and at a lower cost, as well as working on the IVF research."

We approach the cottage again, and I open the sliding doors, let her walk past me, and follow her in.

"Thank you," she says. "For sharing a bit about yourself. I thought maybe you didn't like talking about your family."

"I don't mind at all. I just find that most people aren't really interested and would much rather talk about themselves."

"That's true. Unless they're interested in you." She smiles. "I might have a read for twenty minutes before I start getting ready. I'll just get my book." She goes into the bedroom.

I stand there for a moment. *Unless they're interested in you.* Her words send a frisson down my spine. I can still feel the touch of her lips on mine, and the feel of her soft body pressed against me. God, this is torture. I look at the sofa, picturing myself there tonight, looking up at the ceiling, thinking about her just a few steps away in the bedroom. It would be so easy to toss the covers aside, get up, walk in there, and sweep her up in my arms. I don't think she'd resist me, either. But it's because she wouldn't resist that I need to be strong enough for both of us.

I give a silent groan and run both hands through my hair. Where's your willpower, dude? Pull yourself together!

*

After a brief rest, we decide it's time to start getting ready. We walk into the bedroom, and she retrieves her bag and goes into the bathroom.

"Can I shave while you put your makeup on?" I ask, leaning on the door jamb.

"Sure." She doesn't look up.

"Thanks." I get my razor and can of shaving foam, take off my shirt, and join her at the big mirror.

As I run a sink full of hot water, she huffs a sigh.

"What's the matter?" I ask.

"Nothing." She glances at the tattoo on my back, scowls, then returns to touching up her makeup.

"I can't shave with my shirt on," I point out.

"Of course not," she says sarcastically. "God forbid that I don't get reminded about what I'm missing out on every twenty minutes."

I chuckle and take the lid off the spray foam. "You don't have to look."

She purses her lips, and an impish glint appears in her eyes. She puts down her eyeliner. Then she crosses her hands, takes the hem of her top in her fingers, peels it up her body, and tosses it onto the floor.

"You don't have to look," she says tartly. Picking up her eyeliner, she leans forward to look in the mirror and resumes drawing a line along the top of her lid.

I blink at the sight of her beautiful breasts propped up in the lace demi-cups of a cream bra, and then a stream of foam erupts from the can right across the sink.

"Sorry," I say, scooping it up with my fingers, "I got over-excited."

"We can always cuddle," she says, and giggles.

That makes me laugh, which makes her giggle again, and it takes a few minutes for us to stop setting each other off.

I finish shaving, wash the razor, then pat my skin dry with a towel, my gaze sliding over to her. She's finished her eyeliner and foundation, and now she's brushing the smoky-gray eyeshadow across her lids that gives her a sexy, sultry look.

I do my best not to look at her breasts, but it's nigh-on impossible.

Her gaze meets mine in the mirror, and she raises an eyebrow, cheeky minx. I give her a wry look as I splash on some aftershave, then walk out and leave her to it.

Taking my clothes into the living room, I change into a white shirt and a navy suit, add a blue-and-silver tie, and some black Oxford shoes. Then I sit back and open up my laptop to check my emails while I wait for Heidi to finish.

Ten minutes before six, I hear footsteps and look up to see her approaching. She stops and glances down at herself. "Do I look okay?" she asks shyly. "I want to make a good impression."

Closing my laptop, I put it to one side, then get to my feet. I let my gaze slide down her before returning it to her face. The black sheath dress clings to her slender figure, reaching to just above the knee. The top is covered with a layer of sheer black lace embroidered with big black roses that continues down her arms to her elbows. It's elegant and sophisticated, and also incredibly sexy, mainly because I'm pretty sure from the shape and movement of her breasts that she's not wearing a bra.

"Wow," I say with feeling. "You look magnificent."

She dips her head so her short blonde hair swings forward to hide her blush. "Thank you." Then she looks up again, her gaze skimming over me. "You don't look so bad yourself. You wear a suit superbly well."

"Most men do."

"Not like that. I'm guessing it's bespoke?"

"Yeah. Off-the-peg suits don't tend to fit me right. My shoulders and thighs are too big."

She walks forward to stand in front of me. She's wearing a pair of black high-heels, and although she's still quite a bit shorter than me, they bring her lips slightly closer to mine.

She drops her gaze to my mouth. "Are you trying to turn me on?"

My lips curve up, and I watch hers mirror them. "You've put your lipstick on," I murmur. "Now I can't kiss you."

"That was damn foolish of me."

"Probably for the best."

"Mmm."

We study each other for a moment. Her smoky-gray eyelids have dropped to half mast, and her lips have parted. Her desire rises from her like perfume, and the longing in her eyes is like a silk ribbon, winding around me, ensnaring me.

I want her, so badly. If I don't do something right now, I'm going to rip off her clothes, throw her on the bed, and make mad passionate love to her. I want to kiss her all over, slide inside her, and make her come over and over again.

God... I really, really want to do that...

"We should go," I whisper reluctantly.

She blinks. Her cheeks flush pink. Then she moves back and says, "Yes, of course. I'll just get my purse."

I watch her walk away, my heart—as well as certain other bits of my anatomy—aching for her. I feel bad, as if I've embarrassed her, although we're as bad as each other.

She comes back with her clutch bag, smiles, and says, "Okay! Shall we head out?" She turns and heads for the door.

"Heidi." I stride to catch her up. I take her free hand, and she stops and turns to face me.

"I'm sorry," I say.

She touches my arm. "It's okay. You're right. We shouldn't." She drops her arm. "Just stop taking your bloody shirt off and we'll be all right!"

I chuckle, and she grins and opens the door.

"Wait, shall we call the house?"

"Nah," she says. "Let's walk up."

"In those heels?"

"It's okay, I'm wearing stockings, so they won't rub."

My eyes nearly fall out of my head as I follow her out. "Stockings?"

"Well, holdups." She snaps the elastic at the top of her leg.

I scowl as we walk past the car and onto the grass pathway that leads the other side of the trees to the house. "You're determined to torture me."

"Says the man who ejaculated his shaving foam in front of me," she replied, and we both laugh.

"Come here," I say, reaching for her hand, and I curl my fingers around hers. "Just to look the part," I explain.

"Yeah," she says. "This isn't going to be torture at all."

I grin. "I can't think of a nicer place in which to be tormented."

"That's true. It's very beautiful here."

We walk slowly, Heidi pointing out the birds we come across: house sparrows, gold finches, chaffinches, wood pigeons, and even two blackbirds, serenading us from the trees.

It's just after six by the time we get to the house. We've heard cars passing by on the drive, and we count fifteen parked, with another three or four making their way toward us.

"I thought it was just going to be an informal family thing," Heidi mutters as we near the front door.

"Yeah..." I feel my first tingle of nerves. "Uh-oh."

A young guy who looks like a waiter greets us as we go inside, and he directs us through the reception hall toward the drawing room. We've just walked in when Alan comes over.

"The guest of honor!" he announces. "And his beautiful lady. Welcome to you both."

I look at Heidi, seeing that she's as startled as me. Guest of honor? Holy shit. Is this all for my benefit?

"What can we get you to drink?" Alan asks. "Stephen will be glad to make you any cocktail you like. Or we have several fantastic Islay malts."

"Yeah," I say, "How did you know that's my drink of choice?"

"A little birdie told me." He grins.

"I'd love a G&T," Heidi says.

"I'll have an Old Fashioned, please," I add.

"Of course." Alan gestures to a waiter who's standing nearby, who goes over to the long table that's been set up as a makeshift bar by the drinks cabinet. "How's the cottage?" Alan asks.

"It's lovely," Heidi says, "thank you so much, especially for the After Eight Mints. The little birdie again?"

He chuckles. "I've been talking to Elizabeth Tremblay. She gave me a few tips on what you both liked."

I laugh. "Ah, that makes sense."

"Once you have your drinks," he says, "we'll start making the rounds and introducing you. There are lots of people who are excited to meet you."

I glance at Heidi and run a hand through my hair. "Yeah… about that. We thought this was an informal party."

"It is. Well, I mean, it's not a sit-down do."

"But… you organized it… for me?"

He gives me an amused look. "Of course we organized it for you. Everyone wants to meet the computer superhero who's changing the future of IVF."

"You should have worn your cape and tights," Heidi teases.

"I'm not a superhero," I say, embarrassed.

Alan just chuckles, then takes the drinks from Stephen as he brings them up and hands them to us. "Come on. We're out on the terrace."

He leads the way out through the conservatory onto the large paved area dotted with a few chairs and tables. It's not dark yet, but the place looks like a grotto. Fairy lights have been threaded through the branches of small trees in pots, and strings of them also run above our heads and hang down like a curtain to either side, leaving the front free so the view of the wildflower meadow and the moors is clearly visible. More bottles filled with coiled up strings of lights are placed strategically around on tables and the low walls that run around the terrace. Waiters move slowly through the guests with platters of canapés filled with exquisite-looking nibbles. Music filters through speakers, and with some surprise I recognize *Pineapple Head*—a song by the Kiwi band Crowded House. Alan is originally from New Zealand, but immediately I know the music is for my benefit.

"Hello!" Vicky walks up with a big smile. She's wearing an elegant summer dress and high-heeled sandals, and she has a small red flower in her hair. "Heidi, you look so beautiful."

"So do you, I love your dress."

"And Titus." Vicky reaches up and kisses my cheek. "I'm glad you're here. Carrie's been so low lately. Believe me, I know your work isn't going to be a miraculous cure, but it's exciting to think there's hope, even if it is a few years away."

She gestures for us to follow her and leads us across to where a woman in her thirties is standing talking to a small group of people, although she's watching us. She's tall and very thin, and I can see the impact the years of disappointment have taken on her.

"This is Carrie," Vicky says. "Carrie, this is Titus and his partner, Heidi."

"I'm so pleased to meet you," Carrie says, sliding her hand into mine, and oh my God, she's actually trembling.

"Carrie," I say, placing my other hand on hers, "I've heard so much about you. It's great to meet you at last. And you must be John." I greet her husband, who I recognize from the photo that Alan sent me.

He shakes my hand, too, pumping it up and down. "We're honored you could come," he says. "We've been so thrilled to hear about your work, and it's so cool to meet you at last."

It turns out that the other people with them are Alan and Vicky's other two daughters and their spouses, and we all shake hands and introduce ourselves. Afterward, I turn back to Carrie, seeing from the way that her husband has his arm around her that she's genuinely overwhelmed to meet me. My conversations with people undergoing IVF have enlightened me as to how hard infertility can be on a couple, but for some reason Carrie's obvious emotion moves me more than any others I've met.

"I understand you're a librarian," I say to her. "I've always thought that must be such an excellent job. What library do you work at?"

She brightens and proceeds to tell me about it, and I ask her a few questions before Alan comes up and gently says he'd like to introduce me to a few more people.

"Of course," she says, blushing. "I didn't mean to hog him."

"Not at all," I reply. "I'd love to talk to you more over the weekend, if you're available," I say to her and John. "If it's not too difficult for you to talk about, I'd like to hear your experience with infertility, as the more information I can get, the better."

"We'd like that," John says, because she's too emotional to talk, and I nod and move on, holding Heidi's hand and taking her with me.

"That poor woman," Heidi whispers as we walk away. "She looked close to tears. You're going to make such a difference to people's lives, Titus. I'm so proud of you."

I'm so humbled by her words that I have to have a big swallow of my Old Fashioned to cover my emotion.

"Stay with me," I murmur to Heidi.

"I'm not going anywhere," she tells me, and her fingers tighten on mine.

Chapter Thirteen

Heidi

Titus hardly lets go of my hand all evening. I know him well enough to see how overwhelmed he is by it all, but he's covering it well. He's gone into business mode—turning on the charm without being smarmy, shaking hands, asking questions, and putting everyone at ease.

As well as Alan's family, there are also a lot of business people here—directors and managers from Acheron, and even CEOs and a handful of other members of staff from Alan's two biggest competitors. "This research is bigger than one company," he tells us. "We all need to work together to make it happen."

They aren't shy about grilling Titus, and several times when he starts answering a question, others nearby gather around to listen, so he ends up giving several mini talks to a fascinated audience.

I can't contribute much, and in the beginning I think maybe I should sneak off, have a walk around the garden, and leave him to it. But his hand stays tight on mine, and when I realize he wants me to stay, I keep close to his side.

After about an hour, I tell Titus I need to visit the bathroom, and he says, "I'll come with you."

We excuse ourselves and go inside. "You okay?" I ask as we walk through the house.

"Barely. Can you believe this?"

"He must really, really want you to stay."

"I feel kinda guilty that I've already made up my mind not to. Do you think I should tell him now?"

"I wouldn't spoil the evening. You're making such a good impression. You want to convince him to invest even if you don't stay, don't you? I can't imagine he's going to withdraw his money if you don't, judging by what he's done here for you, but you might as well wait until Monday. Besides, you might change your mind." I add the last sentence playfully.

He glances at me, and his lips curve up, but he doesn't reply. "After you," he says, and I realize we've reached the bathroom.

I slip past him and go inside, my pulse speeding up a little. I shouldn't have said that. But I couldn't help myself. I so wish he was staying here. But I know it's not going to happen. The more I listen to him, the more I realize how important his work is, and what an influential figure he is in the industry. He's not like me, who can get a job teaching pretty much anywhere.

As I wash my hands, I look up at my reflection in the mirror, and for the first time I think about going back to New Zealand. I'm happy here. But what's more important to me? My job, or my love life?

I dry my hands, then frown at my reflection. I've always thought that if a guy loved you, he wouldn't ask you to change for his benefit, but this isn't like that. I know Titus wouldn't ask me to move back. But I'm sure he's hoping I do.

I can't move back just because I've spent a few days with the guy, though. We haven't even slept together. Obviously this is like a holiday romance, that's all, and it feels more exciting and intimate because I've broken up with my boyfriend, and it's summer, and Titus is a touch of home.

Satisfied with my conclusion, I go out, see him leaning against the wall, waiting for me, and my heart bangs so hard against my ribs that I almost keel over.

"You okay?" he asks, eyebrows rising as I clutch hold of a cabinet.

I sigh. "Yeah."

He holds out his hand. "Come on."

I slip mine into it, trying not to shiver as his fingers curl around mine, and together we walk back out to the terrace.

"Titus!" Alan beckons to him. "Come and meet Sam Crewe. She's the CEO of Imagine Enterprises."

Titus pins a smile on his face, and we walk forward to greet yet another businesswoman, who eagerly starts asking him questions.

This goes on for another hour, during which we sample the canapés while Alan plies us with drinks. As well as making sure I eat, I intersperse each G&T with a glass of water, determined not to make a fool of myself by getting drunk. Still, it's impossible not to feel merry, and I can tell from the way Titus seems more relaxed and his easy laugh that the alcohol is having an effect on him too.

The music has been a mixture of both Kiwi and English bands, but now Bic Runga's *Listening for the Weather* comes on, and Titus turns to me with a mischievous look.

"Dance with me," he says.

My eyes widen, and I look around. There's no dance floor here. "Where?"

He looks around too. "Over there." He starts walking to a quieter space in the corner of the terrace, keeping a hold on my hand so I have to totter after him.

"Titus…" I laugh as he stops and pulls me into his arms, embarrassed as a few people cheer, and the rest turn to see what's happening.

"What?" His eyes are a little feverish as he slides his right arm around me. "You've stood by my side all evening. I want to say thank you."

We start moving to the music. His hand is warm on mine, and my skin tingles where the other rests at the base of my spine. Someone whistles, and he chuckles, but he keeps his gaze fixed on me.

"You look stunning in that dress," he murmurs.

I look up into his light-green eyes. It doesn't matter what I tell myself about this being a holiday flirtation. I really like this guy, and my crush hasn't been helped by listening to all these people saying how amazing he is.

"I kinda like dating a computer superhero," I tell him.

He chuckles. "And I don't mind dating the most beautiful girl in the room."

"Are you just trying to get in my knickers?" I tease.

His lips curve up. "Maybe."

My heart skips a beat. "You're going to have to try harder than that."

"Is that a challenge?"

"Are you rising to it?"

He laughs and pulls me a little closer, his lips brushing my temple. "You're a terrible flirt."

"Jesus, pot, kettle, much?"

We dance while Bic tells us she's coming home today, and how the days are getting cold, but that's alright with her, until eventually the song ends. A faster dance tune comes on, and I expect him to release me, but instead he just speeds up the pace and spins me away from him before pulling me back into his arms. I laugh and throw myself into it, doing the best I can in my high heels, and around us, a couple of other couples also join in.

"We're setting a trend," he says.

I grin, thoroughly enjoying myself. We dance to several songs, and it's only a growing thirst that eventually stops us. We rejoin Alan and Vicky, and everyone cheers.

"You make such a lovely couple," Vicky says. "It's so wonderful to see two young people so happy together."

Titus clears his throat, and my face grows hot. For the first time, I feel a touch of shame that we're deceiving this family. If we'd known how nice they all were I don't think we would have done it, but it's too late to tell them now.

It's nearing nine o'clock, and a few people come up to say they're calling it a day, and want to say goodbye to us both. Gradually over the next half an hour the business people depart, and eventually it's just the members of Alan's family who remain—his daughters and their husbands.

The temperature is dropping a little now the sun has set, so we move into the conservatory, and we spend another hour chatting to them over coffee, nibbling from a plate of beautiful small desserts that the waiter brings around: tiny cheesecakes and mini chocolate eclairs you can eat in one bite.

As it gets close to ten o'clock, Carrie and John finally say they're going to make a move, and Titus says, "Yes, I think it's time for us to head back."

"Would you like us to drop you off?" Carrie asks.

Titus looks at me, but I shake my head. "I'm happy to walk," I say, and he agrees.

We all head to the front door, and we shake hands with them all and tell them we look forward to seeing them at the murder-mystery evening tomorrow.

"Thank you so much," Alan says to Titus. "You were fantastic, and you've impressed everyone."

"I've had a great time," Titus replies.

"I'll call for you around eleven tomorrow for fishing?" Alan says.

Titus nods. "Sounds great."

"Here," Vicky says, "take this," and she hands him a torch. "The path is lit with solar lamps, but just in case."

"Thanks." We wave goodbye, then head out of the door and cross the gravel drive to the pathway behind the trees.

As we walk, we hear the cars departing, and then they disappear into the distance. The air fills with the sound of the countryside at night—the hoot of a tawny owl, the rattle of grasshoppers, the light snuffling of a hedgehog in the grass, and the call of a bird, maybe a nightingale or a skylark.

As Vicky promised, the path is lit every few feet by solar lamps pressed into the grass, and the moon is three-quarters full too, so Titus doesn't switch on the torch.

We walk quietly, listening to the nighttime sounds. I feel tongue-tied, acutely conscious of the man beside me. Every now and then I can smell his aftershave, heated by his warmed skin, and my fingers tingle where his hand is still holding mine.

I flex my hand in his. "Nobody's watching now," I say softly.

"Don't care," he says, and he interlinks our fingers.

My pulse picks up speed at his words. He likes touching me.

I'm pretty sure he wants me. I can feel his desire in the air, sparkling between us, a manifestation of the magical evening. I'm filled with a deep longing, an overwhelming hunger for this gorgeous guy.

"You were amazing this evening," I tell him.

"Ah," he says, embarrassed, "don't."

"I mean it. I'm so proud of you."

He squeezes my hand as we reach the edge of the trees and pass by the Range Rover. "That's a nice thing to say."

"You were so knowledgeable. It was really impressive." I take a deep breath. "And very sexy." I stop walking. Titus pauses, then turns to face me.

We study each other for a long time. My heart hammers, and my mouth has gone dry. His eyes gleam in the moonlight. The air between us seems to crackle with electricity.

He doesn't move, though. Is he thinking about the fact that my brother said he could trust him? Rebelliousness flares inside me. We're young, and we're single—why shouldn't we get together? It's nobody else's business.

I don't want him to turn me down, but one of us has to make the move, and I know he's fighting with his principles. It's going to have to be me. Fucking hell, Heidi, just go for it. What have I got to lose? My dignity? I think I lost that with him when I was sixteen and asked him if he'd like to kiss me.

Mind you, it worked then…

My pulse racing, I move a bit closer to him, then slide my hands up his chest to hold his lapels. "Do you want me?" I ask, my voice husky with longing.

He looks down at me, his eyelids sliding to half-mast. "You know I do."

Oh thank God. "I wasn't sure," I admit.

"I've thought about little else since I arrived at your cottage." He lifts a hand to stroke my cheek and sighs as if saying it out loud has made it real. "I don't know what it is… I mean, you're beautiful, and funny, and intelligent… but it's not just that. There's something between us, and every time I try to tell myself there isn't, it flares up again like a firework."

"Oh…" I'm so relieved he feels the same way, it almost makes me tearful.

He lifts his other hand and cups my face as he continues, "I'm crazy about you. I know I should be strong and keep my distance, and the last thing I want to do is make things more difficult for you. But I can't help it. I want you. I've never wanted anyone—anything—so badly."

My breath leaves me in a whoosh. "Kiss me," I tell him. "Please."

"Gladly," he says, and he crushes his lips to mine.

Oh… it's like I'm sixteen again, as we go from zero to a hundred in the space of about two seconds. Fire flares inside me as he delves his tongue into my mouth, and I moan and slide my hands down his jacket, flicking the buttons open. I feel an overwhelming desire to touch his skin, and I tug his shirt free from his trousers, then slip my fingers beneath it and stroke around his waist to his back.

"Jesus," he says, "hold on." He slides the key in the door and unlocks it, and we stumble into the dark house, barely managing to close the door before his mouth is on mine again.

While we kiss, he walks me backward along the hallway to the bedroom, while I slip my hands up his back under his shirt, loving the feel of his warm skin. When I graze my nails down the muscles on either side of his spine, he shudders.

It's no good; I want to see that tanned, smooth skin and those glorious tattoos. I push his jacket off his shoulders, and he lowers his arms to let it fall to the floor. He hurriedly pulls his tie apart, and it joins the jacket. I set to undoing his shirt buttons, but my fingers fumble, and in the end he rips the sides apart, sending buttons popping off in all directions, bundles the shirt in a ball, and tosses it away. Ooh, he's naked to the waist now, and even in the semi-darkness his tattoos are clearly visible, snaking down either arm.

He toes off his shoes and flicks off his socks, and I stop to take off my high heels, groaning as I flex my feet. Next he takes off his trousers, and now he's only wearing a pair of tight black boxer-briefs that leave nothing to the imagination.

Holy moly. Hello, Sir Richard!

Kissing me again, he continues to walk me into the bedroom. It's warm and a little stuffy in here. "Where's the air con?" he asks.

"I doubt there will be any. It doesn't usually warrant it."

"We'll just have to get hot and sweaty then," he murmurs.

"What a shame."

He chuckles, still moving me backward, over to the sliding doors. The curtains are open, but we haven't put on the light, and I know nobody's going to be out there looking in tonight.

He kisses me again, lips searing, sending fireworks shooting off inside me. Oh God, this is really happening. I run my fingers over the defined muscles of his chest, then up to his shoulders and down his arms across his tattoos. I think he's used these magical runes to cast a love spell on me. I feel bewitched, entranced by his hot, damp skin and his fiery kisses.

"Do you have a zipper?" he murmurs, lifting his head, and I nod, turning around to show him. I feel his fingers at the nape of my neck, and then he slides down the zipper and pushes the lace shoulders of the dress off my shoulders. It falls to the floor in a rustle of material, and I step out of it.

While I'm still facing away from him, he moves me forward a few steps until I'm up against the sliding doors to the terrace, and I place my hands on the glass. I have a few seconds to register the beauty of the view, seeing where moonlight has turned the river into a sheet of silver, and then my eyes flutter closed as he rests his hands on my hips.

I'm braless and wearing only a pair of black lacy knickers and my sheer black thigh highs. He runs his hands over the lace stretched across my bottom, then follows the dip of my waist and the line of my ribs. Finally, he cups my breasts in his big, warm hands.

Tipping my head back on his shoulder, I sigh. He groans as he brushes his thumbs over my nipples, teasing them. Slowly, they tighten into firm buttons that he then tugs with his thumbs and forefingers.

Feeling an answering pull deep inside, I turn in his arms and lift up to kiss him, sliding my hands into his hair.

"I'm trying to go slowly," he says huskily, kissing up my jaw to my ear, "but you're not making it easy."

"Good." I shiver as he sucks my earlobe.

He lifts his head. "I want to be gentle with you."

"You mean because of what I said about Jason?"

He nods.

I hesitate. "Can I be honest with you?"

"Of course."

"I don't mind if you're not gentle. It's not about that. I don't mind it… you know… passionate. But Jason… he used to…" I bite my lip. "He verged on violence," I admit. "It's very different. He didn't like women, I don't think, and he took it out on me."

Titus's smile fades, and his eyes harden. He runs his tongue over his top teeth, and I'm pretty sure he's trying to stop himself jumping in the car and driving straight down to give Jason the beating of his life.

But in the end his expression softens, and he takes my face in his hands. "I told you a man should always treat his girl like a princess, and I meant it." He tips his head to the side. "Or maybe like a countess." His lips curve up.

I open my mouth to say something, but I don't get a chance, because he kisses me again. His lips slant across mine, his tongue plunging into my mouth, and my heart hammers. I thought his previous kiss was passionate, but this time he doesn't hold back, and fire shoots through me, while an ache begins deep inside.

He bends, tucks his hands beneath my bottom, and picks me up, and I wrap my legs around his waist. Still kissing me, he climbs onto the bed, then lowers me onto my back. He kisses my mouth, then begins planting kisses down my neck and across my collarbone.

I'm carried away on a wave of pleasure and happiness as he continues kissing down to my breasts, then stops there to cover each nipple with his mouth and tease them with his tongue until they're tight and hard. Only then does he continue down over my belly, moving backwards until he's kneeling between my legs.

Hooking his fingers in the elastic of my underwear, he peels it down my thighs, and I lift my legs so he can take it off. He smooths his hands over my thigh highs with an appreciative murmur, then pushes my legs apart, exposing me to his hot gaze.

I cover my face with my hands as he kisses the sensitive skin of my inner thighs, and then he strokes a thumb up through my folds, and groans. I'm so turned on, I know he's found me swollen and wet.

"Heidi," is all he mutters, before he lowers down, licks up through my folds, and circles the tip of his tongue over my clit.

"Ohhh…" I arch my spine, shuddering at the wave of pleasure. "Oh that feels so good…"

While he licks and sucks, he slides a finger down through my folds to tease my entrance. Then, after a while, he turns his hand palm up and slides first one, then two fingers inside me.

We both sigh, and he strokes me gently, until I'm aching with need, and I'm breathing with deep, ragged gasps.

Only then does he withdraw his fingers and rise up. "I'll get my wallet," he says.

"I have a Mirena fitted," I say. "So you don't have to. But you can if you want, I don't mind either way."

His eyes glitter in the moonlight. "You're sure?"

I nod.

He removes his underwear, leans over me, then glances to one side. "You're so fucking beautiful."

I follow his gaze. I'd forgotten the wardrobe doors are mirrors. Words desert me at the sight of our reflection. The moon has painted one side of his body silver, while the other is in shadow. His tattoos wind up his muscular arms, and I can just see one wing of the raven on his back across his shoulder. I truly believe he's part Viking at this moment.

I shiver. I'm a little nervous, I don't know why. Maybe because I really like this guy, and I'm not hugely experienced, and I want to please him.

"*Du betyr så mye for meg,*" I whisper.

His eyes widen. "Did I say that right?" I ask shyly.

His lips curve up and he nods. "When did you learn to speak Norwegian?"

"I looked it up. I wanted to tell you how I feel about you."

"You mean a lot to me, too," he replies huskily. I think he's genuinely touched.

Then he presses his lips to mine, and I wrap my arms around his neck and lose myself in the kiss.

Chapter Fourteen

Titus

I'm incredibly touched that Heidi has taken the time to learn even a small phrase in my mother's language. This girl surprises me repeatedly with her thoughtfulness and kindness. *You mean a lot to me.* What a lovely thing to say.

It gives me even more of an incentive to pleasure her in bed—not that I needed any encouragement.

I think she's nervous though; her eyes are huge, and she's breathing fast. Holding her around the waist, I roll onto my back, bringing her with me, and she pushes up so she's sitting astride me. "You want me to do all the work?" she teases, a tad breathless.

I give her a wry look, pulling a pillow under my head to make myself comfortable. "I don't want to hurt you. I want you to take me inside you, as slow as you like."

She looks down and rocks her hips, coating my erection all the way up with her moisture.

"You definitely earned your knighthood," she murmurs, eyes wide.

"Concentrate," I scold.

"You're huge."

"I'm really not. I think your ex must have been tiny, that's all."

She rocks again, biting her bottom lip. "Oh my God. It'll never fit."

"Heidi... Relax, for fuck's sake."

"Yes, sir." Giving me a mischievous look, she lowers a hand and slides the tip of my erection down through her folds until I enter her. Then she leans on my chest and pushes her hips down.

She inhales sharply, stops, and closes her eyes. Lifts her hips a little. Lowers them a fraction more. Her teeth tug at her bottom lip as she does it again. Fuck, watching her slowly impale herself on me is the most erotic thing I've ever seen.

"Wait," I murmur as she frowns. "Let yourself adjust."

She opens her eyes and looks at me, a flush filling her cheeks, then bends to kiss me. We exchange a long, luscious kiss and, as she exhales, I hold her hips and slide all the way up inside her.

"Aaahhh…" She closes her eyes again.

"Okay?" I murmur.

She nods, then clenches her internal muscles and groans. "I can feel you all the way up."

I try not to pass out from the exquisite sensation of her squeezing me, and stroke my hands down her back, then around to her breasts. "I'm not hurting you?"

"Of course not. Mmm…" She purrs and rocks her hips. "You feel amazing."

I move with her slowly, letting her get used to the feeling of me inside her. It's grown even warmer in the room now, the heat from our bodies adding to the sultry atmosphere, and her skin glows in the moonlight. Taking her hands in mine, I move them above my head, which brings her breasts in line with my mouth. After kissing her nipples, I run my tongue along the damp skin beneath them, and she twitches and says, "Titus!"

"You'd better get used to it," I tell her as I tease her nipples again, flicking them with the tip of my tongue. "I intend to taste every inch of you before the weekend's over."

"You mean you want to have sex more than once? That's a bit presumptuous of you."

"You can always say no," I tell her silkily. I suck one of her nipples harder, and she moans.

She moves down and kisses me again, delving her tongue into my mouth, and I return it hungrily, moving my hands to her hips so I can thrust up into her. I'm fully coated with her moisture now, and soon the air fills with the slick sound of sex as I plunge into her soft, swollen flesh.

"Ahhh…" She pushes herself upright again and lowers her hand between her legs.

"Oh yeah," I say enthusiastically, glad she isn't shy about pleasing herself. While she circles her fingers, I lift my hands to her breasts and tease her nipples, tugging them gently and rolling them with my thumbs.

Her brows draw together and, eyes closed, she moistens her lips with the tip of her tongue. "Mmm…"

We move together, a beautiful dance that I'm relieved I know the steps to, and gradually she begins to move faster, and her breaths become uneven. I drop my hands back to her hips, holding her firmly as I thrust up into her. I watch as her orgasm sweeps over her, trying to hold onto my sanity as she clamps around me. She tips her head back and cries out, shuddering, and I hold her tightly, glancing over at the mirror to capture the full view of her locked in pleasure.

When she's done, she falls forward onto my chest with a gasp, then opens her eyes and looks at me with something like surprise. "Oh man," she says. "That was intense."

I hold her hips and thrust slowly through her moist, swollen flesh. "You look so fucking beautiful." Her hair is all ruffled, and her face and neck are flushed.

She kisses me, then whispers, "Your turn."

Holding her around the waist, I lift up and twist so she's under me, still inside her. She wraps her legs in their sexy black thigh highs around my hips and stretches out beneath me, lifting her arms above her head. "Come on baby," she says, eyes glittering in the moonlight, "fuck me senseless."

I don't want to hurt her, but it's impossible to go slow when a beautiful girl says something like that. Propping myself on my hands, I set a fast pace, my body taking over from my brain's urging to make it last. I promise myself that next time I'll take all night, and give her more orgasms, but I've been keyed up for days, thinking about her, dreaming about her, and now she's beneath me all soft and moist and warm, and I can't wait any longer.

She's vocal, which I love, crying out with each thrust, saying, "Oh God, oh God," or, "Oh fuck," and muttering, "Come on, baby, that feels so good," and I groan and plunge down into her, lowering my head to kiss her. Not surprisingly, it only takes about thirty seconds before my climax claims me, and I thrust hard, then stiffen and groan as my internal muscles tighten, and I feel the hot, sweet pulses as I come inside her.

"Ah, that's so fucking hot," she says, and I open my eyes to see her watching me in the mirror, skimming her fingers over the tattoo on my shoulders. She brings her gaze back to me, her eyes full of heat.

I sigh, and we exchange a long, lingering kiss.

"I didn't hurt you?" I ask again. After what she said about her ex, I'm very concerned about it.

She cups my face and looks into my eyes. "No, sweetheart. I told you, you don't have to be gentle, as long as you like me."

"I like you a lot," I say honestly.

"I know," she whispers. "I can tell from the way you look at me." She smiles.

I can't imagine what kind of man could look at a woman like Heidi and feel only resentment and hate. She didn't go into detail about what he did to her, so I have to use my imagination. The thought of him inflicting pain on her makes me incredibly angry. The way she tried so sweetly to explain the difference between sex being passionate and violent. Jesus. What kind of guy doesn't understand that?

I return the kiss, rocking my hips slowly, and she murmurs, "Mmm…" and sighs.

I'd like to stay inside her for longer, but eventually I have to withdraw, and I move to the side and stretch out beside her. Leaning across to the bedside table, I retrieve a tissue from the box there and hand it to her. She uses it, then curls up against me, and I lower my arm around her.

"Thank God," she murmurs.

I chuckle. "For what?"

"The sexual tension was killing me. I'm so glad we gave in." She yawns, then kisses my shoulder. "You don't regret it, do you?"

"Nope." I suppose I should, but I don't.

"Good. From the moment you first kissed me when I was sixteen, I think it was always going to end this way." She pushes herself up. "I'm just going to the bathroom."

She slips out of bed and pads across the carpet. I watch her go, thinking how beautiful she is, then look out through the windows. The reflection of the moon lies on the river like a silver plate. An owl hoots in the distance, similar but also different from the morepork in New Zealand.

Maybe Heidi's right about the inevitability of us getting together. She was technically only a child back then, but there was still a connection between us.

I think briefly about Huxley, and feel a flicker of guilt, but I push it away. It's pointless to regret it now, when the act has been done. What's important is how I act going forward. Heidi and I are both aware of the situation. We have a few more days together before it all comes to an end. All we have to do is make sure we keep that in the forefront of our minds.

It's late now, and mid-morning Down Under. I really should call my office and chat to my team, and I should also check in with Saxon. But I'm tired, and for once in my life I have no drive to rise from my bed and get to work.

Heidi comes out of the bathroom, and I go in. When I come out, she's in the process of plugging a standing fan into the socket beside the bed. "I found this in the cupboard," she says, and turns it on.

We get back in bed, and the cool breeze blows across us. "Ah, that's nice," I say.

She glances at me as I slide back under the covers. "Aren't you going to do some work? I don't mind if you want to bring your laptop to bed."

"Not tonight. I've got other things on my mind." I pull her into my arms.

She smiles and settles down. I brush my fingers down her back, drawing circles on her skin, and she draws hearts on my chest.

"You've cheered me up," she murmurs sleepily.

I chuckle. "I'm glad."

"I mean it." She kisses my ribs. "I haven't felt this happy for a long time. Years, even." She sighs.

Still trailing fingers on her soft skin, I whisper. "Neither have I," but I don't think she hears me.

I close my eyes, and we both drift off to sleep.

*

I rouse a couple of times in the night, and each time I reach for the sleeping girl in my bed and pull her close before dozing off again.

It's just after five thirty when I finally wake. The room is filled with light. I'm guessing the sun has just risen above the horizon, because the river outside is a coppery color, a beautiful pinky-orange. A kingfisher is sitting on the fencepost to the left, still as a statue. Its turquoise feathers gleam like a precious jewel.

Heidi is still asleep, facing away from me. Her sunshine-blonde hair is ruffled sexily. The duvet is pulled up to her ribs, but her arm lies over the top, her hand tucked under her cheek.

I study her neck and shoulder blade, the beautiful, pale skin, touched with a couple of freckles. Last night is a bit of a blur. I wasn't drunk, but I'd had enough whiskies to discard the last fragments of doubt I felt about seducing Huxley's little sister.

Or maybe it was because I didn't feel as if I was seducing her. She hardly needed talking into it. Perhaps I should have been stronger and more disciplined, and turned my back on the young, gorgeous woman with whom I felt an instant attraction, but I'm only human.

Do I regret it? I reach out a finger and draw from her neck, over her shoulder. No, I don't. I feel sad, that's all, that our time together is so limited.

I'd better make the most of it, then.

Moving a bit closer to her, so our bodies are flush, I warm her ear with my breath. She stirs, but doesn't wake. I smooth her hair off her neck, then bend and press my lips behind her ear. Very slowly, I begin to kiss down.

I press my lips to her neck, and when I reach the place where her pulse beats slowly, I touch it with my tongue. Then I continue down, to the place where her neck meets her shoulder, then back around her neck to the nape.

"Mmm," she murmurs, stirring. "Titus…"

"Go back to sleep." Sliding my hand under the duvet, I stroke down her back, then under her arm and around her ribs and cup her breast.

She sighs as I tease her nipple with my thumb, my pulse quickening as the soft skin tightens to force a hard bead. Tugging on it gently, I shift on the mattress and start to kiss down her spine.

Oh yeah, I love waking her like this. She's sleepy and she smells warm, the faint scent of her perfume lingering on her skin. I kiss down to the dip at the base of her spine, then roll her onto her back.

Yawning, she stretches beneath me, and I kiss her breasts for a while, licking and sucking her nipples until they're long and hard, and her breathing is starting to quicken. Only then do I duck beneath the duvet, kiss over her stomach, move between her legs, and lower myself down.

Beneath the dark cave of the duvet, I push her knees wide, and she groans and relaxes. Gently, I part her soft folds, then brush my tongue right up the center, and she moans, tilting up her hips to give me better access.

With my thumb, I spread her moisture across her swollen skin, circle the little bean of her clit at the top, then tease it with my tongue, alternating with flicks of the tip and longer licks. At the same time, I stroke a finger down to her entrance, and circle it there for a while before inserting it inside her. She groans, and I turn my hand and join it with another finger, pressing up carefully until I find the small swelling, which I begin to massage.

"Fuck," she says, her hips rocking against my hand, so I know I'm getting to her. My lips curve up, and I slow down, wanting to draw out the pleasure for her.

She groans. "Titus…"

"Go back to sleep." I chuckle and kiss the soft skin on either side, then return to teasing her clit, sucking and giving her long, slow licks. At the same time, I coat my fingers with her moisture, then stroke down to the tight muscle beneath and very gently insert the tip of a finger.

"Oh Jesus…" she whispers.

I groan, tempted to move up and thrust inside her, but while last night was great, I didn't pay her as much attention as I liked, and this time I want it to be all about her. So I continue, teasing her with my fingers and thumb, and flicking with my tongue, listening to her sighs to gauge how close she is.

When I know she's on the verge of an orgasm, I slide two fingers back inside her and cover her clit with my mouth, and hold her tightly with my free arm as she comes. Aaahhh… that feels good, her tight muscles clamping around my fingers as she pulses on my tongue. Five, six, seven times she clenches, and then she exhales and flops back onto the pillow, completely spent.

I withdraw my fingers and kiss up, over her belly and ribs, between her breasts, and all the way up to her lips.

"Mmm," she murmurs as I delve my tongue into her mouth. "Not sure if that's hygienic."

"Fuck that." I kiss her deeply, lying on top of her. "You taste amazing."

She sighs and wraps her arms around my neck, and we kiss for a long time, lying in the early morning sunshine, the fan cooling our heated skin.

When I eventually lift my head, she's smiling. "Lie down," she whispers.

I shift off her and lie on my back, and she sits up. She looks incredibly sexy with her flushed cheeks and ruffled hair.

Expecting her to climb astride me, I'm surprised when she ducks under the duvet and begins to kiss down my chest.

"Ah. Heidi?"

She presses her lips to my belly button, then kisses down over my stomach.

I sigh. "You don't have to…"

"Titus?"

"Yeah?"

"Shut up." She shifts on the bed between my legs, then takes my erection in her hand and closes her mouth over the end.

"Oh… fuck." I cover my face with my hands. Aaahhh… it's been a while since anyone has done this for me. Not every girl finds it a turn on, and I don't like asking if they obviously don't enjoy it.

But Heidi licks up the shaft to cover it in moisture, then strokes me firmly, her hand moving slickly over my skin as she licks and sucks. Oh wow. I was turned on anyway from pleasuring her. This is going to be embarrassingly quick.

I press the heels of my hands into my eyes, doing my best to hold on, but it's impossible. Less than thirty seconds later, her hot mouth, her tongue, and her firm hand have teased me to the edge, and I can't rein it in any longer.

"Heidi," I whisper, "I'm going to come."

Fully expecting her to lift her head, I'm shocked when she slides her lips lower down and takes me deep. Heat rushes up inside me, and I come in her mouth, groaning as her throat contracts, showing me that she's swallowing it all down.

When I'm done, I feel her kissing back up my body. She stretches out along me, kisses me, and delves her tongue into my mouth.

"Oh, gross," I say with a grimace.

"Serves you right." She licks her lips.

I flop back. "Holy fucking shit."

"What?" She laughs. "What's the matter?"

I run a hand through my hair. "That's the first time a girl's ever done that to me."

"What? Kissed you afterward?"

"No. You know. Swallowed."

Her eyes widen. "You're kidding me?"

I shake my head.

"Not even Claire?" she asks.

"Nope."

"But… Christ, that's crazy. You must have had lots of partners over the years."

"Less than you'd think. I'm shy and retiring."

"You're really not."

I shrug.

She studies me, puzzled. "How many girls have you been with?"

"I dunno. Doesn't seem polite to talk about it."

"I'm curious. Go on." She grins at my reluctance. "Do you need a minute to count them all?"

"No. Six."

Her jaw drops. "Is that all? I'd have thought you'd have had a hundred one-night stands."

"Nope. Never had one."

"What? Not one? But you're so gorgeous! Why?"

"Not my thing."

"Not even at uni?"

"Nope. The other guys did sometimes. I just went back to my room and studied." When she gives me a wry look, I add, "I'm not as smart as Mack. It doesn't come as naturally to me. I've had to work hard to keep up with him."

Her expression holds a touch of wonder. "I thought you were such a playboy. You seem so confident and outgoing."

"It's all a front. I'm just an ordinary guy."

She kisses my nose. "One thing you are not, Lawrence Oates, is ordinary, believe me." She kisses my lips then, long and lovingly, while the rising sun bathes us in its golden light.

Chapter Fifteen

Titus

Late morning finds me thigh-high in the cool river. I walked with Alan for about ten minutes to a place where the river widened and there aren't so many overhanging trees to catch your hook on, but it's still beautiful, the edges of the water tumbling over rocks, and the surface filled with dappled sunlight.

As it's warm, we don't need waders, and so I'm wearing a T-shirt and shorts, with a baseball cap and sunglasses to keep the sun out of my eyes.

Alan's started me with a lighter, eight-foot-long rod with a four-weight class, a tapered leader, and a Pheasant-tail Nymph fly with a barbless hook. It takes me a bit of practice, but soon I'm back in the swing of it, and I spend a few hours casting and reeling. I catch two eight-inch brown trout, while Alan manages to land a ten-inch beauty.

Originally, I assumed Alan had brought me out here to talk business, but I'm pleased to find he's happy to stay silent while we're fishing, and it's only when we stop halfway through and make our way to the two fold-up seats on the bank that he begins to chat.

He's brought a flask of tea with him, and he pours us both a cup, then offers me a sandwich from a box. "Cheese and pickle," he says. "I made 'em. Chef was quite disgusted."

"You've been in England too long," I tease, taking one.

"Yeah, maybe."

"Do you get back to New Zealand much?"

"Not since my parents died. I still have two brothers over there, but we're not close, and a phone call a few times a year is enough to satisfy us. My life is here now, with the girls and their families."

I nod, stretching out my legs and having a sip of tea.

"What about you?" he asks. "Are you close to your folks?"

I tip my head from side to side. "They're good parents. I've never wanted for anything. But they're both lawyers, and they work very hard. I was practically brought up by nannies, and I spent a lot of time with my aunt and uncle and their boys."

"Your parents must be very proud of you, though."

"Mum is. She's Norwegian."

"Hence the tattoos?"

"Yeah. She's like a shield maiden. A force to be reckoned with. Dad was very strict and set high standards. He would lecture me for hours if I failed to meet them." Alan's brow furrows and, conscious of sounding a tad bitter, I add, "But I'm glad that they pushed me—they instilled a sound work ethic in me, and a sense of discipline without which I couldn't have gotten where I am. And they've always pushed me to be independent."

"So they won't mind too much if you move here for a few years?" Alan grins, and I give a short laugh. "I know I haven't convinced you yet," he says, "but I still have time."

I have a bite of my sandwich, feeling guilty that I haven't been completely honest with him. I should tell him I came here with no intention of staying, but it's too late to say anything now, so I'll have to continue with the ruse until we leave.

"You've landed yourself a beautiful girl," he says. "Inside and out. Vicky adores her."

"Aw. That's nice to hear." My stomach flips. Is he going to ask for details of how we met, or our lives together in New Zealand? I don't want to have to lie to him again.

But he just says, "You have to hang onto the good ones. They don't come around very often."

"Mm," I agree, thinking about her going down on me this morning.

We sit quietly for a while, eating our sandwiches and drinking our tea. It's a gorgeous morning, and I listen to the water tumbling over the rocks, to the ducks quacking, and the cows lowing in the meadow, and I'm surprised how content, and maybe even happy, I feel.

"Thanks for bringing me here," I say to Alan. "I'm having a great time."

"If you stay, we could do this every weekend." He smiles.

My returning smile is wistful. My own father never did anything like this with me. We never went fishing, or played ball in the garden, and the only time we watched a rugby match together was when he was entertaining in a box and I was allowed to tag along because I wanted to see the game.

It's odd that I seem to get on better with Alan. Obviously, he has business reasons for wanting to keep me in England, but I like to think that's not his only motivation.

"I don't have a son," he says as if he's reading my mind, "and neither the girls nor their husbands are interested in fishing, so it's cool to have someone to go with for a change."

"Do you get out a lot?"

"Not as much as I'd like. You know how it is. Work is all-encompassing, and it's easy to get caught up in it. Vicky's had to rein me in a few times over the years, and drag me away from it all, make sure I take time to smell the roses. It's important. It's why I'm glad you have Heidi. She'll keep you grounded. Does she want kids?"

My eyebrows lift. "Um... I'm not sure."

"Sorry, that was a bit personal."

"It's okay. I'm sure she does. She loves children." She's too beautiful to stay single for long. Soon, she'll meet the lucky guy who gets to marry her and have a baby with her.

I scowl at a frog jumping across the grass in front of me. I'm not going to think about Heidi meeting other men or I'll end up in a bad mood.

Part of me wishes I could confide in Alan, admit what's happened between me and Heidi, and ask for his advice, but I'm sure his business needs would skew his answers. It's up to me to sort it out on my own.

I feel a wave of frustration that our time together is so limited. When we go back to our cottage, we'll only have a day before we're due to leave for New Zealand.

Hmm. What if I could extend our time together, at least until we get Down Under?

Now there's an idea...

*

Heidi

Shortly after Titus leaves with Alan, Vicky arrives at the cottage in a gorgeous BMW X7, and I get in the passenger side.

"Morning!" she says, beaming, and heads off through the big double gates. "How did you sleep?"

"Very well, thank you." I try not to think about the way Titus woke me.

"I'm so glad. Alan really wanted to put you in the tower room, but I thought you'd prefer to have Titus all to yourself in the cottage." She flashes me a grin.

"Very astute," I say, and laugh. "Thank you for a lovely evening, by the way. Titus was quite overwhelmed."

"Oh, I hope he was okay with it. Maybe we should have had a sit-down dinner, but so many people wanted to meet him that it seemed more practical to have a cocktail party. He's a very impressive young man. So incredibly smart."

"He is. He works very hard."

"I bet it's nice for you to have a holiday together. If he's anything like Alan, it's impossible to lure him away from the office. I have to bully him to take a day off. They get it in their heads that it's their job to save the world, and then they feel guilty when they're not working."

"That's exactly right."

"Enough about the boys though. Tell me about yourself, Heidi. You're a primary school teacher, right?"

"Yes." My stomach flips at the thought that she's going to ask me questions about teaching in New Zealand. I really don't want to have to lie to her.

But she just says, "That must be so rewarding. What age group do you teach?"

"The youngest ones, when they're just starting school."

"Aw, is it hard when they get upset?"

"Well, I have to remind myself I'm not their mother. I have an assistant with me, sometimes two, and they're very hands-on. I try to stay practical. As you know, kids are easily distracted, and it's all about keeping them occupied."

"Very sensible. My mum used to say, 'Busy kids are happy kids.'"

I pick up on her use of the past tense. "Is she still here?"

"No, she passed away last year."

"Oh, I'm sorry."

"It was very hard. I miss her a lot. Are you close to your mum?"

"I love her dearly. But she's an artist, a painter, and her art is very important to her. She'd often leave me with my older sisters and brother while she worked." I look out of the window at the Devon countryside flashing past.

"What about your dad? What does he do?"

"He's in finance."

"Are you close to him?"

I don't answer for a moment, and eventually Vicky says, "I'm so sorry, I'm being very nosy. I didn't mean to upset you."

"It's okay. We have a difficult relationship, that's all." I don't really want to talk about it.

"What does he think of Titus?" she asks.

He's met Titus several times over the years when Oliver has brought him to the house, and he knows Julian, Titus's father, so I'm able to answer without lying. "He likes that he's a hard worker."

"Well if he doesn't like him, he's setting his standards a tad high," she says, amused. "Okay, here we are."

She's currently driving through a small village, and I watch, surprised, as she pulls up in front of what looks like a church hall.

"I'd assumed you were heading for Exeter," I say, unbuckling my seat belt.

"No, it's just a small class, I hope that's okay."

"Of course." I get out of the car. Oh my God, this is like the perfect English village. There's a post office, a pub, a church, and even a village green with a duck pond. All it needs is Postman Pat and his cat and it'll be complete.

We cross to the small hall, whose doors are standing open to admit the bright July sunshine. Inside are about eight women who are leaving their bags and shoes at the back of the hall and making their way to the yoga mats at the front. The instructor stands facing them, greeting everyone as they approach.

"Sarah, this is Heidi," Vicky says as we walk up, "she's staying with me, and I said she could come with me this morning, hope that's okay."

"Of course!" Sarah smiles. "Everyone's welcome."

Vicky pushes my purse away and hands over the money, and we find two mats not far from the door. Sunlight falls through the high windows in gold bars across us, and the air smells of herbs and the roses growing by the door.

"We might as well get started," Sarah says. "Let's begin with a warmup, and then we'll do the sun salutation."

As I stretch and move and hold the asanas, I think about how much I'd miss England if I were to move back to New Zealand. Not wanting to spoil my time here, though, I push the thought away and concentrate on stretching my muscles and trying to relax. As the class winds down, Sarah instructs us to lie in *savasana* or the corpse pose for meditation, and she tells us to picture ourselves in a place that makes us happy. I think about my cottage, and the greenhouse where I watch the stars, but as she talks quietly, guiding us through the meditation, my mind instead drifts to the bedroom this morning, to being awoken by Titus' soft kisses, and the way he pleasured me so easily with his mouth.

I'm glad we've managed to steal this time together. I know it's not going to be easy to say goodbye to him when it's time to part, but I don't regret it. He's shown me that it is possible to meet a guy who can make me feel good about myself rather than always putting me down, and for that I'll always be thankful.

*

Just before one o'clock, I'm lying in the sunken bath, surrounded by bubbles, when there's a knock on the bathroom door. "Heidi?" Titus calls.

"Come in."

The door opens, and he peers around the corner. Eyebrows rising, he comes in.

I lift a soapy leg up and wave a foot. "Hello."

He chuckles and leans against the wall, hands in the pockets of his shorts. "Have a nice morning?" he asks.

"I did, thank you. You?"

"Yeah, amazing. Caught several trout."

"Oh, fantastic!"

"It really was. Such a beautiful river, and it was a gorgeous day." His gaze lingers on me, watching the bubbles rising slowly, rainbow-colored in the sunlight. "Talking of beautiful..." He smiles.

I blow some bubbles from my hand at him. "Want to join me?"

"I'm a bit fishy."

"Perfect place to wash it off."

"That's true. Well, if you don't mind." He turns to go back into the bedroom.

"No, strip off here," I instruct.

He turns back wryly, and I wait for him to argue, but instead he toes off his shoes, grabs a handful of his T-shirt by the back of the neck and pulls it over his head, then undoes his shorts and steps out of them. Finally he takes off his underwear, then he steps down into the bath and lowers himself into the water.

It's a big bath, with the tap in the middle, and we sit at either end. He puts some gel in a hand, slides under the surface to soak his hair, washes it, then ducks again to rinse it. He emerges wet and glistening, the water running off his tanned skin.

"Slightly less fishy now," he says.

I smile, my gaze lingering on his shining tattoos. "How's Alan?"

"Good. He brought tea and cheese-and-pickle sandwiches for a snack."

I laugh. "Very English."

"Yeah. We had a chat while we took a break."

"Did you get the third degree?"

"No, not really. He asked about my family in New Zealand. Said if I lived here, we could go fishing like this as often as we wanted."

"Vicky said much the same thing after the yoga."

"Do you think they're working on us?" he asks.

"Oh yeah. But in a nice way. I don't think there's a nasty bone in either of their bodies. They genuinely want you to stay."

He lifts some bubbles on his hand and studies them. I keep quiet. I don't want him to feel as if he's being badgered.

"She said it was difficult to get Alan to take time off," I say eventually.

"Yeah, he said the same, and that it's important to smell the roses. This break has been good for me. I honestly can't remember when I last took time off. Well, Mack's wedding, technically, but I slept through most of that so..."

I grin. "So what have we got planned for the rest of the day?"

"Carrie and John are coming around at two. I asked them to tell me their story."

"Okay, I could chop up some of that fresh fruit in the fridge if you like. Do a platter to nibble, and we could sit out on the patio."

"Sounds great. After that, maybe I'll do a bit of work, then at six we're back up to the house for the murder-mystery evening."

"Did Alan give you your character card?"

"He did. I'm Lord Lawrence Edgmont."

That makes me laugh out loud. "Brilliant."

"I'm a debonair gambler who's a big hit with the ladies, apparently. What about you?"

"I'm the Countess Heidi Carlton. A notorious socialite and good-time girl."

"Countess?"

I grin. "I thought it was appropriate."

He chuckles. "What are you going to wear?"

"I brought the dress that grandma mentioned. Vicky's got a cigarette holder I can borrow, apparently. How about you?"

"Just a suit, and I'll slick my hair back and draw on a mustache."

"Shall we make a pact not to take any photos?"

"Definitely. By the way, you must remind me tonight, Saxon wants a Zoom call, anytime after about eight p.m., so when we get back from the party."

"Okay. Is there a problem?"

"No, I don't think so. Saxon has been running the first tests of the AI program predicting which embryos would lead to a live birth at Wellington Hospital. They've got an eighty-five percent accuracy so far."

"That's great."

"It's good, but I'm hoping we can do better than that. We're just going to have a chat about it."

"I'd like to meet him."

"He'll be at Huxley's wedding." His foot finds mine beneath the bubbles. "I wanted to talk to you about our journey back, by the way."

"Oh?"

"Hux gave me the details of your flight, and I made sure I was booked on the same one— the third of August, right? Wednesday?"

"Yeah."

"You're economy class."

It's a statement, not a question. "Yeah…"

He runs his foot along my thigh. "How about we get you upgraded? Travel with me in first class, in a double suite?"

My eyes nearly fall out of my head. "First class? Jesus."

"I always fly first class. Any idiot can be uncomfortable."

"Yeah, I've seen Palin's *Around the World in Eighty Days*. Wasn't it Alan Whicker who told him that?"

"Might be. What do you think?"

I stare at him, completely taken aback. "Are you serious?"

He laughs. "Yeah."

"But those tickets must be thousands of dollars."

"Something like ten thousand, I think. I'm not sure."

My jaw gapes. "Ten thousand dollars?"

"Pounds."

I make a strangled sound. "Holy fuck."

"Heidi, I can afford it, believe me. Let me spoil you." His gaze is sultry, tempting.

"But it's only days away. There's not enough notice."

"I've already checked. They have one suite free on that flight, so I've put a hold on it. They lower the central divider between two adjacent suites and make a double bed." He flicks his eyebrows up. "Don't you want to join the Mile High Club?"

"Oh my God."

"You get leather seats. A small lounge. A private bathroom. And did I mention the double bed?"

My lips curve up. "You'd really do that for me?"

"As a thank you for coming with me this weekend. It's the least I can do."

Ten thousand pounds… twenty thousand New Zealand dollars. Holy shit. It's a huge amount of money. But then he's a billionaire. It's a drop in the ocean for him. But that's not really the point.

"It's a lot of money to take from a man when we're only having a fling," I murmur.

He shrugs. "I'd do the same for any of my friends."

"Really?"

"No." His lips curve up.

He holds my gaze for a moment, and eventually I smile too. "All right," I say softly.

"Good. I'll go and book it now. We should get out anyway—Carrie and John will be here soon."

I watch him get out of the bath, glorious in the sunshine, all shiny and wet and oh my God he's so fucking gorgeous. He dries himself with the towel, then wanders out, uncaring of his nakedness, and I blow out a long breath before I start to get out too.

He's just being kind, I tell myself. Saying thank you for coming with him this weekend.

But deep inside, I know it's more than that, and my heart leaps.

I don't know why. We're still based on the opposite sides of the world. It's still crazily complicated, and there's no easy answer.

But he doesn't want our time together to come to an end, and that's a start.

Chapter Sixteen

Titus

We spend a couple of hours sitting in the sunshine, talking to Carrie and John, looking out over the river while we nibble from Heidi's fruit platter.

Despite the mostly serious topic of conversation, it's an enjoyable afternoon, maybe because of the setting, or the weather, as the beautiful summer sun continues to shine. Or maybe it's because I'm partly working, so I can shed myself of the guilt that always hovers whenever I'm taking time off. Most likely it also has something to do with Heidi, who sits by my side, joining in the conversation, refreshing our drinks, and catching my eye from time to time, at which point she smiles shyly before looking away.

Whatever the reason, it's a pleasant way to spend my time. Carrie and John are interesting to talk to—John's a GP, so he knows a fair amount about fertility issues and IVF, and Carrie is a chemist and works with her father at Acheron, so she's also interested in the scientific side of things. But they also bring their personal experience, and as they tell me about their journey toward having a family, it becomes obvious it's taken an emotional toll.

"I'm sorry," Carrie whispers at one point, fighting with her tears.

"Don't be," I say. "It's moments like this that make me so determined to help."

"Titus was telling me about his cousins," Heidi adds, reaching out to squeeze Carrie's hand. "One of them is opening a branch of Titus's company in Wellington." She glances at me, obviously not sure how much she's supposed to reveal, but I nod and smile, and she continues, "He's run the first tests of the new AI program Titus has told you about, predicting which embryos will lead to a live birth, and they've had an eighty-five percent success rate."

"That's just an initial test," I say firmly, "it'll improve as we tweak the parameters and run successive tests."

"Whether or not it helps us, it sounds promising," John says. "It sucks to be one of the one-in-four couples for whom a cause can't be identified."

"Well, the important thing is that it's not being caused by some mysterious supernatural force. There's a scientific reason for it. We just haven't found it yet."

Carrie blows out a breath, long and slow. "Do you know," she says, "that's the first time someone has phrased it like that."

"I don't want to give you false hope," I tell her gently. "You've been through some tough times, and you know there are no guarantees. But chromosomal abnormalities are definitely a factor in IVF cycle failure, and determining which embryos have that greater chance of success could be helpful for you."

John sighs. "It's difficult to know at what point to call it a day, you know? I'm thirty-seven now, and Carrie's thirty-five. We all know that your fertility begins to drop as you move through your thirties, and the risk of miscarriage and stillbirth increases. There's also a higher risk of gestational diabetes and high blood pressure. We haven't quite reached that point where we've given up, but we're close."

"We're going to give it one more go," Carrie says. "One more round of IVF. And if it doesn't happen, I think we're going to try to accept it wasn't meant to be."

"Would you want to be a part of the first trial run at Acheron?" I ask.

They exchange a glance, and then turn their hopeful gazes on me. "Dad said we shouldn't ask," Carrie says. "He says you have enough on your plate getting it all organized. But yes, of course, we would love to be a part of it. You can't know how amazing it would be to increase the success rates of IVF. Well, you probably can. I know you've spoken to a lot of couples who've been in our position."

"I have, but I haven't experienced it myself, so I can't pretend to know what you've been through."

She smiles at Heidi. "He's so wonderful. You're a lucky girl, Heidi."

I meet Heidi's gaze and smirk.

"I am," she says. "Lord Lawrence is a real catch."

That makes us all laugh. "Yeah, we'd better head back so we can start getting ready," John says, and they stand to leave.

We see them to the front door, and Carrie stops to give me a hug. "It's been so great to meet you," she says.

"Likewise. I just hope we can help."

She smiles, and they go out to their car.

Heidi closes the door, comes over to me, and slides her arms around me. "All right, Lord Lawrence?"

"Yeah." I kiss her nose. "I suppose we should start getting ready."

"We have time for a kiss though, right?"

"Mmm. Definitely." I lower my lips to hers, moving her back to the wall, enjoying the way her lips part to let me brush my tongue into her mouth. She lifts her arms around my neck, and we indulge in a long, luscious kiss that leaves us both sighing.

"Later," she murmurs. "When we get back…"

"Yeah…" I kiss up her jaw to her ear.

"You gonna fuck me till my teeth rattle, Titus?"

I stop, lift my head, and raise my eyebrows at her. She gives me an innocent look. "What?"

I lean on the wall above her head, and my lips curve up. "You're a bad girl."

She giggles. "I like you."

I chuckle. "I like you too."

"A lot," she clarifies, and blushes.

I look into her beautiful blue eyes, lift a hand, and tuck a strand of her hair behind her ear.

Her blush deepens. "I'm just saying."

"Yeah, I know." I kiss her gently. "There's a conversation coming. I think we both know it. Not yet. Maybe on the plane."

"Okay," she whispers.

I kiss her again. "But tonight, yes, Your Royal Highness, I do intend to fuck you senseless, so I hope you're prepared."

"Ooh. Now I'm going to think about it all evening."

"That was my dastardly plan."

Her eyes sparkle. "I see. Well, two can play at that game."

"So how do you intend to take your revenge?"

She kisses my cheek. "I'll tell you later." Then she ducks under my arm and heads for the bedroom.

I sigh and follow her. She seems to enjoy torturing me.

Luckily, I don't mind one bit.

*

Just before six, we head up the driveway to the main house. A guy dressed as an old-style butler—wearing white gloves, and his coat complete with tails—shows us through to the drawing room, where Alan, Vicky, their girls and their husbands, are already gathered, and they all cheer as Heidi and I walk in.

"Oh, you look fantastic," Vicky says, coming up to admire our costumes. She's wearing a silver 1930s-style dress, with a band around her forehead that bears a single feather. "Lady Victoria Eddington-Jones, pleased to meet you."

I laugh. "Lord Lawrence Edgmont at your service," I say in my best posh English accent.

Vicky giggles and hands the cigarette holder to Heidi. "And you must be the Countess Heidi Carlton."

"Yes, and I'm very pleased to meet you." Heidi's accent is impeccable, but she finishes with a giggle, which makes us all laugh.

"I'm Sir Alan Spencer, Duke of Dottington," Alan says, unable to stop a chuckle as he shakes my hand. "Welcome to Dottington Castle. Let me introduce you to the other guests tonight."

He introduces his daughters and their husbands with their fake names, and asks us what we'd like to drink.

"May I recommend the forty-five-year-old Port Askaig," Alan suggests, and I nod, eager to try another rare Islay malt. When the butler brings it over, I have a sip and sigh. The taste is exquisite—sweet and fruity with a touch of menthol which I adore, although it makes Heidi wrinkle her nose when she tries it.

She sticks with a G&T. Alan says, "Would you like to try a Morus LXIV Gin? It's made from the leaves of an ancient mulberry tree. I was very lucky to find a bottle, and I've been saving it for a special occasion."

"Ooh, yes please."

Alan turns away to talk to the butler, and Heidi whispers, "That must be expensive."

"I've read about it," I murmur. "It's sold in Harvey Nichols in Knightsbridge, and it's a limited edition of only twenty-five bottles. It's the most expensive gin in the world."

"Holy fuck."

I chuckle. "Try to look as if you drink this kind of thing every day."

"It comes in a hand-made porcelain jar," Alan explains as the butler pours the drink, "and a stirrup cup."

The butler hands it to her—a conical-shaped cup wrapped in embossed hide leather.

"You're supposed to sip it neat," Alan explains, "then add a little mineral water several times as you drink it. The gin becomes more flavorful as you keep diluting it."

"Ooh." She sniffs the gin, then takes a delicate sip. "Aw, that's nice. Woody and smokey, and a touch of citrus."

Alan also accepts a glass from the butler and takes a sip. "Mm, yes, I see what you mean. Very nice. It's also supposed to be great as a highball. Maybe we'll try that later."

"Definitely."

I smile at her, surprised and yet also not surprised. She told me she was going to teach me about gins, but I hadn't thought she was serious. I forget that she's Huxley's sister sometimes. I have no doubt he educated her in most of the major spirits before she left New Zealand. He'd have seen it as his brotherly duty to make sure she knew her stuff.

"So," Alan says, "let's go through to the dining room and we can introduce our characters while we have the starters."

We filter through and take our seats at the oak table. Alan and Vicky sit at either end, and Heidi and I are seated opposite each other in the middle. Waiters serve us smoked salmon and prawns in a horseradish cream and lime vinaigrette topped with a small green leaf salad that's absolutely sublime. While we eat, Alan gives an introductory speech welcoming us all to Dottington Castle, and hands an envelope to each of us containing facts about our characters that we need to reveal over the course of the dinner, including who is going to be the murderer. It's not me, so I can relax for the rest of the evening. When I look up, I meet Heidi's gaze, and she grins and winks, suggesting she's enjoying herself.

We finish our starters, and then the waiter is just collecting our plates when there's a high-pitched scream from the kitchens.

"Oh no," Vicky says, putting down her serviette, "I wonder what's happened?"

"We'd better go and see," Alan suggests. "Come on, everyone."

Laughing, we all get up and follow them into the kitchen, where we discover the butler who served our drinks now sprawled on the tiles, apparently 'murdered', with fake blood splashed across his white shirt.

Several members of the kitchen staff are standing around, dressed like servants from an old-fashioned country house, the women in aprons and white hats, the guys in black suits, like characters out of Downton Abbey.

"We'd better interview them," Alan states, "and see if any of them witnessed the murder."

The evening progresses in a similar manner, with facts gradually revealed between the courses. The meal is fantastic—they serve two mains: an incredible beef wellington, and porchetta or salty pork belly stuffed with bacon and brioche that's just to die for. Of course I have to have a piece of both to compare. It's served with mixed roast vegetables including the best roast potatoes I've ever tasted, asparagus with hollandaise sauce, and Yorkshire puddings.

The conversation is light and lively, and I find myself entranced by Heidi, who throws herself into her character with gusto. She constantly makes everyone laugh with her quips and outrageous statements, all delivered in a posh British accent. I'm so glad I asked her to come here with me.

It wouldn't have been the same at all on my own. When I do my usual act of tipping over my wine glass and spilling red wine all over the nice white tablecloth, or backing into the umbrella stand and knocking it over as we make our way into the conservatory, she makes a joke of it and then changes the subject to draw attention away from me, which I appreciate. I know I'm clumsy, but I don't particularly enjoy drawing attention to myself, especially with strangers.

In the conservatory, we discover the murder weapon—a bread knife, hidden in a trunk—and it's at that point that I begin to suspect that Heidi might be the murderer, as one of the maids had mentioned at the beginning that she'd seen the Countess in the conservatory, reading.

As everyone makes their way back to the dining room for dessert, I take Heidi's hand and pull her to one side, behind a large rubber plant in the reception hall.

"I want a word with you," I tell her, pushing her up against the wall. She's taken off her jacket, and while the dress she's wearing isn't revealing at all, it does show off her breasts in a way that's been heating me up from the inside out all evening.

"Why, Lord Lawrence," she murmurs, "I think you're being most inappropriate. If someone catches us, I'll lose my virtuous reputation."

"I think your virtue fell by the wayside some time ago, Countess," I tell her, nuzzling her ear, and she giggles. "I'm beginning to think you might be the murderer," I say, sliding a hand up her thigh beneath her dress.

"That's a shocking thing to say."

"Tell me I'm wrong."

"I wouldn't deign to answer that absurd accusation."

"So it is you, then. I…" My voice trails off as my hand reaches her bottom, and finds only smooth, silky skin. I lift my head and stare at her.

"Told you I'd take my revenge," she says.

I blow out a breath at the thought that she's going commando in that sexy little dress. "Now I'm not going to be able to concentrate for the rest of the evening."

"Well, I need to distract you somehow from your outrageous claims."

I chuckle and kiss her, cupping her bare bottom.

"Hey, we're about to start dessert, so—shit! Sorry!"

We spring apart at John's words, and all three of us give embarrassed laughs. "Sorry," he says again, holding up his hands. "They sent me to let you know."

"It's my fault," I reply, "I'm trying to persuade the Countess to reveal she's the murderer."

He grins. "Let me know if she gives you any clues." He backs away and disappears around the corner.

Heidi giggles, and I laugh. Her cheeks have flushed, but she doesn't seem too embarrassed.

"That was all you," she scolds. "Naughty boy."

"I thought the Countess needed some attention." I nuzzle her ear again, but she slips to the side and starts walking back. "Come on, my lord. Time for something sweet." She winks at me.

I follow her, eyes narrowing at the thought of my hand stroking up her soft skin. I'll make her pay for that later.

We walk into the dining room, and as the others all cast us amused glances and laugh, it's obvious that John has revealed what he saw.

"Sorry," I apologize as Heidi and I take our seats. "I was questioning the Countess."

They all laugh, and Heidi giggles, then says, "Ooh," as she discovers the gin highball that Alan had promised her earlier in the evening.

"Thank you so much for sharing this precious gin with me," she says to him as she sips it.

"Of course," he says, "anything for you two." He smiles at me, and I know his words are genuine. I'm going to miss him and Vicky when I leave.

The waiters then bring in the desserts—served in tiny dishes, so we're able to sample several different sorts. There are coffee and malt biscuit panna cotta, plum ripple ice cream with walnuts, chocolate brownie cheesecakes, mini apple crumble pies and lemon meringue pies, brandy custard choux buns, and banoffee Baileys pies. We work our way through them as we discuss the case, and when Rowena announces she thinks the murderer is Heidi, I mention the waitress's comment about seeing her reading in the conservatory, and we all agree that we think it's her.

With the meal finished, we take our drinks into the drawing room, and Alan officially accuses Heidi, who grins and says yes, she did it, and we all cheer. After that, the butler—who has miraculously sprung back to life—serves us coffee, and then we sit for a couple of hours, chatting about everything under the sun. We talk about the fertility program, but also about their jobs, their hobbies, and life in England in general.

It's with some surprise that I realize it's close to ten thirty by the time the evening wraps up. We all rise and make our way to the front door, and we say goodbye to Alan's family and thank them for a lovely evening.

Alan gestures for me to stay, and so Heidi and I wait while the others filter out. When they've gone, he and Vicky come over and give us both a hug.

"Thank you for making it such a wonderful evening," Vicky says. "It's been a stressful couple of years, and our girls have all struggled in their own ways, so it was great to see them putting it all aside for a bit and just having fun."

"We've had a fantastic time," Heidi replies, "and our compliments to the chef. The meal was amazing."

"What time do we need to get ready for tomorrow?" I ask.

"Five a.m.," Alan says. "Sorry. But they only do the hot-air balloon rides at dawn."

"We can't wait. See you then."

"You sure you don't want a lift back?"

"No, we'll be fine."

We wave goodbye and head out into the night.

The moon is a few days off full, and the sky is cloudless, so the gardens are lit with silvery light. We wander back slowly, hand in hand, along the path behind the trees, listening to the sounds of the evening.

"I had such a fun time," Heidi says. "Thank you so much for asking me to go with you."

I let go of her hand and put my arm around her shoulder, and she slides her arm around my waist. "You were great. I think they were impressed with your British accent."

She laughs. "It's not that different to the Kiwi one so it's pretty easy to do."

I pull her toward me and kiss her hair. "Don't think I've forgotten, by the way."

"About what?"

"The fact that you're going commando. I haven't been able to stop thinking about it all evening."

She giggles. "My work here is done."

I laugh, stop walking, and pull her into my arms. "Come here." I slide a hand to the nape of her neck and hold her there as I kiss her. She murmurs something, then lifts her arms around my neck and presses herself against me.

I sigh, giving myself over to the kiss, enjoying the feel of her soft body, and the way she tilts her head to change the angle of the kiss, her tongue darting out to meet mine.

"Mmm…" My murmur of approval lowers to a growl as a spark lights a fuse at the base of my spine, sending fireworks shooting through me. I don't know how she does it, but she manages to fire me up instantly.

"Are you going to fuck me until my teeth rattle now?" she whispers, lowering her hands to my chest. Through my shirt, she finds my nipples and circles her forefingers over them.

I catch her hands, move them behind her back, and hold them there, gently but firmly. "Whatever the Countess desires," I tell her, and crush my lips to hers, kissing her for ages, while above us the moon rises slowly, and the stars appear on the black velvet sky.

Chapter Seventeen

Heidi

By the time we stumble into the cottage, I'm breathless and aching with desire for the gorgeous guy who seems intent on kissing me until my brain melts.

I've hardly been able to tear my gaze from him all evening. Despite his insistence that he's just an ordinary guy, he shone this evening, entertaining them all with his teasing wit, playing along with the game, and reducing me to mush when he pulled me to one side and felt me up with such boyish abandon.

I can't help it—I'm falling for him, even though I keep telling myself I mustn't, that it's pointless, and he can't possibly feel the same way. Every vibe I get from him screams the opposite, and his words, *There's a conversation coming. I think we both know it,* tell me he knows how I'm feeling, and that he wants to talk when it's time.

But right now I can't think about it because he's kissing me again, while at the same time he slips a hand beneath my dress and slides his fingers up the outside of my thigh. When he finds my bottom still bare, he sighs and strokes it, slowly walking me backward through the cottage to the bedroom, and closing the door behind us.

"Ooh, it's warm in here," I comment, wishing I'd left the door open when we'd left. "Let me turn the fan on."

"Nuh-uh." He pulls me back into his arms. "I want you all hot and sweaty."

"That's gross, Titus. Oh my God!" He strips off my dress in one swift move, leaving me completely naked.

"Oh yeah." He lifts me in his arms and tosses me onto the bed. It's lit by moonlight, and it feels as if I've landed in a pool of silver.

"Hard and fast?" I say hopefully, excited to think of him being unable to rein in his passion.

But although he sheds his clothes quickly, he shakes his head. Once he's naked, he climbs on the bed and stretches out, half lying on me and pinning me there with his weight.

"You've got to ring Saxon," I remember suddenly.

"Fuck Saxon." He props his head on a hand and kisses me.

"He'll be waiting," I protest when he finally moves back.

"He'd understand." He brushes his fingers down my neck to my breasts and teases a nipple with his thumb. "I'm going to make love to you real slow now," he promises. "And make the most of this gorgeous body of yours. I want to taste every inch of you. And I want to make you come over and over again until you're begging me to stop."

I look up into his feverish green eyes, my heart hammering. His impressive erection is pressing against my hip, begging for action, but I can see from the look in his eyes that he's serious. He's going to sex me to death. Oh Jesus. What a way to go.

He starts by stroking me, taking forever to touch every available square inch of bare skin with his fingers, until my body feels like one huge erogenous zone. How can he turn me on by stroking my elbows, my knees, and behind my ears? He kisses me while he's doing this, long, languorous kisses that leave me breathless, and it's only after an ice age that his fingers finally find their way between my thighs.

After parting my knees wide so I'm exposed to his touch, he spends a while stroking the skin of my inner thighs and either side of my mound, and it's only when a moan of frustration escapes my lips that he gives in and slides his fingers into the heart of me.

"Ah, Heidi," he murmurs. "So swollen and wet and ready for me."

I close my eyes, feeling my face flush. "That's rude."

"It's honest. Aaahhh… you're so fucking hot…" He slides his fingers down, right inside me, and I moan again. My eyes flicker open, to look right into his, which are wide and intense. "I'm going to watch you as you come," he murmurs, "so I can share every second of pleasure you feel."

"Oh God…"

"Are you close, baby? Can you feel it coming?"

I close my eyes again. "Yeah…"

"Tell me how it feels."

"Mmm… Like a ball of heat inside me, spreading outward…"

"Am I touching the Countess right?" He circles the pad of his finger over my clit.

"Ohhh… yes…"

He slows, gently teasing. "How about this?"

I groan. "Fuck…"

"Tell me what you want."

"Let me come," I beg. A deep ache fills me inside as he moves his hand away and strokes my inner thighs.

"Look at me."

I open my eyes and look up into his. He returns his fingers, slipping them down into my folds, and this time he strokes firmly. The orgasm claims me immediately, a powerful tightening of muscles inside, followed by the brief, hard pulses that make me gasp out loud. And through it all, I know he's watching me, drinking in my pleasure, knowing it was all down to him.

"Mm," he says, as I flop back onto the pillows. "Good girl."

He kisses me, and at the same time lifts up and moves over me as he starts kissing down my body. He slides his lips up my jaw to behind my ear and sucks my earlobe, grazes agonizingly slowly down my neck, and proceeds to kiss every inch of skin on my arms from my shoulders to my fingertips. Then he moves to my breasts and spends a good while licking and sucking there, until my body starts to stir again, responding to his loving touch.

Only then does he kiss down my stomach, move between my thighs, and part them before burying his mouth in my folds.

"Jesus." I rest my arms over my face, groaning as he slides his tongue down inside me. Moving back a little, he explores with his fingers, taking his time, spending a while teasing my entrance with the tip of a finger before gently sliding two fingers inside me and returning his mouth to my clit. Ohhh… he's so good at this, he knows exactly the right pressure to use with his tongue, how to be gentle but firm. He coaxes pleasure out of me, and it's not long before I feel my muscles begin to tense.

He withdraws his fingers and blows his warm breath across my sensitive skin.

I let out a long groan and look up at the ceiling in frustration.

"Just relax," he tells me, "it'll be worth it, baby."

I try to do as he says, but my body feels like a spring coiled for release, like a clockwork toy wound too tight. His tongue slides through my folds, licking, teasing, warm on my skin, and in less than thirty seconds the pressure begins to build inside me. But once again, he stops, and the ripples die away.

Once more he does it, and by this time I'm so hot I think I'm going to self-combust. I try to slide my hand between my legs to relieve myself, but he moves it away. "Titus…" I whisper, my chest heaving with big, deep breaths, my limbs trembling. "Please…"

"All right, honey, but hang on, it's going to be a strong one." He flicks his tongue over my clit a few times. Then finally covers it with his mouth and gently sucks.

I wait for the orgasm to hit like a truck, but it doesn't; it blooms like a flower opening up and reacting to the warmth of the sun. Pleasure radiates through me, and I cry out at the intensity of it, then shudder as the pulses claim me. Oh God, he was right, it's so powerful, and by the time they release me, I'm exhausted, hot and sweaty and gasping for breath.

I lie there, panting, as he kisses up my body. I'm powerless to stop as he kisses my breasts, then finally crushes his lips to mine. I moan as he delves his tongue into mouth.

"Now I'm going to make love to you," he murmurs, pushing up my knees and sliding the tip of his erection down through my folds. He rocks his hips, and I'm so wet and swollen that he slides inside me in one easy thrust.

"I'm going to do it super slowly, until you come again," he promises, kissing my eyelids, my brow, my cheekbones.

I give a long, heartfelt groan. "Oh my God, stop torturing me, I can't bear it. This is so unfair."

He stops moving. After a few seconds, I open my eyes and look up into his.

"Seriously," he says. "You're complaining about the number of orgasms I'm giving you?"

My lips part, and I fumble for words, trying not to laugh. "No, I meant… um…"

"Right." He withdraws and grabs my left arm. I giggle and try to remove it, but he rolls me onto my front easily, and positions himself between my legs. He's heavy on top of me, and I have no chance of fighting him off.

"Titus!" I can't do anything for laughing. "I'm sorry."

He slides the tip of his erection down until he enters me, then pushes forward, burying himself deep inside. I squeal, then give a long moan at the sensation of being filled so completely. "Yeah…" I whisper, "go for it." He's fired up now, and I'll be happy if he takes his pleasure from me, as it'll probably only take him thirty seconds, and then I can go to sleep.

But he lowers his mouth to my ear and murmurs, "Oh no, you don't get away that easily. I'm going to fuck you until you come, Heidi Rose."

I groan. "I'm spent. You'll come before I do."

"Oh, I can promise you that won't happen. I can go on all night. So you'd best relax and just let it happen."

I rest my forehead on my hands, realizing he's serious. "I can't. I'm exhausted."

He rocks his hips, then pushes forward, burying himself so deep inside me that I squeal. "Are you trying to spear me to the bed?" I say over my shoulder.

He pulls down a pillow. "Bite on this if you need to."

I flop onto it. "I'm going to sleep."

He chuckles and starts thrusting. "You're welcome to try."

Of course, there's absolutely no chance for me to doze off, because he plunges deep into me, while he slides a hand beneath me to caress my breast and tug on my nipple.

"Ah Heidi…" he mutters, kissing my neck, and then he turns my face toward him and crushes his lips to mine. He's totally overwhelming my senses: the smell of his aftershave mixed with the scent of sexy hot male, the taste of his mouth, the heaviness of him on top of me, the feel of him inside me.

I'm convinced I can't come again—it doesn't matter what he does, I'm finished. But then he moves his hand down between my legs, his fingers finding my clit, and oh my God, despite my protestations that I'm done, the first flickers of pleasure flare inside me, and I moan.

"Come on, Countess," he whispers, starting to move faster. "Come for me. You know you want to."

"I can't…"

He kisses my cheek, my ear. "Yes you can. Do it for me."

It's so hot, and our skin is sticking together, peeling apart whenever he moves. The fact that I'm powerless to stop him is somehow such a turn-on that all it does is increase my passion. The air is filled with the sound of sex, his hips meeting my butt with a smack, the slick sound of him inside me, his deep groans, and the gasps that he forces from my lips with each thrust.

I'm going to come again. I can feel the pleasure gathering in my stomach, building up, and I bury my face in the pillow.

He obviously senses it because his hips move faster, pumping hard, and that's it, I can't control it, it's like a hot desert wind blowing across me, a pleasurable sirocco, and I cry out with each powerful pulse, consumed by exquisite gratification. Propped on his hands, he thrusts me through it, until I'm a quivering heap of bliss.

But he doesn't stop—he continues to thrust, and I clench the pillow with my hands and hang on for dear life as he rides me hard and fast for another thirty seconds until finally his climax hits. He groans and shudders, swelling inside me, and I feel his pleasure in every cell of my body.

He gives delicious little movements of his hips, sending aftershocks through me, before he finally withdraws.

He kisses my ear and murmurs, "Are you okay?"

"I can't move. All the bones in my body have disappeared. I'm so fucking hot."

"Aw. I'll put the fan on." He gets up—how does he have the energy to move?—goes around the bed, and switches the fan on, and I sigh at the blast of cool air over my heated skin.

I hear him leave the room, but I still can't move. I listen to him in the kitchen, opening the fridge, and then he comes back into the room and climbs onto the bed.

"Cold water," he says, handing me the bottle.

"I can't move."

He laughs, leans across to put the bottle on my bedside table, then lies beside me, head propped on a hand. I turn my head to look at him, but it's all the movement I can manage.

He looks amused. "You did ask," he says.

Oh yeah. He's right. *Are you going to fuck me until my teeth rattle?*

"Me and my big mouth," I mumble, and his lips curve up.

My gaze skims lazily over his face, his broad shoulders, the muscles of his chest, all painted with moonlight. He lifts a hand and moves a strand of hair off my face where it's stuck to my cheek. Then he trails a finger down my back to the dip at the base of my spine.

"You look amazing," he says.

"You mean I look soundly fucked."

"Yeah."

We both laugh.

"I mean it," he says. "You're incredibly beautiful."

I turn my head and bury my face in the pillow. "Stop it," I say, my voice muffled.

"I think I'm a little bit in love with you, Heidi Rose Huxley."

I go still. Did I hear him right?

I turn my head back. He smiles.

"I'm a little bit in love with you, too," I whisper.

We study each other for a while.

"It was a bit dumb to sleep together, wasn't it?" I say.

"Just a bit."

"We should have known."

"Yeah."

I know I should be worried or upset. Heartache is on the cards, one way or another. But I can't feel anything except joy at his words.

"Thank you for the three orgasms," I say.

He laughs. "You're welcome."

"I didn't mean to complain after the second."

He moves a bit closer to me and nuzzles my ear. "I know. It was an excuse to torture you, that's all."

"I quite like being tortured."

"Good."

"Even though now I've lost the use of my limbs."

He chuckles. "You're the sexiest girl I've ever met."

"I think that says more about the girls you've met than about me."

But he bends his head and kisses my lips, and I sigh, powerless to stop him, even if I wanted to, which I don't.

When he finally moves back, I say, "You should ring Saxon now."

He groans. "Shit, I forgot. Yeah, I should." He sighs. "Do you mind if I do it from here?"

"In bed? Doesn't sound very professional."

"It's only Saxon. He won't care. He's rung me from the bath before."

I chuckle. "All right." I push myself up with a groan. "God. I feel as if I've been run over."

"Good sex should always make you feel like a cartoon character flattened by a piano," he says. Laughing, he leans over the bed to collect the laptop case sitting beside it.

I poke my tongue out at him, finally manage to get to my feet, and pad over to the bathroom. "So rude," I mutter, going inside.

I take off my makeup and splash some water on my face. Then I spot one of Titus's T-shirts lying on a chair, so I put it on. It's far too big, but it smells of him, which I like. I go back out, just as he says, "Morning." He's sitting up in bed, his back against the pillows, lit by the lamp.

"Hey," Saxon says. "I guess I should say good evening?"

"Yeah, it's eleven p.m. here." Titus's gaze slides to me as I come out. His lips curve up as he sees me in his T-shirt, and he nods as I gesture to the bed, so I slide in beside him, making sure to stay out of camera shot.

The guy on the screen is in an office that's obviously a few floors up because behind him I can see across the harbor. The sea is an iron-gray, topped with white horses, and wintry rain beats against the window. Saxon looks enough like Titus that it's clear they're related—good-looking, dark-haired, although he has a neat beard and mustache. He looks smart in a navy suit, white shirt, and blue-and-silver-striped tie. He lifts his eyebrows. "Not alone, dude?"

"No," Titus says, "so be polite."

"Hello, Heidi," Saxon says with a smirk, even though I'm sure he can't see me.

I stare in surprise at Titus, who looks embarrassed. "I might have mentioned you," he says.

"Extolled your virtues for two whole pages in his email, more like," Saxon replies.

Titus rolls his eyes. "Jesus. Don't exaggerate."

"A page and a half, then. Don't I get to see the lovely lady?"

"I've just taken off all my makeup," I say with a laugh, but I turn the laptop so I'm visible in the picture in the corner, and shyly smooth back my hair. God, I still look just-fucked. "Hello."

He smiles. "Hey, Heidi," he says softly. "Pleased to meet you."

"Likewise. It looks a bit wintry out there. Is that Auckland Harbor behind you?"

"Yeah, I'm in Titus's office. It's fucking horrible today, pardon my French. The biggest rainfall in July for something like fifty years. You're definitely in the best place. What have you been up to?"

"I... uh..." I blush scarlet.

"I meant during the evening," he says with much amusement.

Titus laughs and turns the camera back to himself as I cover my face with a hand. "We've been to a murder-mystery evening with Alan

Woodridge. It was good fun. Heidi turned out to be the murderer. I should have guessed."

"She looks like the shady sort." He grins. "Glad you're having a good time, and I'm sorry about this."

"No, it's okay. Everything all right there?"

"Yeah. I had a long meeting with Mack, Elizabeth, and your team. Mack's just finished another version of Stork using the adjustments I passed on to him."

"That's the nickname we've given to the IVF program we're running at NZAI," Titus tells me. "How does it look?" he asked Saxon.

"Pretty damn good. We're going to start the second set of trials next week, if you're in agreement."

"Of course."

"Should give you some more ammunition to persuade Acheron to invest even if you don't stay."

"I'm hoping Alan will agree. He genuinely wants this to work, and he's willing to put his money where his mouth is."

"It'll be cool if you get to stay in New Zealand, eh?"

Titus glances at me for a moment, hesitating. Then he looks back at the screen.

"Ah," Saxon says. "Right."

I slip out of bed. "I'm going to make us a coffee," I murmur.

"Okay."

I feel Titus's gaze on me as I cross the room and go out into the kitchen, and hear him murmur as he continues his conversation. I don't know whether he'll talk to Saxon about me—I know guys don't tend to confide in each other about this kind of thing—but at least he has the option if I'm not in the room.

The tiles are cool beneath my feet. I cross to the coffee machine and open the box beside it. Ooh, there are rows of coffee pods containing all different types and strengths of coffee. I take two out, slot one in the machine, set it going, then fetch some milk from the fridge.

I think I'm a little bit in love with you, Heidi Rose Huxley.

My lips curve up, and I hum to myself as I pour the milk into a jug. I need to practice mindfulness, I tell myself. Right here, right now, life is pretty sweet.

Chapter Eighteen

Titus

I watch Heidi disappear around the corner and hear her go into the kitchen, and bring my gaze back to Saxon. He's watching me, a lopsided smile on his lips.

"You okay?" he asks.

I sigh. "Yeah. I've been an idiot."

"I could have told you this would happen. It was obvious from the way you spoke about her."

I huff a sigh.

He chuckles, then purses his lips. "Is she likely to move back here?"

"I don't know. She loves England, and she's all settled here. I can't ask her to do that."

"But if she offers?"

I hesitate. I don't think she will. I know she repeated my line about being a little in love, but we've only been together a few days. It's no time at all to ask someone to change their life for you.

I slide down the pillows a bit. "Can we talk about something else?"

"Sure."

"Like... what's this about you moonlighting?"

He frowns. "What do you mean?"

"I hear you've been earning some spare cash as a stripper."

His jaw drops, and then his eyes narrow. "Fucking Huxley. Can't keep his mouth shut."

I laugh. Huxley emailed me this morning to give me the rundown. Saxon has been up in Auckland keeping an eye on things in my absence, and they went out last night. "What happened?"

Saxon looks up at the ceiling for a moment before returning his exasperated gaze to me. "Hux wanted to try out a new bar he'd heard about. I went out with him, Elizabeth, Mack, and Sidnie. I… ah… might have had one too many."

"I'm shocked."

He gives me a wry look. "There was a group of girls there, well, women, but young, early twenties."

"Ah."

"Yeah. It was a leaving do. Apparently they'd organized a stripper, but he hadn't turned up. One of them asked me to stand in."

"Tell me you didn't," I say, already knowing the answer from Huxley's story.

"I declined politely. But the others were all cheering, and then Hux and Mack joined in, and, well, I sort of unbuttoned my shirt a bit just for a laugh…" He scratches the back of his neck.

I chuckle. Huxley told me that Saxon went a bit further than that, but I decide not to push it. "Hux said you disappeared with a redhead."

"Um, yeah. She came back to my hotel room." He plays with a pen for a moment before lifting his gaze back to me. "I liked her."

I lift my eyebrows. "Really?"

"Yeah. But I won't be seeing her again. She was moving away."

"Did you get her name?"

"Yes," he says sarcastically. "Catie. With a C."

"Pretty."

"She was."

"I meant her name."

"That too." His gaze drifts away as he obviously remembers a moment from the night before. Then it comes back to me, and he sighs. "When I woke up this morning, she'd gone."

"Ah, fuck. No number?"

"Nope. Huxley didn't know her or the group she was with. I've got no way of tracking her down."

"Maybe the bartender?"

"She obviously didn't want me to find her. It's a fine line between being interested and stalking, you know? It was fun, but I've got to let her go." He looks wistful. Then he sighs. "You want to go through the report?"

"Yeah, okay."

He talks for a while, summarizing the results and discussing his take on them.

Heidi comes into the room as Saxon is finishing up, and I say goodbye to him and tell him I look forward to catching up with him at Huxley's wedding.

As Heidi climbs on the bed, I close the laptop and lean it against the bedside table, then take the mug she passes to me. "Thank you."

She smiles and curls up next to me, pulling the duvet over her legs. It's cooler in here now, although her cheeks still hold a touch of the flush that bloomed in them while we made love.

"All good?" she asks.

"Yeah. I was teasing him because Huxley emailed me and told me Saxon got drunk last night and did a striptease in a bar."

She laughs. "And my brother didn't leap to his rescue and stop him?"

"Nah, he stood there and watched. So did Mack, by all accounts. It sounds like it ended well." I tell her about the redhead.

"Aw," she says afterward, "that's a shame. She did a Cinderella?"

"Sounds like it, except she didn't leave the glass slipper behind."

We study each other for a moment. I hold my arm up. She moves closer to me, and I lower my arm around her.

"So Saxon isn't with anyone?" she asks.

"No. His girlfriend moved out a while ago. She said he didn't spend enough time with her. It's tough when you work long hours and you give your all to your job, and then your partner resents you for it."

She looks up at me. "Are you speaking from experience?"

"Maybe."

"Are you talking about Claire?"

I hesitate. I am, but it doesn't feel right to criticize her.

"It's all right," she says softly, "you don't have to say anything." She kisses my cheek. "You really are very sweet sometimes."

I put my empty mug on the bedside table, and she finishes off hers and does the same.

"Come on," she says. "You look tired. We've got an early start tomorrow. Let's get ready for bed."

We clean our teeth and turn off all the lights. It's warm, but Heidi turns the fan on, and we snuggle under the duvet. I cuddle up to Heidi's back, pulling her against me.

"Goodnight," she murmurs.

"'Night, sweetheart." I kiss her hair.

I could have told you this would happen. It was obvious from the way you spoke about her.

I sigh, and close my eyes.

*

Five thirty a.m. on Sunday finds us at an airfield close to Exeter Airport, watching the huge red balloon being filled with hot air.

Alan and Vicky are coming with us, and they join us in the wicker basket. William, who's taking us on our adventure along with his wife, Ria, opens the blast valve that adjusts the burning of the liquid propane, and the balloon rises gradually into the sky that's filled with the blush of early morning.

Heidi stands close to me as we lift into the air, and I put my arm around her. "I forgot to ask if you were scared of heights," I say.

"Not like Oliver," she replies. "But it still makes my heart race, all the same."

"I know what you mean. It's exhilarating." I've never done this before, and it's a whole new experience to be open to the fresh air as the balloon begins to head west toward the city of Exeter.

"This is amazing," I say to Alan, who grins.

"I know. We've done this a few times because it's such a fantastic experience. I had to organize it for you both when I knew you were coming."

I look away. He's doing everything he can to try to persuade me to stay. And that's fair enough. I guess I'd do the same if I was in his position.

"We're lucky that the summer weather has held for so long," Vicky says.

"It's been gorgeous," Heidi agrees. "Last year July was a washout." She blinks, then bites her lip. "So my grandma said, anyway."

My heart skipped a beat, but neither Alan nor Vicky seem to have noticed her slip. Heidi meets my gaze and grimaces before looking away. I give her shoulders a squeeze. I was the idiot who didn't put Alan straight when he assumed we were a couple, and I don't want her to feel bad.

The hot-air balloon flies at about ten miles per hour, and it gives us plenty of time to see the sights and admire the view. We fly slowly over the city of Exeter, while Ria starts pointing out places of interest, like the remains of the Norman Rougemont Castle, the winding River Exe, and then the cathedral, resplendent in the middle of the green, and she traces the playing-card shape where the Roman fortress once stood.

After that we continue to head west, out across the patchwork quilt of the Devon countryside. William takes us to the edge of the moors, and when Ria tells us we're flying over the town of Briarton, Heidi peers over, looking for her cottage, although we're too far up to make it out.

It takes us about ninety minutes to fly as far as Haytor, where we drove to the other day. We look down at the brown, purple, and green bruise of the moors, the ancient gray rocks, and the tiny ponies.

"It's an amazing country," I murmur to Heidi. We're cuddled up as it's quite fresh up here in the air, despite us both wearing jackets—plus I can't keep my hands off her.

"I love it," she replies. "I feel so at home here, in a way I don't in New Zealand. I don't know why."

I kiss her brow. "Maybe because you're half English."

"Yeah, maybe."

My lips rest against her temple. I suspect it's more to do with her escaping her father's control and being able to live her life the way she wants here, although I don't say as much.

The more I'm with her, though, the more I realize it would be a mistake to try to persuade her to return to New Zealand. She's happy here. She has friends and a great job. She is British now, for all intents and purposes. Her life is here. And when her visit to New Zealand is over, I'm sure she'll be relieved to get back.

Our journey has come to an end, and William begins to return to the airfield. This time, he takes us east to the coast, and then we fly up the coastline, looking down at the thin strips of golden beaches and the deep blue water before we float back up over the kaleidoscope of fields. It's a fantastic flight, and it's made me wish I was seeing more of the country.

It's past nine a.m. by the time we land. We thank William and Ria for the marvelous experience, and then Alan drives us back to Hawkerland Manor. They ask us to join them for breakfast, so we go up to the house and sit with them at the table in the conservatory. Alan calls the chef out, and he asks us to choose from a long menu of possible breakfasts, including a full English breakfast with eggs, bacon, and sausages, as well as things like kedgeree, ricotta hotcakes, omelets, pancakes, and waffles.

I go for the full English, while Heidi chooses the chef's recommendation of spiced oatmeal fritters with coconut caramel pears.

"Does he work here all the time?" Heidi asks when the chef excuses himself to cook our meals.

Alan chuckles. "No. We used to have a full-time housekeeper when the girls lived at home, and she did a lot of the cooking because we were always so busy. But now they're gone, she only comes part-time. She does leave us some meals that we just throw in the oven when we don't feel like cooking, but when we have guests, we hire a proper chef from a local firm."

"What would you like to do this afternoon?" Vicky asks. "We were wondering if there was anywhere nearby you'd like to visit? We thought maybe Bath?"

Heidi's eyes light up. "I'd love to go to," she says breathlessly.

"Did you have any plans?" Alan asks me.

"I was thinking about doing some work," I say, "but I guess I can be talked out of it."

"Of course you can!" Vicky protests.

"I can hire a helicopter at the flying school," Alan says, "and we'll pick up a car the other end."

"Sounds terrific." Part of me would like to have spent the day in bed with Heidi, but as appealing as that sounds, I know how much she'll love going, and I'm interested to see somewhere Roman."

So after we've eaten breakfast, Alan flies the four of us up to Bath, then drives us from the airport to the site of the Roman baths. It completely blows me away, and Heidi is in her element. We end up spending a couple of hours walking around the Sacred Spring, the Roman Temple, the Roman Bath House, and then the finds belonging to the ancient people of Aquae Sulis, with Heidi giving us a rundown on the history and archaeology. She's fascinated by the numerous objects that were originally thrown into the baths as offerings, including over twelve thousand Roman coins, and curse tablets— messages inscribed on sheets of lead or pewter, rolled up and thrown into the spring. I love her passion for the place, and I'm glad I was able to visit it with her.

"I guess you know how strange this feels," I say to Alan as we stand in front of the gilt bronze head of the goddess Sulis Minerva, while Vicky and Heidi have a look around the shop. "It's two thousand years old. I mean, I know our country is young, but I've never really thought about how it must feel to live in a place where people have walked before you for thousands of years."

"I'd love to visit Tanzania," he says. "Imagine walking through the Olduvai Gorge where Homo habilis lived 1.9 million years ago. Or Laetoli, where Lucy walked 3.6 million years ago. There's so much of the world to see, Titus. We have to be careful not to shut ourselves away in our offices for too long. Vicky has taught me that. You make sure that you let Heidi drag you away from your desk once in a while. Not all those who wander are lost."

I smile. "Heidi said those very words to me not that long ago."

"She's got her head screwed on right, that one."

"Yeah," I say with feeling. "She certainly has."

I feel oddly lightheaded, maybe even a little dizzy, which I think is possibly lingering jet lag mixed with tiredness because we rose so early this morning, so I don't protest when Alan finally suggests we head back. He flies us to Exeter airport, and then drives us back to Hawkerland Manor, dropping us off at the cottage around four p.m.

"We'll pick you up at six-thirty," he says as we get out, "and take you to The Green Man for dinner, okay?"

"Sounds great." We wave goodbye and head inside.

"I'm going to make a coffee, do you want one?" Heidi asks.

"Not for me, thanks. I might just catch up on my emails."

"Okay, sweetie." She goes into the kitchen, and I head into the living room.

I sit on the sofa, prop up my feet, and open up my laptop. I have a ton of emails, and several reports I need to read and make notes on.

But it's warm in the room, and my head is buzzing. I slide down a little, and think to myself that I'll just close my eyes for five minutes, which should be enough to perk me up.

*

I jerk awake, and for a moment have no idea where I am. I'm lying on a sofa, and I can hear the water lapping, ducks quacking, and the call of various other birds. Then I remember—I'm at the cottage in Devon. I must have dozed off.

"Hey, you."

I turn my head and see Heidi curled up in the armchair opposite, reading.

I yawn and stretch. "What time is it?"

"Five thirty, don't worry. We've still got about an hour."

"I don't know what happened. I crashed right out."

"Yeah, you looked very tired. Can I get you anything?"

"I could do with a kiss," I tell her.

She chuckles, puts down her book, and comes over to me. Bending down, she presses her lips to mine, then squeals as I grab her and pull her on top of me.

"Come on," I scold, "did you really think I was going to let you go after one peck?"

"I was hoping you wouldn't." She looks down at me, her hair swinging forward like a curtain, her blue eyes like circles cut from the sky outside, and kisses me properly, delving her tongue into my mouth.

I sigh, wrapping my arms around her, and we kiss like that for ages, warm in the summer sunshine, with the smell of the lavender outside blowing through the house where Heidi must have opened the sliding doors to let the cool breeze in.

"Mmm," she murmurs after a while, and moves her hips from side to side, brushing her mound against my erection. "His lordship is hoping for some action, I think."

"How's the Countess? In good form?"

She giggles. "She'd be happy to receive some attention." She gets up off me, slips off her jeans and underwear while I sit up, then climbs back astride me. I help her off with her top and bra, and now she's naked, which somehow seems adventurous when it's so beautiful outside, and the doors are open.

I feel blissfully happy, having her in my arms, the two of us taking time to kiss and arouse one another. I cup her breasts and pluck at her nipples, while she lowers her hands to the zipper of my jeans, slides it down, then moves closer so she's nestled right against my erection. We kiss like that for a while, as she rocks her hips and arouses herself on me, and it's not long before she whispers, "Are you ready?"

I nod, push down my boxer-briefs, and release my erection, and Heidi guides it beneath her, then sinks down onto me. "Aaahhh…"

Her exhalation turns into a moan, and her teeth tug at her bottom lip as she moves her hips, coating me with her moisture so I can sink further into her.

"Titus," she whispers, cupping my face and kissing me.

We move together, her skin glowing and slightly damp from the warmth, her face and neck filled with the subtle blush of sexual arousal. Fuck, that's sexy, and it makes me push up inside her, and she moans and arches her back.

"You're so beautiful," I tell, beginning to lose it. I stroke my hands down her back, then bring one around her waist and slide my thumb down between us until I find her clit. She's moist and swollen, and as I circle my thumb over the tiny button, she moans and delves her tongue into my mouth.

"I love doing this with you," she whispers, rocking her hips.

"I could do this with you every day for years and never get bored," I reply truthfully. There's something about this girl that just fills me with joy. I can't put my finger on it. I've known more beautiful girls. Women who are more confident, more intelligent. But she brings it all together in one package, and it's created this gorgeous, sexy, funny young woman who rings all my bells.

"Ah, Titus," she murmurs, "I wish…" She kisses me, still moving, her breath hitching.

"What?" I ask, but she shakes her head, closes her eyes, and bites her bottom lip, and I watch pleasure sweep over her, sweet and golden as the rays of the sun. She cries out, clamping around me, and that proves my undoing. My climax hits me seconds later, and the two of us lock together, like the statue of two lovers, frozen at the height of passion for eternity.

Chapter Nineteen

Heidi

At six thirty, Alan and Vicky arrive to take us out for dinner. We drive a few miles into the English countryside, and Alan pulls up outside a building with a thatched roof and white cob walls, with a sign hanging out the front that says, "The Green Man".

"It dates back to 825AD," he tells us as we get out. "It was originally a nunnery and a farm, and it's in the Domesday Book."

It goes back to the time of William the Conqueror? "Wow." I'm thrilled, and I can see that Titus is genuinely impressed.

"It's supposed to have a couple of ghosts, too," Vicky teases as we go inside.

"Even better."

The long bar that spans the length of the room is made from solid English oak, and blackened beams run along the ceiling and down the walls, filled in with cob. One wall contains a beautiful stained-glass window, which Alan tells us is an original from the fourteenth century.

Rectangular tables with high-backed chairs fill the restaurant section, and we're shown to a reserved table. Titus sits next to me. He looks gorgeous tonight. He's wearing black jeans and a plum-colored dress shirt with a lighter plum color pattern on the front placket and the inside of the collar and cuffs that he's rolled up a couple of times.

I think I'm a little bit in love with you, Heidi Rose Huxley, he told me, and I returned the sentiment, but I know now it wasn't true. I'm not a little bit in love. I'm completely and wholly in love with this guy.

I know it's not real love—it's like a snowflake, or a bubble—insubstantial and fleeting. I know it's not enough to build a future on. And I know I can't give everything up for him. I know, I know, I know… It's a holiday fling, a crush. That's all.

But I'm still shocked at the intensity of the emotion I'm feeling. When he looks at me, it's as if I've touched a live wire, and it makes everything seem to swell inside me—my heart, my lungs, my… other bits. Especially my other bits. All the time he's around, I've got sex on the brain. He was only inside me half an hour ago, and I'm already thinking about the next time we're going to make love… although that might have something to do with what's happening under the table. I'm wearing a short skirt, and he rests his hand on my knee, then slides it up a few inches so it's warm on my thigh, his fingers drawing light circles on my skin. I glance at him, but he's talking to Alan, so I don't even think he's aware he's doing it.

I don't know why he has such an effect on me. Jason never reduced me to mush like this. In fact, no other man has ever made me feel this way. It's as if I thought I liked chocolate, but I've just discovered that I've only ever eaten plain bars, and suddenly I've been presented with a box of the most sumptuous truffles in the world, full of all kinds of flavors that burst on the tongue.

And now I'm thinking about covering him in melted chocolate and sucking it all off, and I'm back to sex again.

"Heidi?" Vicky asks, snapping my attention back to the present. A waiter is standing by the table, and they're all looking at me.

"What do you want to drink?" Titus asks softly, his eyes sparkling. I know then that he's well aware of what he's doing beneath the table, and the effect it's having on me. I nudge his knee with mine, and he squeezes my thigh.

"I'll have a half of the local cider, please," I say, spotting it on tap.

"I'd like to try a beer," Titus says to Alan. "What do you recommend?"

"If you prefer a cold beer, you'd be better off with lager. The ales are served at room temperature here."

"I usually drink lager, but I'd be happy to try a draught ale."

"How about a Spitting Feathers bitter? It's from a local microbrewery, and I think it's one of the best local beers."

"Sounds great. I'll have a pint of that," Titus says, and the waiter nods and goes off with our order. "Spitting Feathers?" Titus says, amused. "Does it make you angry, then?"

"Here it also means thirsty," I tell him. "In Shakespeare's Henry IV, Falstaff says 'I brandish any thing but a bottle, I would I might never spit white again.' I think it's from that." My face warms at his smile. "More useless information," I add.

"You fascinate me," he says.

My blush deepens as Alan and Vicky exchange a glance. "Young love," Vicky says, sighing as she turns her attention to her menu.

I glance at Titus. He doesn't look upset at Vicky's comment, and he winks at me before lowering his gaze to the menu.

I look at mine, although it's tough to concentrate on the words. Titus and I are supposed to be faking love this weekend. How did it turn into the real thing?

*

It turns out to be a lovely evening. The four of us get on really well, and there's no shortage of conversation as the meal progresses. We spend a long while talking about New Zealand. Alan has only been back once, many years ago, to show Vicky the place of his birth, and we exchange memories and discuss how much it's changed. They then talk about the UK and different places they've visited, insisting that at some point we should do a tour of the country to see all the amazing historical sites.

I keep waiting for them to push the subject of us moving to England, or to try to influence Titus in some way, but they don't, and for that I'm grateful. I wonder whether they're aware of how much they're selling the place without that added pressure.

Then I realize that of course they're aware. They've presented the very best face of the country—the gorgeous countryside, the history, and luckily the best weather. Like all countries, England has many faults, but its landscape and historical sites aren't two of them.

When we've finished our meal, we linger over coffee, and then eventually Alan drives us back to Hawkerland Manor.

"Such a shame the weekend's almost over," I say sadly. "I've had such a great time."

"It would be wonderful if you lived here," Vicky says, looking over her shoulder from the front seat. Alan nudges her, though, and she bites her lip and turns her gaze out of the window.

In the back seat, Titus glances at me, so he obviously spotted it. He must know that, to a certain extent, they're trying to influence us. I think he's just relieved it hasn't been too overt.

"What time are we off tomorrow?" he asks Alan.

"I'll pick you up at eight a.m. We'll do a tour of the plant, meet a few of the team, and then in the afternoon it's the board meeting."

"Okay."

"I'm sorry I can't take you out tomorrow," Vicky says to me. "I'm meeting friends in London."

"Oh, that's fine. I thought I might have a swim in the pool, and a walk around the grounds."

Alan pulls up outside, and we say goodbye and go into the cottage.

"That was an amazing meal," I say, taking off my sandals and going through to the kitchen, the tiled floor cool on my feet.

"Yeah, I think they enjoyed themselves." Titus follows me out and pulls me into his arms. "Thank you for coming with me."

"It's my pleasure. I've had such a great time." I kiss him. "Are you nervous about tomorrow?"

"A bit."

"Will the board members grill you about your work?"

"Almost certainly. I don't mind that. The research is sound. I suppose I'm more nervous that our time with Alan is coming to an end, and he's going to want an answer."

"Can you say you'll think about it, then tell him via email?"

"I could, but I think that's the coward's way out. I'll play it by ear, but I'm planning to tell him tomorrow."

I rest my cheek on his chest, suddenly emotional. Once he's admitted to Alan that he's not staying, it'll put the onus of our relationship—such as it is—on me. He said there's a conversation coming between the two of us, maybe on the plane, but I can only think that he means he's going to ask me to move back to New Zealand.

He wraps his arms around me, and we stand there like that for a while.

I can't bear the thought of not seeing him again. But what's the option? I give up my life here? But even if that's what he's hoping for—and there's no guarantee he's interested in anything long term—what would happen if it didn't work out between us?

He presses his lips to my hair, and I feel him give a long sigh. If there was an easy option, maybe he would like to continue to see me. But there's not. And I think maybe he feels as sad about that as I do.

Chapter Twenty

Titus

"Did you sleep well?" Alan asks.

It's about 8:30 a.m., and we're on our way to Acheron Pharmaceuticals, on the outskirts of Exeter. "Great, thanks," I say. "It's so quiet in that cottage, apart from the ducks and the owls and the moorhens and the swans…"

He grins. "Yeah, the bird life is guaranteed to get you up in the morning even if your alarm clock fails." He takes the slip road off the motorway and drives down to a roundabout, then indicates at the second turning. I assume he's heading toward the signposted industrial estate, but he passes the turnoff and continues north out of the city.

We're both in business mode today. I'm wearing a dark-blue, three-piece, bespoke wool suit with a white shirt and a smart navy tie with white spots, because donning it makes me feel as if I'm putting on a suit of armor. Not that I'm preparing for battle, but when I'm suited up, I feel ready for anything.

I got a lovely surprise this morning when, as I was dressing, Heidi retrieved a velvet box from her bag and handed it to me.

"What's this?" I asked, surprised.

"A good luck charm." She gave me a nervous smile.

I opened the box to discover it contained a silver tie pin and cufflinks, each bearing a small Roman coin.

"They're only copies of Roman denarii, of course," she said shyly. "I bought them in Bath. You don't have to wear them if you don't want to."

"Of course I'll wear them." Genuinely touched, I took them out carefully, slotted the pin over my tie, and inserted the cufflinks into the cuffs of my shirt. "I love them. Thank you so much."

I brush my fingers over the tie pin now, thinking about how she hugged me afterward and wished me luck. It was such a sweet gesture. I try to ignore how it feels like a parting gift, because I hope that's not how she meant it.

Alan's wearing a dark-gray suit, and he's obviously taken as much care over his appearance as I have—his hair is neatly combed, he's shaved, and he's polished his shoes. I think he's a bit nervous about today. Obviously it's his company, but he needs the board's approval for such a large investment, and they're going to want reassurance that NZAI will be able to carry out the research.

He slows the car as a sign for Acheron Pharmaceuticals looms ahead of us and turns left. The long drive is lined by trees, and it's only when we turn the corner that I finally see where we're heading.

My eyebrows rise. It's a huge site, formed from what look like new buildings covering a few acres of land. Clear signs on the walls ahead of us indicate that the road left leads to a separate private hospital. I'm guessing Acheron has close connections with this, and it's where the clinical trials will probably be carried out. Straight ahead is the main office block for Acheron Pharmaceuticals. To our right, the road curves around to the laboratories and the facilities where the medications are manufactured.

Alan drives ahead to the office block and draws up out the front—he has his own, named parking space, of course—and we get out and walk into the office block.

It's everything I've come to expect from Alan Woodridge—elegant, smart, and swish, as Heidi likes to say. In the main lobby, the reception desk and the paneling on the walls is made from a light wood, while the carpet tiles are pale gray, making it feel large and spacious. There's a generous waiting area with a coffee machine and a water cooler. Everywhere looks clean and sparkling. I have no doubt that he's had people scrubbing and repainting the place. I bet this is how the King feels wherever he's touring.

Alan signs me in at the front desk, introducing me to Iris, a woman in her forties who looks no-nonsense and efficient, but who gives me a warm smile when she finds out who I am. "I've heard a lot about you, Mr. Oates," she says.

"Titus, please," I tell her. "And stop, you're making me blush."

She chuckles, and Alan grins. "Let's go up to my office," he says, "and meet my team. Then I'll take you on a tour."

We head across the lobby, stopping three times so he can introduce me to people. Each time, he says, "This is the famous computer engineer, Titus Oates, from New Zealand." After the third time, I chuckle and tell him, "Less of the famous, Alan."

"Credit where credit's due," he says, pressing the button to call the elevator, and walking in as the doors open.

The elevator is glass walled and gives us a view across the offices as it rises to the fifth floor. We exit into another lobby, this one quieter. The carpet is plusher here, the wood of a darker hue, and there are oil paintings on the walls. We walk past an impressive boardroom with a table that seats twelve, and along a corridor that looks over a large central office filled with people starting their day, hanging up their jackets, and taking coffee cups to their desks.

"Everyone looks happy to be working here," I comment, noting the smiling faces and the relaxed manner of the employees.

"We work hard here to have a pleasant working environment," Alan says. "We have lots of social functions, competitions, rewards, that kind of thing. I like to think of myself like Dickens' Fezziwig."

That makes me laugh. "You're not fat enough."

He grins, leading me into an open-plan semi-circular lobby from which half a dozen offices radiate out. "Morning, Jade."

The woman in her thirties with blonde hair in a bun smiles and gets up as we approach. "Mr. Woodridge, good morning. And you must be Mr. Oates."

"Titus, please," I say, feeling as if I'm fighting a losing battle. I hold out my hand, and she shakes it.

"Lovely to meet you at last—we've heard so much about you."

Alan grins at my wry look. "You'd better get used to hearing that. This is my office through here. Would you like a coffee?"

"Please."

"Jade?"

"Coming right up, sir."

"Thank you." He leads the way to the office at the far end. It's the biggest one, of course, bright and spacious with a view over the lawns behind the building. A large desk stands at an angle to one side, and at the other end a light-gray sofa and chairs surround a low coffee table. Paintings of seascapes decorate the walls. "Rowena's," he says, referring to his daughter.

He puts his briefcase on his desk and says, "You can leave yours here if you like. It'll be safe."

I put mine by the chair in front of his desk. "Come with me," he says, "and I'll introduce you to the team while we're waiting for our coffee."

He leads me back out and along the line of offices. Five of them are occupied, and I get to meet the men and women who help him run the firm—the heads of the financial, scientific, commercial, people and culture, and marketing departments. They all shake my hand warmly and say they're looking forward to talking more when we meet up for lunch in the boardroom.

The last office is empty. Alan takes me in, though. It's a good size, with an attractive view, very light and spacious.

He turns to me with a smile. "This would be yours, if you decide to stay."

My eyebrows rise. "You'd want me up here?"

"Of course. You'd be an important part of my senior leadership team, Titus." He claps me on the back. "Come on. Jade will have got the coffee ready by now."

I follow him out, taken aback by his comment. I'd assumed that if I were to move here for the two years he's requested, I'd be based with the rest of his engineers in the main computer room. I certainly didn't expect to become part of his management team. I know how important my AI program is, and what potential it has for the medical industry, but even so, it's difficult not to be flattered by his words.

My stomach flutters, and I brush my fingers over Heidi's tie pin. I've spent a long time traveling alone, and I'm used to coping on my own, but I wish she was here with me today.

We spend twenty minutes chatting over coffee while he tells me a little about the structure of the company, and then he takes me on a tour. We walk through a large portion of the office building, exiting at the rear and then walking across to the laboratories. After showing me around these, he takes me through the manufacturing facility before leading me back into the last section of the office block: the computer rooms.

"She's not a patch on Marise," Alan says when he shows me their main computer, referring to Mack's supercomputer back in New Zealand, "but she's smart, and she's getting smarter. Due in no small measure to our resident genius."

He introduces me to Elliot, the engineer who runs their computer science department. Two geeks fluent in computer code, we hit it off immediately, and Alan soon wanders off, leaving us to chat for an hour about NZAI and the Stork program.

Eventually Alan returns, and I say goodbye to Elliot reluctantly and follow Alan out. "Last bit," he says, and he leads me across to the front entrance and out of the building. Turning right, he takes me on a short walk to the private hospital.

"This is where we run our clinical trials." He takes me inside.

It's cool, clean, and smartly decorated in pastel colors no doubt meant to relax and reassure the patients. He signs us in, and we've literally just sat in the waiting area when a woman comes out of one of the doors and walks over to us.

"This is Dr. Meera Pawar," Alan says. "She's a reproductive endocrinologist, and the head of the fertility clinic."

"Mr. Oates," Meera says without Alan saying my name, "I'm so very pleased to meet you."

"Likewise, and please, call me Titus," I tell her.

She beams. "Come this way, Titus, and let me show you around our clinic."

Meera is proud to show their facilities and introduces me to dozens of people—more reproductive endocrinologists, embryologists, sonographers, nutritionists, and of course the all-important nurses and administrative staff. Everyone stops what they're doing to greet me, perpetuating the feeling of being royalty.

"We really look forward to working with you further," she says when our tour comes to an end.

"Goodbye." I head out with Alan, who gives me a regretful look as we start walking back to Acheron.

"Sorry about that," he says. "I have made it clear that it's not a foregone conclusion."

"It's okay." I smile, even though my stomach flips. I'm starting to dread the thought of the coming discussion we're going to have later.

"Sorry if it's been a bit overwhelming," he adds as we walk into the lobby. "I know it's been a whistle-stop tour, but there's a lot of ground to cover."

"It's okay, I've enjoyed it," I say honestly.

We return to the fifth floor and head toward the boardroom to discover Jade in the process of organizing caterers to lay out the lunch on the big table. "We discussed whether we should take you out for lunch," Alan says, "but we were advised you'd prefer this."

Advised by whom? I go to ask, but he's busy talking to Jade, and the other members of the leadership team are filtering in, so I take a seat at the table and resolve to ask him about it later.

Alan might have decided against a four-course meal at a posh restaurant for lunch, but they've pulled out all the stops. The food is exquisite—everything bite-size and easy to eat: turkey, ham, and cheese wraps rolled and cut into slices, chicken taco salads in mason jars, hot bites like pizza-stuffed crescent rolls and chicken meatloaf muffins, and a variety of other attractive salads, with plenty of vegetarian options.

We talk while we eat, and it doesn't take long to see that Alan has surrounded himself with like-minded people—intelligent and hardworking, but likable and with a sense of humor. They all seem keen to make me feel comfortable and at home, and ask me lots of questions about my work, as well as about New Zealand.

It's an enjoyable lunch—not in the least because I'm ravenous— but as it draws to a close, the butterflies in my stomach begin to flutter again as the time for the board meeting nears.

I don't know why I'm so nervous. Mainly because I don't want to let Elizabeth and Mack and Saxon and all the others who are involved down.

"Right," Alan says as if reading my mind, "are we all done? Titus, let's go back to my office and get you ready for the meeting."

I say goodbye to the members of the team, visit Alan's private bathroom, splash cold water on my face, and check to make sure I don't have any spinach in my teeth. I check my phone then, the first time in a while, and smile as I see a message from Heidi.

Good luck! Hope it goes well. xx

Me: *Thanks! So far so good. About to go into the board meeting. Wish you were here.*

Her: *Aw, me too! I'll be with you in spirit, if that means anything.*

Me: *It does. Miss you, sweetheart. Looking forward to tonight.*

Her: *Me too. Love you! x*

My eyebrows rise, and my heart skips a beat.

Seconds later, she sends another text.

Her: *Shit, sorry. I didn't mean to get heavy. I just meant… jeez, you know what I meant.*

My lips curve up.

Me: *Yeah. And in the spirit of reciprocity, I love you too. Gotta go x*

Her: *Good luck* <3

I pocket the phone, feeling warm all the way through. Whatever happens today, I know she's there waiting for me.

I head out into his office. He's out talking to Jade, so I take a few minutes to center myself and get in the right headspace for the meeting. Focus, Titus. Don't think about what you're going to get up to with Heidi tonight. About her soft thighs, and the way her golden hair swings forward when she kisses you, and how her face and neck flush when you're having sex. I give a silent groan. Now it's all I can think about.

"Ready to go?" Alan asks, coming into the office.

I clear my throat. "Yep."

"Come on, then."

He leads me out, but instead of turning toward the boardroom, he heads the opposite way along the corridor, then opens one of a pair of wooden doors and gestures for me to precede him. I go into a much bigger boardroom, and realize the previous one must have been just for internal meetings, whereas this is geared for visitors and meant to impress. Twenty comfortable-looking leather chairs are tucked under the long wooden table, and there's a huge interactive whiteboard and a TV. A coffee machine sits on top of a sleek sideboard that probably contains office stationery. In front of each chair is a notepad and pen and a glass, and in the middle are bottles of still and sparkling water, and plates of cookies and small cakes. The table also contains several areas where you can plug in your laptop, and numerous USB ports.

"I'll help you set up," Alan says. He takes the seat at the head of the table and sits me on his right side, then shows me where to plug in my laptop and how to project what's on the screen onto the interactive whiteboard. We've just finished when the door opens, and the first people start coming in.

There are twelve members on the board, and Alan introduces me to them all. The men and women are an impressive mix: there's an ex-member of parliament and cabinet minister, a senior lecturer at the University of Exeter, healthcare executives, a director of a Chartered Accountancy firm, and several doctors and scientists, most of whom are leaders in their own field.

Once they've all helped themselves to tea and coffee and taken their seats, Alan stands and begins the meeting by welcoming everyone and giving me a formal introduction. He then hands over to me for my presentation.

I've done this a hundred times, and I know it all inside out and back to front, so it's not onerous, but I feel the weight of responsibility on me today as I explain the research and deliver the results of our initial trials. I don't need to embellish the results because I believe personally they're impressive enough, so I stick to the facts, and let the numbers speak for themselves.

When I'm done, I get a round of applause, and then the questions start.

They grill me like a twelve-ounce ribeye, for a total of two hours. Perhaps grilled is too strong a word. They're not aggressive or confrontational. They're knowledgeable and interested, even fascinated, and there's a sense of excitement and wonder in their questions at what the future holds if they have access to the kind of research that my company is producing.

Despite their pleasant manner, by the end of the meeting I'm damp under the arms beneath my jacket and relieved it's over.

Alan takes me back to his office, then excuses himself and returns to the boardroom to finish up the meeting.

Jade sticks her head around the door. "That was a long one."

"I'm knackered," I say with feeling.

She laughs. "Would you like a cold lager?"

"Oh my God, seriously? Yes, I would kill for one."

She smiles and goes out, then returns after thirty seconds with an opened bottle of Speight's.

"Don't tell me," I say, accepting the Kiwi beer, "Alan's doing."

She grins. "He wanted you to feel at home. Can I get you anything else? Would you like something to eat?"

"No, I'm good, thank you."

"I don't think he'll be long."

"No worries."

She goes out, and I take the beer over to the comfortable chairs by the sofa, sink into one, and prop my feet on his coffee table. I have a long swig of the beer, sigh, and lean my head on the back.

I should text Heidi and tell her how it went, but a wave of tiredness washes over me. Instead, I rest my hand on my tie pin, and think once again about having her in my arms tonight.

Less than five minutes later, the door opens and Alan walks in.

"I see Jade sorted you out," he says with a laugh, coming over and sitting on the sofa. He's holding a beer, too. Blowing out a breath, he flops back. "Sorry about that. It was a long one, eh?"

"Hopefully I did okay," I say, having another swig of beer.

He gives me a strange look. "You're kidding me, right?"

I blink. "Uh, what do you mean?"

He studies me for a moment, then leans forward, elbows on his knees, dangling the bottle in his fingers. "Titus, you totally blew them away."

My eyebrows rise. "They want to invest?"

"Of course they want to invest. That was never in doubt."

"If I stay here," I clarify. "Right?"

"Titus," he says softly, "We'd love you to stay, and our scientists are very keen to work with you. But I understand that your life is in New Zealand. Acheron will invest in your project regardless of your location. I'm sorry. I should have made that clearer."

My heart lifts. "Seriously?"

"Of course. This work goes beyond ownership and location—it's of international importance. The only question is, are you willing to share your research with us?"

It's then that it hits me. Alan wasn't nervous about the board's reaction, and whether they'd agree to the funding. All along, he hasn't thought of my visit as an interview. He sees it as me interviewing him. He's afraid that I'll be precious about the research. That I'll want to keep it to myself.

He smiles at my bewilderment. "You truly are the most modest, humble, unpretentious guy I've ever met."

I stare at him dumbly.

"Son," he continues gently, "your work is groundbreaking. You're going to change the future of fertility treatment. You're going to make a difference to millions of lives. Think of all those babies who will be born because of you. Why do you think everyone's been so excited to meet you today? Everyone wanted to shake hands with the guy who's going to change the future of IVF."

"It's not just me," I say, my voice husky. "It's all of us—Elizabeth, and Mack, and Saxon..."

"I know, and the fertility drug that Elizabeth has formulated is revolutionary, and it's going to play a huge part in this. But it's the AI part of it—the selection of the embryos—that will change the face of everything. Imagine telling people who'd struggled to have a child a hundred years ago that we would be able to ensure they could carry a healthy baby to full term?"

"We're not there yet."

"No, but you're damn close. I still don't think you truly understand what an impact this is going to have. So I hope you can see why I'm so keen to work with you."

His brow furrows—he really means it.

Slowly, I sit up and put the beer bottle on the table. My heart's racing.

I can't hide the truth any longer. Alan is too nice, too decent. He values honesty and loyalty, and I can only imagine how he's going to feel when he knows that I've deceived him.

"I've got something I need to tell you," I say. "I know it's going to disappoint you, and I'm so sorry."

Chapter Twenty-One

Titus

"It's all right," Alan says. "I know."

I'm conscious that my jaw is sagging, and I snap it shut. "What?"

"That you plan to go back to New Zealand." His eyes are gentle. "And I also know that you and Heidi weren't an item when you came here."

I stare at him. "What?"

He scratches the back of his neck. "This is... ah... a bit embarrassing to admit. But you have to understand how much I want you to stay." He gives an embarrassed grin.

"I don't understand."

"Well, you know I've been talking to Elizabeth. When she said she was pregnant and wouldn't be coming, I asked her, half-jokingly, how I could convince you to stay when you came over. She said that she thought you and Heidi might be... you know... attracted to one another, and it might be fun to put you together and see what happened."

"So that day we arrived at Hawkerland Manor, you put us in the cottage on purpose?"

"Yep. Vicky thought it was great fun. We half expected you to protest and explain you weren't a couple, and when you didn't..." He grins.

I'm so taken aback, I can only stare at him. Eventually his smile fades, and he says, "I'm sorry. It was part practical joke, part hopeful matchmaking. You seem so good together, and the last thing I'd ever want to do is upset you, so—"

"Relax," I say softly, "I'm not upset. Taken aback, yes. Heidi bollocked me for not putting you straight that first day, and by then it was too late, so we thought we'd better pretend to be a couple. And then…" It's my turn to look embarrassed. "Well, I guess it was inevitable."

His lips curve up. "She's a catch, to be sure."

I sigh and run my hand through my hair. "I guess you know, then, that she lives here, in Briarton. She's a primary school teacher there."

"Yes, Elizabeth told me."

"She's happy here. And Alan, I'm happy in New Zealand. My business is there. I'd already decided when I came here that I wouldn't be moving. The plan was hopefully to convince you to invest even though I was going back."

"I know. And we will. There's no question of that."

It still hasn't sunk in. Acheron is going to invest. Holy shit.

He tips his head to the side. "I'm surprised at just how unassuming you are. Heidi mentioned to Vicky that your father hasn't always been supportive of you."

"Did she?" That surprises me.

"He's not proud of you?"

"He's never said as much." I hesitate, unused to putting my feelings for him into words. It feels disloyal, and I haven't even discussed it with a therapist. But somehow it feels right to talk about it with Alan. "I think he's jealous of me. I think he resents my success. He's always lectured me against being conceited or arrogant. He's always dismissed my achievements."

"And yet still you try to win his approval," Alan says. "I hope you realize you're never going to get it."

I look at where my hands are clasped. I guess I've always known that. But to hear it said out loud is more of a shock than I expected. "I owe him a lot," I say, my voice husky.

"He's your father. You don't owe him anything. You'll understand when you have children. It's a debt you pass on. My father worked hard to provide for his children. He went without sometimes so that I could have everything I needed to go to university and start up my business. But I don't owe him for that. It's what you do. Instead, I provide for my girls and do everything I can to set them up in life. I wouldn't expect them to feel as if they have to pay me back. I just hope they get the chance to pass that on to their kids one day."

I frown. "I get what you're saying, but he likes to remind me that I got where I am because I'm privileged and had his support. He told me I'd be nothing without him, and he's right."

Anger flares in Alan's eyes. "Bullshit. You'd have been successful at whatever you turned your mind to, even if you only had a penny to your name. Look, you don't need him, or me, or anyone to tell you that you're successful. I think you should stop trying to seek his approval, and stop worrying about what you think he might say about the decisions you make. You've earned the right to live your life the way you want. Do I wish you'd move here? That's a resounding yes. You're like the son I never had, and I would love to spend more time with you both socially and at work. I think with your brains and my company we could achieve amazing things, and I know our scientists and computer engineers would love to work with you. But you've done enough. I know you're not my son, but I'm incredibly proud of you for what you've achieved. If you'll let us work with your program, we'll pick up the baton and run with it, and do what we can to improve it. And if you don't win the Turing Award for your work, I'll be very surprised."

It's dubbed the Nobel Prize of Computing, the most prestigious and sought-after technical award. I'm so shocked that my throat tightens, and for a long moment, I can't say anything. Alan picks up his beer and has a swig while he waits for me to regain control.

"Sorry," I whisper. "It's a lot to think about. And I need to decide what to do about Heidi."

"Do you love her?"

The question takes me back. I'm not used to discussing emotions like this. Men rarely do it anyway, and certainly not with strangers. But I can see he genuinely cares about me, and his query is honest. He wants to help.

"We've only been together for a few days," I reply slowly.

He blows a raspberry. "I decided I was going to marry Vicky two hours after I met her."

That makes me laugh. "Really?"

"Yeah. I'd never met anyone like her. I met her at a party at university. She was there with another guy. But we started talking, and she was funny and clever, and right there and then I told her to ditch her boyfriend and go out with me."

"And she said yes?"

"Not at first. But I was relentless." He smirks.

I smile. "I understand what you're saying, but it's not really an answer for my predicament. I like her a lot. And... I have told her I'm a little in love with her."

"Does she feel the same way?"

"Uh, yeah. I think so."

"But being in love is different from loving someone, right? That comes with time. And it's a gamble for either of you to make big changes to your lives after such a short time."

"Yes, that's right. But it's not just that. She also has a difficult relationship with her father, and she's worried about going back for the wedding. She's flourished since she's been here. I can't ask her to go back there permanently."

"Well, all I will say is that I don't think you should make decisions for her. Maybe the time she's spent here has given her the confidence to stand up to her father. The last piece of advice I will give—and I appreciate you haven't asked for any—is that love, true love, doesn't come around very often. And it's always better to regret something you've done, than something you haven't."

I know he's right. But I still don't know what to do. Hopefully the path will become clear to me in time.

I have several long swallows of my beer, finishing off the bottle, and put it on the table. "So... is this the point where we shake hands on the deal?"

"You're sharing the research with us?"

I laugh. "Of course I'm sharing the research!"

He grins, stands, and extends his hand, and I do the same. We shake firmly.

"We're going to make history, Lawrence Oates," he says, his eyes alight with excitement.

I feel a swell of happiness. "I hope so."

"Come on then. Let's get you back to your girl."

*

Heidi

At around 5:30 p.m., I hear a car outside, put down my book, and go to the window. It's Alan's Merc, and I watch Titus get out and wave goodbye before walking along the path to the cottage.

My stomach flutters. I haven't heard from him since lunch, so I have no idea how his day has gone. I open the front door and smile as he approaches. He looks tired, although he smiles back when he sees me."

"Hey," I say, standing back to let him in.

"Hey, you." He puts down his briefcase. Then, immediately, he pulls me into his arms, wraps them around me, and gives a long sigh. "I missed you," he murmurs.

"I missed you, too." I bury my face in his shoulder. "You smell so good."

He sighs. "You smell of chocolate and mint."

"Busted. I just had some After Eights."

He chuckles. Lifting his head, he looks at me for a moment, then lowers his lips to mine for a long, sweet kiss.

When he eventually moves back, I frown. Something about his mood worries me, and I'm almost afraid to ask, but I take a deep breath and say, "How did it go?"

"It went great. We shook on it. They're giving us the funding."

Delight fills me, and I beam a smile and say, "That's wonderful news!"

He returns the smile, but there's just something in his eyes that gives me pause.

"Is their investment conditional on your move here?" I ask.

There's a long pause. Then, eventually, he says, "No. It's unconditional. I don't have to move."

We study each other for a long moment. He gives a small, somewhat wistful smile, and it's then that I realize. A small part of him was hoping it *would* be conditional, because it would have been almost impossible for him to turn down the investment. He would have felt obliged to move here, and then he wouldn't have to make the difficult decision to leave New Zealand.

At first I feel devastated, but then I think: is that really what I wanted? For him to move here because he had to?

No, my girlish heart wants a big, romantic happy ever after, for him to say he's fallen in love with me, that he can't bear to be apart from me, and that he's choosing to move here. But I know how childish that is. I'm sixteen years old all over again, snogging the older guy in the kitchen, imagining it's love at first sight, and that he's going to propose the next day. Jeez, I'm so foolish. Insanity is doing the same thing over and over and expecting different results. I really am fucking nuts.

Conscious that I've let too much time go by, I pin a big smile on my face. "That's great news," I say with as much enthusiasm as I can muster. "I'm so pleased for you."

His frown lifts, although I can't tell if he's regretful or relieved. "Thanks," he says.

"How about you sit down and I get you a drink? You can tell me all about it—or not, if you'd rather."

"Oh I'm happy to talk."

"Whisky?"

"I'd love one, thank you. I'm just going to change." He walks into the bedroom.

I go out to the kitchen, toss some ice into two tumblers, take them through to the drinks cabinet, and slosh a decent amount of whisky over one, and some gin over the other.

Then I stand there for a minute, realization sinking into me slowly like a stone tossed into treacle. Our little affair is nearly over. It was only ever going to be a fling. I knew that, deep down, but I've still fallen for him. Oh my God, Heidi, you're such an imbecile.

I shouldn't have asked him to stay with me. Shouldn't have spent all those days in Devon with him. And I certainly shouldn't have slept with him.

But it's done, and I don't regret it, because I've had a wonderful time. I need to stop acting like a teenager and accept it for what it was—a fun diversion, after all the hassle I've had with Jason. Titus has proven there are decent guys out there, and that not every man wants to control me.

Tears prick my eyes, but I hear him coming out of the bedroom, and I blink them away, turning with a big smile.

He's changed into a faded tee and a pair of track pants. He looked amazing in his suit, but he still looks super sexy. I think I'd find him attractive if he wore a black rubbish bag.

He throws himself onto the sofa, accepts the glass I hold out, then pats the cushion beside him. "Come here," he instructs.

I lower down beside him and curl up, and he puts his arm around me. He has a big mouthful of the whisky and lets out a long sigh.

"Are you hungry?" I ask. "Would you like me to fix you something to eat?"

"Maybe a sandwich later. I had quite a big lunch."

"Okay." I kiss his shoulder. "I'm so pleased for you. Elizabeth is going to be thrilled."

"Yeah, I'm glad it's going to happen for everyone involved."

"Come on then, tell me what happened. In glorious detail."

He chuckles and begins to tell me. He goes through the day, explaining how Alan showed him around, then tells me about the board meeting, and finally his conversation with Alan at the end.

His voice grows husky as he reveals that Alan said he was proud of him, and when he comes to the bit about winning the Turing Award, he has to stop talking.

"I wouldn't," he says fiercely. "He was just being kind."

I know Alan wouldn't have said that unless he believed it—Titus is being unassuming, as usual. But as remarkable as it is, Alan's mention of the award isn't what's touched him. This is about the fact that some guy he barely knows is prouder of him than his father has ever been.

I put my arms around his neck and hug him, and he hugs me back, his arms so tight they almost crush me.

"He said he'd want me on his senior leadership team," he whispers. "He's allocated an office near his for me." He releases his arms and slides down on the sofa a little, looking up at the ceiling. "I thought he was just flattering me, trying to get me to stay, but he said he'd decided from the beginning that he'd invest. He said he should have made it clearer that he only wanted me to move here because he wants to work with me, and for me to liaise with his scientists and engineers."

"He believes in the work."

He nods. "I can't tell you what that means to me."

"I can see that, honey." I cup his cheek and turn his head so he's facing me. Brushing a thumb across his lips, I murmur, "It's only what you deserve. You've worked so hard."

He looks into my eyes. "I've thought about you all day. I kept touching my tie pin every time I needed courage."

"There, see? I told you it would bring you luck."

He sighs. Then, holding me, he falls back so he's lying on his side on the sofa, his arms around me. I shift until I'm facing him, and we wriggle until we get comfortable.

"Do you need to call Elizabeth and Mack and Saxon?" I murmur.

"It's too early there. I'll do it later."

"Okay." I don't need persuading to lie there and cuddle up to him.

I rest my cheek on his shoulder. I'm wearing a mini skirt, and my left leg is hooked over him. With a finger, I trace a heart on his T-shirt. He brushes his hand down my back.

"I talked to Alan about you," he murmurs.

My hand stops, while my heart skips a beat. "Oh?"

"He knew we weren't an item when we came here. He and Vicky—and Elizabeth—set us up."

My jaw drops. "Are you angry about that?" I ask after a few moments.

He chuckles. "No. I think it would have happened anyway." He slips his fingers beneath my tee and touches my bare skin. "He said it's always better to regret something you've done than something you haven't."

I lie still, and try to stay calm. "I suppose that's true."

"You know I'm crazy about you, don't you?" he says.

My lips slowly curve up. "I'm crazy about you, too."

We lie there quietly for a while as thoughts whirl around me like pieces of paper tossed into the air. Then, eventually, I lift my head.

I rest my chin on his shoulder and study his profile. His arms have loosened around me, and his breathing is deep and regular. He's asleep, exhausted from all the nerves and emotion.

It's always better to regret something you've done than something you haven't.

Maybe our fling isn't as over as I thought it was.

Thank you, Alan, I say in my head, and then I rest my cheek back on his shoulder and close my eyes.

*

I doze for a while—I don't know how long, but it's still light when I open my eyes. The sunshine has deepened to the color of honey. I lift my head to look at him, and catch my breath. His eyes are open, and he's watching me.

He doesn't say anything, and I lower my chin to his shoulder again and just study him.

He lifts a hand and cups my face, then brushes across my bottom lip with his thumb. I open my mouth and catch it in my teeth, close my lips around it, and suck.

His lips curve up, and his eyelids lower a fraction, his eyes taking on a sultry gleam.

"You're so fucking sexy," he murmurs, his voice like cream, smooth and rich.

My pulse speeding up, I wash my tongue over the pad of his thumb and suck again, and he shifts his hips, giving me a wry look as I spot his erection and inhale. Carefully, he extracts his thumb from my mouth, and then he places both hands on my waist and lifts me on top of him, so our faces are level.

Then he cradles my head with a hand, and brings my lips down to his.

He kisses me for a long time, nipping at my bottom lip with his teeth, sliding his tongue into my mouth. I respond with thrusts of my tongue, tipping my head to the side so I can slant my lips across his and deepen the kiss, making my heart bang against my ribs and my pulse race.

My breathing quickens, and I move my hips against his, arousing myself on his erection, and making him give an approving murmur.

I push up, and he shifts onto his back so I can straddle him. There's not a lot of room, but I'm not complaining. I strip off my T-shirt, then take off my bra, and he fills his palms with my breasts and teases my nipples with his thumbs.

I groan and kiss him again, rocking my hips against his and moaning at the feel of his rock-hard erection pressing on my sensitive mound.

"That feels good," I whisper, setting up a rhythm, and he matches the movement with rocks of his own, still stroking my breasts. I sigh against his lips, feeling sleepily turned on, temporarily filled with the bliss of summer, the two of us bathed in the honey sunlight, so sweet I can almost taste it.

We kiss while he strokes my back, my hair, my face, and plays with my breasts, but eventually a sense of urgency rises within me, and I push up and fumble at his track pants. He helps me out, releasing his erection from his boxers, and I pull my underwear aside and hitch up my mini skirt. Guiding him beneath me until the tip parts my folds, I sink down onto him.

We both exhale with an, "Aaahhh…" as he slides deep inside me.

"Fuck," he says with feeling.

"That feel good, baby?" I rock my hips, driving him in and out of me.

"It feels amazing." He cups my breasts and rubs his thumbs over my nipples. "You look so beautiful."

I glance down at myself, seeing our bodies coated in the late sunshine, and push up his T-shirt, enjoying the sight of his glowing abs and pecs. Then I stroke my hands down his arms, admiring the sight of his tattoos painted in gold.

"You're like an Adonis," I whisper, thinking how gorgeous he is. "I'm so lucky."

His brow flickers with a frown, as if he's puzzled at my words, but he doesn't say anything, blinking slowly as desire spirals up inside him.

"Mmm…" I tip back my head, arching my spine so I can push my breasts into his hands, starting to lose control.

"Jesus," he mutters, and then he rears up, slides a tight arm around my waist, and somehow manages to turn on the sofa so I'm pinned beneath him. Our clothing twists and wraps around us, my arm's caught under him, and he's leaning on my hair, but he immediately starts to thrust, and at that moment I don't care about anything except the feel of him sliding inside me.

I suck my bottom lip, torn between closing my eyes so I can concentrate on the pleasure flooding me, or keeping them open so I can watch him. I choose to watch him for a while, and slide my hands up under his T-shirt so I can dig my nails in his back.

Growling, he lifts up, tears off the top, and tosses it onto the floor, and then I get the full glory of the sight of his muscles painted with copper sunlight. I scrape my nails lightly down his arms, and he shudders. Pushing up my knees and wrapping my legs around his waist, he changes the angle of his thrusts so he's grinding against me, and instantly I feel the first flutters of an orgasm deep inside.

"Ahhh… I'm going to come," I whisper.

"Yes," he says in triumph, "come for me," and so I close my eyes and my lips part as the exquisite feeling sweeps over me. Everything clenches deep in my belly, like a drawstring being pulled tight, and it's slow and beautiful, making me cry out loud before the six or seven hard pulses take my breath away.

"Ah God," he says, "ah, Heidi, you feel so fucking good," and with another half a dozen thrusts he comes too, shuddering with the force of his climax. I dig my nails in his back and tighten my internal muscles as tight as I can, clamping around him. In response he lets loose a string of swear words, some of which I'm sure I haven't heard before, as he releases inside me.

I lift my hands and sink them into his hair, and pull him down for a fierce kiss. He's such a fantastic blend of passionate and gentle. He's so perfect for me.

First I kiss his cheeks, his nose, and then his mouth, long and soft. My heart is light as a feather, filled with hope after his earlier declaration that he's crazy about me. I don't know what's going to happen, but I'm excited to think it might not be over, and there might be a future for us to explore.

Chapter Twenty-Two

Titus

After a snooze and an earth-shattering orgasm, I discover that I'm ravenous, despite my large lunch. Heidi offers to cook something, but Alan has urged me to make use of their chef, so I call the house and ask whether he'd be prepared to make us something. "Anything, sir," is the answer, so I ask him for something Chinese and spicy. After a while, there's a knock at the door, and a young guy delivers a bag full of containers. We take them into the kitchen and unpack them with whistles and cheers when we discover kung pao chicken, twice-cooked pork, king prawns in ginger and garlic, and a superb crispy chili beef, along with fried rice and homemade vegetable spring rolls.

Heidi and I pour ourselves another drink, serve up the food, take it out onto the terrace, and sit at the outdoor dining table to eat. It's a beautiful evening, warm and sunny, and we work our way through the dishes while we talk about the day. She asks lots of questions about the board meeting and what Alan said, and I tell her a bit more about Stork and what Alan's hoping to achieve at Acheron.

When we can't eat any more, we sit until it starts getting dark, and then pick up our plates and take them inside. After we've washed up, I collect my laptop and make myself comfortable in the armchair, and call Elizabeth, then Mack, then Saxon on Zoom while Heidi goes off to have a bath.

I keep the calls short, and Heidi's still in the bath when I finish. I stand in the doorway, listening to her singing, and smiling at the sight of her immersed in all the bubbles.

She sees me and her face lights up. "Hey! All done?"

"Yep." I walk in and sit on the chair beside the bath.

"I'm guessing Elizabeth was pleased?"

"They all were, and relieved."

"I'm so glad." She looks genuinely thrilled for me, which brings a lump to my throat. I saw the look on her face when I walked in and told her that Alan's investment was unconditional. I'm sure she'd been hoping that my moving here would be a condition. Instead, I don't have to make that difficult decision between taking the money and leaving my home country and my business behind.

"I was just about to get out," she says. "Hand me that towel?"

I hold it out for her as she rises, wrap it around her, and then pull her into my arms. Her skin is warm and glistening, and her hair is damp at her temples when I nuzzle there.

She leans her cheek on my shoulder, and we stand there like that for a moment. Then I kiss the top of her head. "Fancy a movie?"

"Sure, why not?"

So we watch a movie, then go to bed. Despite my snooze, I'm tired out from the day, but it doesn't stop me lying awake for ages after we've turned out the lights and snuggled up together. From her breathing, I'm pretty sure she's awake, too. But we lie there in the darkness, lost in our thoughts, as the full moon rises slowly in the night sky.

*

The next day, Alan and Vicky come to see us just after eight a.m. to say goodbye.

Heidi hugs them both and I hug Vicky, and then I go to shake Alan's hand, and he laughs and pulls me into a bearhug.

"So great to meet you," he says. "Call me when you land, okay?"

"Will do." I go to pull away, but he hangs onto me for a few seconds longer before he finally releases me. To my surprise he actually looks a little choked up at having to say goodbye, and that makes my throat tighten.

We've already put our bags in the car, and we lock up the cottage and give them the keys, then wave goodbye, get in the Range Rover, and head out of Hawkerland Manor toward Exeter.

I glance at the country house in the rearview mirror as I drive, feeling a pang of wistfulness at the thought that I might not see it or Alan again.

"You okay?" Heidi says softly.

I clear my throat. "Yeah. Sad to go, in a way."

"I know what you mean." She sighs. "All systems go for New Zealand now, right?"

"Yep. What time do you want to leave tomorrow?"

"Shall we leave at midday?"

"Sounds great."

I hold out a hand, and she slips hers into it.

We don't say much more on the journey back.

*

The rest of the day passes quickly. Heidi goes out to visit her grandparents, then spends the rest of the day sorting out her clothes, washing, and packing. I do some laundry, pack my case, and then work quietly, catching up on emails and then reading Saxon's new report on progress with Stork at Wellington Hospital, making some notes.

In the evening, Heidi makes us a pizza, and we sit on the sofa and eat it while we watch another movie. When we finally go to bed, she leads me into her room without asking, the quirky little room with its blackened oak beams, the coffin hatch in the floor, and the tiny window overlooking the street, and she strips off her short T-shirt dress, puts her arms around me, and presses her soft body against mine as she lifts up to kiss me.

We make love slowly, and as I kiss her and slide inside her, looking down at her flushed cheeks and eyes filled with emotion, I can't help but wonder why I'm doing this to myself. I should have stopped this as soon as I knew she liked me, and I realized I felt the same way. Instead, I told her I'm crazy about her, even admitted that I love her after she declared the same in a text. And I still don't know how it can possibly work out.

All I do know is that I can't walk away from her. And as I come inside her, wrapped in her velvet warmth, I know I'm in big trouble.

*

The next day, we finish off our packing, then head out around midday. Heidi locks up her cottage, and we pack up the car and head east, taking the long A303 road. She's quiet, which doesn't surprise me as I know she's nervous about seeing her father again. I don't force her to talk, but put some music on instead. As I suspected, it's impossible for her not to sing along to the songs she knows, and I soon have her smiling and laughing as we sing together.

It's with some surprise that, halfway through our journey, I suddenly see a very familiar site on the horizon in front of us.

"Stonehenge?" My jaw drops.

She smiles. "I wondered if you realized we'd be passing."

"I didn't. Holy shit." Unfortunately we haven't left ourselves enough time to look around, but I slow as we pass, captivated by the sight of the magnificent stones in their horseshoe shape, stark against the countryside to our left.

"And look at all the Bronze-Age barrows," Heidi says, pointing to the mounds visible on the skyline. "It's such a beautiful, ancient landscape."

Her face is filled with wonder, and I find myself staring at her rather than the view before I finally tear my gaze back to the road.

The conversation we need to have is looming, and I know what I need to say, but she's not making it easy.

*

The next few hours, as always, are long and drawn out, as we hand over the car, find our way to the right terminal, check in and get rid of our cases, then make our way with our carry-on luggage to the flight lounge. We buy a sandwich and a coffee, head to the gate, hang around until it's time to board, and then eventually the call comes through for first-class passengers to make their way on.

I've been looking forward to this bit, and sure enough, Heidi's face is a picture as we're shown to our first-class double suite. Consisting of two suites with the central partition lowered, the two single beds on either side of the partition have been converted into a double. The crisp white sheets have been sprinkled with red rose petals, and there's a tray bearing a bottle of champagne in a cooler and a selection of handmade chocolates I know she'll love. Either side of the bed is a cream leather recliner with a table for eating or working, and both face large-screen TVs. Each side also has a small private bathroom with a shower.

"Oh. My. God," she says once the flight attendant has left the room. "Titus!"

I laugh. "What?"

"Do you travel like this all the time?"

"In a single suite, yes, when I can." I grab her and nuzzle her neck. "You can thank me later."

"There will definitely be some thanking going on, believe me."

I chuckle. "It'll be good to finally join the Mile High Club. I think we get badges."

"Really?"

"No, Heidi." I kiss her, and she pouts.

Then she says, "So you haven't joined it before?"

"Nope. First time traveling with a girlfriend."

She doesn't reply, and I catch myself and say, "Ah, well, you know what I mean."

"Mm," she says, then turns away to investigate the free toiletries in the bathroom.

I purse my lips before making my way over to my seat. Auckland is eleven hours ahead of London because of British Summer Time, so even though it's only Wednesday night, and we'll be landing on the fourth of August—Friday—at 8:35 a.m., we actually have just over twenty-four hours together. My stomach flutters. I'm both excited and nervous at the thought of talking to her about it.

She buckles herself into her seat, and we talk about the jet lag, deciding it makes sense to try to stay awake as much as possible on the first leg, then sleep on the second after we change planes, so that when we land we'll be waking up ready for the day ahead. Easy to say, not so easy to do, especially on such a long journey. But it's a lot easier in the comfort of first class.

After only an hour in the air, we're served dinner, a sumptuous three-course meal. First we have antipasti of wagyu *bresaola* and roasted chicken with herbs, served with parmesan and marinated vegetables; then Heidi chooses Chicken Bzar in a traditional Arabic spice marinade served on aromatic rice with friend onions and pistachios, while I opt for the pan-fried beef tenderloin served with steamed snow peas, carrots, and new potatoes with herbs. Moving to sit on the bed together for dessert, we both finish with the chocolate mango tart, rolling our eyes at the taste of the layered chocolate and mango mousse topped with dark chocolate ganache and served with mango jellies.

The flight attendant tops our glasses up regularly with champagne, removes our dishes, then dims the lights and leaves us, insisting we call if there's anything we need. Stuffed to the brim, Heidi and I cuddle up and finish the bottle of champagne while we watch a couple of in-flight movies.

By this time, it's about three a.m. London time, and we're finding it increasingly difficult to keep our eyes open. Eventually we give in, get into bed, and cuddle up, and we catch about three or four hours' sleep before it's time to get up and start preparing for landing.

Less than two hours later, we're in the air again, heading toward Auckland.

It's now around ten a.m. London time, but the plane is running on Auckland time, which is around nine p.m. Neither of us feels like another dinner, so we opt for a bowl of chunky fries and a coffee, watch another movie, then head to bed again.

"I'm so disorientated," Heidi says as we snuggle down beneath the covers.

"I know what you mean. We'll get some sleep soon, and then we'll feel more normal when we wake up and it's morning in Auckland."

"Soon?" she queries. "You have something else planned then? Want to watch another movie?" Her eyes sparkle in the low light.

"Nope." I pull her toward me and roll onto my back, bringing her with me, and she laughs.

"Are you sure about this?" she whispers.

"I've locked the door. We won't be interrupted." I'm already hard for her, and I move her hips so she can feel how much I want her.

Her eyes widen. "You don't hang around."

"I want you, Heidi Rose. Right here, right now."

Her lips part, and then she sighs as I bring her head down to kiss her, plunging my tongue into her mouth. She's wearing a T-shirt and underwear, but I divest her of them quickly, and my clothing joins hers on the floor in seconds. Now we're both naked, and hunger for her sweeps through me, as I smooth my hands down her back and clutch the muscles of her bottom, holding them so I can rock her against the root of my erection.

I don't know what it is—the thrum of the engines, maybe, the excitement of doing this on a plane, or the fact that our emotions are running high at the moment—but passion sweeps through me with the heat of a thousand suns. I roll her beneath me, kiss down her body, and suck her nipples hungrily, and when I slip my hand down between her legs I find her already wet and swollen, more than ready for me. Still, I take a while to arouse her, but it doesn't take long before she's begging me to slide inside her, and I don't need any further encouragement.

She gives a long moan as I enter her, and I give a short laugh and kiss her, murmuring, "Shhh!"

"Sorry. I can't help it." She bites her bottom lip as I begin to thrust, wrapping her legs around me and tilting up her hips.

"This is going to be hard and fast," I say, my voice husky with lust, "so hold on."

She gives me a helpless look and nods, and I lift up and start moving, giving in to my body's urge to take both of us to the edge. She moans and closes her eyes, moving with me, and it takes less than thirty seconds before she sucks her bottom lip and her brow furrows with a frown.

I thrust harder, plunging down into her and making sure I grind against her clit, and she inhales and holds her breath, then lets out a long, fierce series of moans as she comes. I kiss her to cover them, then, when it doesn't work, cover her mouth with a hand, trying not to laugh while she shudders and clenches around me. When she's done, I finally lift my hand, and she opens her eyes and gives me an apologetic look as she whispers, "Sorry, was I being noisy?"

"Loud enough to wake the dead." I chuckle and kiss her again, continuing to thrust, feeling the first tremors of my climax approaching. "Ahhh... Heidi..." I plunge deep into her, and she's warm and soft and wet, and it's only seconds before it's too much for me, and I come hard.

Her hand covers my mouth, and I realize I must be making too much noise as well, but I can't control it. My breath warms her fingers as I gasp and groan, and it's only when my body releases me from its tight grip and I sink down on top of her that she takes her hand away.

"Naughty boy," she says, and she kisses my jaw and nips my earlobe.

"Ow."

She giggles, then wraps her arms around me. "Now we're official members."

"Mm." I take my time to kiss her, enjoying her soft mouth, and then eventually withdraw and shift to the side so I'm not squishing her. I pull her into my arms, and we cuddle up together.

We lie there quietly for a while, listening to the thrum of the engines, and I think about us flying high above the clouds, circling the Earth through the darkness to greet the sunrise on the other side.

I kiss the top of Heidi's head, and she trails a finger down my chest, playing with the hairs there.

"I think it's time," I say.

She draws a heart. "I know." She pushes herself up. "I could do with a drink."

"Let's ring for the attendant."

"Hold on." She pulls on her T-shirt and underwear, and I do the same, then unlock the door. We sit up in bed, and then we press the buzzer. Twenty seconds later, there's a knock at the door, and the attendant appears. We order a couple of drinks—an Islay malt for me, G&T for her. The attendant brings our drinks, then withdraws and leaves us to it.

We sip from our glasses. I inhale, then blow out the breath slowly.

"I didn't expect to fall in love with you," I begin.

She looks up at me with her big blue eyes, and then her lips curve up in a beautiful smile. "That'll teach you to touch the standing stone," she says, and I chuckle. "I'm in love with you, too," she whispers.

"I don't know how much to trust what I'm feeling," I admit. "We've only been together... what? Seven, eight days? I know most people would say it just feels more intense because it's a holiday fling."

"That could be true."

"So maybe it would be wrong to make major decisions about our lives based on a crush."

"Good point."

I sigh. "I know you love England, and you've made a life there. I know you don't want to move back to New Zealand. And you know that my life is there—my friends and family, my business."

She gives a small nod.

"I don't want to ask you to move," I tell her. "Why should you give up your perfect life for me? It's not fair to demand that of you when there's no guarantee it would work between us. But I suppose we have to face the truth that one of us is going to have to make that sacrifice if we want to try to make it work."

"I know," she whispers.

I take her hand in mine and brush my thumb over her knuckles. "I'll be honest with you, Heidi. I don't know if I can make that sacrifice. I feel like a heel for saying it. I'm not saying that my job is more important than yours, or that I don't have feelings for you, because I do, or we wouldn't even need to discuss it. But I'm on the verge of this big breakthrough, and I need to be near my team, and near Mack's supercomputer, and to be able to meet Saxon and visit Wellington, and I can't do all that from the other side of the world."

"I understand," she says, and I can see her trying to be brave, even though I'm sure her heart is breaking.

I squeeze her hand. "I suppose what I'm saying is… is moving back something you'll consider? Will you think about it? Or do we both need to accept right now that it's just not going to happen? In which case, does it make sense to prolong our parting by seeing each other in New Zealand? Or is it just going to make it more painful?"

Chapter Twenty-Three

Heidi

My heart sinks.

I knew this was coming. How could I not? Despite his polite assertion that his job isn't more important than mine, it is, in the big scheme of things. He's running a company developing research that could change hundreds of thousands, if not millions, of lives. I might love my job, but I teach children. Technically, I can do that anywhere.

Deep down, I feel a stab of resentment, but it's small, and it's short-lived. He's not being selfish, or belittling my career and my problems. His brows have drawn together, and I know it wasn't easy for him to say all that. He doesn't want to ask me to move for him. He's just stating the obvious—if I don't move back to New Zealand, our relationship—or our fling, our affair, however I want to define it—is over.

I feel a rush of emotion, and swallow hard, dropping my gaze to where he's holding my hand. He sighs, leans over to the small table at the side to put his glass down, then comes back to pull me into his arms. "Come here," he murmurs, and he hugs me tightly, while I bury my face in his neck.

"I can't believe I've just found you," he says, "and I feel close to losing you. I don't know what to do about it."

I hug his strong body, feeling his sorrow in my bones. I keep trying to tell myself that it's only been a week, and it can't mean anything. I hate stories and movies about instalove, and I've always mocked them when I've seen them. But I can't deny how I feel right now.

The intensity of our passion will fade once we're apart. I don't need to be told that. But I can't vouch for regret. I have a sneaky suspicion it will consume me once I let him go.

"I don't want to lose you," I whisper.

"I don't want to lose you, either."

"It's not enough time to make a decision like this."

"I know."

"But walking away from you is going to kill me."

"Ah, Heidi. Me too."

There are plenty more fish in the Pacific. Lots of other men who will treat me well, who are sexy, and gentle, and clever. Who'll make love to me passionately, while holding me as if I'm something precious. Who'll make me feel loved, and wanted. Aren't there?

Or is Titus the one man in the world I'm meant for? My soul mate? Is there such a thing? What if there is, and I'm about to walk away from him?

I rest my forehead on his shoulder. "I wish we had longer together. It would be wonderful if we had months to get to know each other so we could decide how serious this is. But we don't have months."

"No, we don't. I suppose that all we do need to know, right now, is if we want to be with one another. If we want to try to make it work."

We sit quietly for a moment.

"Do you?" I ask in a small voice. My heart races as it occurs to me that he might be trying to pluck up the courage to tell me it's over.

He looks into my eyes for a long while, long enough that I think I might go into cardiac arrest if he doesn't say something soon.

Then he blinks, and the corner of his mouth quirks up. "All I can think is that the thought of letting you go makes me feel as if someone has reached into my chest and is pulling my heart out with their fingernails."

"Me too," I squeak, overwhelmed at the thought that he doesn't want to let me go.

He nods. Then he pushes himself up on the pillows. I sit up with him, sensing a change in his mood. A determination that wasn't there before, now we've admitted to each other that we don't want it to end.

"Okay," he says firmly. "We don't have months. But you are in New Zealand for three weeks. You're supposed to be staying with Chrissie, aren't you?"

"Yes. She has a spare room in her apartment."

He reaches over for his drink again and has a mouthful of whisky. "Would you rather come and stay with me?"

My eyes widen. "Really?"

"Yeah. I mean, I'll be working, but you can go and visit your friends and family during the day, and then we could meet up in the evening…"

Joy fills me at the thought that we don't have to say goodbye. Yet, anyway.

It's not an answer to our conundrum. But I do understand that he's saying he doesn't want to let me go, and he's going to do everything he can to try to keep me.

*

We don't talk much more about it. It's late, and so we finish off our drinks and then settle down to try to get as much sleep as we can before we land.

But we stay as close together as it's possible to get, wrapped around each other, and I think he's as overjoyed as I am at the thought that, if nothing else, we want to be together.

A few hours later, we finally rouse and decide it's time to start preparing for landing. I take a shower—a shower! On a plane! Soon after, the flight attendant brings us breakfast. Titus has scrambled eggs with chives on sourdough toast and veal sausages, while I have French toast with poached peaches and vanilla mascarpone, and we both have several cups of steaming hot coffee.

Finally, the pilot announces it's time to get ready for landing, and we take our seats and buckle ourselves in. I look out of the window as the plane approaches Auckland. I'm coming home. New Zealand will always be the place I was born, and super special to me. But I'm surprised not to feel more excited. I don't feel emotional. I can feel Titus's gaze on me, as if he's half-expecting me to be tearful, but I keep my gaze on the window, watching the approach of the city in the early-morning sunlight, and have to admit that my heart is still in England.

Once we've landed, we're let off the plane first. I say a silent goodbye to our private suite, sad to see it go, and walk with Titus through the airport. We both have Kiwi passports, so it's a relatively quick process through passport control. We wait for our cases, go through customs, and then we walk out into the arrivals lounge.

I come through first, and I'm not expecting to see anyone I know, so it's a real surprise to see Mack standing up and waving.

I turn as Titus comes through and goes to take my hand, moving mine out of the way. He raises an eyebrow, and I murmur, "Mack's here."

"Oh." He glances at me, but doesn't say anything.

We exit the gate and go up to him. I've known him longer than Titus—since Huxley first brought him home when they were about thirteen. He was gorgeous then—a sprinter, long and lean—and he's still gorgeous now, a rich, powerful, smart guy, who nevertheless always acts like he's my uncle.

"Hey, you!" He throws his arms around me, and I give him a big hug. "Good to see you again, sweetheart," he says. Then, over my shoulder he says, "Hey man, didn't know you were arriving today."

"Yeah, we got seats together as we were on the same plane," Titus says easily, obviously picking up that I don't want Mack to know about us, not yet.

"What are you doing here?" I say to Mack. "Not that it isn't great to see you."

"Huxley wanted someone to meet you, and Elizabeth has a scan this morning that he didn't want to miss, so he asked me to pick you up."

"Oh, is she okay?"

"Yeah, yeah. All routine stuff. She's healthy as, and the baby's fine." He looks at Titus. "Want me to drop you off as well?"

"No, it's okay, I'll catch a cab. I'm going home first, then heading off to the office." Titus looks at me and hesitates. I meet his eyes, and we exchange a small smile. "Catch up with you later?" he says.

"Yeah, okay."

"See you later," he says to Mack, and heads toward the exit.

I watch him go, then look back at Mack. He's studying me, interested. Ah shit.

"Have you got a minute?" I ask. "Can I get a coffee?"

"Yeah. Come on, I'll get us both one."

We go up to the small coffee van and he orders two lattes. Then we stand to one side as we wait for them to be made.

Mack doesn't say anything, but his eyes are alight with humor.

"What?" I say irritably.

"How long has that been going on?" he asks.

"How long has what been going on?"

He just tips his head to one side.

I scowl. "Mind your own business."

"Does Huxley know?"

"Yes, Mack, the first thing I did when I wanted to fuck my brother's best mate was ask his permission."

He raises an eyebrow.

"You're only four years older than me," I snap, "so stop treating me like I'm fourteen."

"I'm just concerned, that's all. He's a softie. If you two get involved, he won't find it easy when you leave."

My jaw drops. "You're worried about *Titus* getting hurt? Jesus."

"You girls have a habit of turning us guys into mush."

I drop my gaze to my feet. "It doesn't always happen that way," I mumble.

He sighs then, and he pulls me into his arms. "Ah, yeah, I forgot about your ex. Shit. I'm sorry."

I drop my forehead on his shoulder. "Don't berate me. I didn't mean for it to happen, and neither did he." I turn my head and rest my cheek on his chest. "He was so good to me. He drove across the country to make sure I was all right when Jason turned up on my doorstep. He's just the best guy I've ever met. He's smart and funny and kind and sexy. And he lives on the other side of the fucking world, and I don't know what I'm going to do."

Suddenly my face is wet, and all the emotion that I've been keeping a lid on threatens to bubble over.

"Hey, it's okay." He tightens his arms. "I'm sorry, I thought it was just a fling."

"It is. But I really like him, Mack."

"Does he feel the same way?"

I nod without looking up. "I'm going to stay with him while I'm here."

"Aw, and he's had to catch a cab. You should have told me."

I wipe my face and move back as the barista calls Mack's name. "You caught us by surprise."

He fetches our coffees, and then we sit on a couple of seats by the van. I have a sip of mine, letting out a shaky breath as the hot liquid warms me through.

He mirrors my pose, leaning forward, elbows on his knees, holding his cup, and bumps his shoulder against mine. "If it's meant to be, it'll work out. He's very resourceful."

"I know. But either I have to move here or he has to move there. It's pretty simple." I bite my lip.

Mack has a swig of coffee. "Let me tell you a little story about Lawrence Oates. When he was seventeen, he went camping with some of his cousins in Kahurangi National Park. They planned to follow the river and camp for a few days, but fog set in, and they got disoriented. They walked further than they realized, and they lost their bearings. Saxon slipped down a steep gully, sprained his ankle, banged his head, and got a concussion. He was pretty groggy, and Titus was really worried about him. It started raining heavily, and the temperatures were minus eight at night. But Titus stayed level-headed, and got them to make camp in a clearing by some fresh water. When their food ran out after five days, he found cabbage tree shoots, supplejacks, and mushrooms to eat for another two days. He lit a fire to keep them warm, and told them stories and jokes to keep their morale up. A rescue helicopter spotted the smoke from the fire and winched them to safety."

My jaw has dropped. "Shit, really? I didn't know."

"Titus just laughs it off, but I think he probably saved their lives. People have died out there in the bush. What I'm trying to say is that when this guy wants something bad enough, he tends to find a way. So have a little faith and let him work it out. He'll get there."

I wipe under my eyes and blow out a long breath. "I'll try."

He bumps my shoulder again. "Come on. I'll take you to his place."

We rise, and he shoulders my flight bag and insists on pulling my case for me as we walk out of the airport and cross to the car park. He presses the button on his key fob to a gorgeous Aston Martin, and hefts the case and bag in the boot.

"No Jamie today?" I ask as I get in the passenger side, referring to his brother, who's also his driver.

He gets behind the wheel and buckles in. "No, would you believe his wife is also at the hospital seeing her midwife today?"

"Oh, I didn't know she was pregnant. When is she due?"

He starts the engine, and the car purrs into life. He heads off toward the state highway. "At the end of August. He's very excited. They got married earlier in the year. They only wanted a quiet wedding in the local registry office. He's so happy with Emma."

"That's nice. And I hear you're a happily married man now, too."

He grins. "Yep."

"Who'd have thought it? I didn't think any girl would ever be able to lure you away from Marise."

"Oh, I still love her dearly. But Sidnie has better legs."

I chuckle. I ask him about what he's working on at KoruTech, and he chats away about the new microprocessor he's developing while I look out of the window, watching the busy suburbs of Auckland fly by. It suddenly occurs to me that I don't know where Titus lives—he never got around to giving me his address. Mack is heading toward the CBD, and he passes the Sky Tower, then pulls up in Albert Street, at the base of a brand-new tower block. At the bottom, the sign declares it's the location of The City of Sails Hotel.

"Oh," I say, surprised. "He lives in a hotel?"

"It's mixed-use development. There are twenty-four luxury apartments on the top eleven levels. They have access to the hotel's services and amenities—the restaurant, gym, that sort of thing."

"I keep forgetting he's *rich as*."

He chuckles. "Nice having a wealthy boyfriend, is it?"

"He's not my boyfriend," I say, embarrassed at the term.

"Sorry," he says sarcastically, "I didn't think he'd appreciate the term fuck-buddy."

"Mack!"

"You started it." He gets out of the car. Mumbling, I follow him.

He hefts my case out of the boot. "You want me to bring it up?"

"A world of no. But thank you for the lift." I reach up and kiss his cheek. "That was very sweet of you. I know how busy you are."

"Always time for my favorite niece." He smirks as I roll my eyes. "I'm guessing you're coming to Huxley's 'welcome-back-Heidi' party at the club tonight?"

"Do I have to?" I grin at his wry smile. "I'll see you there."

I wave goodbye, and he gets back in his car and drives off.

I sit on a bench on the roadside for a moment, needing to catch my breath. Ooh, it's cold today. I forgot it was midwinter here, and I'm not wearing a jacket. At least it's not raining, but the sky is the color of dishwater, promising it'll be wet later.

I was only half joking when I asked Mack if I had to go to the party this evening. Oliver wanted to celebrate my return, and I didn't have the heart to say it's the last thing I wanted. I know my parents are going to be there because Mum mentioned it the last time I spoke to her. I really don't want to go. But I don't want to let Oliver down.

I blow out a shaky breath. I can get through this.

First I text Titus. *It's me. I told Mack. He was fine about it. So is it okay if I still come to yours?*

A message pings up in seconds: *Of course! Where are you?*

Me: *Downstairs.*

Him: *Floor forty-one. Number two. See you soon!* He finishes with a heart emoticon.

I smile. *I'll be up in five.*

Next, I ring Chrissie. "Hey!" I say when she answers, "it's me!"

"Heidi! Are you in Auckland?"

"I am, I landed about half an hour ago. Look, sweetie, I hope it's okay, but I'm going to be staying somewhere else." I'm convinced she won't mind. She shares the flat with her boyfriend, and I'm sure she'd rather be alone with him.

"Aw, that's a shame! But of course, no worries. Where are you going? Not home?"

"No. Um… I'm going to be staying with Titus."

"Oh…" She laughs. "Is that so?"

"Yeah. We got on really well, and… you know…"

"You don't have to explain to me, darling. Go and have fun. I'll see you at Huxley's tonight."

"Thanks for understanding."

"Hey, your sex life always has to come first."

"Damn straight. Catcha later." I grin and end the call.

Lastly, I call Mum. Knowing Dad will be at work, I call the landline. It rings a couple of times, and then someone answers.

"Hello?"

Fuck. It's my father.

I freeze. For a few seconds, I have to fight with myself not to just end the call as an icy finger trails down my spine.

But I'm not the girl I was before I left for England. He's still my father. I'm sure I can have a conversation and not crumble into dust.

Taking a deep breath, I say, "Dad? It's Heidi."

He's silent for a moment. Then he says, "You're in Auckland?"

"I am. Landed about half an hour ago. I was hoping to reach Mum."

"And you got me instead. Sorry about that."

I can't tell if he's being sarcastic or if he's smiling. Probably sarcastic, knowing him.

I decide to ignore the jibe. "How are you?" I murmur.

"I'm well, thank you. And you?"

"Yes, fine, thanks." Polite as strangers.

He's quiet again. I screw up my nose, trying to think of what to say.

"Where are you staying?" he asks.

"With a friend."

"Anyone I know?"

Resentment swells inside me, destroying any intention I had of trying to remain civil.

I could lie, I guess. But then I think, why should I? "It's Lawrence Oates," I say, my tone clipped.

"Titus?" He gives a short laugh. "Of course. Julian said his son had blown off the principal of King's College for you." He's talking about Titus's father. Shit—I'd forgotten that they know one another. "He wasn't too happy about it," he continues. "I'm surprised at you, Heidi. Titus isn't a schoolboy anymore. He's a Chairman and CEO. You can't just cry and ask him to come running to help you."

I blush scarlet. "I didn't! My ex showed up while we were talking, and he was drunk, and Titus was worried about me."

"Yes, I heard about the issues you were having. If you'd called the police when Evie said, you wouldn't have needed rescuing, would you?"

I stand up. "Please tell Mum I called and that I've landed okay. I'll ring her on her mobile next time."

"Heidi—"

I end the call.

Grabbing the handle of my case, I go into the hotel foyer. I'm too angry to take much notice of the place, but I'm aware of metal-framed, reeded-glass partitions and high ceilings with bright lighting that make me think of Exeter cathedral before I find the elevator.

I travel up to floor forty-one. I'm shaking now, trying to hold in my emotion, as the numbers gradually climb.

When I get to the floor, I go out and look up and down the corridor. There are only two doors—one to the left, and the other to the right. I go right to number two. Then I pause.

Leaving my case and flight bag outside the door, I walk down the corridor to the end. Out of the window, I can see straight across to the Sky Tower.

I can't go into Titus's apartment like this. I'm so angry, mainly because Dad's words hit right to the center of my fears. He was right.

Titus isn't a schoolboy anymore. Just look at this fucking apartment block. He's a billionaire CEO; why on earth would he be interested in me? I'm sure he only asked me to stay here out of pity. He's probably already regretting the offer. Maybe I should go back down to the lobby and get myself a drink while I think about this.

"Heidi?"

I spin around. Titus is standing there, his hands in the pockets of his jeans, watching me.

"You okay?" he asks.

"Not really." I glare at him. He looks so fucking gorgeous. I want this man more than life itself.

Without warning, emotion explodes inside me, and I burst into tears.

Chapter Twenty-Four

Titus

Grabbing the handle of Heidi's case, I hold my other hand out to her. "Come inside."

Pressing her fingers to her lips, she moves forward a few steps, then stops and says something. Her voice comes out as a squeak.

"I think only dogs could hear that," I reply and, palm uppermost, flick my fingers up. "Please come inside."

She picks up her flight bag, puts her hand in mine, and I lead her into the apartment.

Once she's inside, she drops her flight bag, and I leave her case next to it. "Come and sit down," I instruct, leading her through to the living room.

Wiping both her cheeks, she stops in the middle and looks around, eyes wide. "Holy shit. Look at this place."

I glance around, seeing it through her eyes. Floor-to-ceiling glazing means the apartment has a spectacular sweeping view across the city, and is full of daylight. The living area has a plush gray carpet with a cream suite, while gray and cinnamon-colored cushions bring a touch of color. Chevron timber flooring, porcelain tiles, and lots of gray marble in the kitchen give it a striking design with clean lines. The dining table, where I also work, has cinnamon-colored chairs, and a beautiful view of the harbor.

"It's nice," I concede.

She gives a short laugh. "Yeah, Titus, it's very nice."

I take her hand again and lead her over to the sofa. She sinks onto the middle cushion, and I sit next to her. Her spine is stiff. Resentment and anger oozes out of her.

"What happened?" I ask. "Did Mack say something?"

She shakes her head and puts her face in her hands. "I called Mum, and Dad answered."

"Oh…" I watch her as she fights for control. "Do you want to tell me what he said?"

She bends her head, sinking her hands into her hair. Then she lifts her head, leaning her elbows on her knees and giving me a small smile. "Let's just say he has the gift of making me doubt my sanity."

I frown. I've deliberately not pushed her to talk about her father before, because I can see how much even thinking about him upsets her. But now I want to know.

"Come on," I say, "You can talk to me."

She gives me a mutinous glance. "I don't want to."

"Why?"

"Because nobody understands. Everyone thinks I'm overreacting. Even my sisters. Everyone thinks Dad is witty and charismatic. They don't see the other side of him."

"What is the other side?"

"He's a controlling bastard." The words burst out of her. "And I was always too fucking weak to stand up to him. Abigail, Evie, and Chrissie all took after him, and they were all rebellious. They managed to give as good as they got. But I took after Mum. She never argues with anyone, and she used to beg me not to argue with him or upset him. I was the baby, the good girl, who did what she was told. I hated confrontation, and he absolutely dominated me. My school years were fucking miserable."

She wipes away the tears that continue to spill out of her eyes. "It carried on when I went to university. Because he was paying for the course, Dad demanded I live at home rather than on campus. Other kids might have rebelled, slept around, gone to parties, but I was too terrified of his disapproval." She puts her face in her hands.

My heart aches for her. "Heidi…"

"It's so hard to explain," she says, lowering her hands again. "Men—and even a lot of women—don't have a clue how hard it is for others to stand up for themselves. They say things like, 'Oh I'd have just told him to fuck off and walked out.' They make it sound so easy, and they tell you you're weak. They don't get how some people are so overbearing. It's like trying to stand up in a cyclone."

"Did you ever talk to your sisters or Huxley about it?" I ask curiously.

She shrugs. "My sisters all thought I was exaggerating. They said I was being a wuss and I just needed to stand up to him. Oliver was more understanding, and he tried to help. He spoke to Dad about it once—they had a huge argument. Oliver said that Dad needed to let go a little, give me a bit more freedom. But Dad just turned on him, mocked him, told him to mind his own business. Oliver had his own problems with him."

"Yeah, I've seen them clash over the years."

"He tried to talk me into moving out, to go into halls of residence, or even to live with him. I did think about it, but I backed down in the end. I couldn't bear the weight of Dad's disapproval. It's so hard to explain."

"Heidi—I understand. My own father is like it, maybe not quite to the extent of yours, and of course I'm a guy, which makes it easier in many ways. But it's only recently that I realized how long I've been trying to get Dad's approval. It was Alan who told me I'm never going to get it. It was a revelation for me. And liberating. But the point is, I understand. So, anyway, what happened after that?"

"I'd been emailing Grandma—she was the only person I could really talk to about it. She knows what he's like, of course. She's seen the way he's treated Mum sometimes, and she hates it. I was in my last year at university, close to being qualified. I was still living at home. I told her I wanted to leave but I didn't know if I was strong enough. And she said why not come over to England for a while? I had citizenship because of Mum, so I'd be able to work. As soon as she said it, I couldn't stop thinking about it."

"What happened when you told your dad?"

She inhales, and blows the breath out slowly. "We had the argument to end all arguments. Dad began by yelling at me, saying I wasn't going, I was being ridiculous. Normally I'd have caved, but I'd booked my ticket, and I'd done a phone interview with Lucy, my headmistress, and gotten the job, so I felt that I couldn't back out. And that gave me the courage to stand up to him. I said I was going whether he liked it or not, and I was sick of him trying to control me. He had a meltdown, called me all the names under the sun, said I was ungrateful, told me I was delusional if I thought he'd let me go. I asked what he was going to do—chain me in the cellar?"

"Jesus."

"I suddenly realized he only had as much power over me as I was willing to give him. He said he'd stop my allowance, even cut me out of his will. I realized that when I was earning my own money and could support myself, I wasn't beholden to him, so I told him to do it. Like you said, it was liberating."

She sighs and leans back. All the color has drained from her face. I know it's tough for her to re-live this. "That last hour at the house was just horrible. I packed my bags, all while he was yelling at me. Mum was in their room, crying. I should have called Oliver or one of my sisters, but I just wanted to get out. I threw everything in two suitcases with him standing over me, shouting. I took them to the front door. He came with me, and he tried to pull the cases out of my hands. I opened the front door, and he stepped in my way and told me to go back indoors. I refused and said I was leaving, and that I hated him. And then…" Her bottom lip trembles, but she lifts her chin. "He hit me."

My jaw drops. "Ah no."

"A backhander, across the face."

"Oh, Heidi…"

"I think he knew he'd gone too far. I walked out, and he didn't try to stop me. I got my cases, ran to the car, threw them in, and drove away. And I haven't been back to the house since."

I'm so shocked, I'm not sure what to say. "Did you tell Huxley or your sisters?"

She shakes her head.

"Why not?"

"I don't think they'd have believed me. I didn't want to talk about it, anyway. I was so glad to get on that plane, I can't tell you."

"Did he mention it the next time you spoke to him?"

"I haven't."

I stare at her. "You haven't spoken to him since you left New Zealand?"

"No. He hasn't called me, and I haven't contacted him. I speak to Mum once a month or so. And obviously I'm still in touch with my sisters and Oliver."

"Do you resent them for not doing more for you?"

She studies her hands. "I've tried very hard not to be bitter about it. They didn't really see much of it firsthand. Abigail, Chrissie, and

Oliver had left home by the time I was in my teens, and Evie was out all the time. They never understood, and you can't explain it."

She sighs. "I thought he'd ruined me for other men. Especially after Jason. I felt I was doomed to be dominated by overbearing men. I can't believe I chose someone like him." Her gaze drifts to me, and her lips curve up. "And then I met you." She gives a small laugh. "I hope I haven't changed your view of me. It must be tough having a wuss for a girlfriend."

I study her for a moment, trying to keep calm. I'm burning with anger toward her father, but I'm determined not to show it, because that's the last thing she needs right now.

"You mentioned you knew Hal King," I say eventually. "So you probably know his cousin, Leon?"

"Yeah. He works at Noah's Ark as well, doesn't he?"

"That's the one. I met him at Huxley's—he stays at the club when he's in Auckland. We got chatting, and he told me how he and his wife have done some work with the Women's Refuge. His wife, Nix, visited one, spoke to a lot of the women there, and wrote a report for him, and he said it was incredibly eye-opening, and that I should read it. It was quite shocking for me."

"What did it say?"

"One of the biggest things that came out of it for me is that the women didn't see themselves as victims. Most of them were incredibly brave, and stayed in destructive relationships not because they were cowards but because they literally had no other option. It showed me how it's so easy to judge when you've not been in that position."

I lean forward and take her hand. "You're not a wuss, Heidi. You're not weak. And you're not a failure. You were a child when it started. The one person who's supposed to protect you and look after you is the one who failed. Abusive parents know your weak spots, and how to use them effectively against you. Nothing you did caused him to be abusive, and you can't change him."

She's shaking a little. "I try hard to forgive him, and not to be angry toward him or Mum, but it's so hard."

"Heidi, it's okay to be angry. I read a quote once, something about your anger being the part of you that knows your mistreatment and abuse are unacceptable, and that your anger is the part of you that loves you."

She stares at me.

"Have you not seen a therapist about this?" I ask gently.

She shakes her head. "I just want to forget about it."

"I think we both know that's not going to happen. You should see someone. I'm sure they'd help you understand it all better."

"I might do that."

I hold up my arm. She moves up close and snuggles against me, and I lower my arm around her. "Now I understand why you've been nervous about tonight."

"Yeah. I'm not looking forward to it. Part of me wishes I hadn't come back." She draws a pattern on my T-shirt.

I rest my head on the back of the sofa. And there's me asking her if she'd consider moving back here. No wonder she went pale when I suggested it.

She sighs and rests her head on my shoulder, and I kiss her hair.

I look out of the window, at the stormy gray sky. For a moment, the clouds part, and I see a chink of blue. It's the smallest bit of blue sky. Nowhere near enough to make a sailor a pair of trousers, as my grandmother used to say. Maybe a tiny handkerchief. But it's there.

True love doesn't come around very often. And it's always better to regret something you've done, than something you haven't.

Lost in thought, I stare at that patch of blue for a long time, as slowly an idea begins to form.

*

After a while, I get ready for work. Heidi says she's going to see her sisters. I give her a key to the apartment, and tell her to hang her clothes in the wardrobe and settle in, then leave her to it.

I drive to the office, say hello to my team, grab a large coffee, and go into my room. I spend a couple of hours catching up on work, and have lunch with the team. In the afternoon I attend a few meetings.

All the time I'm working, the idea I had this morning simmers away in the background like a pot of porridge on a stove until eventually, around four p.m., I go back to my office. I sit up at the architect's desk I had installed in front of the window, pin a fresh piece of A3 paper onto the desk, and grab a pen.

This is real blue-sky thinking, I muse, remembering the moment I saw the chink of blue through the gray clouds, and my lips curve up.

And then I start jotting down my thoughts.

*

Normally I'm in the office until nine or ten p.m., but that night I'm home by six, and Heidi and I order a takeaway, sit at the table, and talk about our day while we eat. Then we get changed and start heading down to Huxley's Club around seven.

We're both jet-lagged and fighting tiredness. Heidi's nervous, and at any moment I expect her to say she wants to go home. I confess to feeling a tad anxious, too. I presume that Mack has told Huxley by now that she's staying with me. I'm not sure how he's going to feel about that. I'm guessing there's a conversation coming about it.

Huxley's is a business club, with a smart-casual dress code, and although he wouldn't care if anyone wore jeans tonight, both of us have dressed up a little. As a kind of armor, I think, she's wearing black trousers and a scarlet top, and she's done her hair and makeup, and she looks absolutely stunning. I'm also wearing black trousers and a dress shirt.

As it's not far, we decide to walk, and don jackets and take an umbrella against the blustery rain. I put my arm around her, and she cuddles up to me, shivering as the icy rain occasionally blows across us.

When we arrive at the club, we make our way up in the elevator to the first floor. We go in and make our way through to the Churchill Lounge, where Huxley's organized for Heidi's friends and family to meet.

Just outside, Heidi pauses and takes a big breath.

"Are you okay?" I murmur.

She nods. She's very pale, but I can see from the determined set of her chin that she wants to do this.

We walk in, and there's a huge cheer as everyone sees her and comes rushing over. Huxley is first, and he gives her a bearhug and says, "Missed you so much!"

"I missed you too." She squeezes him back, then glances around. "Where are Mum and Dad?"

"Not here yet."

She blows out a relieved breath. "Okay."

"I'll get you a drink," I tell her, thinking she needs the Dutch courage. I go over to the bar, order her a G&T, and me a whisky.

"Hey." Mack appears and claps me on the back. "Good to see you again."

"Likewise."

"Sorry about earlier," he says. "You should have told me you and Heidi were an item. I'd have given you a lift home."

"I wasn't sure if she wanted to tell anyone," I admit. "Have you told Huxley?"

"Nope."

"Told Huxley what?" It's Elizabeth, looking gorgeous in a gray pregnancy top over black trousers, who comes up to give me a hug and a kiss on the cheek.

"Nothing. Hello, you." I kiss her back, then glance over at Heidi's brother, who's making his way over to us. Heidi is surrounded by her sisters and friends, and she's laughing, so she seems okay.

"Titus." Huxley holds out his hand, and I shake it. "Good to see you back," he says.

"Thanks."

"And great news about Acheron. Well done."

"Yeah, it was a huge relief."

"Can I have a word?" Huxley says. "Privately?"

"Uh…" I look at the G&T that the bartender has just put in front of us.

"I'll give it to Heidi if you like," Mack says.

"Okay, thanks." I pick up my whisky and follow Huxley as he gestures with his head to a quieter corner of the room.

He stops and turns to face me. "Sorry about this, I thought it best to talk to you rather than Heidi."

"Okay…" I have a mouthful of whisky.

"As you know, we're having the wedding at the Jewel Box Lodge. There's limited accommodation, so we're having to balance the guest list carefully. I just wanted to check—I've put you and Heidi together—that's okay, right?"

I stare at him, surprised. "Oh. I… uh… didn't realize you knew. About us, I mean."

"Yeah, Elizabeth told me." The corners of his mouth quirk up. "Sorry, is it supposed to be a secret?"

"No. I wasn't sure how you'd react, that's all. You said you could trust me, and I wondered whether you'd see it as a breach of that trust."

"Fuck me, Titus, I was joking. Heidi's twenty-five. I think she can make up her own mind who she dates now."

I give a short laugh and study my shoes for a moment. "Yeah, okay."

"Thanks for sorting out her ex," he says. "She doing all right over there apart from that?"

"She's doing great." I have a sip of whisky, glancing over at her. I hadn't been sure whether I was going to mention it. I don't want to betray her confidence, but equally Huxley is a good friend, and I think he should know. "She's better now she's away from your father."

He rolls his eyes. "Yeah. I know he was a bit controlling of her when she was here."

"I think it was more than a bit. From what she tells me, he completely dominated her while she was at home. She doesn't like talking about it," I say as he frowns, "because your sisters think she's exaggerating, but it sounded pretty bad. Hux… I hope you don't mind me saying, and tell me to back off if you want…"

"Go on."

"The day that Heidi moved out, she had a big argument with Peter."

"Oh. What happened?"

"I think you should know… He hit her."

Huxley goes still. He stares at me for about ten seconds. Then, slowly, he puts his glass down on a nearby table before he turns back to me and says, in a low, deliberate tone, "What?"

"She told me this morning. He was yelling at her while she packed. Her mum was in her bedroom, crying. Heidi got to the front door and tried to go out, and he gave her a backhander."

Huxley goes white. "Fucking bastard."

"I'm so sorry, man. I wasn't sure whether to tell you. I don't want to stir up trouble. That's the last thing she wants. She's trying to move on. But she's terrified about seeing him again. I mainly wanted to warn you in case something kicked off either tonight or at the wedding. I'm sure it won't. But I thought you'd rather be forewarned."

Hands on his hips, he stares at the floor for a moment, breathing heavily. Then he looks up at me. "I knew he was overbearing and controlling. He tries to be the same with me, and it's tough to stand up to him sometimes. I've seen him with Heidi, of course, but she never said anything to me." He looks over at her, a pained expression on his face, and runs his hand through his hair.

"She's embarrassed about it, would you believe. She thinks she's weak because she found it difficult to stand up to him."

"Ah, don't, you're breaking my heart."

"I know, I felt the same. You read Nix King's report, right?"

He sighs. "Yeah."

"It's domestic abuse, Hux. Pure and simple." I have a mouthful of whisky, hating that we're having this conversation. "Have you ever seen any signs of it with your mum?"

He hesitates, then looks at the floor. "He's always overpowered her. Talked over her. Put her down. But he's the same with everyone. I never saw any sign that violence was involved."

"She doesn't like talking about it, but I get the feeling she's resentful toward your mum for not standing up for her more."

He looks back at Heidi. I follow his gaze, smiling at the sight of her surrounded by her sisters and friends.

"Is it serious?" he asks. "You and her?"

I look back at him. "I'm going to marry her, if that's what you mean."

His eyes widen, and then he laughs. "Really?"

"I won't ask her yet though because I'm still ironing out some kinks."

"Like living on opposite sides of the world, you mean?"

"That would be one, yes."

"If she came back, she needn't have anything to do with him. You could live in Wellington, or the South Island."

"I'm working on a solution."

"All right." He smiles.

"What about your dad? Should I have told you?"

His smile fades. "I'm glad you did." He glances at the door. "They should be here soon. I'll head them off at the pass, I think. I don't want her to have to see him tonight."

"Want me to come with you?"

He hesitates.

"Nothing wrong with moral support," I say.

He nods then. "Okay."

I finish my drink, and as we head out, I leave the glass on the bar. I see Heidi glance over at us, but I don't meet her eyes and instead follow Huxley out of the lounge.

Chapter Twenty-Five

Titus

"Are you sure about this?" I ask Huxley as we walk along the corridor.

He nods. "More than I've ever been about anything. Apart from convincing Elizabeth to marry me. And if I can do that, I can do anything."

Still, I can see him breathing fast. He's nervous. Jesus, what is it with fathers? Why do some men feel the need to control their children? I think briefly about my dad, and I know there's a conversation coming there, too. I'll worry about that later, though.

We reach the lobby and wait in front of the desk. Huxley smiles briefly at a couple of Heidi's friends who come out of the elevator and stop to say hi, and he directs them down to Churchill's Lounge. Then we wait, not speaking,

Only a few minutes later, the elevator pings, the doors open, and Peter and Helene Huxley come out.

Peter's eyebrows rise at the sight of the two of us waiting. "A welcome party," he drawls. "To what do I owe this honor?"

"Is Heidi all right?" Helene asks anxiously.

"She's fine," I reassure her.

"Can you follow me?" Huxley says and, without waiting for an answer, he turns and walks along the corridor to the meeting rooms.

"What's this about?" Peter demands, but Huxley doesn't reply. The two of them follow him, and I bring up the rear. We go into the nearest meeting room, and I shut the door behind him. I stand back, feeling uncomfortable, half wishing I hadn't volunteered to go with him. There's something about Peter Huxley that sucks all the positivity out of the room.

"Where's Heidi?" Helene asks.

He ignores her. "I want to talk to you about something," he states to his father.

"What?" Peter sounds bored.

Hands on his hips, Huxley glares at him. "When Heidi left home, she said you two had an argument."

Peter mirrors his son's pose. "So?"

"She says…" Huxley frowns, pained. "She says you hit her, Dad."

Helene's jaw drops.

"She's lying," Peter states without batting an eyelid.

Huxley blinks. I don't think he'd expected his father to deny it outright.

"He wouldn't do that," Helene says to him, shocked. "He loves Heidi. Oliver, what a horrible thing to say."

Huxley clenches his jaw, but doesn't say anything. He glances at me, and I can see he's not sure whether she was telling the truth.

I think of Heidi's anguish, how upset she was. Why would she make it up? She's not the type of person to score points. She's not a drama queen. I don't have any doubt.

I move forward to stand beside him. "Heidi wouldn't make up something like this."

Peter turns his glare on me. "What the fuck has this got to do with you?" Then he gives a short laugh. "Oh yes. You turned down the principal of King's College for her. You idiot."

I slide my hands into the pockets of my trousers so I don't hit him, but I'm furious with both him and my father. "I know she was telling the truth," I say to Huxley as calmly as I can. He meets my eyes, and then nods.

Peter looks from me to his son, thoroughly amused. "So you've brought me in here to sort me out? Laurel and fucking Hardy? I'd fight you both with my eyes closed."

Huxley gives him an impatient look. "Fight? We're not fourteen." His voice is filled with loathing. "I brought you here to tell you that I want you to leave my club. And also to say that you've been uninvited to the wedding. I don't want you there. I didn't anyway, but I asked you for Mum's sake." He glances at her. "I'm sorry, Mum, but you must have had some idea of the way he treated Heidi. Why didn't you say anything?"

Her eyes fill with tears, and she presses her fingers to her mouth.

"You're welcome to stay," he continues, his voice rough. "And to come to the wedding. But Dad isn't."

"You're being ridiculous," Peter says, managing to make his son sound as if he's a complete idiot.

Huxley moves closer to him, shaking with anger. "All those speeches you gave me about respect and being a better man. You've got a fucking cheek."

Peter doesn't reply. He's breathing heavily, too. I think he's finally beginning to realize that his son is serious. He meets his son's eyes. And then he lowers his gaze to the floor. He's ashamed.

Huxley inhales. I think up until that moment, he wasn't a hundred percent sure that Heidi wasn't making it up, but one look at his father's face shows that she was telling the truth.

"She's tiny, Dad," Huxley whispers. "Just five foot five. She weighs, like, a hundred and twenty pounds. And you hit her? How could you?"

"You don't know the whole story," Peter says defensively. "You weren't there. She—"

"Say she deserved it," Huxley says. "I fucking dare you."

Peter closes his mouth. Huxley twitches, and for a moment I think he's going to hit his father. I put a hand on his shoulder. Peter might deserve it, but Huxley doesn't want to lower himself to his level.

Huxley turns around and walks out, opening the door with such force that it bangs on the wall, and he disappears down the corridor.

Helene bursts into tears. I feel sorry for her, especially as I'm sure Peter is as controlling of her as he was of Heidi. But Heidi is my first priority.

"I think you should leave," I say to Peter.

He turns to face me, his eyes blazing. "Fuck off," he snaps. "Just because you've gotten between Heidi's legs doesn't mean you have a say in what happens in this family."

She'd told me how he appears charming to outsiders, and how even her sisters don't fully believe her, but it's the first time I've seen his mercurial nature for myself.

I move closer to him. I'm two inches taller, thirty pounds heavier, and thirty years younger, and I know he's aware of all of that as his eyes widen. He wasn't expecting me to front him up. He thought I'd back down. Clearly, he doesn't know me at all.

I don't care if he insults me—he means nothing to me, and therefore he has no power to hurt me. I don't care if he insults Hux, either. The dude's almost as tall as me, and he can fight his own battles.

But insulting Heidi like that—his own fucking daughter—is a whole other matter. I'm all for girl power. But I'm enough of a man to feel a need to defend my woman.

"You're a bully," I say, my voice heavy with disgust. "And I'm not scared of you. You're Heidi's father, and because of that I'm sure she still loves you, despite what you've done, which is why I'm going to walk away now. But I tell you, man to man, if you come within half a mile of her without her permission, I'll punch your teeth so far down your throat your dentist will have to access them via your arsehole."

He holds my gaze, clearly furious. But he doesn't say anything.

I look at Helene. "Are you going to be okay?" I don't want to leave her with a fuming Peter, who could take it out on her.

She's still crying, but she looks at me and nods.

I turn and walk away. I go back to the lobby and turn toward the Churchill Lounge. Then I stand in the shadows and wait.

A few minutes later, Peter marches past. Helene follows him, head down. The two of them wait for the elevator, not talking, go inside, and the doors close.

Blowing out a breath, I head down to the lounge.

*

Heidi

Titus and Oliver still haven't returned. I have no idea where they went. I sigh, turning my attention back to my sisters. Evie has a glow about her she didn't have when I left. The source of it becomes clear when Victoria appears beside her and slides an arm around her waist. Tall, blonde, and beautiful, the transgender woman who has been one of Oliver's best friends since high school has been dating Evie for a few months now, and as the normally gruff Evie—a police officer who doesn't suffer fools gladly—actually blushes as Victoria kisses her cheek.

"I don't know what you've done with Evie," I say to Victoria. "You've turned her into a pussycat."

Evie glares at me, and Victoria chuckles. "She's like a Baked Alaska. She's all crisp on the outside and soft in the middle."

That makes me and Chrissie laugh, and we exchange a smile as Victoria kisses Evie's neck, and Evie blushes again and elbows her.

"Heidi." It's Mack, with a tall, slender woman by his side with wild, blonde curly hair. "I'd like you to meet my wife."

"You must be Sidnie," I say, holding out my hand. "Oh, it's so lovely to meet you."

"Likewise." Sidnie slides her hand into mine. "Mack's told me so much about you."

"Oh dear."

"All good things," she says, laughing. I can see immediately why he likes her. She's beautiful and bubbly, and when she looks at him, she has stars in her eyes.

"How's life with the workaholic," I ask her, "do you get to see him at all?"

"Actually he's home by seven most days."

"Amazing what the power of the pussy will do," Chrissie says. Mack glares at her, but Sidnie giggles.

"Where's Titus?" Sidnie asks. "I was going to ask him how his trip went."

"I have no idea. Do you?" I look at Mack, but he shakes his head.

"Hey!" I grin as Abigail appears beside him, holding a very special little parcel. It's my nephew. "Aw, look at him! He's gorgeous, Abi. What's he doing here—it's past his bedtime, isn't it?"

"Ah, I thought you'd like to see him," she says. "Want a cuddle?"

"Oh my God, of course." I hold out my arms and she lifts him into them. Oh, he's beautiful, with downy fair curls, flushed cheeks, and the brightest blue eyes. "Hello, Robin," I murmur, nuzzling him. "You smell amazing." I smile at Elizabeth as she joins us. "You'll be having one of these soon."

"I know. Difficult to believe, isn't it?" She comes over and strokes his hair.

"Look at you, gorgeous boy," I murmur, moving from side to side as I hum to him.

"Don't tell Jim you're singing Miley Cyrus to his son," Abigail says. "He'll never let you hold him again."

I laugh, kissing the baby's head, and continuing to hum *Flowers* as I move with him.

"Here's Huxley," Mack says, and we glance over as he comes into the room. To my surprise, he doesn't walk over to us, but instead goes up to the bar and orders a drink. We watch as he downs it in one.

"Uh-oh," Elizabeth says. "Something's wrong."

Puzzled, I exchange a glance with Evie, and then we watch Oliver order another drink and bring it over to us.

"Hey," Elizabeth says. "Everything all right?"

"Yep," he says.

"Where's Titus?" I ask.

He glances over his shoulder. "On his way, I expect." He has a sip of his drink.

"Out with it," Chrissie says. "What's going on?"

He hesitates. Then he looks at me.

I hand Robin back to Abigail. "What's the matter?" I ask, my heart starting to race.

"I'm sorry," he says. He puts down his glass. Then he comes over and puts his arms around me.

Baffled, I slide my arms around his waist and rub his back. "Come on, tell me, what's going on? Is it something to do with Titus?"

"No, no. It's Dad."

I move back. "Is he all right?"

"Yes. But… Titus told me."

I go still. I know what he's referring to.

"What do you mean?" Evie asks. "Told you what?"

Oliver looks at his sisters. "When Heidi left the house, she had a big argument with Dad."

"Yeah," Chrissie says, "we know. She told us."

"Did she tell you that he hit her?"

They all blink, then turn to stare at me.

"What?" Evie demands.

Abigail's jaw has dropped. "You're kidding."

"A backhander across the face," he says. Now I understand. I thought he was upset, and he is, but that's not his strongest emotion. He's absolutely furious.

"You've spoken to him," I whisper.

He looks back at me, lowering his arms. "I asked him to leave, and I told him he's not coming to the wedding."

My mouth opens, but no words come out.

"Shit," Mack says.

"Oh my God," Chrissie whispers, looking at me. "He hit you?"

I swallow hard. "He was upset. He didn't want me to go."

Oliver turns on me then, eyes blazing. "Don't you dare defend him," he snaps. "Don't you dare."

My bottom lip quivers, and Elizabeth touches his arm. "Steady," she murmurs.

He glances at her, then runs a hand through his hair. "I'm sorry. I feel terrible, that's all. I knew what he was like, we all did. You tried to tell me it was worse for you, and I should have listened. I should have gotten you out earlier."

Tears have sprung into Chrissie's eyes. "I know you said sometimes that he was hard on you, but I thought you were exaggerating. Oh my God, Heidi, I'm so sorry."

"I can't believe it," Abigail says, "I never thought he'd do that to you, of all people, Heidi. That's awful."

"It's okay." My voice comes out as a squeak. "He was just so different when you all left and we were alone."

I look over as someone comes through the door, feeling a rush of relief when I see it's Titus. He comes over, and obviously realizes what we're talking about by the looks on our faces.

"Are you okay?" he asks immediately, coming up to me.

I nod and bury my face in his shirt. He wraps his arms around me. "I'm sorry I told Hux," he murmurs. "But I had to do something."

"It's okay," I whisper. "I'm glad."

He blows out a relieved breath—he was worried I'd resent him getting involved. He has no idea how much it means to me that he did that.

"He's gone," he says to Oliver.

"Did he say anything else?" Oliver asks. Oh, so Titus was in the room? I lift my head, but he doesn't let me go.

"Yes," he says. He doesn't elaborate.

"Was it about me?" I ask.

He just looks at me. Then he kisses my forehead.

"What happened?" Chrissie asks.

"I adapted a line from *The Fate of the Furious*," Titus says.

Mack and Oliver both give a short laugh. "What was it?" I ask.

Titus tucks a strand of my hair behind my ear. "I told him if he came within a mile of you without your permission, he'd have to answer to me."

I'm shocked that he was able to speak to my father like that. Christ, Dad must have said something terrible to provoke that reaction. "What did he say about me?" I ask.

He just shakes his head. He won't tell me. It must have been bad. Resentment wells inside me that my father would put me down in front of him.

But even more overwhelming is an internal glow that Titus stood up for me.

Oliver clears his throat. "Heidi's home for a while, so we've got plenty of time to talk about this more. But tonight's supposed to be a celebration. It's great to have you home, Heidi, and I'm also thrilled that you and Titus are an item. Let's raise our glasses and toast—Heidi and Titus."

"Heidi and Titus," everyone echoes. I look up at Titus, and he grins and kisses me, as they all raise their glasses.

*

It doesn't turn out to be a bad evening in the end. I can see my sisters are upset, and at one point Huxley takes them aside, and I discover he's arranged for us all to meet up to talk about it tomorrow.

It is upsetting, but I'm also glad that everyone knows now—it makes me feel less alone. It's also a huge relief to know I'm not going to have to see Dad. It's not until now that I realize just how terrified I was of him. I know how much courage it must have taken Oliver to ask him to leave, and to uninvite him to the wedding, and I'm touched that he did for me.

But I'm even more touched about what Titus did.

It's not the last surprise of the evening, though. At one point, Oliver says to him, "So have you set a date yet?"

I blink. Titus gives him an exasperated look and says, "Dude."

"Jesus," Elizabeth scolds, giving me an apologetic glance, "I'm so sorry. The man can't hold his drink."

"I thought you'd asked her," Oliver protests.

"I said I was ironing out the kinks," Titus replies. My eyebrows rise. "Not that sort of kinks," Titus adds.

The others laugh, and he grins and pulls me to one side.

"Tell me more about these kinks," I murmur, and he chuckles. My heart's racing again, though. "What did Oliver mean?" I ask.

"I don't want to say," Titus states.

"Why?"

"Because it sounds arrogant and controlling, and I think the last thing you need is more of that in your life."

I push him. "Titus..."

"I told him I was going to marry you."

My jaw drops for about the third time this evening. "What?"

He shrugs. "I realized it on the plane. I don't want to be apart from you. I want you in my life permanently."

"But we've only been dating, if you can call it that, about ten days..."

"Yeah, which is why I said it sounds arrogant and controlling and I haven't asked you yet. But I know what I want, and I'm working out a way to get it." He sounds determined, and unashamed of it.

I'm so taken aback that I can't think what to say. Eventually I settle for, "Mack said you were resourceful."

"Yeah. When I put my mind to something, I normally get it."

"I... don't know what to say. I'm incredibly flattered. But marriage?" I'm full of so many emotions right now.

"Alan told me he knew two hours after meeting Vicky that he was going to marry her. I don't mean yet. I'm just saying, we are going to get married one day. When we're ready."

"Holy shit, Titus..."

He bends his head and brushes his lips against mine. "Wouldn't you like to wear my ring? To promise to love me forever?"

Emotion rushes through me, making my throat tighten. I can't answer, so I just nod.

"I'll ask you properly," he murmurs, "when the time's right. But you should know, there's a conversation coming." He smiles, because it's the same thing he said before.

I lift my arms and wrap them around his neck as he kisses me properly. Around us, my family and friends cheer, but I don't care. I want everyone to know how much in love I am with this man. He's the best thing that ever happened to me, and even though I'm still not sure how it's all going to work out, something tells me that Titus has an idea, and all I have to do is leave it to him.

Chapter Twenty-Six

Titus

The next ten days or so pass quickly. Heidi has been much happier since that evening at the club. The next day she met up with Huxley and their sisters, and they had a long conversation about what had happened, and what they were going to do. She told me all about it when she came home, wrung-out and emotionally drained, but as if a weight had been lifted. Her siblings had all apologized for not taking her more seriously when she'd complained about their father and told her they'd support her with whatever stance she preferred to take with him.

The next day, they met Helene Huxley in town, and had a difficult talk with her. Apparently she cried a lot, and they were shocked when she admitted she knew how difficult it had been for Heidi, but that she'd felt unable to do anything about it. Huxley told her she was welcome to come and stay with him if she wanted time away from Peter, but Helene then revealed that they'd had a big argument after what had happened at the club. He'd gotten drunk, then he'd broken down and confessed to her privately that he was ashamed of what he'd done, and told her that he was going to try to be a better man. His children thought it was the drink talking, and Heidi remains dubious whether he'll actually change when he's sober, but she's glad for her mother's sake that he's going to try.

My days are filled with work, and Heidi goes out and sees her friends and her sisters, but our evenings are spent together, sometimes with Hux and the others, but mostly alone. Since I confessed that I'm planning to marry her, and especially since the stuff with her father, Heidi has relaxed, losing some of her nervous energy, and growing in confidence, which has been lovely to see.

To her credit, she hasn't pushed me for details of what I'm planning, apparently content to believe my claim that I'm working out a way to get what I want. And so the weekend of Huxley and Elizabeth's wedding approaches, and with the kinks I mentioned mostly ironed out the week before, I fly to Lake Tekapo with a clear head, ready to put my plan into action when we get back.

Tekapo is a small rural town at the southern end of the lake that lies in the heart of Mackenzie country—a basin near the center of the South Island—with the Southern Alps to the west. We're staying at The Jewel Box Lodge, named after the star cluster in the Crux or Southern Cross constellation, which can only be seen in the southern hemisphere. The Jewel Box is an exclusive resort often used for weddings and other special occasions because it's parked right on the edge of the lake, with a large collection of villas for guests, a big function room, an award-winning wine cellar, and a collection of hot pools where you're encouraged to lie and look up at the stars.

The lake is in the Aoraki (which is the Māori name for Mount Cook) Mackenzie International Dark Sky Reserve—the largest gold-standard International Dark Sky Reserve in the world, with some of purest skies on the planet. I've been to the University of Canterbury Mount John Observatory at Lake Tekapo a few times to talk to experts there about astronomy and Artificial Intelligence, but I've never stayed at The Jewel Box, so I'm really looking forward to it.

Huxley has arranged for a flight for the guests from Auckland to Wellington, and then several smaller flights to transport us all to Lake Tekapo. There are only going to be about forty guests in total—not many at all considering Huxley runs a club and knows a huge number of people, and Elizabeth has a lot of contacts in her business. But they wanted to keep it small and intimate, then hold a larger party at the club for wider acquaintances the following week when they return from their honeymoon, where they're going on a boat trip around Milford Sound, then driving slowly back through the South Island, sightseeing as they go.

Peter Huxley is noticeable by his absence. Both Hux's paternal grandparents have passed away, and Peter is an only child, so Huxley doesn't have any other relatives on his dad's side to contend with. But Helene has surprised us all by coming even though we all know it must have been a difficult decision, possibly helped by the fact that her parents—Heidi's grandparents that I met in England—arrived a few days ago for the wedding, and are able to support her. She's also looking after Hux's daughter Joanna over the weekend.

We arrive on the Friday afternoon before the wedding on Saturday the thirteenth of August, and we're shown to our villas. While guests continue to arrive, we settle in and getting ready for dinner. Heidi and I cuddle up on the bed, looking out over the gorgeous view of the lake while we chat, and then I lie there and pretend to read a report as I watch her get ready. She tortures me by walking around in her sexy underwear while she does her hair and makeup, and resisting my advances with a laugh when I try to grab her as she walks by, protesting that she needs to get ready for dinner.

Eventually I join her in the bathroom for a shave, both of us laughing as we remember the shaving cream incident, and then we get dressed—me in navy trousers and a blue shirt with lighter blue flowers inside the cuffs and collar, Heidi in a gorgeous dress I haven't seen before that's a deep blood-red with long sleeves and a flared skirt. With her bright blonde hair neatly combed and a pair of black high heels, she looks absolutely stunning.

We head for dinner and discover Huxley and Elizabeth waiting at the entrance to the restaurant so they can greet everyone as they arrive. Elizabeth is now twenty weeks pregnant, with a gentle swell to her figure and a bloom to her cheeks, glowing with health and happiness. They hug us both, and we go into the restaurant where people are still walking about and greeting one another.

"Titus!"

I turn and grin at the sight of Saxon Chevalier, my heroically named cousin. He's spent a lot of time with Mack, Huxley, and me over the past year since he's been coming to Auckland more frequently, and we've all gotten on well, which is why Hux decided to invite him to the wedding.

"Hey, man," he says as we exchange a bear hug. "It's great to see you. And Heidi. Good to see you in the flesh, so to speak." He holds out his hand and shakes hers. He's wearing a navy pinstripe suit, a white shirt, and a spotted tie. Heidi's gaze drifts down him from his sticky-up hair to his white Chucks, and her lips curve up. "Going for the Doctor Who look?" she queries.

"She's got you sussed," I reply, amused, "and you're not even wearing your David Tennant coat."

"The tenth Doctor rules," he states, sliding his hands into the pockets of his trousers.

I chuckle. "So, who have you brought as your date, then?"

He purses his lips. "I'm going stag, to a stag party. There should be a prize for that."

Heidi giggles and slides her arm in his. "I'm sure Titus won't mind sharing me for the weekend."

"Titus minds very much. But you won't feel as odd once dinner's over." I'm referring to the fact that after dinner, Huxley is taking the guys off for a few hours for a whisky-tasting session, while Elizabeth and the girls will have a similar wine-tasting event, which is apparently also promising a plethora of chocolate. Afterward, we're all meeting up in the hot pools for a float under the stars.

"Not much of a consolation," he mumbles, but he lets Heidi lead him over to one of the tables, where Mack and Sidnie are just about to take their seats.

"Hey, Saxon," Mack says, and the two of them shake hands. "I don't think you've met my wife yet. This is Sidnie. Sidnie, this is Saxon Chevalier."

"Great name," she says, shaking his hand.

"Don't mock me. I know I sound like a stripper."

"I would never mock a person's name," she replies, shaking out her serviette. "My maiden name was Beaver."

That makes him laugh, and Heidi grin. Then I knock over my wine glass, which gives her a fit of the giggles.

"Titus has arrived," Mack says, and I give him a wry smile as I sit.

We're soon joined by Helene Huxley, Joanna, and Heidi's grandparents from the UK, Laura and Graham Craven. Two seats are left free on each table, and we discover that Huxley and Elizabeth are going to join tables for different courses.

At first, I wonder whether having Helene there without Peter is going to be awkward, but it turns out not to be at all. Saxon is sitting next to her, and when he discovers she's there on her own, and that she has a sense of humor, he declares she's going to be his date for the wedding and flirts outrageously with her, making Joanna giggle almost constantly.

"I'm not single," Helene protests as we're served our starters, even though I know she's enjoying the attention. "And I'm twice your age."

"Out of sight is out of mind," he states. "And I like older women. Besides, I heard you're a terrific artist. I thought you might be looking for a new life model."

"I paint abstracts and still lifes," she points out, blushing.

He purses his lips. "I'm sure a joke exists about plums and a banana, but I'm not going to go there."

That makes us all laugh, and Joanna giggle even more. "You're incorrigible," Heidi scolds.

He grins. "I pride myself on it."

A bit later, when he excuses himself to go to the bathroom, Heidi whispers to me, "He wouldn't make a move on her, would he?"

I chuckle. "If she wasn't your mum? Maybe."

Her eyes widen. "Really? But she's, like, twice his age."

"Saxon doesn't give a fuck what anyone thinks of him. If he liked her, her age wouldn't stop him. But he wouldn't seduce the groom's mother at a wedding. Even he has some boundaries."

"Are you sure about that?"

We watch him walking back across the room, stopping occasionally to talk to someone and make them laugh. He's always walked as if he owns the joint. "I know he seems cocky," I say softly, "but I'd trust him with my life. He's one of the good guys."

She smiles as he rejoins us and takes his seat. "Mack told me what happened when you went camping as kids," she says to us both.

"Yeah, that wasn't the most fun vacation I've had," I reply. "It got pretty scary when the temperature dropped below freezing, especially when Saxon got a concussion."

"I'm just surprised it wasn't you who fell over," Mack states.

"I'm only clumsy with inanimate objects," I say. "Saxon's the one who's broken every bone in his body and knocked himself out half a dozen times."

"Don't exaggerate," he says.

"All right, how many have you broken?"

"Fifteen. That's nothing," he says as Heidi inhales in shock and the others exclaim, "Evel Knieval had four hundred and thirty-three fractures."

"How have you broken so many?" she asks.

"I like motorbikes. They don't always like me, though."

"He's got a death wish," I tell her. "He's always jumping out of planes or bungee jumping or snowboarding or something."

"Jeez, don't tell Oliver," she says.

"Don't tell Oliver what?" It's Huxley, with Elizabeth, coming to join us for the main course.

"Saxon likes skydiving," Heidi states.

Huxley holds Elizabeth's seat for her, then sits and shudders. "I thought jumping off the Sky Tower was bad enough. I couldn't do it out of a plane."

"Not even to show me how much you love me?" Elizabeth asks.

"Sorry sweetheart," he says, "but if you don't believe me after I fell over six hundred feet, I don't see why I should plummet for ten thousand."

We all laugh, and the conversation continues while we eat. It's midwinter at the moment, and while it's not snowing, the clear skies mean it's freezing, so they're serving mulled wine and hot toddies, and there's a magnificent hot cocoa bar where you can help yourself to various toppings like marshmallows and chocolate flakes. The menu is just as impressive: we start with a hearty vegetable soup, then there are traditional roasts for the mains, including venison and pheasant, vegan pasties with mushrooms, lentils, and red wine, root veggies roasted with thyme, Portobello mushrooms stuffed with cranberry and pistachio and onions with sun-dried tomatoes and hazelnuts, and huge roast potatoes, all served with a rich gravy.

"Oh my God, I'm so full," Heidi complains when she scrapes the last fragment of a roast potato up.

"There won't be any water left in the hot pools once we all get in," Huxley says.

"Especially when I join you," Elizabeth states with a groan, smoothing a hand over her bump. "I must weigh about five hundred pounds now."

He chuckles, nuzzles her ear, and whispers something in it.

She groans again. "Not until my dinner's gone down."

"Dessert first," Mack says, as the waiters bring it around, and we all blow out a breath, but it's amazing how you find the space to squeeze a bit more in when it's so delicious, and it's not long before the baked spiced plums with Chantilly cream or sticky toffee puddings with steaming vanilla bean custard and thick clotted cream have all disappeared.

By now it's eight p.m., and the sun has set. Huxley advises everyone that we're going outside for a sky tour, and so we should all 'rug up'—

Kiwi for wrap up warm. We break for ten minutes while we return to our villas and pull on jackets, boots, hats, scarves, and gloves, then return to the stargazing area in front of the restaurant. We take our seats, and they dim the restaurant lights. They have two magnificent telescopes set up that they promise we'll be able to look through after our talk.

Staff members from The Jewel Box hand out blankets and heated wheat packs, and continue to supply us with mulled wine as we listen to one of the experts from Mount John Observatory give us an introduction to what we can see in the sky tonight. The skies are absolutely breathtaking. The Milky Way is at its brightest at this time of the year, and there's only a sliver of moon, which is better for stargazing. The guide points out Mars, Jupiter, and Saturn, and constellations including Scorpius, Libra, Sagittarius, and the Southern Cross, explaining that one of the telescopes is set up to show us the Jewel Box star cluster from which the resort gets its name.

He tells us that we might get to see the Aurora Australis—the Southern Lights—if we're really lucky, and if we're still up when the skies are darker. I'm excited to see them as I've only watched them online, and the conditions are perfect, so there's a good chance.

It's too cold to stay out long, but we all get to look through the telescopes at the Jewel Box and the Eta Carinae Nebula before we head back inside.

At this point, Elizabeth calls the girls to go with her to another room for the wine- and chocolate-tasting session. I give Heidi a hug, and she smiles before heading off with the others.

Despite the fact that she's been laughing and joking, she's been a bit quieter since we came here. I wonder whether it's starting to play on her mind that it won't be long before her vacation is up. No doubt she's concerned about what's going to happen between us. Well, hopefully I'll be able to reassure her about that very soon.

Huxley takes us through the restaurant to a separate function room. Here there's a roaring log fire, and the fifteen or so guys present take a seat at the chairs and tables where our next guide is preparing a presentation on New Zealand whisky.

Huxley's gaze drifts away for a moment, while the conversation continues around him.

"Thinking about your dad?" I ask quietly, knowing that his father is the one who introduced him to malt whisky.

He looks back at me, one corner of his lips quirking up. "Yeah."

"Do you regret not asking him to come?"

"No," he says firmly. "I just regret that he's such a fucking bastard."

"Fair enough."

He blows out a breath. "I'm not going to think about him tonight." And he turns his attention to the guide as he begins to talk.

The presentation ends up taking over an hour, with much laughter as we sample all the whiskies, losing the plot about halfway through when everything starts to blur. Even though we insist we're full, the hosts bring out some bowls of potato wedges with chili sauce and sour cream, and they all disappear over the course of the evening.

When we're finally done, we drift out to the hot pools, change into our swim shorts, and lower ourselves into the steaming water. More hot toddies are brought out, and we sip them as we float on our backs, looking up at the stars. The horizon to the south flickers with a pinky yellow light, a sign that the Southern Lights are going to be bright later tonight.

We talk for a while, pointing out different constellations to each other. Gradually, some of the guys go back to their villas, and others congregate in small groups to chat. Eventually, I end up in an area of the pool with Mack, Huxley, and Saxon. And on the spur of the moment, and probably connected to the alcohol I've consumed, my plan spills out of me.

"Guys," I say, "can I talk to you about something?"

"Yeah," Huxley says. "Can't guarantee I'll remember it in the morning, though."

"You've got a point, and it really deserves a more formal setting, and I apologize for that. I hope you don't think I'm playing it down, because I'm not. I was going to call a meeting when we got back. But I felt a bit less nervous after a few whiskies, so I thought I'd seize the bull by the—"

"Bollocks?" Mack suggests. "Spit it out, mate. What's going on?"

I look up at Sirius, the brightest star in the southern hemisphere, a mighty diamond in the night. "I'm planning to move to England."

After about ten seconds of silence, I look back at the others, who all seem to have sobered up.

Huxley looks surprised. Mack is thoughtful. Saxon is smiling.

"Heidi?" he queries.

I give a small shrug. "Ninety percent Heidi, yeah."

"You'd move to the UK for her?" Huxley asks.

"Yes. After what happened with your father, I don't want to ask her to move here."

"You wouldn't have to live in Auckland."

"I know. But she's happy over there. And I want her to be happy."

His lips curve up. "Fair enough. I'd be sorry to see you go. Are you thinking just for the two years that Alan Woodridge asked for?"

"In the first instance. I'd come back every few months, probably. Long term? It depends. I've been talking to my team about it, trying to iron out any issues." I look at Mack and Saxon. "Obviously, it depends in part on you two, and Elizabeth. We're at a vital stage in our research, and I know it won't make things easier me being in the UK."

"The only issue I can foresee is the timing of any meetings," Mack said. "But I don't see why we can't schedule for early mornings and the occasional late evening here. We'd either hold them on Zoom, or you could join us on Zoom while the rest of us meet up in person. Everything else can be done online. Like Hux said, I'd miss you, but you've got to follow your heart."

I nod. I look at Saxon then. "How do you feel about running both the Wellington and Auckland branches of NZAI?" I ask softly.

His eyebrows rise, and he sits up a little straighter. "You wouldn't want Jeff to take over?" Jeff is one of the most senior members of my team in Auckland.

"He'd oversee the work when you weren't there. But I'd prefer it if you'd head the business. It would mean some travel on your part. Maybe a week in Auckland, a week in Wellington? Or a few days in Auckland anyway. You'd make the decisions. Run the show. I'd always be on hand if you want to discuss anything, but I'd mainly concentrate on the new research with Acheron. What do you think? You don't have to decide now."

"I'm incredibly flattered you've asked me." He looks genuinely touched.

I grin. "Why? You're my cousin. And we work well together."

"Yeah, but… it's your company."

"And?"

"And I'm… me," he finishes lamely, in an uncharacteristic display of modesty. "Do you trust me to be at the wheel?"

"Dude, you're practically running the Wellington branch already, and anyway you're twice as smart as me." He gives me a wry look, and

I say, "Alcohol makes you tell the truth. You're smart as, Saxon, but you don't take yourself seriously enough. You're more than capable of doing this. If you want to."

"I want to. And thank you for saying that."

"Are you going to cry?"

"Possibly. Look the other way."

I chuckle and flick some water at him. "We need to work out some details," I tell them. "But in general you're okay with it?"

"With you putting my sister first?" Huxley asks. "I think so."

"We'll find a way to make it work," Mack says. "Go for it."

Saxon glances over at the building. "The girls will be on their way back soon." He smiles. "Are you going to tell her tonight?"

"I hadn't planned to."

"Well, either way, I'm pleased for you. And incredibly jealous. She's gorgeous, and nice with it. You don't deserve her."

I sigh as I watch the Southern Lights flicker. "Tell me something I don't know."

Chapter Twenty-Seven

Heidi

The hour or so that I'm with Elizabeth and the others is the most enjoyable I've spent in a long time. We test a whole raft of New Zealand wines, Elizabeth asking for details as she can't drink, and I sample so many chocolates that they'll need to reinforce the plane when I get back on it.

We spend most of the hour drinking, talking about boys and babies, even my mother, Elizabeth's mother, and my grandmother, who all giggle as though they're fifteen. Joanna's gone to bed in the villa next door, so the conversation inevitably turns risqué as time goes by and we get more tipsy.

But it's only as we finish the last sample of wine that Evie says, somewhat slyly, "So, Heidi... how's it going with Sir Richard?"

"Yeah," I say, choosing a last chocolate from the box, "this is really a conversation I want to have."

"Who's Sir Richard?" Victoria asks.

Chrissie snickers. My face grows hot as the rest of them, including my mother, look at me.

"Shall I tell them?" Evie asks, "or do you want to?"

"I don't really want anyone discussing the size of Titus's appendage, thank you very much."

"Good grief," my grandmother says. "Evie!"

"Exactly," I scold. "Someone please change the subject."

"How much longer do you have here?" Abigail asks.

"Just under two weeks."

"What'll happen then?"

"I'll get on a plane in Auckland and miraculously land in London, I'm guessing."

"You know what I mean. What's going to happen with Titus?"

"I don't know," I say. I bite my lip for a moment. "He said he wants to marry me."

They all stare, shocked, then erupt in a thrilled cheer.

"He hasn't asked me formally," I add. "And I think we need to spend some proper time together first. But he's said he's going to when everything's sorted."

"What does that mean?" my mother asks.

"I think maybe he's going to suggest we live in Wellington, or even the South Island."

"Aw," my grandmother says.

"I know."

"Would you move back here?" Elizabeth asks.

I hesitate. "I'd think about it. I'd miss England. I love it there, and I adore my little school. But I want to be with him. It's not an easy decision."

Elizabeth rubs my arm. "It's funny how often things work out. Come on. Why don't we get back to the guys? I'm sure they're missing us."

"I think I'll go back to my room," Mum says as we all start getting up.

"Saxon will be disappointed," Evie teases.

Mum blushes scarlet. "Evie! I'm a married woman."

"While the cat's away…"

"And he was only joking," Mum scolds.

"I don't think he was," I say with a laugh. "Titus said Saxon doesn't give a… damn what anyone thinks, and if he liked a woman, her age wouldn't stop him."

"I'm not listening to this," Mum states, but I can see she's flattered. "I'm off to check on Joanna. Goodnight everyone. See you tomorrow."

"Yes, I'm off too," Grandma says, and some of the others excuse themselves.

The rest of us go back to our rooms and change into our swimsuits and bikinis, then grab a blanket and meet by the stargazing platform before we head off to the hot pools.

Ooh, it's cold tonight. It's nearing ten o'clock, and the sky is clear of clouds and full of so many stars it makes me catch my breath.

The guys are in the nearest pool, and they all cheer as we approach, drop our blankets, and hurriedly slide into the pool next to them. Titus puts his arm around me and gives me a long kiss.

Only Elizabeth pauses on the side.

"What's up?" Victoria asks, looking stunning in a black all-in-one costume with orange flowers across her breasts.

"I just wanted to check that nobody minds me getting in," Elizabeth says, clutching her towel around her a little shyly.

We all look at her, puzzled. "What do you mean?" I ask.

"Well, I've heard that some people aren't keen to go swimming with pregnant women…"

That comment is met with a slew of comments like, "Jesus, Elizabeth, just get in," and "Oh for God's sake, seriously?"

Oliver stares at her, shocked. "What are you talking about?" he asks as she sinks beneath the surface of the hot water.

"One of the women at my ante-natal class said she went swimming at the public pools last month, and a guy there said it was disgusting and it shouldn't be allowed."

"Holy shit," Saxon says. "I hope she told him to go fuck himself."

"I think she got out," Elizabeth states. "She was embarrassed and upset."

"I don't get that at all," Saxon replies. "I think pregnant women are sexy."

"You think all women are sexy," Evie points out. "You've got sex on the brain."

"Harsh," he says. "But true."

We all chuckle.

"You made my mother blush," I tell him.

He grins. "Good."

"Fuck me, I don't want to know that," Oliver says. "For Christ's sake, change the subject."

"All right, I will," I say. "So, Saxon, tell us about this redhead you met a couple of weeks ago. Titus said she asked you to strip for her and her friends, and apparently you obliged?"

"Oh my God," Evie says, "more details, quick."

He scowls. "I don't think I'm ever going to live that down."

"It was quite the show," Mack states. "Especially the white boxers with red hearts you were wearing."

"I did not reveal my boxers," Saxon declares. "Did I?"

"Do you own a pair with red hearts on?" Sidnie asks him.

He opens his mouth to deny it, and then his lips curve up, and we all laugh. "Shit," he says, "I didn't think I went that far."

Mack smirks. "Oh yes, my friend. There was very little left to the imagination."

"Red hearts?" Evie queries.

Saxon pulls a face. "They were a Christmas present from my mother."

"At least they stayed on," Elizabeth says. "Until you got back to your hotel, anyway."

He just gives a smug smile at that.

"You took her back to your room?" Victoria scolds. "Saxon!"

"What? We were both single, consenting adults."

"Even so," Victoria continues. "A one-night stand? I'm shocked."

"Did you use protection?" Evie wants to know, eyes twinkling.

"Jesus Christ," he says as Sidnie and I giggle. "Yes, Evie, I packed my own parachute."

She giggles too, and he grins.

"What was her name?" I ask.

"Catie. With a C." His expression softens.

"That's unusual."

"It might not have been her real name," he admits. "I told her mine was Norman."

That makes us all chuckle. "Was she older than you?" I ask.

He obviously guesses I'm referring to his admission that he likes older women. "No… She was twenty-three. Tall, like Sidnie. Legs all the way down to the ground. And she had this red hair that was up in a bun, but when she took it down…" He gestures as if to indicate it tumbling over her shoulders, and sighs. "It was like fire."

"Was it natural?" Chrissie asks.

"Yeah," Mack says, "did the carpet match the drapes?"

Saxon bears the teasing and laughter with a wry smile. "I don't kiss and tell."

"She's hardly going to find out," Evie scoffs.

"That's not the point."

She raises her eyebrows. He flicks water at her.

"What did you like most about her?" I ask softly, because it's clear that he did.

He hesitates then. "I don't want to say."

"Why?" Evie asks. "Is it rude?"

"Jesus, Evie, no. Because you'll all mock me."

"Now you've got to tell us," she demands.

He blows out a breath. "She could name all the Doctor Whos in order."

We burst out laughing and his lips curve up. "She sounds nice," I say. "I wish I could have met her."

He sighs. "Yeah. She was..." He drifts off. I wait for him to answer, starting to smile as he continues to gaze off into space. Then he looks back at me and his lips curve up. "I was trying to think of the right word."

"And?"

"Sublime pretty much covers it."

"Aw. And you can't find her?"

He sighs. "Nah. Anyway, enough about me. Time someone else was the topic of conversation."

"Yeah, it's time we mocked the groom," Chrissie states. "Mack, you must have some stories about the two of you."

"Oh yeah," he says with feeling. He meets Oliver's eyes and grins. "You'll never guess who I saw the other day."

My brother gives him a wary look. "Who?"

"Simone Lafleur."

"Oh God," Victoria says, and the three of them start laughing.

"What's this about?" Elizabeth asks suspiciously.

"We went to school with a friend called Kai," Mack explains. "He works with me now at KoruTech. Well, when we were seventeen, he was dating a French exchange student called Simone Lafleur. We went over to his house one day. We were in the living room with Kai and Simone, playing on the PlayStation. His sister, his parents, and his grandmother were also there."

"Mack had a Labrador called Moose," Oliver explains. "Unbeknown to us, Moose had run off into Kai's bedroom where Simone had obviously stayed over."

"The dog came running in, carrying something," Victoria says. "He dropped it on the carpet in front of us all. It was Simone's vibrator."

"Oh no!" I clap a hand over my mouth, while Sidnie dissolves into giggles, and everyone else laughs.

"Kai still gets embarrassed about it now," Mack says. "Poor guy."

"It's a great story," Chrissie states, "but not nearly embarrassing enough for Huxley."

"We don't embarrass our mates," Mack replies. Then he looks at Saxon. "Apart from you, obviously."

I chuckle. Saxon just snorts.

"Huxley embarrassed you well enough at your wedding," Evie points out.

"That's true, and I intend to return the favor in my speech," he says. "Just not right now."

"Well, we have some news instead," Victoria says. She glances at Evie, who wrinkles her nose, then smiles at us. "Evie and I have decided to get married."

"Oh my God!" I squeal, and everyone whoops and cheers. The two of them laugh as we surround them and exchange hugs and kisses.

"When?" Oliver asks.

"In the summer," Victoria says, and she smiles at him.

"I'm so pleased for you," he murmurs, and they have a big hug.

I cover my mouth, overcome with emotion. They've been friends for a long time, and Oliver has helped her through her transition over the years.

Saxon looks at Titus then. "Maybe now's the time?" he asks.

Titus shakes his head, but Evie overheard and says, "What's this?"

"Nothing that won't wait," he says, but she persists.

"Come on, if we're all sharing news…"

"I don't want to steal your thunder."

Evie rolls her eyes. "Titus!"

Exasperated, he glances at me. "I wanted to do this privately. Sorry."

"What's going on?" Elizabeth asks.

"I need to go over the details with you later," he tells her mysteriously. Then he looks back at me. "I've talked to the guys about it tonight, that's all. I had to speak to them first because I had to be sure they were up for it, and—"

"Titus!" Evie barks in her best police officer's voice.

His lips curve up. Keeping his gaze on mine, he says, "I'm moving to England."

There's a second of silence, and then everyone cheers again. I'm caught up in a whirlwind of hugs and kisses, but I can't respond because my head's whirling.

"Wait…" I push everyone away and stare at him, heart hammering. "What do you mean?"

"In September," he says carefully, "once I've got everything sorted here, I'm moving to England."

"But… what about your company?"

"Saxon is going to take over here."

I glance across at him. He pulls an eek face, then grins.

I look at Mack. "But doesn't he need to be near Marise?"

"Well, you see, there's this invention that we think might be quite useful," he says, "it's called… what is it, Hux?"

"It's to do with spiders. The Intra-web?"

"Something like that."

"Oh, shut up." I look back at Titus. In a small voice, I say, "You'd do that? For me?"

He removes a strand of my hair where it's stuck to my wet cheek and tucks it behind my ear. "The short answer is yes. I'd do anything for you." His lips curve up as the others all go, *Awww!* But he keeps his gaze on me. "The longer answer is that I don't want you to feel that you're making me do it. Alan wants me to move there, and the truth is that I love it there. And it's going to be an exciting couple of years, and a fascinating project to work on. I can't wait. And the company will still be here if and when I come back."

"Probably," Saxon says, and Titus chuckles.

"I'd love to go to England," Oliver states. "All those motorways fascinate me. I keep telling Elizabeth I want to take her up the M1, but she says she needs to get some lube first."

We all burst out laughing. Elizabeth rolls her eyes at him. "How many whiskies have you had?"

"I lost count. Hey, it's my stag night."

"We should have gotten married after I had the baby," she grumbles. "All that wine, and I didn't get to drink any of it."

"Aw." He pulls her into his arms and nuzzles her neck. Her lips curve up, and she splashes him.

"Oh my God," Sidnie says, "look!"

We all follow her gaze to the south, and stare in wonder at the flare of pink and yellowy-green light brightening the sky. As we watch, a shooting star speeds above it, like a wish flashing through the darkness.

We watch it for a few minutes, talking quietly. I lean my head on Titus's shoulder, and he kisses my hair. My mind is still spinning, my heart racing. He's moving to England! I can't believe it. Will we live together? I know he'll be working a lot—how often will I get to see him? We'll be able to see more of Alan and Vicky too, which will be nice, as I liked them both. And it must be good for Titus—he'll be able to use all the resources that Acheron has to further his research.

"Okay, I think we're off," Huxley says. "I don't want Elizabeth to get cold."

"Fusspot," she says, but she doesn't complain. She lets him help her out of the pool, and then as we all wave goodbye, they head in.

The rest of us also start getting out. The staff have brought us warmed bathrobes and blankets, and we wrap ourselves in them, say goodnight, and head toward our villas.

Inside ours, it's warm and toasty. We brush our teeth and get ready for bed, then turn off the lights and sneak under the covers, delighted to discover that the staff had put on the electric blankets while we were in the pool. To our amazement we can see the Southern Lights dancing in the sky through the open curtains.

"Wow." Titus props himself up on the pillows. "That's quite a view."

"It sure is." I can't tear my gaze away from him. He's wearing a black T-shirt and boxer-briefs in bed as it's cold. The sleeves of the tee stretch across his impressive biceps. The material is taut over his muscular chest. His hair is ruffled where it got damp and he couldn't be bothered to brush it.

He glances at me and grins. "I was talking about the lights." He holds up his arm, and I curl up next to him. He pulls the duvet up and tucks it around us.

"Are you sure?" I whisper. "About moving?"

"It's all sorted. I've already talked to Alan."

"Oh." That surprises me.

He strokes my back. "I hope you don't mind. It's not that you were last on the list."

"I know, honey. Your business is important."

"It is, and thank you for saying that, but it's more that I wanted to make sure it would work. I had to know that Mack and Saxon were on board, and just to iron out a couple of practical matters with Alan—the transfer of data, that kind of thing."

"And it all went well?"

"Yes, perfect. The main thing was getting Saxon on board to run the company this end."

"You think he's up to it?"

"Oh, definitely. I wasn't joking when I said he was smarter than me. He'd give Mack a run for his money. But he's a creative rather than a critical thinker. I analyze and evaluate. And he…"

"Makes stuff up?"

He laughs. "Yeah. We work well together. Critical thinking is logical, objective, based in reality and probability. Creative thinking is intuitive, subjective, and based in possibility. He forms hypotheses, and I test them. One's no good without the other."

"I think you're putting yourself down, because you seem very creative to me, but I understand what you're saying."

"Basically, he comes up with the ideas and I put them into practice, but you're right, of course, there's a lot of crossover. He's good with people, as you've seen, but I was hoping to ease him into running the company by starting with the new branch. Instead I'm kinda throwing him in the deep end. But he'll cope, and I think he's excited about the challenge."

"I wonder if he's knocking on my mother's door at the moment."

He chuckles and kisses the top of my head. "I told him what had happened with your dad. He knows she's been through it a bit, and she's here on her own. He wanted to cheer her up."

"So he wasn't hitting on her?"

He tips his head from side to side, and we both laugh.

"He really seemed to like that girl he hooked up with," I say, as he slides down the pillows and gets comfortable.

"Yeah. It's a shame when that happens. That's why you have to hold onto the good ones when you find them." He tightens his arms around me.

I wish we could make love now, but I'm tired, tipsy, and full of good food, and I'm so cozy, under the covers with the man I love.

He doesn't say anything more, and soon his breathing evens out, and I know he's falling asleep.

He's going to move across the world to be with me. Oh my God. I still can't believe it.

My lips curve up, and within a few minutes, I'm asleep.

*

When I wake, it's still dark, but the horizon is filled with the blush of dawn. It's lovely and warm in bed, and someone is kissing my neck.

Smiling, I turn my head and let him kiss my lips. "Morning," I murmur.

"Morning." He nuzzles my ear, then moves up closer so our bodies are flush, my back to his chest. "Sorry, did I wake you?"

"Mmm, but it's the absolute best way to wake up." I move a hand behind me and slide it down to grasp his erection in his boxer briefs. "Morning, Sir Richard."

He chuckles and rocks his hips. "He says good morning."

"Feels as if he wants some action."

"He's got his fingers crossed."

That makes me laugh. I turn to face him, hooking my leg over his, and he rolls onto his back, bringing me with him.

Brushing back my hair with both hands, he studies my face, his eyes filled with something akin to wonder. "How do you look so amazing when you've just woken up?"

"I think you need to get your eyes tested."

He smiles, but says, "I mean it. You're the most beautiful woman I've ever seen."

"Little tip—you don't need to flatter me. I'm a sure thing."

He slides his hands down over my back, then around to cup my breasts in my T-shirt nightie. "In that case, I'd better take advantage of my good luck."

"Definitely."

It's the last word either of us says for a while. We're too busy kissing, licking, sucking, and stroking, taking time to arouse each other, as the sun slowly fills the room with its thick, buttery rays.

He kisses down my neck to my breasts, and cups and nibbles them through the tee, while he strokes between my legs through the thin fabric of my underwear until it's soaked with my moisture, and I'm begging him for more.

I brush my fingers over his erection through the cotton of his boxer briefs, then eventually slip my hand beneath the elastic so I close my fingers around him, and marvel at how hard and long he is, arousing him with firm strokes until he groans and flips me onto my back.

Pulling the duvet over us so we stay in our snug den, and stripping off my underwear, he presses the tip of his erection down into my folds, and slides inside me easily. I sigh and wrap my legs around him, and he plunges his tongue into my mouth and kisses me deeply as he begins to move inside me.

Oh, the bliss of making love in the early morning, when you're warm and safe and with the man you love. I like sex hard and fast; sometimes it's fun to be a little rough and passionate. I enjoy trying new positions, and oral sex is just heaven. But my favorite is like this— slow and languorous, lazy almost, in missionary where I can look up at him, and he can drive the pace. And this morning he wants to go slow, and we sort of drift toward a climax as if we're on a punt in the river, gliding downstream.

The nice thing is that I don't have to reach or make any effort at all to get myself there. With Titus, it's like he's gently steering the punt, making small alterations so I don't drift into the bank, but I know he's going to get me there in the end, and all I have to do is lie there and dream as I look up at the sky.

I don't just lie there, of course, I put a bit more effort in than that, but that's how it feels.

He seems unhurried, keeping up the same slow rhythm for ages, but my body stirs, moistens, swells for him, my muscles loosen, my skin grows warm, my nipples and lips and everywhere, in fact, grows super-sensitive, and eventually deep in my tummy I feel the first exquisite flickers of an orgasm.

"Ahhh…" he says, so I know he can sense it, and he increases the pace of his hips and lifts up onto his hands so he's looking down at me.

I catch my bottom lip between my teeth, torn between wanting to watch him climax and needing to close my eyes so I can concentrate on my own pleasure. In the end I have no choice, and my eyelids flutter closed as he thrusts me closer to the finish line.

I'm hot now, under the covers, and our skin is sticking together. He tosses the duvet aside, and I welcome the cooler air as it brushes across our skin. The rich honey-colored light of the sun falls across us, filling me with a sense of sweetness and warmth. The muscles of the man above me glow as he moves. Jesus, he's so fucking beautiful.

"Ah God, don't stop," I urge, even though I know there's no chance of that.

"I won't," he reassures, demanding, "come for me."

The pleasurable sensation spreads out from my core and claims me with several fierce pulses that leave me gasping as I fall back onto the pillows. Ooh… mmm… that felt good, and it's still not over because now I get to watch him climax, which is almost—not quite, but it's a close thing—as sweet as my own orgasm.

He thrusts harder, faster, his eyes closed, and I know he's focusing on the similar sensations deep inside, feeling those flickers in his tummy, that fantastic clenching of muscles. He shudders, no doubt feeling the heat of his gorgeous silky fluid rushing up through him, and then he comes inside me, hips jerking, giving sexy, throaty groans.

When he eventually opens his eyes, he looks into mine, blinks, then blows out a long breath.

"Do you want kids?" I ask.

His eyebrows rise, then he laughs as he withdraws and flops onto his back. "Yeah," he says. "I guess." He watches as I lift up and lean on his chest. "Do you?"

"Mmm." I draw a heart on his chest. "I was just thinking how amazing it is that what we just did could make a baby."

"Yeah. Every time I study the process, I think what a fantastic design it is."

"God was so sweet making it such a pleasurable experience."

"It was a sneaky trick to make sure we procreate."

I laugh. Then I kiss his chest. "I love your sperm."

That makes him laugh. "Your eggs are pretty cool, too."

"We're so romantic, aren't we?"

"Yeah. Perfect for a wedding."

"Oh, of course! I forgot. Oliver and Elizabeth get married today. What time's breakfast?"

"Eight," he says. "We'll have a shower in a minute."

"Yeah. In a minute." I rest my cheek on his chest, looking out at the sunrise. "No rush."

Chapter Twenty-Eight

Titus

We all meet up for breakfast in the restaurant and spend a leisurely hour or so over the wonderful spread. We can choose from several cereals, fresh fruit, toast, croissants, and a variety of jams, or cooked breakfasts that include sausages, bacon, mushrooms, and eggs cooked however we want them.

Afterward, we have several hours to pass before the wedding in the afternoon. Heidi and I join some of the other guests at the skating rink and make fools of ourselves on the ice. Afterward, we take one of the helicopters that Huxley has hired for the day and fly up to the Tekapo side of the Two Thumb Range of mountains where there's a ski area. Neither of us particularly wants to ski, but there's a magnificent café perched on the side of the mountain overlooking the slopes, and we get ourselves a couple of Irish coffees and take a seat outside to watch the skiers and snowboarders. Evie and Victoria are out there skiing, and so are Chrissie and her boyfriend, and we also get to see Saxon on a snowboard, performing on an obstacle course, jibbing over ledges and walls and miraculously managing to avoid breaking any bones.

It's while we're sitting there sipping our coffees that Heidi gets a text message.

"It's from Dad," she says.

My eyebrows rise. "You don't have to read it." I don't want him to spoil the day for her.

But she blows out a breath and pulls it up. "I'll only keep wondering what it says." She reads it out to me.

Heidi, I'd like to see you before you leave for England. I understand if you'd rather not, but I've done a lot of thinking, and I hope you'll agree. Love Dad.

She looks up at me, her brow creasing in a frown.

We study each other for a while. "What do you think it means?" she asks eventually.

"If I was being cynical, I'd say he wants a final opportunity to convince you to stay so he can keep control over you."

"And if you weren't being cynical?"

"It's possible he's had a chance to think about what he did, and what happened the other night at the club, and he wants to make it up to you."

She examines her hands for a moment. "I didn't say anything to you, because I know how you feel about him, and I was dubious myself. But Mum told me he's been seeing a therapist about his anger management issues. Maybe they've helped?"

"Maybe."

"You don't think so?"

"I'm not sure how much a person can change in ten days. But if he's truly remorseful? Who knows?" I hold her hand. "I don't want you to get your hopes up only to have them dashed again, that's all."

"Yeah, I know what you mean. I'll think about it."

"Okay. Hey, speaking of fathers, there's something else I want to talk to you about. I wondered if, after the wedding, you'd come with me to visit my folks. I'd like to introduce you to my mother. Unfortunately it means meeting my father, too."

She chuckles. "Of course I'll come. I'd like to meet them."

"All right. I'll let them know."

The skiers are making their way back, and so we finish our coffees and start heading for the helicopters. It's a beautiful journey back over the snow-covered mountains and fields, with the lake glinting in the late morning sunshine like a huge mirror.

Back at The Jewel Box, we visit the restaurant for a light lunch. Elizabeth has already disappeared with her mother and sister to start getting ready, and it's not long before the rest of us head to our villas to do the same.

It doesn't take me long to get my suit on. I leave Heidi putting on her makeup, go down to Mack's villa, and knock on the door.

"Just checking on the groom," I say when Sidnie opens the door.

"Come in." She looks stunning in a light-blue dress with a pleated skirt, her blonde curls bouncing around her shoulders. "He's a bit nervous," she whispers, gesturing at the guys in the living room. "I'll leave you to it. I want to finish my makeup." She goes off to the bedroom.

I walk into the room and discover Mack sitting in one of the armchairs, leaning back, ankle resting on the opposite knee, watching Huxley pace up and down in front of the windows. Thankfully, they're both dressed, in dark-gray suits, with wing-tipped collars and bow ties.

"How are you feeling?" I ask.

Huxley glances at me but doesn't answer.

"He's a bit queasy," Mack says.

"Better or worse than jumping off the Sky Tower?" I ask, amused.

Huxley swallows. "Ten times worse."

"Jesus. Why?"

"You'll understand when it's your turn," Huxley states, and Mack raises his eyebrows and nods as if to say, *He's right.*

"Are you worried she's not going to turn up?"

Huxley stares at me. "Well, now I am."

I laugh. "I didn't mean it was a possibility. She's not going to back out now."

"She said no to me every month for ten years. I'm kinda used to being rejected."

"She's having your baby," Mack reminds him.

"Yeah…"

"Dude," I say, "the girl's crazy about you. She's not going anywhere."

Huxley just gives us a helpless look.

"I'm getting worried," Mack says. "You've gone the same shade of green that you went up the Sky Tower."

Huxley puts a hand to his mouth, then says, "Excuse me," and strides off to the bathroom.

I meet Mack's eyes, and we both laugh. "He's such a wuss," Mack says.

"Were you nervous on your wedding day?"

"Yeah. I was shaking by the time of the ceremony. Didn't throw up, though."

"What about if I go and check on Elizabeth? Make sure everything's okay?"

"That's a great idea."

"All right. Be back in a bit." Leaving Mack to watch the groom, I leave the villa and walk across to where Huxley and Elizabeth were staying.

I knock on the door. After a few seconds, it opens to reveal Victoria, looking gorgeous in a cream trouser suit.

"Hello," she says, surprised. "Everything all right?"

"Yeah. Hux is freaking out, though. I thought I'd just check on Elizabeth, and then I could report back that she's still planning to tie the knot."

She laughs and looks over her shoulder. "Elizabeth, is it okay if I let Titus in?"

"Yes, of course," Elizabeth calls.

Victoria stands back, and I walk past her into the villa.

Quite a few women are in the large living room, either fussing around Elizabeth, who's standing in the middle of the room, or making coffee, or just sitting chatting, including her sister, her mum, Helene Huxley, Joanna, Evie, Chrissie, and Victoria.

"Titus," Evie calls out, and they all cheer.

"Hey." I smile at Elizabeth as she turns to face me. She's wearing a plain white satin dress with a high waist, so the material flows over her small bump. It has a V-neck and small lace sleeves, and it's simple and beautiful. "Wow, you look like a million dollars."

"Only a million?" She smiles back. "You don't look so bad yourself."

"In this old thing?" My navy bespoke suit was incredibly expensive, but it fits like a dream. Chrissie whistles, and I grin at her.

"He said Huxley's freaking out," Victoria states.

Elizabeth's smile fades. "Oh no. What happened? He's not... having second thoughts?"

"Jesus," I say, "don't you start! Of course not. He's worried you're not going to turn up."

She rolls her eyes. "Seriously?"

"He said he's ten times more nervous than when he jumped off the Sky Tower."

Everyone in the room goes, "Awwww!"

She smiles. "Silly arse. Go and tell him I have no intention of letting him off the hook."

I laugh. "I will."

"How's Heidi?" Evie asks.

I give her a wry look. "Don't start."

"I hope she's giving Sir Richard plenty of exercise…"

I mumble under my breath and leave the villa, a ripple of laughter following me out.

After crossing to Mack's place, I knock on the door again, and he lets me in.

"How is he?" I ask.

"He's thrown up twice. I swear the guy went the same color as that." He points to a fruit bowl on the table that's a vivid forest green.

"It's strange," I comment. "They're so happy together. She's obviously going to turn up. All he's got to do is say a few words and it'll all be over."

"Like I said, wait until it's your turn. It's so much more than that."

"I just can't see why making that commitment is scary." The thought of marrying Heidi doesn't frighten me; if anything, I feel exhilarated at the thought.

"It's not that," Mack says. "It's humbling to think someone else is promising to be with you for the rest of their life. You start asking yourself: what happens when they realize you're not worth it? It's terrifying."

I stare off into space. "Thanks. That's gonna fester."

"Anytime."

The bathroom door opens, and Huxley comes out. He's white-faced, but he looks a little better than when he went in.

He sits on the sofa and looks at me like a puppy dog.

"Elizabeth's fine," I say, trying not to laugh. "She said she has no intention of letting you off the hook."

"Do you think she meant it?"

I smile. "She was in her dress."

That makes his face light up. "How did she look?"

"White."

"Titus…"

"She was absolutely stunning, Hux. The dress has a high waistline so the skirt falls here," I mirror the shape of her bump. "Right over your baby."

Mack grins at him, and Huxley gives a shy smile.

"She's so excited to marry you," I tell him. "She was worried you were having second thoughts."

"Jesus, seriously?"

"I soon put her straight. So, only half an hour and then it'll all be over and you'll be able to relax. Can I leave you now without worrying you're going to freak out?"

"He'll be fine," Mack assures me.

"All right. I'll see you there."

I leave them to it and go back to our villa. As I go in, Heidi comes out of the bedroom, in the act of slotting in an earring. "How is he?" she asks.

"Terrified. But I went to see Elizabeth, and once he found out she's not planning to do a runner, he felt better."

She laughs. "What an idiot."

"Yeah." I walk up to her, my pulse speeding up. "Wow, you look amazing." She's wearing a long-sleeved cream knitted dress that reaches to just above her knees. My gaze drifts down and spots her black boots. "Whoa."

Her curtain of blonde hair swings forward as she bends her head to follow my gaze. "You like?"

"I do."

"I can keep them on tonight, if you want."

The thought of Heidi Rose Huxley, naked except for the boots, does strange things to my thermostat. "Oh yeah." I slide an arm around her. She's put on her lipstick so I don't want to kiss her and smear it, but I nuzzle her neck and nip her earlobe.

"Ow." She shivers. "Mmm. I can't believe we had sex this morning and I'm still filled with lust for you."

I chuckle and kiss along her jaw. "We've still got about fifteen minutes before we need to leave if you want a quickie."

That makes her laugh. "You're such a naughty boy."

"I wasn't, until I met you."

"So it's all my fault?"

"Totally." I kiss her forehead. "And now I'm going to walk away, or I won't be held accountable for my actions."

*

In the end, the wedding goes smoothly. Both bride and groom turn up, and I'm not ashamed to admit that seeing Huxley's face light up when Elizabeth appears in the doorway brings a lump to my throat.

The ceremony takes place in the conservatory of The Jewel Box, which is a special function room with glass on three sides that overlooks the glimmering waters of the lake. If it was summer, they could have exchanged their vows outside on the grass, but it's snowing today, so they choose to have it inside.

The service is short and simple, without any frills, carried out by a local celebrant, and yet it's still beautiful, with the two of them framed against the view of the lake, with eyes only for each other. Heidi's hand slides into mine as they promise to love each other until death parts them, and I'm not surprised to see her eyes shining.

Afterward, the organizers open the sliding glass doors and the happy couple go outside for photos, with Elizabeth donning a thick white wrap, and the rest of us smiling through our shivers. It's not long before we're back inside, though, accepting cups of cocoa and hot toddies, and making our way toward the restaurant, where the tables have been laid for dinner.

Relieved that his bride turned up, ecstatic to be married to the woman he's been chasing for ten years, Huxley is high as a kite, and he remains so for the rest of the day. Always the perfect host, he's the life and soul of the party, and he and Mack, his best man, make sure the rest of the day passes without a hitch. Food and drink flow, and after dinner the music starts, and we eat, drink, and dance well into the evening, until the Southern Lights brighten the horizon, their strange, mesmerizing patterns flowing across the sky.

*

The next day

"Are you nervous?" Heidi asks me as our plane lands in Wellington.

"What makes you ask that?"

"You're almost breaking the bones in my hand."

I release her fingers where I've been squeezing them. "Sorry."

"It's okay. Is it your father you're worried about meeting?"

"Both my parents stress me out. I'll be glad when it's over. But it's got to be done."

We don't say much more as we leave the airport and catch a taxi. I give the driver the address in Oriental Bay, and he heads out into the windy streets. It rarely snows here, but the rain that whips across the windscreen is icy cold.

It's not long before he draws up outside the house. Worth over four million dollars, it perches high on the hill, with magnificent views over the city to the left and the harbor to the right. They bought it a couple of years ago, so it's not my childhood home, and I find it a tad sterile and old-fashioned, the deep-red wooden floors and gray tiles in the kitchen making it darker than it should be with all its windows.

"Titus, sweetheart," Mum says. She kisses me on the cheek, then gives me a big hug. I've always thought she could easily have been a Viking shield maiden. She's still tall, blonde, and striking, but she's lost weight since the last time I saw her, and she's even more pale than usual.

As she draws back, I gesture to the woman at my side. "Mum, this is Heidi."

"Heidi, it's so lovely to meet you." Mum's voice still has a trace of a Norwegian accent, even though she's been here over thirty years.

Heidi shakes her hand. "It's great to meet you, too. I've heard so much about you." She speaks easily, reminding me that she's a schoolteacher, used to dealing with parents older than herself.

"Come in," Mum says, leading the way through to the living room. Two pristine white sofas overlook the stormy gray harbor. Heidi perches on the edge of one. I'm sure she's as terrified as I am of marking the cushions. "Can I get you a drink? Tea, coffee, herbal tea?"

"A coffee would be lovely, thank you."

"Titus?"

"Yeah, coffee thanks."

"Do you still have thirty cups a day?" she scolds, heading out of the room. "You should really switch to decaf."

I cross my eyes, and Heidi stifles a giggle. "Stop it," she mouths. "Don't make me laugh."

I go to reply, but at that moment my father appears, and both of us get to our feet again. "Hey, Dad," I say.

"Titus." He comes over and shakes my hand. We've never hugged, and he's never been overly affectionate, but to my surprise he rests his other hand on top of mine. "It's good to see you."

"Titus?" I ask, amused. "You've never called me that before."

He hesitates. He's as tall as me, strong and imposing, but he doesn't look quite himself either today. "Yeah, well," he says, "you're not a boy anymore. You have the right to call yourself whatever you want."

He moves back. Not sure what to say, I take Heidi's hand and bring her forward. "Dad, this is Heidi."

I'm not sure how he's going to greet her. The last time we spoke, he accused me of throwing away my career for a woman, and I hope he's not about to accuse her of leading me astray.

But he takes her hand in his, and shakes it warmly. "Heidi, it's lovely to meet you. You seem to have won my boy's heart."

"Oh." She flushes. "That's a nice thing to say."

"I hear you're a schoolteacher in the UK," he says, leading her toward the sofas. "I've always thought it must be such a rewarding job, teaching."

"Oh definitely," she says, "especially with the young children who aren't used to being away from their mothers. It's great to see them gain their independence."

He asks her about the curriculum over there and, seeing she's comfortable with him, I leave her to it and go out into the kitchen.

Mum is leaning against the worktop, waiting for the coffee machine to fill one of the cups. She smiles as I walk up. "Hello, my darling," she says. I hug her again, and she slides her arms around my waist. "I've missed you," she murmurs.

"Is everything all right?" I ask. "You and Dad seem... different."

She rests her cheek on my shoulder. "Ah, it's been a bit of a difficult week."

"Why? What happened?"

She sighs. "I wasn't going to tell you."

"Mum, come on. It's clear something's bothering the two of you."

After a moment, she lifts her head. She studies my shirt, brushing out an imaginary crease. "He admitted he's been having an affair with his secretary."

Shocked, I can only stare at her as she moves back.

"I know you knew about it," she says quietly.

"I didn't know," I say, just as softly. "I guessed. It's over?"

She nods. "She's left the company." She presses her lips together, obviously fighting against showing her emotion.

I hug her again. "I'm so sorry. You should have called me."

"Ah, it's something a man and woman have to sort out between themselves. He wants us to stay together. He says he's determined to make it work." She moves away and changes the cups in the machine.

"How do you feel about it?" I ask, still reeling.

"He's been very different. Mainly since he spoke to Peter Huxley after Heidi returned."

My eyebrows rise. "Seriously?"

"Yes. Peter admitted what he'd done… striking Heidi." She gets some milk from the fridge. "Peter admitted he thought he'd lost her, and Oliver, too. He cried on the phone. Julian was so shocked."

"Jesus. I didn't know that."

"He told me that evening. It all came spilling out. About his affair with Sarah. And your argument on the phone when you were in England. I don't think it ever occurred to Julian that a father could lose his kids. That they might not want to see him anymore. He's so proud of you. But he knows he's been hard on you. We both have. We wanted so much for you, so we pushed you and pushed you… And you've exceeded our expectations a hundredfold. You've done so well. But at what cost? We know we've alienated you." She presses her fingers to her mouth.

"Aw, Mum, come on, you've not alienated me. I'm so grateful for all the encouragement you've both given me, and all the opportunities I've had. I wouldn't have gotten where I am if it wasn't for both of you."

She rubs her nose. Then she gives me a bright smile. "Heidi is a lovely girl."

"She is. Mum, I'm going to move to England to be with her, for a couple of years to start with."

Her eyebrows rise. "I didn't realize it was that serious."

"Yeah. It is."

"Oh, I'll miss you," she whispers. "But I can make a diversion when I go to see Grandad and come and visit you."

"That'll be nice. Speaking of which… I was wondering whether you'd consider giving me Grandma's engagement ring." My grandmother died a few years ago, and my grandfather gave Mum her ring.

She meets my eyes, and smiles slowly. "For Heidi? Of course. What a wonderful idea. Here, finish the coffee, and I'll go and get it."

Trying to stay calm after the revelation she's just given me, I pour the steamed milk over the espressos. I'm finding it hard to believe that my father's done a complete U-turn. But then it sounds as if both he and Peter Huxley have had quite a shock over the past few weeks. Is it enough to force both of them to change? Once, I would have said no way. But now? Maybe it is possible for an old dog to learn new tricks.

Mum comes back out as I'm placing the cups on a tray and holds out a small velvet box. I open it. It's not the biggest diamond in the world, maybe two carats at most, but the ring was handmade, and it's very meaningful to me. The gold band is inscribed with tiny Old Norse runes both inside and out.

"Do you remember what they say?" Mum asks.

I nod, close the box, and pocket it. "Thank you." I watch her place some cookies on a plate. "Are you going to be okay?"

She puts the plate on the tray, then turns and smiles at me. "I'll be fine. *Is i magen!*"

I smile. It means 'Ice in one's stomach,' or stay in control and play it cool. "Yeah. *Is i magen.*"

Chapter Twenty-Nine

Heidi

I was nervous about meeting Julian Oates, bearing in mind the issues Titus has had with him, and I feel a moment of panic when Titus goes out to the kitchen and leaves me alone with him.

But Julian is nothing but polite and genial. He asks me questions about my job, my family, and where I live in the UK, and I tell him a bit about the weekend Titus and I spent together there, where we met Alan Woodridge, and about his country manor.

"Alan must be thrilled to have Titus working with him," I say. "I know he's put an office aside for him."

Julian stares at me. "He's moving to the UK?"

I stare back. Holy shit. My face burns. "I'm sorry," I say quietly. "I thought he'd told you."

"No." Julian glances out to the kitchen. "I'm guessing he was going to save that for today."

Fuck. I look at my hands, wishing the ground would swallow me up. No doubt his father is livid that he's the last to find out.

But as he looks back at me, I can see he's stricken at the thought of his son moving away. Does he realize part of the reason is because of his attitude toward his son?

He says softly, "He must be very in love with you to make a decision like that."

My blush deepens. "I don't know... we haven't known each other very long. And I would never stand in the way of his career. This is a great opportunity for him to learn from English scientists and computer engineers. He's very excited about their investment, and what it'll mean for the advances in IVF. I'm sure that's the main reason he's moving there."

He smiles. "That's a very modest answer. I can see why he likes you." He picks a thread from his trousers. "Did Lawrence—Titus—tell you that he was conceived through IVF?"

My jaw drops. "No. I didn't know that."

"Ingrid and I had trouble conceiving. It was my fault. We went through two cycles that failed. She fell pregnant with the third. It's why he's an only child. It put a strain on our relationship, and we didn't want to go through it again."

I'm not quite sure what to say to that.

Footsteps echo on the floorboards, and Titus and Ingrid come back into the living room. He puts the tray on the table, and sits beside me as Ingrid hands out the cups.

"I didn't know you were conceived with IVF," I say.

"Mm. Sorry, did I not say?"

"No." His innocence doesn't work—he purposefully didn't tell me. I wonder why? It makes more sense why he's so interested in it now. I wonder whether his parents told him what Julian just revealed about the strain it put on their relationship. Titus told me he thinks his father is having an affair with his secretary. Maybe he thinks the pressure of having to go through IVF created the first cracks in their marriage, and he hopes to help other couples from having to go through that.

"Heidi tells me you're moving to the UK," Julian says.

"I'm so sorry," I say to Titus, "I didn't realize you hadn't told them yet."

"It's okay, I was going to tell them today." He squeezes my hand. "Yeah, Acheron Pharmaceuticals has requested I run the project from there for a minimum period of two years, and I've decided to accept, mainly because I want to be near Heidi." He smiles at me.

"It sounds like a great opportunity," Julian says. He hesitates, then he adds, "I'm proud of you."

Titus looks as if his father has just slapped him around the face with a wet fish. "Oh."

The two of them stare at each other for a moment. Then Julian turns his gaze to me. "I want to say that I'm sorry to hear about what happened with your father."

I stiffen. Titus's hand tightens on mine.

"I've known Peter Huxley a long time," Julian says. "We've both made mistakes we're sorry for."

It doesn't come close to explaining away the years of control I've had to endure from my father, and the violent act he carried out at the end. But Julian glances at Titus, and I know this isn't really about me. He's trying to say sorry to his son. It doesn't come easy to proud men, and this is probably the closest he's going to get.

Ingrid sips her coffee and says, "So where are the two of you going to live?"

"We haven't actually talked about that yet," Titus says, looking relieved at the change of subject. "Heidi rents a cottage in the village where she works. I'll be working about half an hour away. We'll talk about that over the next week or so."

"When will you be moving?" Julian asks.

"Heidi flies back on the twenty-sixth of August. I'll be staying for another week or two to make sure everything's set here, then I'll follow her over."

Julian continues talking about life in the UK, politics, and Brexit, and thankfully we don't return to the topic of my father or anything personal. Ingrid doesn't say much. At one point, Julian extends his hand to her. She looks at it, waits a moment, then slips hers into it, and he squeezes her fingers. It's an innocuous gesture, but Titus glances at me.

It's then that I realize why the house feels strange. It's heavy with sadness. Nobody ever knows what goes on between two people. But it's clear that Julian and Ingrid have had their problems. Whether they're able to overcome them, I don't know.

We don't stay for much longer. We finish our coffee, and then Titus declares it's time to leave, and we get to our feet. The two of them see us to the door. Julian shakes my hand while Titus hugs his mother. Then Ingrid gives me a hug.

Titus faces his father and extends his hand. This time, Julian moves forward and puts his arms around his son in a bearhug.

Titus stiffens. Obviously, this doesn't happen often. For a moment, I think he's going to stand like that until Julian moves away. But eventually, Titus hugs him back, and they stand there like that for a moment before they release.

"Stay in touch," Julian says gruffly.

Titus nods, and we walk down the steps.

Once we're on the pavement, he says, "Let's have a walk along the beach." It's stopped raining, so I nod, and he leads me across the road and along the promenade.

We stand there for a moment, the brisk wind tugging at our clothes. He inhales deeply, then blows out a long breath as he releases a lifetime of tension and disappointment.

I slide my arms around his waist, and he hugs me back.

"Why didn't you tell me you were conceived through IVF?" I ask.

He sighs. "I don't like talking about it much. I know the pressure of getting pregnant put a huge strain on my parents. They had two failed cycles, and at that point Dad wanted to stop, but Mum pushed him into trying one more time. I think they came close to separating— she even moved out at one point. And then she fell pregnant. They've stayed together all this time, so I guess it says something for their marriage, but I don't think things were ever the same after that. But Mum's just told me that he's admitted he was having an affair, and he's ended it."

I pull back, shocked. "Really?"

"Yeah. He spoke to your dad on the phone. Your dad told him what he did to you, and about the argument he had with Huxley, and apparently your dad cried. I think it really shook my dad up. After that, he told Mum, and... well, you saw what he was like with me. He's never hugged me like that before."

I let him pull me tight against him, but my stomach is churning like the choppy waves. Dad cried while on the phone to Julian? That doesn't sound like him at all.

Is it possible that he regrets what happened between us? I won't know unless I go and see him.

I don't want to do it. But not seeing him is cowardly, and I'm bigger than that now.

I bury my face in Titus's chest. As long as he comes with me, I'll be okay.

*

A few days later, it's my turn to face my parents.

The weather mirrors my mood—gray and blustery. Titus pulls his car up in front of the house, turns off the engine, and looks across at me. "Are you sure about this?"

"No." I'm shaking like a leaf.

"We can leave at any time. Remember that. He has no control over you now."

I let out a shaky breath and nod. "Okay."

"Come on. I'll be with you the whole time."

We get out of the car, and he takes my hand. Holding it tightly, I lead him around the side of the house to the deck at the back, and we climb the steps.

"Heidi!" It's Mum, coming out of the house, and she walks up to me and gives me a big hug. "I'm so glad you came." I hug her back. Then she turns to Titus and hugs him as well. "Thank you so much for coming," she says. She gives him a meaningful look that I'm sure means, 'Thank you for getting Heidi to come.'

"It's nice to see you again," he says.

"Come in." She walks through the open sliding glass doors into the living room.

We follow her, and discover my father already there, standing waiting. His face is wan, and he's lost a little weight.

I still find it difficult to believe that Dad cried on the phone to Julian. He's never cried in front of me, and he's always been so sure of himself. Looking at him now, though, pale and thin, suddenly I know Julian was telling the truth.

Dad watches us walk in and swallows. "Hello."

"Hello." I stop by the sofa, hands in my pockets, shoulders hunched. I don't want to hug him. Fuck me, this is horrible.

Titus clears his throat. "Hello, Mr. Huxley."

"Peter, please." He holds out his hand, and Titus shakes it. "Can we get you a drink?" Dad asks. "Tea, coffee, or something stronger? Heidi? Would you like a gin and tonic or something?"

Although Dad loves whisky, and was keen to train Oliver to appreciate a fine malt, he would lecture me for hours if he heard I'd been drinking. So for him to offer me a G&T is a surprise.

"Coffee will be fine," I say. "Thank you."

"And for me," Titus says.

"Let's go into the kitchen," Mum says brightly, "we can sit at the table."

We follow her out there, and Titus and I sit. I glance over at the kitchen worktop. This is where Titus first kissed me, all those years ago, when I was sixteen. He grins at me, and I know he's remembering, too.

I've come a long way since then. I'm a qualified teacher, and I've moved to the other side of the world, where I manage very well on my own. Titus is right—Dad has no control, and no power over me now. It gives me courage, and I try to relax a little.

"How are Grandma and Grandpa?" I ask. Mum's parents are staying with them while they're in New Zealand.

Mum turns the coffee machine on. Usually Dad leaves her to it, but this time he gets the milk out and starts pouring it into a jug while she makes the espresso. "They're good," Mum says. "They've gone down to Matamata to see the Hobbiton set. They'll be back tomorrow. They enjoyed the wedding."

I glance at Dad. He doesn't look up and concentrates on steaming the milk.

"It was good to see Huxley finally tying the knot with Elizabeth," Titus says. "It's been a long time coming, and they seem very happy together."

"We're looking forward to having another grandchild, aren't we?" Helene asks Peter.

He nods, but doesn't say anything.

He brings over a plate of muffins that Mum must have made that morning. Titus takes one, but I'm too nervous to eat. Mum and Dad carry over the coffees and sit at the table, on the other side from Titus and me.

It's started to rain, and the wind blows the droplets against the window. "Horrible weather," Mum says. "At least it's summer in the UK."

"Mm." I sip my coffee.

Mum offers Dad a muffin, but he shakes his head. "Oliver called yesterday," he says.

My eyebrows rise. He and Elizabeth are still on their honeymoon.

"I think Mack told him you were coming to visit," Mum reveals.

I roll my eyes. "Figures." I meet Dad's eyes as he looks at me. "Have you forgiven Oliver for knocking her up yet?"

When he first found out Elizabeth was pregnant, Dad accused Oliver of being irresponsible in not wearing a condom, oblivious to the fact that he purposefully got her pregnant because she wanted a baby.

He drops his gaze to his coffee. "I apologized to him for that. I told him I hope I can make amends, because I'd like to be a part of my grandchild's life. He told me I had to make amends to you first."

"So that's why you want to see me? So you don't lose your son and grandchild?"

Mum winces. Titus glances at me. But I feel bitter and uncomfortable. I've waited two years for an apology, and Dad showed no remorse at all until Oliver confronted him at the club.

"No," he says, "I'd already asked to see you. Heidi, I owe you an apology."

I sit there, stiff and resentful, and glare at him. "For what? For the years of control when you wouldn't let me out of your sight? Or for taking your anger out on me when I finally announced I was walking away?"

"For all that."

"It's too late, Dad. Far too little, far too late."

"I know." His lips tremble, and to my shock, tears tumble over his lashes and roll down his cheeks. "I know what I've said and done, and I wish I could undo it, but I can't." He covers his face, and his shoulders heave.

Holy fuck. There's little worse than seeing a grown man cry, especially when he's your father.

A small part of me feels a sense of smugness that, at last, he's feeling a fraction of the pain he's caused me over the years.

But then I look at Titus, who's brow is furrowed with pity, and I feel a sting of shame.

It's not easy for men like Peter and Julian to admit they're wrong, and to say sorry. I'm not a practicing Christian as such, but through my work at the primary school, I have an understanding and an appreciation of the values we try to teach the children, and I know the importance of forgiveness.

Titus looks at me, and obviously reads it in my face. He gestures to himself and then the door, and when I nod, he gets to his feet and says quietly to Helene, "You have a lovely home. Would you like to show me around?"

Biting her lip, she nods, and the two of them go out. Soon I hear them talking in the living room.

Slowly, I get up, walk around the table, and sit in the chair Mum has just vacated. Reaching across to the kitchen towel, I tear off a sheet.

"Dad," I murmur, handing it to him.

He takes it, wipes his face, and blows his nose. "I'm sorry," he whispers.

We sit there for a moment while he composes himself. The rain blows against the windows. I can hear Titus and Mum talking as she shows him through the house. Once again, I remember the moment in this kitchen, where he pushed me up against the worktop and kissed the living daylights out of me. It fills me with warmth, and banishes the coldness I'd felt when I first walked in.

"I am sorry," Dad says again.

"I know." I take a deep, shaky breath. "And that's important to me. It's… it's going to take a while for us to mend what's broken between us. But I do want to mend it."

He looks at me then. "Really?"

I nod. "One day, God willing, Titus and I might have children. If we do, they deserve the right to know their grandparents. Stopping them from seeing you would be revenge, and that's not an emotion I want to experience."

His lips curve up, just a little. "He's moving to the UK to be with you. He must be serious about you."

Obviously, that's not the only reason he's moving. But I just nod and say, "Yeah. I think he is."

"I'm glad. He's a good man."

"He is."

"He'll take care of you."

"I don't need a man to take care of me, Dad. Even though Titus drove across the country after he heard my ex turn up at my house, and I was more than pleased to see him, I'd already dealt with Jason. It's important to me to be independent." I don't add, *Because of how you treated me.*

He nods. "I'm glad that you are. I'm proud of you for moving all the way to England, getting a job, and managing on your own."

My eyes sting. "I wish you'd said this two years ago."

"So do I."

He puts a hand on the table, palm up, maybe sensing that I'm not yet ready for a hug. I slide my hand into his. And we sit like that, listening to the rain, until Mum and Titus come back.

*

A week later

"Well, I'd better go," I say to Titus.

It's nearly nine p.m. and the two of us are in the flight lounge. My flight is in an hour. I've already checked in my luggage, and I need to get through security and find my way to the right gate.

"Yeah," he says. "I wish I was coming with you now."

"I'll be fine." More than fine—he's booked me into first class again. "It'll only be a couple of weeks anyway, and you'll be following me over."

"Yeah."

I go to pick up my flight bag, and he catches my hand. "Just a minute."

I look at him in surprise. "What?"

"I've got something for you." He takes a small velvet box out of his pocket.

My heart bangs against my ribs. He hasn't mentioned marriage again. But his words at Oliver's wedding ring in my ears: *There's a conversation coming...*

He rubs his thumb over the box. "This is my grandmother's engagement ring. She died a couple of years ago. I asked Mum for it when we went there. I'd like you to have it. If you'd rather me buy you one of your own, that's absolutely fine, and I'll be happy to do it."

I can only stare at him. "Oh, Titus..."

"I know we haven't been dating long. And I know it makes sense to wait, to live together for a while, make sure we're a good fit, all of that. But I don't want you to leave before... I mean I want to show you..." He frowns. "I should have written it down."

My lips curve up. "I'm not used to seeing you at a loss for words."

"It doesn't happen very often." He takes a deep breath. "Heidi Rose Huxley, I'm asking you if you'll marry me. I know a proposal should be romantic and organized, and I'll ask you again when we're in England, and we're settled, and you're sure. But I didn't want you to leave without..." He looks at the box.

"Without your ring on my finger so any man I meet knows I'm spoken for?" I smile.

His brows draw together. "That sounds a bit prehistoric."

"Am I in the right ballpark?"

"Maybe."

I look at the box. "Can I see the ring?"

"Oh. Of course." He opens it up and passes the box to me.

The diamond on the top glitters in the electric light. To my uneducated eye it looks huge. It's stunning, but it's the band that draws my attention. It's inscribed with what look like runes. I take it out and turn it around, examining them. They're on the inside and the outside.

"It's Old Norse," Titus says as I give him a querying look. "It loosely translates as 'You are my Valkyrie, and I would follow you across the nine realms and into eternity.'"

My jaw drops. "Oh Titus." I press my fingers to my lips. "It's beautiful."

"I don't know if it'll fit. Will you try it?"

"Of course." I take it out and slide it onto my fourth finger. It's a fraction too big.

"You can get it altered in England, if you like," he says.

I turn my hand back and forth, watching the diamond glitter. I absolutely adore the words on the band.

I look up at him, overcome with emotion. "Yes, I'll marry you," I whisper.

He gives the most dazzling smile. "I love you."

"I love you too."

He pulls me to my feet, and I lift my arms around his neck as he lowers his lips to mine.

While he kisses me, I open my eyes just a little and watch the diamond sparkle in the light over his shoulder.

Chapter Thirty

Heidi

The school year starts on Monday the fifth of September, the first day of the autumn term.

I've already been in school for a few days, cleaning my classroom, organizing wall displays, resources, school supplies, and getting ready for the manic first week. I have a whole new classroom of children, most of whom are nervous and unused to being away from their parents full-time. Some of them have attended the nearby playgroup or some form of nursery school, but even so, going to big school can be daunting and overwhelming for even the bravest kids.

The first week is taken up with basic tasks. I sit the children in a circle, and teach them that they have to be quiet until their name is called, and they learn each other's names. We work on life skills—they learn to hang up their coats and bags, put their own shoes on, and get changed for PE. There are sniffles and tears and one or two accidents as they get used to using strange bathrooms, but my assistants and I take it in our stride and explain it doesn't matter.

Much of the week is concentrated on play, so I can watch how the children interact, and decide what activities to plan going forward. I need to see who can count up to twenty, and which of them is familiar with the letters of the alphabet. Our topic for the week is 'All About Me,' and we talk about their families, friends, and pets, and about going to the shops, and places they might visit on a regular basis like the doctor's surgery and dentists.

Of course, a big part of the first week is settling the parents, too. Those who already have several school-age children know it's best to walk away without looking back, but for many this is the first time they've had to leave their little ones, and they're as stressed as the kids. I reassure where I can, and if the child is upset, promise I'll ring Mum or Dad at break time to let them know they've settled, which they invariably have.

On top of all this are staff meetings and all the paperwork that goes along with teaching—noting each child's level of progress. It helps that it's not my first year, and I've learned from my mistakes. I already have detailed lesson plans, and I know the importance of getting organized before classes start.

As the week draws to a close, I feel the usual exhaustion that accompanies it, but I also feel a seed of excitement settle in my stomach. Next Wednesday, Titus is due to arrive. Since I left New Zealand two weeks ago, we've spoken on Zoom every day, usually when it's evening here, once Titus has arrived at his office in the morning. He also texts and emails me, and I'm used to feeling my phone buzz against my hip half a dozen times through the morning.

I miss him terribly, and I can't wait for him to get here. We've decided that we'll stay at the cottage in Briarton for a few weeks at least, and then once he's here and settled in at Acheron, we can talk about where we go from there. I think we'll probably rent somewhere between here and Acheron, maybe in Exeter. I'm excited to look at properties, and to move in with him.

I had his grandmother's ring altered, and now it fits comfortably on my finger. I've shown all my friends and the other teachers who've noticed and asked about it. I adore it, and I'm so touched that it belonged to his grandmother. It means a lot more to me than a huge diamond that's just for show.

On Friday afternoon, I wait for the last pupil to be picked up after three p.m., then spend an hour tidying the classroom, replenishing the supplies, and jotting down some observations. At four there's a staff meeting, and that takes forty-five minutes, so it's close to five p.m. before I'm finally done for the day.

It's only four a.m. in New Zealand, so I'm not expecting to hear from Titus yet. Occasionally he has texted me that early if he's woken up, but usually the first I hear from him is in the evening. I keep my phone in my pocket anyway, just in case.

He's been a bit distracted the last few days. I'm not surprised—this close to leaving, he's got to be feeling the pressure of handing over the running of his company. I know he's been training his team in Auckland, and also meeting with Saxon several times to make sure he's comfortable with the organization.

Unfortunately he had to skip our usual Zoom call last night because he had an important early morning meeting with his research team, so it's been a couple of days since I've spoken to him. He did text me this morning, and he was as chatty and loving as ever, but I still miss him. Still, Wednesday isn't long. I'll keep myself busy this weekend, and weekdays always fly by.

I lock up my classroom and walk across the playground. It's a beautiful autumn evening. The oak trees that ring the school are beginning to turn, and the leaves are falling in a riot of color—yellow, orange, red, and brown. I bend to pick up a couple, thinking that maybe I could do some hand painting with the class next week. They could draw around their hands and then paint them to look like autumn leaves. That might be fun. Maybe on Monday we'll do a little nature walk around the grounds and collect some of the leaves first.

A few members of staff are walking to their cars, and we call goodnight and wish each other a great weekend. I get to the edge of the car park and look for my car. I parked it over by the school hall. Finding it, I walk a few paces. And then I stop. A man is leaning against the car, hands in the pockets of his jeans, watching me. As our eyes meet, he smiles.

I inhale sharply. My heart bangs against my ribs.

Then, a smile spreading from ear to ear, I run across the car park and jump up into his arms.

Laughing, he swings me around, then lowers my feet to the floor and gives me a long, hard kiss.

"What are you doing here?" I demand, breathless, when he finally releases me.

"I thought I'd surprise you." He smiles. "I hope that was okay."

"You're here? To stay? You're not going back?"

He shakes his head. "I'm all yours."

He's wearing a light-blue sweater over a white shirt and jeans, and he looks young, fit, healthy, and gorgeous.

Pressing my fingers to my lips, I burst into tears. He laughs and wraps his arms around me. "You old softie."

"Oh my God, I missed you so much." I bury my face in his sweater.

"Hello," he says, and I realize another teacher must have approached us.

"You must be Titus," a voice says—it's Lucy, my headmistress. "Heidi has told us all about you, and she showed us her beautiful ring. I'm Lucy."

"Very pleased to meet you." He holds out a hand behind my back, and I feel them shake hands.

Pushing myself back, I wipe my face and laugh as Lucy says, "Aw!"

"He surprised me," I tell her, accepting a serviette that he finds in his pocket and hands to me. "I wasn't expecting him until Wednesday."

"What a lovely thought. And now you have all weekend together. I hope you have an amazing time. See you Monday, Heidi." She smiles and heads to her car.

I blow my nose, wipe my face, then poke him in the chest, worried he's a figment of my imagination. "You're really here?"

"Looks like it." He cups my face in his hands. "Shall we go home?"

"To the cottage?"

"Yeah. I haven't seen you for two weeks, and I have an urge to get you into that tiny bed and make mad passionate love to you."

I look up into his eyes. "I can't wait. I love you, my Striking Viking."

"And I love you, my little Valkyrie." And he presses his lips to mine, while the autumn leaves gently flutter to the ground.

Newsletter

If you'd like to be informed when my next book is available,
you can sign up for my mailing list on my website,
http://www.serenitywoodsromance.com

About the Author

USA Today bestselling author Serenity Woods writes sexy contemporary romances, most of which are set in the sub-tropical Northland of New Zealand, where she lives with her wonderful husband.

Website: http://www.serenitywoodsromance.com
Facebook: http://www.facebook.com/serenitywoodsromance

Printed in Great Britain
by Amazon

22416606R00165